14.00

PRAISE FOR

ENRAPTURED

"Filled with sizzling romance, heartbreaking drama, and a cast of multifaceted characters, this powerful and unusual retelling of the Orpheus and Eurydice story is Naughton's best book yet."
—*Publisher's Weekly*, starred review

TEMPTED

"Endlessly twisting plots within plots, a cast of complex and eminently likeable characters, and a romance as hot as it is complicated." —*Publisher's Weekly*, starred review

"Ms. Naughton has taken the Greek Argonaut myth, turned it on its head, and OWNED it!"
—*Bitten By Paranormal Romance*

ENTWINED

"An action-packed creative wonder guaranteed to snag your attention from page one." —*Fresh Fiction*

"Do NOT miss this series!"
—*NY Times* bestselling author Larissa Ione

MARKED

"Naughton has tremendous skill with steamy passion, dynamic characterization and thrilling action." —*Publisher's Weekly*

"Elisabeth Naughton's MARKED gives an incredibly fresh spin on Greek Mythology that is full of humor, action, passion and a storyline that keeps you from putting down the book."
—*Fresh Fiction*

WAIT FOR ME

"Full of twists and turns, lies and deception, and the ultimate revenge, Wait For Me is a great romantic suspense read."
—*Night Owl Reviews*, Top Pick

"This book blew me out of the water. Wonderfully written with characters whose emotional turmoil seemed to jump off the page and grab you." —*Cocktails and Books*

STOLEN SEDUCTION

"This third book in the Stolen series is full of intrigue, secrets and undeniable love with characters you can't get enough of...an awesome read!" —*Fresh Fiction*

"An adventurous story of twists and turns, this story will keep you guessing until the very end. And the chemistry between Hailey and Shane is sizzling hot. Naughton combines passion and danger in one fast-paced story." —*News and Sentinel*

STOLEN HEAT

"This book has got it all: an adventure that keeps you turning the pages, an irresistible hero, and a smoking romance."
—*All About Romance*

"Stolen Heat is an awesome combination of deadly suspense, edgy action and a wonderful romance with characters that you'll laugh, cry and yell with." —*Night Owl Romance*

STOLEN FURY

"A rock solid debut...Naughton's intelligent adventure plot is intensified by the blazing heat that builds from Lisa and Rafe's first erotic encounter." —*Publisher's Weekly*

"Naughton deftly distills deadly intrigue, high adrenaline action, and scorchingly hot passion into a perfectly constructed novel of romantic suspense." —*Chicago Tribune*

LOSING IT ALL

Theron brushed a finger down Acacia's cheek, watched her back rise and fall in deep sleep. Studied the way her lashes formed spiky crescent shapes on her pale cheeks. Her courage still awed him. Last night she'd been ready to take him on. There was no other female in the universe who would dare stand up to him when he was in one of his moods, but it hadn't stopped her. She was fearless. And as selfless as he'd told the king. Everything he'd never wanted but now couldn't imagine living without.

He'd known she was his from the first taste. Long before he'd ever slid deep inside her. If he'd been more in tune with his humanity, he would have recognized it the first time he'd kissed her back in her small house. But he hadn't. Because he'd needed her to unlock that side of him he'd always repressed.

She was his curse. His soul mate. His life. And there wasn't a damn thing he could do to keep her from dying.

Titles by
Elisabeth Naughton

Eternal Guardians Series
(Paranormal Romance)

ENRAPTURED
TEMPTED
ENTWINED
MARKED

Stolen Series
(Romantic Suspense)

STOLEN SEDUCTION
STOLEN HEAT
STOLEN FURY

Single Titles

WAIT FOR ME
(Romantic Suspense)

Anthologies

BODYGUARDS IN BED
(with Lucy Monroe and Jamie Denton)

MARKED

ELISABETH NAUGHTON

For Alice,
who listened to the idea for this book first
and encouraged me to write it.
Alice, I blame you.

And next I caught a glimpse of powerful Heracles.
Around him cries of the dead rang out like cries of birds
Scattering left and right in horror as on he came like night...
--THE ODYSSEY

CHAPTER ONE

Some nights, a woman just wanted to bash her brain against a wall to keep from screaming. For Casey Simopolous, this was one of those nights.

"Yo, sistah. My tongue's not getting any wetter over here by itself." The blond frat-boy wannabe at the other end of her section threw his arms out wide with a could-you-be-more-stupid? look on his face. "We gonna get those drinks or what?" The two idiots seated next to him at the small circular table laughed and slapped him on the shoulder in a you-da-man move that made Casey grind her teeth together.

Oh, she could think of a number of comebacks for that one, but like the bad girl she wasn't in this den of indecency, she bit her lip instead. She plastered on a smile she didn't feel, dropped off the beers at table eleven and headed toward the troublemakers.

She hefted the full tray over her head as she zigzagged through XScream. Around her, heavy bass echoed from speakers hidden in the walls, vibrating the floor beneath her feet, sloshing her brain against her skull in the process. She had a killer headache, and that low-level buzz she'd been experiencing for the last thirty minutes was wreaking havoc on her usually cool-headed mood. If she hadn't eaten recently, she might have chalked it up to low blood sugar, but since Dana had forced her to choke down a burger during her break, she knew that wasn't the case. And she was tired of trying to figure out just what was wrong with her anyway.

Stop stressing already, would you? Sheesh...

She shook off the thought and picked her way around tables, past loggers and teachers and even the town's mayor. Far be it from her to judge who got their thrills in a place like this. To her right, Anna was onstage, working it for all she was worth, and from the corner of her eye, Casey caught a bra—or was that a G-string?—fly through the air, but she ignored that, too. Just as she did every night.

The college kids who'd been flicking her crap all evening whooped and hollered as they watched Anna turn with a lusty grin, bend over at the waist and shake her size-zero behind. They obviously didn't catch the fact that Anna's seductive wink and lip-licking was motivated by nothing but dollar bills, but then that wasn't exactly a surprise. These three yahoos were anything but Rhodes scholars.

They barely spared Casey a glance as she drew close, which was just fine with her. The micromini schoolgirl ensemble Karl insisted all the servers wear wasn't the most flattering outfit on her five-foot ten-inch frame, and she couldn't wait to be done with her shift so she could get out of it as fast as possible.

She set the first beer on the table in front of troublemaker number one, moved around behind the blond who was shaking his head in a yeah-baby move while salivating over Anna, and reached for the next beer on her tray. But before she could wrap her fingers around the chilled glass, a body slammed into her from the side, jostling the drinks and her and sending frothy golden liquid spilling over her tray.

"Hey!" she exclaimed, trying to right the tray before she lost everything on the table at her side. "Watch it!"

That buzzing picked up in her head, and before the words were even out, a tingling sensation lit off in her hip to radiate outward across her lower back and knock her equilibrium out of whack.

Casey swayed, reached out for the table but only caught the edge with the tips of her fingers. She had a moment of *Oh, crap* as she went down, heard chairs scrape the dingy floor and the college kids' shouts of surprise. But before her body hit the ground, an arm of steel that seemed to come out of nowhere wrapped around her torso, and another darted out to rescue the falling tray.

She didn't have time to do more than gasp. The mystery man who'd nearly knocked her to the ground turned her in his arm as if she weighed no more than a feather and set her on her feet. He handed her the tray, nodded and said in a thick accent, "Excuse me."

And Casey lost all ability to speak.

He was huge. Easily six and a half feet tall and at least two hundred and fifty pounds of solid muscle. His legs were like tree trunks, his chest so wide it was all she could see. And that face? *Greek god* came to mind, with that olive skin, the shoulder-length hair the color of midnight and those black-as-sin eyes. But it was the way he was looking back at her that really threw her off guard. Like he recognized her but couldn't place her. Like they'd met, but the idea didn't thrill him. Like she was the last person on the planet he wanted to be staring at right now.

"Jesus," one of the college kids behind her exclaimed. "Are you brain-dead or what?"

Oh, damn. Those stupid college kids.

She was just about to turn to defuse the situation, but the Greek god beat her to it, shooting them a withering look that could have turned flesh to stone. The kid's smartass mouth snapped shut, and the comments died behind her. Neither of his friends piped up to berate her more.

For the first time all night, a little of Casey's headache dissipated. She wanted to turn and look at the stupefied expressions on the troublemakers' faces, but she couldn't tear her gaze from the man in front of her. He must have noticed her staring, because he cast another bewildered look her way, then gave his head a swift shake and headed off to the other side of the club.

And it wasn't until he was all the way across the room that she finally drew in a breath.

Holy cow. What was that?

Her lungs suddenly seemed one size too small. She sucked in air, rubbed a hand over her brow and tried to regulate her breathing as she continued to stare. He stopped at a booth near the back wall, and though Casey couldn't see his face, it was clear he was talking to someone seated in front of him.

Someone who was female and blonde and petite and who had come in alone a half hour ago, then slinked into the shadows to watch the show.

At the time, Casey hadn't paid the woman much mind—occasionally women came into the club alone—but now she did. Now that *her* hero in black had zeroed in on the blonde beauty, Casey definitely wanted to know more about each of them.

"You gonna stare all night or get busy?"

The voice at her back shook Casey from the fog brewing in her head. Turning, she pulled her attention to the three college kids, studying her like she was a complete moron, their irritation with her obviously usurping the earlier intimidation from her mystery man. The tray wobbled in her hand, but she caught it before the half-empty glasses spilled again.

"So sorry," Casey muttered, grabbing a rag from her tray and mopping up the mess on their table. What was wrong with her? "I apologize."

"Geez," the blond muttered, shaking beer from his fingers. "What are you, mentally challenged or something?"

Casey ignored the comment and finished cleaning the table. "I'll get you three more beers—on the house, of course."

"Damn right," the one to her right snapped, as he turned to look back at the stripper feet from him up on stage.

She ignored that too as she finished grabbing empties, then glanced toward the hulking shadow several tables over.

"Those guys giving you trouble?" Nick Blades asked as she drew close.

"No more trouble than normal." Carefully, Casey picked up the wadded napkins on his table and dropped them on her tray. He was nearly as big as the Greek god, but that's where the similarities ended. Nick's blond hair was cut military short, he sported a series of strange tattoos and piercings, and it was hard not to stare at the jagged scar that ran down the left side of his face from temple to jaw. He always sat in her section, and though she'd told herself a thousand times he was harmless, a part of her just couldn't convince herself of that. She'd been there. She'd seen what he could do. And though she was grateful, she didn't want to see it again.

He watched her carefully, but she didn't make eye contact. "You seemed a bit distracted there."

Casey's hand paused as she thought back to the hulking Greek god, and warmth spread up her cheeks as she went back to cleaning Nick's table. It made perfect sense a guy like that would glance right past her and go after a looker like the woman in the corner. Men didn't generally notice stick-skinny Amazon women when curvy, petite blondes were anywhere close.

"You want another one, Nick?"

At his silence, Casey finally glanced up, and that's when she noticed Nick wasn't watching her but was staring across the club with narrowed eyes and a tight jaw. Staring toward the Greek god and his blonde bombshell. But he wasn't looking on with admiration or intrigue or even jealousy. No, Nick was watching them with malice, and very clear recognition.

Weird. How would someone like Nick know a guy like that? "Nick?"

Nick cut his eyes from the corner, his face turning impassive. "Might as well."

That tingling intensified again across Casey's lower back as she backed away from his table. "I'll get that for you and be right back."

She left him sitting in the same spot and headed for the bar, reminding herself the whole way she didn't want to know what Nick Blades thought of anyone. She had enough of her own problems to worry about. On a long breath, she set her tray on the shiny surface and handed Dana, the bartender, her orders.

Dana pulled the tap and filled three pints for the boys Casey had spilled on moments before. Then she glanced toward the middle of the room. "I see your admirer's here again tonight."

Casey frowned. She didn't like to call Nick an admirer. Didn't like to call him anything, for that matter. But she'd never shared the real reason with Dana, and she wasn't about to now. "I know."

"It's kinda sweet," Dana said. "Though he doesn't strike me as your type."

Casey didn't think it was sweet. Lately it was bordering on creepy. But she shrugged for Dana's benefit. "I don't have a type."

Dana smirked and set the beers on Casey's tray. "And if you did, it definitely wouldn't be the bad-boy biker type."

It got under Casey's skin, just a little, that she was so predictable. "Don't judge a book by its cover, Dana."

Dana pinned her with a look as she poured vodka into a glass and added orange juice from a pitcher. "Spoken like a true bookseller. How's the shop anyway?" She dropped a cherry into the drink and set it on the tray.

"Fine. Not as busy as this place, but then I don't serve up sex between the pages."

"Maybe you should."

Casey couldn't help smiling. "Yeah, maybe I should."

She waited while Dana finished her order, and tapped her fingers on the bar to the beat of Justin Timberlake's "SexyBack." Jessica was onstage now, already shimmying out of her hot shorts, and Nick was barely paying attention. Casey's gaze swept over the room, and for a fleeting moment, she wondered what her grandmother would say if she could see her now.

"Acacia. Meli, what has happened to you?"

"Nothing, Gigia. It's only temporary.

"It's always temporary with you, meli.*"*

"You off in a few?"

Dana's voice pulled Casey from her musings and she nodded. "Yeah. Thank God. Fifteen more minutes, then I'm free for the weekend. The bookshop's closed tomorrow and Monday."

"Good. You work too hard, Casey. I don't know how you do it. All day at the shop, nights here. Ease my worry, honey, and tell me you've got a hot date planned."

Casey reached for the tray. "Yeah, with a good book."

"You need to get out more, Case. Find a good-looking guy who'll remind you what life is all about."

Casey thought back to the Greek god. She just bet *that* guy could remind her what life was about.

She shook off the thought as she hefted the tray and turned to leave. "I don't have time for hot dates. I'm too busy."

"After you deliver those," Dana said at her back, "cut out early. I'll cover for you."

Casey glanced back. "You sure?"

Dana shrugged and smiled as she wiped out a glass, her soft red hair glinting under the dim lights. "Yeah, sure. Go on. Something comes up, I'll get Jane to cover your tables."

"Thanks," Casey said on a sigh, feeling suddenly tired.

"One thing before you go. When you get home, would you check to see if I left my phone there the other night when I came over? I can't seem to find it."

"Sure thing. I'll call you."

Dana winked. "Appreciate it. Have a good weekend, Casey. You deserve it."

Casey stopped at the college kids' table and delivered their beers, then glanced toward the back corner. The blonde was pushing herself out of the booth, but she stumbled when her feet met the ground, which was weird because Casey was sure the woman hadn't had anything to drink. The Greek god was right there to catch her, though, just like he'd done with Casey.

No, not like he'd done with Casey. Her eyes narrowed as she watched. He was much gentler with this woman. He pulled her close as if she were made of glass and seconds later swept her up in his arms and whisked her out the back door of the club, straight out of a scene from *An Officer and a Gentleman.*

Only this guy was ten times bigger and a million times hotter than Richard Gere ever was.

Warmth rushed to Casey's cheeks again as she watched, and envy—the only word she knew to describe that strange tightness in her chest—stabbed at the center of her. What would it feel like to have a guy like that so focused on her?

The door snap closed behind him, leaving only the darkness and thumping bass of the club in its wake. With a frown, Casey took a deep breath and turned.

No sense worrying about something she'd never have. No sense worrying about something she didn't have time for anyway. She needed to finish her shift so she could get home and sleep off this weird virus she'd been fighting the last few days. Then pull herself together so she could do it all over again Tuesday morning.

She crossed to Nick and handed him his Coke. "I'm heading out, Nick. You need anything else, Dana will take care of you."

He lifted his fresh glass. Long sleeves covered his arms, and the fingerless gloves he always wore kept all but the tips of his fingers from view. "Will do. And Casey?"

She stopped midturn and glanced back. "Yeah?"

"That guy who ran into you? If you see him around town, I want you to let me know."

Casey's brows drew together. "Why?"

"Personal reasons."

Okay, *that* was weird, too.

"And you'd be smart to stay away from him if you do see him," he added in a low tone. "Far away. He's dangerous."

That spot on Casey's lower back tingled again, and she lifted her chin. There was looking out for her, and then there was telling her what to do. And even though something instinctive told her she'd never see the Greek god again, right now, coming from Nick, she wasn't wild about either.

"Yeah, Nick," she mumbled as she turned and headed for the dressing room. "I'll be sure to do that."

* * *

"Theron, put me down." Isadora's free hand pushed against Theron's chest, but her protest did little more than annoy him.

He wouldn't lose his temper. The fact that he'd spent four days tracking her down was inconsequential at this point. So was the fact that he'd left his kinsmen to come after her. He would simply take her home before the Council discovered she was gone and all hell broke loose.

"Theron, I mean it," she said again, as the door to the human skin club snapped shut behind them and he headed away from the building.

"It's time to go home, Isadora. You've had your fun."

Isadora glanced over his shoulder back toward the building with a defeated look in her eyes. "You don't understand. I need her."

Need *her*? Like hell. He was the only one she needed right now. If her father found out what she'd been up to...

He gnashed his teeth at the thought and kept walking. If it were up to him, no one would know where she'd been these last few days or what she'd been up to. The last thing he—the leader of the Argonauts and a descendent of Heracles, the greatest hero ever— needed was for his warrior brothers to know his future wife had a human-female fetish.

He cringed at the thoughts. Both "human female" *and* "future wife."

Isadora squirmed in his arms again, but finally gave up with a sigh. And that was just fine with Theron. He wasn't in the mood to play nice.

The air was cool, but Theron barely felt it. A muffled thump-thump-thump echoed from the club behind him as he walked. Quietly, Isadora said. "She was beautiful, wasn't she? Graceful and tall. I...I didn't expect her to be so tall."

More frustrated by the second at Isadora's strange behavior, Theron picked up his pace. It wasn't until Isadora sighed again and rested her head against his chest that he remembered how inebriated she was and how tightly he must be holding her.

He loosened his grasp and forcibly gentled his voice, though even he knew it came out rough and stilted. "Isadora, you cannot just run off like this."

"I...I know," she breathed against him, her body growing lax in his arms. She shivered and tried to burrow closer. "I just wish..."

Her fading voice made him remember how she'd had trouble standing in the club. For the first time, he realized there hadn't been a single glass on her table. Not even a watermark from one that had been recently cleared away. Gathering her in one arm, he reached around and felt her forehead. Her skin was cold and clammy.

His aggravation morphed to urgency. She wasn't drunk at all. She was sick.

Skata. He had to get her back to Argolea. Like, *now.* "Hold on to me," he said firmly in her ear, repositioning his arm under her legs again. "I'll get you home."

She closed her eyes and, after a moment of what looked like incredible pain and heartbreak, nodded in what he could tell was great reluctance. "Yes. Yes. You're right. It's long past time. Take me home, Theron."

He took one step forward with her in his arms and felt the air change. It went from moist and warm to frigid in the span of a nanosecond. And he knew without looking that they were not alone.

Four daemons, beasts of the Underworld caught between mortal and god, horns sharp, teeth bared, appeared as if from thin air. One directly ahead, two to Theron's right, one to the left. They had bodies of men, covered in leather and trench coats that flapped behind them as they moved, with hideous faces, something of a mix of lion and wolf and goat.

Isadora's muscles relaxed in Theron's arms. He wasn't sure if she'd fallen asleep or if the sickness that racked her body had pulled her into unconsciousness, but at the moment he didn't care. It was better for her if she didn't see what they faced.

"Release the princess, Argonaut, and your life will be spared," the daemon directly ahead announced in a raspy voice.

A humorless sound bubbled from Theron's chest even as his mind spun with options on how to get out of this one. His kinsmen were nowhere close. He'd come looking for Isadora on his own. "Since when have daemons been known for their mercy?"

The leader growled. "Our mercy is the only thing that will save you. Unhand her. Now. You will not be given another chance."

They were about out of chances, as far as Theron could see. He glanced down at Isadora, out cold in his arms. For nearly two hundred years he'd served his race because it was his duty. Even though it hadn't been his first choice, he'd been willing to marry her if it meant preservation of their world. Tonight, though, he knew he would serve the *gynaíka* who would one day be Queen of Argolea, in order to save her life and that of their people. Even if it meant losing his own.

The two daemons on his right moved closer. Theron closed his eyes and used every ounce of strength within him to form a protective shield around Isadora. The effort drained him of his powers. He had nothing left for the fight to come.

Knowing she was now safe from the daemons, he slowly set Isadora on the ground at his feet. She curled onto her side on the cold asphalt but showed no other signs of consciousness. He rose to his full height of six feet, five inches and stared at the four daemons who still towered above him. "If you want her, boys, you'll have to come and get her."

The one in the middle, who was clearly in control of the others, chuckled, though the sound was anything but humorous. "So arrogant, Argonaut. Even when you're trapped. Atalanta will be most amused by your brashness."

"Atalanta is a petty hag with a perpetual case of PMS. And let me guess… As her number-one whipping boy, you get what? The right to wipe her ass?" He laughed, though he knew all it did was enrage the beasts in his midst. If he was going to go out, though, he might as well go in a blaze of glory. "Let me ask you this, dog face, just how inconsequential is your race that Hades would so easily hand you off to a bitch on wheels like Atalanta, anyway?"

The four growled in unison. The leader's eyes flashed green. "Taunt all you want, Argonaut. In mere minutes, you'll be begging for us to kill you."

They moved forward in a unit, as if of one brain. And without hesitation, Theron brought his fingers together until the markings on the backs of his hands glowed from the inside out. The portal opened with a flash and closed seconds later, leaving him alone with the daemons in the cold parking lot.

In the split second of silence that settled over them like a dark cloud, fury filled the face of each daemon, followed by a roar the likes of which only a god has ever heard.

"Sending the princess home was the last mistake you'll ever make, Argonaut," the leader growled.

They struck as a pack, taking him down to the pavement hard before he had time to reach his weapons. Teeth bared, fangs unsheathed, they tore into his flesh.

As his back hit the unforgiving ground and the last vestige of strength rushed out of his body, Theron had one fleeting thought.

This was going to be bad. Before it was over, it was going to be very, very bad.

CHAPTER TWO

In the club's locker room, Casey changed quickly back into her jeans and white fitted tee. She slipped on her Keds, threw her pathetic excuse for a uniform into her backpack and headed for the service entrance on the side of the building.

She chanced one quick look back into the club as she pushed the door open, and saw Nick was watching her.

Her nerves jumped a notch, but she told herself there was nothing to worry about as she fingered her keys and crossed the parking lot to her car. The mid-September night in the foothills of the Cascades of western Oregon was balmy, with just enough bite to remind her fall was right around the corner. In another week or two she'd need a sweater when she came out here after work.

After unlocking the door of her Taurus, she slid behind the wheel. She knew without looking that Nick was standing at the door, watching her. Sure enough, once she started the ignition, flipped on her lights and glanced back, he was there.

Don't think about it.

She wouldn't.

She pushed the thought aside and told herself to be thankful instead of creeped out as she turned the key in the ignition. He'd saved her once. If he'd ever intended to do her harm, he would have done it long ago. She turned up the volume on the CD player as she rounded the building, then slammed on the brakes when she saw the group of animals scavenging what had to be the carcass of some poor unsuspecting raccoon or opossum or deer.

Her first thought was *dogs*, but it changed to *wolves* as she got a closer look at their ears. But when the one closest to her lifted its head and turned to face the blare of her lights, her mind went blank.

A chill slid down her spine. Not a dog or a wolf or anything else she'd ever seen in her life. This thing had the face of a lion, the ears of a dog and the horns of a goat. And, holy hell, it was wearing clothing. Dressed...like a man.

She shook her head, closed her eyes and opened them again, sure what she'd seen was a figment of her imagination. And that's when she noticed that what the animals or things—she didn't know what to call them—were feasting on wasn't a carcass, but a human body.

In that instant, she was back in that empty lot, the hard, cold earth pressing into her back, the two powerful men tearing at her clothing as she screamed in futility and tried to get away. Sickness pooled in her stomach as she saw herself there on the ground with no one to help her.

Before she knew what she was doing, she jerked the car into neutral, pushed the door open and jumped screaming from the driver's seat, arms waving wildly in an attempt to get the animals to leave the person alone.

Four sets of glowing green eyes turned her way as she ran at them. Four low growls echoed in her ears. It wasn't until she was nearly on top of them that common sense finally kicked in and she realized she was in deep shit.

She skidded to a halt and froze.

The closest rose to his feet, and she saw, with vivid clarity, that he did indeed have the body of a man. Only he was huge. Easily seven feet tall and close to three hundred pounds, with crimson blood trailing down his face to drip onto his chest. The other three, equally large, rose quickly at his back and joined ranks behind him.

"Get back in your car, human. This does not concern you."

Holy crap, it talked.

Cemented in place, all Casey could do was stare wide-eyed at something that couldn't possibly be real. She glanced down at the man behind them, covered in blood, as the contents of her stomach lurched up her throat. "Oh, God. What—what happened here?"

The creature who'd spoken stopped midstep toward her. He sniffed, long and hard, as if trying to draw her into his lungs. His eyes widened, and something like shock, or maybe recognition—if you could call it that—raced across his catlike face before he turned and spoke in garbled words to the three at his back.

They all stared at her in wonder and then, in a puff of smoke, disintegrated into thin air.

Casey gave her head a swift shake. Smacked her hand against her forehead. Told herself what she'd just seen couldn't possibly be real. Good Lord, she needed to stop purchasing those vampire romances for her grandmother's store.

When the man on the ground moaned, Casey glanced down sharply. No matter what had happened, there was definitely a man hurt in front of her.

Head still spinning, she rushed to him, dropped to her knees and stared down at his face. The Greek god. From the club. The one who'd swept out of there with that blonde woman in his arms like a knight in shining armor. He was hurt bad. Cut and bruised and bloody over nearly every part of his body. For a moment, Casey didn't know what to do. Then he tried to move, and her brain kicked into gear.

"No, don't get up. Oh, God. I'm going to call for help. You're—" She forced back the bile. "What happened to you?"

"No...help," he croaked in a deeply accented voice. "Rest. Just...need...rest."

The man was delirious. He needed a hospital and a gallon of blood and doctors who knew what to do to help him. Good God, were those bites on his arms? It looked as though his flesh had been gnawed clear to the bone.

She tried to keep him still, but even hurt as he was, he was too strong for her. He pushed up so he was sitting. His head lolled around like it might just fall off his body.

"Please," he rasped. "Just...get me out of here before they come back."

At those words, Casey looked up and around. There was no wind, no crickets chirping or cars moving on the street beyond. No other people, either. The woman he'd left the club with had vanished. There was only silence. An eerie, strange silence completely at odds with the normal night sounds of Silver Hills, Oregon.

Since he was already rising to his feet, she helped him by slipping an arm around his back and draping one of his over her shoulder. By some grace of God they made it to her car, though she wasn't entirely sure how. As he dropped into the passenger seat like a ton of dead weight, Meatloaf pumped out of the stereo, singing about what he'd do for love. Casey grunted as she lifted the man's legs inside the car and shut the door after him.

Nausea continued to pool in her stomach as she hustled around to the driver's side, but she stopped at her open door and momentarily thought of the blonde again.

She glanced over the asphalt to the empty lot beyond and the copse of trees that turned to forest past that. Where the hell was she? Casey considered looking for her, but the man moaned once more, the sound pulling at her attention.

"Please," he croaked out. "Hurry. They'll be back."

Remembering what she thought she'd seen, Casey climbed into the car, turned down the stereo and hit the automatic door locks, just in case.

Okay, think. She'd take him for help, then call the authorities to come back and look for the woman. Figuring that was as good a plan as any, she glanced at the man to her right and started the ignition. "I'm taking you to the hospital."

His hand snaked out so fast, she barely tracked it. It closed around her wrist with stunning force for someone who looked to be on his deathbed. His index finger pressed against her pulse point. "No hospital. Rest." The fight slipped from his words, and in his heavily accented voice she sensed something…familiar. Dark eyes focused in on hers until all she saw were pools of obsidian, black as night. Warmth rushed through her limbs until every muscle in her body relaxed. "All I need is rest. Then I promise I'll leave you. I won't hurt you."

It was a strange comment coming from a man who couldn't even keep his head up. The safest thing to do would be to head straight for the hospital or police station or simply run back inside the club, where she knew Nick was sitting.

But she didn't. Instead, she nodded slowly, unable to stop herself. A strange fogginess filled her head, one she tried to shake off but couldn't. As she put the car in gear, pulled out of the parking lot and attempted to turn toward the hospital, a tingling vibrated across her lower back. The car made a right-hand turn onto Old Cornell Road almost as if it had a mind of its own, heading for her house at the lake.

"Thank you, *meli*," he whispered as he released her arm and closed his eyes. "This will be over soon. I promise."

Nick Blades kicked the apartment door closed and tossed the keys to his Harley onto the small card table in the middle of the empty living room. He peeled off his leather jacket and threw that over the keys, then pulled out the desk chair and sat, cheap vinyl creaking beneath the weight of his body as he did.

Something didn't jell.

He flipped open his laptop—the only expensive thing in the shabby apartment he kept here in Silver Hills—and waited for the machine to boot. As Windows blinked onto the screen, he chewed on the inside of his lip and ran his hand over the stubble on his chin.

He'd recognized the blonde in the corner of the club the moment he'd walked in. No telling how long she'd been there, but the way she'd been staring at Casey set his instincts on alert. What in hell was an Argolean doing in that club, trying to pass herself off as a human?

He rolled his finger over the keyboard and called up his instant messaging. He hoped Orpheus was on so he could get some of these damn questions answered.

Sure enough, the one link he had in Argolea was there.

Computer nerd.

He started typing.

Niko: *Need answers. Can you chat?*

Orpheus: *What up, my man? Been a while. How're those human women treating you?*

Nick frowned as his fingers flew over the keys.

Niko: *Like a stallion. Why the fuck do you think I stay here?*

A laughing smiley icon rolled across the screen.

Orpheus: *You are the biggest frickin' liar I ever met. And I am jealous as sin. What do you need?*

Niko: *What rumblings have you heard from the Council?*

The cursor blinked, and Nick leaned back in his chair, one hand on the armrest as he waited to see if Orpheus would answer. The guy was the most techno-savvy person—mortal or god—Nick had ever met. He gobbled up human technology like a child in a candy store and morphed it with what his race was doing, which was the only reason Nick could chat with him like this. If there was a chance Orpheus thought their conversation was compromised, he wouldn't risk answering.

Orpheus: *What makes you ask?*

Niko: *Curiosity.*

Orpheus: *You know what humans say happened to the curious cat.*

Niko: *I've already been dead once. Remember? I'll take my chances.*

Orpheus: *Fine, wiseass. But you didn't get this from me.*

Niko: *I never do.*

Orpheus's uncle was one of twelve Council members who advised the king. In actuality, the Council defied the king more often than not, and it was no big secret they were itching for a shift in power. Because of that, Orpheus had the skinny on everything that went down in the Argolean kingdom—good and bad. And he was Nick's one link to something he'd turned his back on years before.

The cursor blinked and then started moving.

Orpheus: *The king is dying. Some say he'll be dead before the next full moon.*

Niko: *The Council must be overjoyed.*

Orpheus: *They're not. In fact, they're mad as hell. Isadora is scheduled to marry the guardian Theron by week's end. It was announced only days ago.*

The two faces he'd seen in the club finally clicked. The blonde wasn't just any ordinary Argolean. She was the *gynaíka* who would become queen of her race. And the colossal Argonaut who'd come to get her wasn't just one of her guardians, he was their leader. The Argonauts' blood ties were the strongest of any Argolean, all the way back to the original seven heroes. Their power was far-reaching.

No wonder the Council was in an uproar. Isadora was the only living heir King Leonidas had produced. And everyone knew she was a weakling. Small and frail and meek. The *gynaíka* was no leader. But with Theron as her mate, the Council wouldn't dare challenge her. And the heirs he and Isadora produced would safeguard the monarchy for millennia.

Not that Nick gave a flying fuck what happened to any of them. After what had been done to him, he cared little if the entire Argolean race imploded in on itself.

But why had the princess been in a seedy human strip club? And why had she been fixated on Casey?

Nick chewed on that question as he resumed typing.

Niko: *Were the Argonauts in attendance at the announcement?*

Orpheus: *Yes. All seven. Even Demetrius. He didn't seem thrilled by the news.*

Nick clenched his jaw. No, he doubted Demetrius would be happy to hear Theron would command even greater control.

Orpheus: *Rumors are circulating, though. No one's seen Theron since. Or Isadora, for that matter. Some say they've already eloped to avoid backlash from the Council.*

Nick knew for certain they hadn't eloped. The Argonaut had been pissed when he'd found Isadora in the club; that'd been written all over his face. But that sure as hell didn't explain why the princess had been in XScream in the first place.

Niko: *Thanks for the info.*

Orpheus: *You thinking about coming back?*

Niko: *For what?*

Orpheus: *I dunno. Been a while since you've been interested in anything happening in the kingdom. You know my uncle Lucian has pull with the Council. He'd jump on your situation. With your brother—*

Nick didn't bother to read the end of Orpheus's sentence. His fingers flew across the keyboard.

Niko: *He's not my brother. And I have no desire to return to Argolea, now or in the future. For my safety, and the safety of others, I like to remain in the know, that's all.*

Orpheus: *I take it things have been peaceful on your end then.*

Niko: *As peaceful as they ever are.*

Not that Nick was about to cop to anything with Orpheus. Especially anything related to where he was and what he was doing. He trusted Orpheus enough to believe the news the Argolean passed him was accurate. But that was as far as it went. Nick had learned long ago not to reciprocate. If the Argonauts ever found out where he was or what he was doing, they'd hunt him down and slaughter him without a second thought.

And that was one more reason the Argonaut Theron's presence in Silver Hills tonight was of even greater concern to Nick. Something was brewing under the surface. Something even Orpheus didn't know about.

Nick signed off and closed the laptop. And as he sat in the darkness of the quiet and empty run-down apartment near XScream, he thought back to how Isadora had been staring at

Casey most of the evening. If the *gynaíka* had been on the hunt for a female to satisfy her appetite, she'd easily have picked one of the others.

No. She'd wanted Casey. Which meant the *gynaíka* knew exactly who Casey was.

He stood quickly from his chair, grabbed his jacket and pulled it on. A growing sense of unease rushed through him, a need to see for himself that Casey was indeed safe and sound.

He picked up his keys and slammed the door at his back. And didn't once think about the fact it was close to three A.M. or that Casey was probably sound asleep in her little house up by the lake.

CHAPTER THREE

Casey dropped the injured man sprawled over her shoulder onto her bed with a grunt, not entirely sure how she'd gotten him from the car to her house without collapsing herself.

He flopped onto the mattress, rolled to his back and groaned long and loud in pain. Fresh blood from numerous cuts seeped through his torn black T-shirt, ran down his massive forearms in rivulets. His black jeans were ripped at the thigh, and blood continued to pour down his pant leg and over his boot. His face wasn't much better, a myriad of scrapes and scratches over almost every part of it.

Nausea pooled in Casey's stomach as she took a good look at his injuries. She pressed the back of her hand against her mouth to keep from losing her dinner.

He needed a hospital. He needed an IV and medical professionals who knew what to do to help him. He needed—

"*Meli*, help me."

His outstretched hand, coated in his own blood, beckoned her.

She moved forward, almost as if someone were pushing her, and hesitantly slid her hand into his. His eyes remained closed, but his fingers tightened around hers with stunning force.

Okay, that didn't seem right. Something was off here. She tried to clear the fog from her brain, which seemed to be hanging like a shroud.

"T-Tell me what to do to help you," she whispered.

"Lavender."

"What?" No way she'd just heard him say—

"Fresh"—he hissed in a breath—"lavender. It grows. Here. Does it not?"

"Um, yeah," she said as her mind spun. He tried to shift his big body farther up the bed. Letting go of his hand, she helped him lift his legs. He groaned when she touched his injured limb.

"I'm sorry," she said on a cringe, then remembered what he'd asked for. "I don't understand. Why do you need—?"

"You must get it for me. Steep the lavender in boiling water," he said from between clenched teeth, as he fisted the once-white comforter at his sides. "Soak rags and bring them to me. Hurry."

Casey stared at his wounds, momentarily transfixed by the damage. Her head was spinning. Nothing seemed to make sense. Not who he was or what had happened to him or how she'd gotten him here, into her house. And now he wanted lavender? That request was more ludicrous than anything else he'd—

"Now," he rasped in a firm voice. "You must bring the lavender now. Before it's too late."

She felt herself nodding, but didn't know why. And then her legs were moving and she was rushing out of the room, filling a stock pot with water in the kitchen and setting it on the stove to boil before she ran out of the house.

Lavender. Have to get lavender for him, because he needs it.

Outside, the moon peeked over the tall Douglas fir, splashing shadows across the surface of the lake as she moved and her mind battled some unseen force that seemed to be spurring her on. Somewhere in the distance an owl cried, the sound almost eerie in the stillness. The few houses nestled around the lake were separated by forest and distance, the nearest at least an eighth of a mile away, and tonight she was glad.

She pulled up short at the edge of her small yard and yanked a handful of lavender from the flower bed. Back inside she went right to work, setting a pot to boil and tossing the herbs inside to brew. While that heated, she raced for the linen closet off the hall bathroom and grabbed as many washcloths and hand towels as she could find, then hauled them back to the kitchen. She tossed the washcloths into the pot, grabbed the stack of clean hand towels and headed for her bedroom.

Halfway there a wave of nausea washed over her, and she paused in the hallway, one hand on the wall, to catch her breath.

It's okay. I'm okay. It's just seeing that blood. And the weird virus you're fighting. Nothing more.

She swallowed once, twice, and waited until the dizziness passed, then moved forward.

The sight that greeted her tore a gasp from her mouth and brought that sickness right back to her stomach. Her patient was sitting up on her bed, bare to the waist, tearing his pants at his injured thigh. His face was scrunched up tight and his lips were compressed in obvious pain. Dark hair fell over his face. In the light from the hallway, the cuts and gashes and—oh, God, claw marks?—across his torso were a thousand times worse than she'd imagined.

She forced herself to go into the room, though she wanted to run away, and flipped on the bedside lamp. "I—oh, God."

He was drenched in sweat. An ear-shattering roar tore out of him as he ripped his pant leg in two all the way to his waistband, then fell back against the pillows.

Casey immediately rounded the bed, dropped the wad of towels near his feet and took the top one, pressing the soft cotton against the gush of blood to slow the stream. Swallowing hard, she continued to apply pressure even as he growled low in his throat and writhed beneath her.

This was insane. He needed a doctor. He'd die if the wound wasn't closed, continue to bleed out all over her grandmother's antique white lace duvet. Somehow she had to get him back to her car and take him into town, where he could get real help. Why on earth had she brought him here in the first place?

Frantic, she glanced toward the doorway, then back at his leg. She didn't want to leave him, but she needed to get to the phone.

"Have to stitch it closed."

His gravelly voice brought her head around, and she looked at his face, this enormous dark and dangerous man who'd stalked through XScream earlier tonight with the arrogance of a warrior, now mere feet from death's doorstep.

"I…I can call someone. If you hold this, I'll go—"

"No!" He leaned up quickly, though she saw the shot of pain in his contorted features as he did so. He grabbed her wrist tight. That warmth spread through her body again. "Needle. And thread. You have those, don't you?"

The haze returned. Thicker. Denser. Surrounding her body and blocking out her peripheral vision until all she saw were his dark-as-night eyes. Until all she heard were his words. Until all she felt was his finger stroking her pulse point, over and over again.

Slowly, she nodded, as she had before, like he was willing her to do so.

With his free hand he pressed down on the towel over his wounded thigh, then ground his teeth together. "Get those and come back."

She hesitated. Stared at him. And had the strangest sense she'd met him before. Somewhere. Or maybe not him. But definitely someone like him.

Crazy. He was a stranger. Someone who had obviously gotten in over his head tonight. He could be a criminal. A mercenary. A madman. But even as the thoughts flickered through her mind, she dismissed them. Right now, he was nothing more than a man who needed her help.

Heart pounding, Casey turned and left the room, and when she came back with her sewing kit, she saw he wasn't holding it together nearly as well now. His breathing was labored. Sweat dripped down his forehead. His skin was pale, his eyes clouded. She suspected he was fighting with everything he had left in him to keep from passing out.

Her hands shook as she dug through the kit and found a needle, then stilled as another thought struck. "It's cotton. The thread is cotton. That's not good, right? I mean, hospitals use something sterile. I need—"

"Cotton's fine," he rasped. "It'll be absorbed into my skin within hours."

She wanted to ask how that was possible, but he lifted those cloudy onyx eyes to hers before she could, and she got that fuzzy-headed feeling again, like someone else was controlling her from the outside in.

"I may pass out. I'll try to stay awake, but I'm not sure I'll be able to...take it. After you stitch up the wound, bring the lavender towels back." He squeezed his eyes shut tight. Blew out a breath. "Bring the towels, wring them out and lay them over my wounds."

"But how will that—?"

"The lavender has healing properties. Trust me. On three. Alright, *meli*?"

His eyes locked on hers. And something passed between them in that moment. A connection she couldn't explain. A familiarity that touched her somewhere deep inside. As her heart raced, all Casey could do was nod.

He nodded back, then lifted his hand from his injured leg and dropped back on her mattress with a groan.

Casey's stomach flipped around like a fish out of water as she went to work. After cleaning the needle, she tried not to think of what she was doing or the way blood ran down her hands as she worked. She made methodical stitches and remembered her home-ec teacher's words from high school: *Small, even stitches, Casey. Don't rush.*

Oh, Lord, if Mrs. Stevens could see her now.

She tried to stay focused, to keep her hands from shaking. At some point she realized the man in her bed had stopped groaning and that his muscles had gone lax. She looked up only to discover he'd passed out sometime after she'd started, though she didn't know when. Fear that she'd killed him nearly paralyzed her. She reached up quickly with her bloodied fingers, felt his pulse. Weak but consistent. She breathed out one sigh of relief, then forced herself to refocus and kept stitching. Only when she had the wound completely closed and she was snipping the end of the thread did she notice the blood flow had slowed considerably.

At least that's one good thing.

She'd used all the towels she'd brought to mop up blood as she worked, and there were other cuts on his arms and torso that needed tending. One quick glance down and she realized her T-shirt was ruined, soaked clear through in places from his blood. Seeing no reason to salvage it, she lifted the cotton over her head and bunched it up against a nasty-looking wound beneath his ribs. He moaned, tried to move slightly, and that's when the breath Casey hadn't realized she'd been holding came out of her on a rush.

He definitely wasn't dead. He was sleeping.

Probably better. She didn't know how he could have endured that pain without anesthetics. She'd have been dead already.

She was hesitant to stitch up any other wounds, even though she thought they might need it. He'd only been concerned with the one, and he was a man who'd obviously been through his fair share of fights before. She noticed then, as she looked across his bare chest and toned abdomen, the myriad of scars that crossed his skin.

And the strange tattoos on his forearms that ran down to his fingers. Ones she was almost sure she'd seen before.

Who was this guy? And what had really happened to him tonight?

"Meli," he said in a rasp, turning his head toward her.

She used the ruined shirt in her hand to wipe the blood from his face as gently as she could as she bent over him. And out of nowhere, a wave of tenderness she couldn't contain whipped through her as she looked down at this big, strong, hulking male who was so completely vulnerable to her right now.

The emotion was completely out of place. She didn't know him. Didn't have any tie to him. And yet, she couldn't have turned away from him if she'd tried.

Maybe it was because she'd watched her grandmother die only months before. Then she'd been powerless to help. Now she wasn't. As she studied his chiseled features, ran her fingertips over his silky eyebrows, she felt that flash of familiarity all over again.

Then again, maybe it was something more.

"Shh," she said softly, shaking off the strange thought. "It's over now."

He lifted a hand, as if in slow motion, and ran his fingers over the bare skin of her arm. A shudder ran down her spine, and electricity raced over her skin. "Towels," he said weakly. "Lavender."

"I'll get them," she whispered. "Just lie still and breathe."

His hand dropped to the mattress as she turned and left the room. In the kitchen, she used tongs to lift the soaking washcloths from the steaming water, transferred them to a colander and squeezed out as much moisture as she could. While they cooled in the sink, she poured juice into a cup and dug through the cupboards until she found a box of bendy straws she'd bought for her grandmother, when she'd been too weak to lift a glass. She put everything she needed on a tray and took it back into the bedroom.

She laid a damp rag over each of his wounds. He flinched as the towels touched his tender skin, then sighed in what she could only describe as relief when each of his wounds were covered. Amazing. She'd always loved the scent of lavender, but who knew it could be so totally calming?

She lifted his head with one hand and gave him a sip of the juice, then placed the glass on the side table as the soothing fragrance wafted through the room. Glancing down at his body, she realized his blood-soaked pants needed to come off, so she went to work cutting them from his legs as carefully as she could.

It wasn't easy. And after ten minutes with the scissors, making no progress whatsoever, she went into the garage and came back with wire cutters. The fabric—it was like nothing she'd ever felt before—sort of a cross between leather, superstrong vinyl and…Kevlar. But that didn't make sense, did it? She looked closely as she pulled the garment free of his body. It was thick. As strong as steel. And he'd torn it with his bare hands? On closer examination she discovered the inside housed unusual holsters for tools—weapons?—in strange pockets she'd never seen in any pair of pants before.

Okay, that was weird.

She was about to open the first of the many holsters to see what was inside when she glanced back at her patient and realized…he wasn't wearing underwear.

A flush heated her skin as her eyes took in the sight of him there, splayed naked in front of her on the bed. Even beat to hell, bloodied and bruised, he was stunning. Strong roped muscles in his shoulders and arms and pecs, taut abs and trim hips, and lower…

That flush turned to a white-hot burn she felt *everywhere*.

Oh, yeah. Do not *go there.*

She turned away, calling herself ten kinds of idiot as she put his things on a nearby chair and moved to the closet, where she grabbed a blanket from the top shelf. The comforter beneath him was soaked with his blood, but she didn't want to move him just yet. Gently, and without looking at his hips again, she laid her grandmother's quilt over his battered body and tucked it up around his neck to keep him warm. Then she brushed the back of her hand against his forehead to check his temperature.

Stay professional. You're just being a Good Samaritan. But oh, hell. She had an overwhelming urge to be anything but.

He moaned, tipped his head her way, eyes still shut. Absurdly thick, dark lashes any woman would die for fanned over the soft skin beneath his eyes. He didn't feel hot, so she figured that was a good sign.

"Just breathe," she whispered. "And sleep now." She reached over to turn off the bedside lamp and forced herself to step away. "I'll check on you in a little while."

"Thank you, *meli*," he whispered as she walked out of the room.

She hesitated in the doorway, struck by the fact he'd used the same term of endearment her grandmother had always used. His accent was definitely European, but not like any she'd ever heard. Eastern European maybe? But even that didn't fit. Her grandmother had been born outside Athens, then immigrated to the United States when she was just a girl. And though Casey's roots were Greek on her mother's side, she knew for certain the endearment *meli* was not a Greek one.

Strange, she told herself, *but not a biggie*. In the grand scheme of things, what this man called her was trivial at most. Making sure he didn't die on her watch was all that mattered.

CHAPTER FOUR

"You are certain of this?"

Atalanta looked out across the River Styx in the belly of the Underworld and ground her teeth at what she had just learned.

"Yes, my queen," her archdaemon said. "There is no mistake. Her essence was strong."

She turned to look back at Deimus, the creature she considered her number-one daemon, and narrowed her eyes. Her bloodred robes spilled over her bare shoulder, the hems pooling on the blackened ground where she stood. "He was wise to keep her from us."

"Yes, my queen. Wise but not perceptive. To think she would not be found was an oversight on the king's part."

"Hm," was all she said. "And what of the princess?"

A low growl rumbled from Deimus's chest. "The Argonaut Theron sent her back to Argolea before we could apprehend her."

"I see." She knew, of course, that Theron's sending the princess home had drained the Argonaut of his powers. Just as she knew he still lived due to her daemons' ineptitude. She lifted one eyebrow in challenge. "And he is dead?"

"No, my queen. The human woman interceded. She... When we recognized her, we came directly to enlist your guidance."

"I see," she said again, with perfect calm. She linked her hands behind her back and stared down at Deimus, three steps below on the blackened ground. He was tall, but being one of the original heroes, so was she. And he had not even a tenth of the powers she did. "Tell me of the princess."

He breathed out what sounded like a sigh of relief. "She is fragile, my queen. For her, it is a matter of time. This one, however…" He hesitated. "She could strengthen their cause if left unchecked."

"And yet you said she is but human."

Deimus nodded. "Human and weak, my queen. Like all humans."

Deimus didn't know of the prophecy, but Atalanta did. The temper she'd so carefully tamped down rumbled deep in her soul. "Then explain to me why she still lives!"

He bowed his head in submission. The hesitation confirmed what she suspected.

Spineless.

Disgust roiled through her. She turned her full fury his way. "Do I not bleed for what I have created? Have I not sacrificed myself for what I have built?" She lifted her arms and looked to the swirling sky, now red and glowing from the rage that spilled forth from her body. "Did I not give up all that was within my grasp for immortality, to lead you and your rogue band?"

In two quick steps she was on level ground. His head darted up at her swift movement. She watched his surprised eyes as she deftly pulled the sword from his hip guard and, without looking away, threw her arm out sideways. The blade sliced the jugular of the daemon at Deimus's left, sending him to his knees in a gasping gurgle of blood.

He made no move to help his brother in battle. Deimus's shocked eyes quickly shifted from the daemon, who moments ago had stood with him in the human parking lot, back to Atalanta. His head dropped lower. "Yes, my queen."

Atalanta's disgust grew as she thrust the bloody sword to the ground and kicked the writhing daemon to his back. Useless. All of them. Was she forever going to be surrounded by imbeciles?

"A human woman will not be the fall of what I am on the verge of commanding," she yelled. "I have not spent the last three thousand years in the bowels of hell to fail now. Argolea belongs to *me*. And I will take my rightful place on the throne and rule that which should have been mine eons ago. Not the fool-hearted king, nor the hapless princess, nor the mightiest of the Argonauts can stop me from attaining what is mine. And I relish the day they are banished from my kingdom forever. She is but a human, as you so eloquently pointed out, Deimus. Find her. Kill her. And bring me her head."

Green, catlike eyes lifted to hers. And smoldering in them was true fear. "But she is—"

"Do you dare question my authority?" she bellowed. "*I* am the goddess. You are but a servant in *my* realm. My dominion over the daemons is all-encompassing and the choices I make regarding that rule are mine alone. No god, including Zeus, can overrule my authority. Make no mistake, Deimus, if you cannot do the job that is before you, I will turn you over to Hades myself. You think this is bad?" She gestured to the limp daemon at her feet and slowly shook her head. "Your time in my kingdom will feel like heaven compared to what awaits you with him."

Deimus's head dropped once more, and though the tense line of his shoulders remained defiant, his acquiescence was palpable. "Yes, my queen."

She waited until Deimus and his incompetent warrior fools dragged the mutilated daemon out of her stone temple, then turned her attention back to the River Styx. She drew in a steadying breath to calm herself as she climbed the steps again and stared out at the water.

Oh, how she hated them all. Every single Argolean. Especially the Argonauts. There'd been a time…

She ran her hand over her lips and thought back. Yes, there'd been a time when she'd wanted only to join them. But that time was long over. Their dominance was nearing an end. Argonauts were merely mortal beings with longer-than-average life spans. They could be killed. They *would* be killed. She lived for the day the Argonauts—every last revolting one of them—was wiped from the face of the Earth and the Argoleans they protected were hers for the taking.

She'd had it with the Underworld. Her time was now.

She took another deep and calming breath. The prophecy would never come to pass. She had stopped it before. She would do so again at all costs.

A smile worked its way across her face as the knowledge relaxed her further. And ice, as cold and wintry as the winds that blow across the Arctic in the human world, solidified in the space that had once held her heart.

* * *

Casey was halfway to the living room, where she planned to lie down on the couch and get at least thirty minutes of sleep before she went to check on the mystery man in her bed again, when she heard a knock at her front door.

She froze, glanced at the clock on the wall—3:14 A.M.—then at the door. And for a moment had a paralyzing flash of seething wild animals in the lot behind XScream.

Which was off-the-charts insane, because such things just didn't exist.

The knock turned to a heart-thumping pounding. Her adrenaline shot through the roof.

Oh, God. What if that was…

"Casey?" A muffled voice called from beyond the door. "I know you're in there. Your light's still on."

Nick.

Panic turned to bewilderment to apprehension. What was Nick Blades doing at her house at three o'clock in the morning?

"Nick?" She took two steps toward the door.

"Open the door, Casey," he said in a more forceful voice.

Her hand hovered over the doorknob as she glanced down at her feet and suddenly realized she was wearing nothing but ruined Keds, blood-stained jeans and her bra. "Um. Hold on. I need to get, um… I'm not decent. Just…wait."

She ran to the hall bathroom and grabbed her white terry robe, only to realize her hands were covered in dried blood. Crap. She didn't have time to scrub them. Nick's earlier warning zipped through her mind, and she knew for certain she couldn't let him know about the injured man in her bed.

She tugged the robe on over her bra and cinched it tight, curling the collar up so it hid any blood that might have splashed onto her chest. Then she unrolled the sleeves as far as they'd go until they hung over the tips of her fingers. Confident her hands were now hidden, she glanced in the bathroom mirror and swallowed a gasp at what she saw.

Her hair was standing at odd angles, and dark circles had formed under eyes, but she figured, screw it. Whatever Nick wanted, she'd just find out quickly, then send him on his way.

On a deep breath she hoped would calm her nerves, she walked to the front door and at the last second remembered her shoes.

"Dammit," she muttered under her breath as she toed off the bloody Keds and kicked them behind the door. Then she pulled the heavy wood back a crack and peered through the darkness to where Nick stood on her front porch.

And this time she did gasp. Silhouetted by utter darkness, his scarred face highlighted only by the light coming from her kitchen behind her, he was huge. Like a Mack truck come calling. He towered above her, a dark and dangerous badass biker dude, just as Dana had pegged him, with narrowed eyes studying her as if he expected her to do something completely unpredictable, like attack him.

That night three months ago flashed in her mind without warning. And as it did whenever the memory hit, her stomach pitched all over again. She'd left the club at two A.M. that night, headed for home. Halfway to her car, the two drunk guys who'd repeatedly tried to manhandle her inside stepped in her path and not so politely offered her a ride home. She said no, but they had other plans. Three minutes later she was flat on her back in the dirt of the adjacent empty lot, not more than a hundred yards from the club where she served drinks night after night. She knew they were going to rape her, possibly kill her, just as she knew there wasn't a thing she could do about it.

And then like out of a dream—or a nightmare—Nick had materialized behind them. A towering, menacing threat from above. Even now she could hear the screams. Smell the blood. Conjure up the horrifying sounds that still woke her sometimes in the night. She'd covered her ears and rolled away in the dirt to get away from the horror. Where, thankfully, she blacked out.

She'd awoken in the hospital the next morning. Dana was there, holding her hand. Her friend told her one of the dancers had found her in the parking lot moments after she'd left the club, that she'd slipped on an oil patch on the pavement and hit her head. But Casey knew that wasn't true. She still wasn't sure what exactly had happened to those two losers, but she'd never seen them again. Nick, on the other hand, hadn't missed a night at the club since.

This is Nick, she reminded herself. *He saved you once. He's not here to murder you in your sleep.*

"Um, hi, Nick," she said in what she knew was an unsteady voice. "It's a little late. What can I do for you?"

It's three A.M., her mind warned. *What the hell do you think he wants you to do for him?*

Stop it!

"Everything okay?" he asked, tipping his head to the side, almost as if he'd heard her arguing with herself.

She nodded too quickly. Kept one covered hand clutching the lapels of her robe together, the other firmly on the door. "Yes. I was just about to go to bed. Is there something…wrong?"

His eyes narrowed to thin slits. He eyed the outside of her house. Looked over her head through the small gap in the door and into her living room.

Casey stiffened. "Nick?"

His gaze ran back to her. Rolled from head to foot. Not a steamy sweep, like she'd seen some men do at the club, but more of an observation. Like he was satisfying a curiosity.

"Cooking something?" he suddenly asked.

"Oh. Um." Could he smell the lavender? She drew in a deep whiff without realizing it. "Just tea. I always have some before bed," she lied. "Was there, uh, something you needed?"

His gaze settled back on hers, but she couldn't read his stone-faced expression. Had no idea what he was thinking.

"There was a commotion at the club after you left," he finally said. "Those college kids that you spilled beer on. They were asking about you, where you lived and stuff. That dancer, the one you don't get along with—"

"Paula?"

"Yeah. Paula. She was talking to them. I thought maybe she gave them your address. Figured I'd drive up here on my way home and check on you, just to be safe."

"Oh." Confusion at his sudden appearance turned to gratitude, though something in the back of her mind screamed, *Don't you think it's odd he feels so protective of you?* "Thank you," she said, pushing that thought aside. "I'm fine, though." She tried a smile she hoped reached her eyes and didn't give away any of what she'd dealt with tonight. "Just tired. But safe and sound. So there's no reason to worry about me."

He didn't look convinced. His gaze swept over her again, but he nodded, as if he knew not to press the issue. "Okay," he said, backing off her porch and down two steps, until he was on the ground but still taller than she was. "I'll let you go back to bed then. Sleep well, Casey."

He made it halfway down her front walk before common sense finally kicked in. "Nick?"

He turned slowly. "Yeah?"

"How did you find me?"

"Dana."

Her eyebrows drew together. "Oh. But—"

"G'night, Casey."

Her mouth snapped closed. By the time she thought to ask just how he'd wrangled that info from Dana, he was already on his Harley, revving the engine. Seconds later he was gone, and all that was left was the sound of his bike whining through the trees off in the distance.

Casey closed the door with a click, latched the dead bolt and turned the lock. Still reeling from Nick's strange visit, she wove through the house to the hall bathroom.

Her mind was a tumble of activity as she slowly peeled the clothing from her body, then climbed into the shower and turned the water on hot. Fifteen minutes later, with the mystery man's blood cleaned from her skin and her nerves somewhat steadier, she wrapped the terry robe around herself once more and went to find clean clothes.

Her patient was still sound asleep in her bed, in the same position she'd left him—flat on his back, with his head tipped slightly to the side, his dark hair fanning over her pillow. Why hadn't she taken him to the hospital before? Tentatively, she walked to the edge of the bed and felt his forehead again. Finding he was still cool, she lifted the towel covering his wounded leg and drew in a sharp breath.

It was already healing. A scab had formed over the wound as if it had healed for two days already. Unable to believe what she was seeing, she lifted another rag on his chest to see that the gash over his ribs was healing in the same way. Another on his arm. One on his chest. And looking closely at his face, she realized the swelling had already gone down near his eye and that his scrapes weren't nearly as fresh as they'd been only an hour ago.

"Just who are you?" she whispered aloud.

He didn't answer. She knew he wouldn't. Whoever he was, though, he was a medical miracle.

Suddenly more exhausted than she'd been before and too tired to come up with answers of her own, Casey replaced the towels and blanket and headed for the couch. She left the bedroom door open so she could hear him if he needed her in the night, but something in her gut told her he wouldn't.

She blew out a breath as she lay on the worn cushions, pulled the afghan over her and looked up at the ceiling. A thousand questions raced through her mind as her eyes slid closed and sleep tugged at her, but the only thing she could focus on was his words.

Thank you, meli.

That husky voice of his seeped into her thoughts, whirled around and around until it was all she could hear. And then she wasn't listening anymore. She was dreaming. Of cotton fields and cannons and soldiers in gray coats, charging. Guns firing from across a valley. The clash of weapon against weapon. Ear-piercing cries of agony and heart-stopping shouts of victory.

And on the fringe, the man in her bed dressed all in black, standing in the shadows of the trees, watching the battle with a keen eye. Beside him, another man, this one older, with a similar facial structure and the same strong body, and wide, broad shoulders.

"This all will be yours," the older man said with a sweep of his hands. "All of it. Yours to guard. Your birthright. Do not disappoint me."

Before Casey could hear her Greek god's response, the world went black.

Theron was wedged into the hottest, tightest, slickest place in Argolea. And he was loving every moment of it.

He lifted his hips. Twisted to get higher inside the *gynaíka* straddling his lap and breathing heavy against his neck. She tightened around his length until he was sure he'd explode. On a moan, she moved so the pressure eased. He groaned in frustration, thrust up into her burning wetness as she began to ride, and in reward, the climax he'd been seeking came screaming back, tightening his nuts to almost painful levels.

Where his climax hung. Teasing him. Taunting him. Just out of his reach.

With a curse he rolled her onto her back. Thrust deep, as sweat slid down his temple and dropped onto her face. Her nails scored the base of his spine as he pumped hard over and over. She kicked her dark head back against the pillow and screamed out her release. But he couldn't get there with her. No matter what he did, he couldn't finish. Frustrated, he kept pounding away at her. Reaching. Seeking. But nothing worked.

On the verge of screaming himself in agony, he flopped onto his back again. The sound of a door slamming somewhere in the distance brought his eyes immediately open.

His heavy breathing was the only sound in the dark room. Footsteps echoed from somewhere nearby. Slowly, he pushed up on his elbows and realized he was in bed. Naked. Alone.

Skata, he'd been dreaming. Dreaming of screwing some sexy, faceless *gynaíka*. And judging from the state of affairs between his legs, he hadn't just been dreaming, he'd been humping away at the mattress to no avail.

Strange memories filtered through his hazy mind as he eased back down. A dark-haired beauty saving him from a group of daemons. The same mysterious *gynaíka* tending his wounds. A soothing voice. Kind, violet eyes. She, leaning over him, wearing nothing but a white lace bra that at the time hadn't seemed significant but that now made his dick harden into a rod of steel.

Who was the *gynaíka* who'd left him in a fit of sexual despair the likes of which he couldn't remember experiencing? It definitely wasn't his bride-to-be. Isadora didn't exactly excite him. He was weak, knew he'd been in some kind of fight and that sex should be the last thing on his mind, but it wasn't. At the moment, all he could think about was his dream *gynaíka* and where the hell she was when he needed her most.

He kicked off the hot covers with his good leg, closed his eyes and saw her body. Slim waist. Small, firm, plump breasts that fit his hands to perfection. Luscious lips an *ándras* could sink into.

A tingle ran down his stomach as he imagined those beautiful lips of hers wrapped around the tip of his erection. The torturous erotic vision tore a groan from his chest. He threw his arm over his eyes and nearly came right there without any kind of physical stimulation.

Knock, knock, knock.

His eyes popped open when he realized he wasn't alone after all.

"I heard you moving around in there," a sultry female voice called from the other side of the door. "Can I come in?"

Holy *skata*. What in Hades was this?

He scrambled for the quilt and pulled it over his very aroused body. And as the sexual haze cleared from his mind and his night vision sharpened, he realized this wasn't his bed.

No, not his bed, not his house, and that *definitely* wasn't a voice he recognized.

"Are you okay in there?" That voice now held an edge of panic. The doorknob rattled and turned.

Theron's nerves kicked in as he pushed himself up against the headboard. He gritted his teeth at the stab of pain in his leg and glanced around the room. He couldn't see his clothes. Or his weapons.

Double *skata*.

He caught his breath as the door pushed open. Then exhaled on a smothered groan when a tall, dark-haired beauty with eyes like a violet sunrise stepped into the room.

She wore faded jeans and a white V-neck sweater. Dark wavy hair fell around her shoulders. Her nose was straight, her chin slightly pointy, her cheekbones sharp as they caught what little light was coming through the windows. But none of that was what made him swallow back a resurging burst of lust.

No, it was looking at those plump, delicious pink lips framing a sultry mouth, which curved into a nervous smile. A smile he recognized. Just the sight sent his cock screaming for release once more.

His dream *gynaíka*.

It all came back in a rush. She was the one who'd rescued him in the parking lot behind that club. The same one who'd brought him to her home, tended his wounds, tucked him into her bed and whispered reassuring words in his ear.

Just breathe.

His skin went hot at the memory of her sexy voice. She was the one he'd fantasized about only moments before. The same one he desperately wanted to get inside right now.

Only she wasn't Argolean. No, this gorgeous beauty was human.

Human.

Just the word revolving around in his brain dimmed his arousal and set off a buzzing in his chest that set him on guard.

She stepped to the end of the bed and stopped. It was then he noticed the plastic bag in her hand. His spine stiffened. "You look better. Your color's already perked up. Are you hungry at all?"

His eyes narrowed on her face. Her *familiar* face. He'd seen her somewhere before—he just couldn't quite place her.

As if she could read his mind, she dropped her gaze to his legs, covered by the blanket. He lifted his knees to form a tent to hide what was still going on under the covers and crossed his arms over his bare chest. She looked back up and tried to smile, though he could tell it was forced. "My name's Casey, by the way. We didn't exactly meet. Officially. Last night."

He nodded, only because he knew it was expected of him, and kept watching her like a hawk. "Theron."

"Theron," she said as if trying the name on for size. "How are you feeling tonight? You've been asleep all day. You didn't even move when I rolled you over and changed the bedding."

He'd been out? All day? He glanced to the windows and the darkness beyond. His injuries must have been worse than he remembered. "I'm fine," he said. "A little stiff."

Craaaap. Great word choice. He was more than stiff in places he was sure she didn't want to know about.

Silence fell between them. He knew his lack of conversation was making her uneasy, but he wasn't entirely sure of her motives just yet, and the knowledge the *gynaíka* he'd been fantasizing about had turned out to be human was still wigging him more than he liked.

She glanced around the room as if she didn't know where to look and was embarrassed about meeting his eyes. As she did, he remembered the way she'd gently stroked his hair after stitching up his wound. The way she'd wiped the blood from his face and leaned over him in nothing but that sexy white bra.

His erection came pounding back, though he fought like hell to keep it down.

She lifted the bag in her hands. "I got you some things to wear. Your pants were ruined, so I threw them away."

A blush rushed over her cheeks. And he realized then she was the one who'd stripped him bare. He glanced around again. What in Hades had happened to his weapons?

She looked away from his eyes. "You had some, um, strange tools in your pockets. I put them on the dresser." His eyes followed the sweep of her hand, and he felt instant relief. Everything was there. Still in their individual holsters. As if she hadn't even opened them. The only thing that was missing was his blade. And that, he remembered in a rush, he'd stuck under the bed when he'd ripped off his shirt last night, while she'd been gathering supplies.

She peered into the bag. "I wasn't sure on the size. I couldn't find a label on your, um, pants." She set the bag on the foot of the bed and stepped back. "I made some soup, if you're hungry."

His eyes narrowed on her face again. What did she want from him? In his experience, humans took what they wanted, thought only of themselves and rarely cared about others. So why, exactly, was she helping him?

She folded her hands in front of her in a hesitant move when he didn't answer. "I could bring it in here if you're still too tired or sore to get up."

"No," he said slowly. "I will get out of bed." And get his weapons. Check out the house. See where he was. Get the lay of the land. Make sure she wasn't planning on slicing and dicing him in his sleep. Just to be safe.

She nodded. "I checked your leg a while ago when you were sleeping. It looks a lot better. I'm still not sure how that's possible, but…well, I'm glad to see you're recovering so quickly."

She seemed sincere, as if she'd honestly been worried about him. He thought back to the panic in her eyes when he'd been half-conscious and dealing with the pain of his wounds. Remembered how together she'd been and how she'd done what needed to be done without freaking out. And though he didn't want to, he was impressed by her composure.

Then his brain skipped to the visual of those long, slender fingers touching his naked flesh beneath the blanket as she checked his wound. His whole body trembled with a renewed rush of hot arousal.

Which shouldn't be happening.

She glanced toward the door to her left. "There are towels in the bathroom, if you want to take a shower." When she looked back, a fresh flush crept up her cheeks. "If you need any help getting up—"

"No," he said quickly, knowing he didn't need any help in *that* department. He was already far *too* up for his liking. "I can manage."

She smiled in what he could only describe as complete relief, though color still stained her cheeks.

He nodded once but couldn't bring himself to thank her.

As if she knew what he was thinking, she hesitated. Looked up until her violet eyes locked on his. And stared at him as though she knew him.

That déjà vu flared again. Just where had he seen her before?

She stepped back so quickly, she hit the doorjamb with her shoulder. Then jumped as if the wood had bitten her in the ass.

And he just couldn't stop it. Amusement lifted his brow. Had he thought this woman was a threat? She was no more dangerous than an ant.

"Okay," she managed. "I'll, uh, be in the other room if you need me." She turned and fled.

Alone, Theron's curiosity faded as he stared at the open door. Her exit had not only robbed him of her unusual company but also of his arousal.

Confused as to what was happening to his body and why, he decided maybe he wasn't as well as he'd first thought. He pulled the covers back and looked down at his injured leg. The stitches were barely visible, and the wound was no longer red or inflamed. In another day or so it would be nothing but another scar to add to his collection. Judging from the other marks on his body, they'd heal equally well.

Unfortunately, though, the strange sensations buzzing around in his chest and head warned him he wasn't back to normal, and given that, it wouldn't be wise to try to open the portal and send himself back to Argolea just yet. In his weakened state, he'd be a prime target for the daemons, and he didn't even know if he had enough power to get home once he made the connection.

No, he decided. A better idea would be to stay here tonight. To eat the food this unusual but harmless human had made for him. To relax, to regain some of his strength so that tomorrow— maybe—he could head home.

As he tossed his sore legs over the side of the bed and rolled to his feet, his jaw tightened at the stab of pain in his thigh. He reached out to support his weight on the footboard and bit back a groan. Oh, yeah, definitely not well enough to try to make it home. Even the strongest of the Argonauts had limits, not that he was about to admit that to any of his kinsmen.

He ground his teeth to keep from whimpering like a little *gynaíka* as he shuffled to the bathroom. Inside he flipped on the light and started the shower, then moaned in relief as the hot water cascaded over his aching body and washed away the last sting from his cuts and bruises.

And though he didn't mean to, as his eyes slid closed, he couldn't help but think of the woman in the kitchen and imagine her fingers and lips running down his damp skin, instead of water.

Good gods. A woman? He was definitely more injured than he'd thought. His lusting after a human was clear proof he wasn't right in the head. It didn't matter how sexy she was or what her reasons were for helping him. She was human, and for him that meant off-limits. Forever.

CHAPTER FIVE

"What do I smell?"

The spoon in Casey's hand clattered to the stovetop, bounced off the surface and hit the tile floor at her feet. Soup splashed onto her sweater and jeans, and she hissed in a breath.

"*Skata,*" Theron said, moving toward her. "Are you all right?"

"I'm fine." Casey reached for the hand towel hooked over the oven-door handle. She swiped at the mess on her stomach and down her thighs.

Smooth, Case. Real smooth.

"I did not mean to startle you."

Her hand paused at the sound of that sexy accent, then she gave herself a mental shake and continued wiping her clothes. The man moved like a silent shadow, even injured as he was. She was sure she'd only heard the shower turn off moments ago.

"You didn't," she said, trying to sound nonchalant. "I was thinking about something else."

Yeah, right.

He bent at her feet to retrieve the spoon. She looked down and followed him with her eyes as he pushed to stand, then wished she hadn't.

He towered over her. Nearly six and a half feet and at least two hundred and fifty pounds of pure muscle. His hair was damp from his shower, brushed back from his face and just long enough to curl at his collar in a way that begged her to run her fingers through the damp mass. The long-sleeved black T-shirt she'd bought for him was snug against his muscled chest and arms, the faded Levi's riding low on his lean hips. Beneath the cuffs of his jeans, his bare feet peeked out, looking ridiculously masculine against her pale pink tile floor.

She swallowed a groan as she flashed on what that body looked like stark naked. The long roped muscles, chiseled angles, hollows and planes that she could now envision way too well. The scars across his chest lived in her mind now, along with that arrow of dark hair that pulled her attention down until just the memory made her blush.

Injured, she'd found him wildly attractive, but now, semihealed and well rested, he was more than that. He was danger on a stick, dangled out in front of her like candy for a child. Every woman's sex fantasy come true. And for some insane reason he was standing in *her* kitchen, watching *her* with wary eyes.

She still wasn't entirely sure how that had come to pass, and if he weren't looking at her right now, she'd probably have chalked it up to a dream. But it wasn't. He was real, smelling of Ivory soap and a hint of her favorite shampoo. She had to block images of him wet and naked in her shower, using her bath products against his naked skin, because just the thought was too much to handle. And because she knew she must look like a moron right now, practically drooling over him, with soup staining the front of her outfit.

She blinked and turned for the cupboard, forcibly breaking the spell she seemed to fall under whenever he looked at her. "What you smell is soup. You must be starving. Have a seat at the table and I'll get you some food."

He shuffled across the floor and dropped onto a chair at the round oak table. Only when he grunted did she remember he was injured. "How's your leg?"

"Better," he said as she set a steaming bowl in front of him. His eyes barely flicked over the soup before returning to her. "A little sore." He leaned over and took a deep whiff while she opened the drawer and pulled out a clean spoon. "What is this?"

"Cheddar broccoli. My grandmother's recipe." She handed him the spoon, set butter and a plate of warm rolls on the table near his arm. When he continued to stare at her, she choked on a laugh. "Don't worry, it won't poison you. I do know how to cook."

Frown lines creased his forehead, but he spooned up a bite, blew on it, then cautiously tasted a small amount. His dark eyebrows lifted in surprise. "It's good."

Casey smiled as she pulled the refrigerator open and grabbed a soda. She popped the top and set it in front of him, then spooned up a bowl of soup for herself. "I know modern women aren't supposed to like to cook, but, well, I do. Makes me feel like I've accomplished some small feat during the day."

She slid into the seat across from him and lifted her spoon to taste it herself. He waited and watched, and she had the strangest sense he was checking to make sure she didn't keel over from food poisoning. She took a second bite and smiled.

The lines across his forehead relaxed, and he resumed eating. He glanced at the can she'd put in front of him, seemed to study it intently, then lifted it and looked inside the hole on top. "What is this?"

"You don't like soda?"

"Soda?" he asked, turning the can and reading the side. Again he looked at her, waited while she lifted her can and took a drink. Only when she set hers down and went back to eating did he lift his to his lips and take a long swallow.

Then proceeded to spew Diet Dr. Pepper all over the table.

Casey leapt from her chair and grabbed the kitchen towel again. She pressed it into his hand and against his mouth. "Not a fan of diet, huh?"

Hack, hack.

"Let me get you something else."

She opted for a Coors from the refrigerator, since she never bothered to buy regular soda, and handed him that. He downed half of it before he pulled the bottle from his mouth with a frown and glanced at the label. "It tastes like water."

She grabbed another towel to mop up the soda. "Well, it's not a Guinness, but it's definitely not water. Where the hell are you from that you don't drink diet soda or light beer?"

He finished coughing and studied the can of diet soda on the table as if it might just jump up and bite him. After polishing off the rest of the beer, he set the empty bottle on the table before he said, "A small village. We...do not have a lot of foreign trade."

No kidding. Casey slid back into her seat. "A small village where?" On Mars?

He finally tore his gaze from the can and looked up into her eyes. Familiarity sparked again as she studied his face. What was it about him that made her feel like they'd met before?

"A small village near the Aegean."

"The Aegean Sea?" He nodded. Well, that sort of made sense, actually. She'd known he wasn't American. Casey went back to her soup. "So you're Greek."

"No, not exactly." Just when she was sure he wasn't going to go on, he said, "The...political arena where I'm from is ever changing."

He had the strangest way of putting words together. Like he was trying too hard to sound normal.

"I see," she said. Though she really didn't. She knew the Yugoslav wars in the 1990s had changed the landscape of the Balkan region. Though she could trace her roots to the area and she was good with geography, even she wasn't sure how countries had been divvied up after the gunfire had ceased. "So what brought you to Oregon? It's a pretty long trip for you."

He nodded and reached for a roll. "I was looking for a friend."

The woman at the club.

Casey swallowed back a spurt of jealousy she didn't understand and continued eating. But a lump of remorse settled hard in her stomach when she realized what she had to tell him next.

She set down her spoon and wiped her hands on her napkin, laying it next to her bowl on the table. "I don't know what happened to the woman you were with. When I found you in the parking lot, she was gone."

He didn't look up from his food. "She's fine."

Just what the heck does that mean?

"How do you know? You were already hurt by the time I reached you. Where did she go?"

Almost as if he realized he'd said too much, he lowered his spoon and met her eyes. She saw knowledge and secrets in his dark gaze. Coupled with the flat-out truth he wasn't going to explain anything to her.

She leaned back in her chair and narrowed her gaze, trying to look at him objectively and not as the sex symbol she'd been fantasizing about earlier. "You know, I'm starting to think something about you just isn't right. What did happen to you? Someone attacked you in that parking lot, didn't they? You weren't hit by a car. No matter how many times I've tried to tell myself that's all that happened, I know it's not. I think it's about time you were honest with me."

He clasped her arm on the table before she even saw him move, turned her palm up, slid his fingers down the center of her hand and hooked his pinky around her thumb, pinning her hand with ease. Slowly, he circled his index finger over the center of her palm, down to the heel of her hand, lower, until electricity burned along her wrist. Sparks shot straight to her spine and a warm, almost liquid sensation rushed through her entire body.

Her breathing slowed. The pupils of his eyes grew until she found herself staring into pools of obsidian dark as night. And suddenly she had trouble remembering just what it was she'd gotten so worked up over only a moment before. Though she knew there was something. Some reason. Hanging on the edge of her subconscious. Why couldn't she reach it?

But the thought was overridden by the way he was touching her. So...sinfully delicious and...oddly peaceful.

"Listen carefully," he said slowly. "I was walking across the parking lot when you turned the corner in your car. It was dark. You were tired. You didn't see me until it was too late. Your car hit me. You brought me here because you were worried about me and felt guilty. I'm not familiar with American hospitals and didn't want to go to one if I didn't have to. You helped me heal. You did a good thing."

Yeah, that had to be the way it happened. Casey's heart rate slowed as she relaxed further into his gentle caress. He had the softest fingers. His hands were warm and tantalizing. She couldn't help but imagine those strokes running over her shoulders, down to her abdomen and finally up to her breasts.

"You want to continue to help me," he said in an even softer voice. One that sounded like velvet and sandpaper all at the same time and ignited a rush of hormones deep in her body. "Anything I need."

Of course she needed to help him. His injuries had been her fault. But...anything? Her cheeks warmed. Visions of his naked body laid out like an offering on her white comforter rushed through her mind again.

And that's when she saw the wicked smile curling one side of his mouth, almost as if he could read her thoughts. "Yes, *meli*," he whispered. "Anything I want, you will do for me."

Heat snaked through her abdomen, dripped lower until she felt the unmistakable wetness of her arousal. And then he broke the contact with her hand as quickly as he'd grasped it.

She blinked several times. Felt oddly lightheaded. Though he went back to his meal, her skin tingled as if he were still caressing her wrist. And something unfurled inside her then, some hidden part of her that had been waiting. Waiting for…this moment her whole life.

"Your soup is getting cold, *meli*,"

Casey tore her gaze from his rugged good looks and glanced down at her bowl. Riiiiight. Dinner. That's what she was supposed to be focusing on. Not on him and some strange feeling that didn't make a lick of sense.

Slowly, because her hand was trembling, she lifted her spoon and took a small bite. But didn't taste a thing. Because what she suddenly wanted on her tongue wouldn't come close to fitting on a spoon.

Some kind of instrumental music filtered through speakers in the ceiling as Theron sat in the kitchen watching Casey clean up the dishes from dinner. A candle in a large hurricane lamp flickered in the center of the table, casting warm light and the scent of vanilla across the room. But what held his attention wasn't the candle or music, but rather the woman in his line of sight.

Woman. Holy Hades. A human woman. One he couldn't seem to stop thinking about. He'd changed his mind right there during dinner. When he'd held her hand in his and recognized the desire in her eyes. For some reason, the Fates had given him this respite here with her while he healed. Why should he fight it?

Her back was to him as she washed their dishes. He'd offered to help, but she'd told him to sit and relax and not irritate his injuries. If she knew what he was planning, she wouldn't be standing there looking so at ease.

Snug jeans molded to her body like a second skin. Her simple white V-neck sweater was somehow hotter than any lingerie the Argolean *gynaíkes* he'd been with over the years had ever worn. Watching her, blood rushed to his groin and tightened his jeans until he had to shift in his seat to release the pressure.

He lifted the lager in his hand and took a small sip to cool the heat building in his veins. He'd had better, but this wasn't too bad. And it beat that carbonated crap any day. Humans had some strange tastes, though this one he sort of enjoyed. And he could go on watching the woman in front of him move all night long.

Which was ironic, considering he'd given his kinsman Zander such a hard time about his unhealthy obsession with human women. And yet, here he was.

Theron's watched her lean down and place a pan in a bottom cupboard. The denim stretched across her heart-shaped ass, the waistband dipping low over her back until he saw a glimpse of white lace peeking from beneath. His pulse kicked up and the blood roared in his head.

She opened a cupboard to her right and eased up on her toes to put a bowl away. When it was obvious she was having trouble reaching the highest shelf, he rose slowly and moved to help her. The pain in his leg had dimmed to a dull throb, but there was no reason to tell her that.

Citrus and lavender drifted to his nose when he got close, remnants of the same shampoo he'd used in her shower and something else that could have been lotion or perfume, he wasn't sure which. He eased in behind her and took the bowl from her hand. "Let me help."

She stiffened as their fingers brushed. The muscles in her arms and legs went rigid. His chest brushed her back as he set the bowl on the top shelf, and his elbow ran down her forearm in a barely-there brush of skin against skin.

"Thank you," she said softly, easing back down on her feet. The motion brought his hips into contact with that delectable ass he'd been admiring before, and the erection he'd been fighting all night came roaring back.

He knew she felt it because she went still. All through dinner, as they'd made mindless small talk about the area and the lake and her neighbors, she'd been looking at him like she wasn't sure what he would do next. For a while he'd thought it was fear making her wary, but now he knew that wasn't the case. The way her body tensed, the way she drew in a sharp breath and held it without moving at their contact was a clear sign of arousal.

Neither of them spoke, and in the silence he could hear her heart beating its erratic rhythm. He lifted a lock of hair from her shoulder and ran it between his thumb and forefinger. It was smooth and silky, and he had a wicked desire to see the dark mass spill over his abdomen as her lips trailed south along his body. He lifted the lock to his nose and sniffed. "Oranges or grapefruit?"

She swallowed. "Bed Head."

His brow lifted, and he knew she caught his confused expression from the corner of her eye. "It's a type of shampoo." She turned slowly and eased back just enough so her sweet behind brushed against him and then was gone. "You really do live in an isolated area, don't you?"

He nodded, watching the way her eyes flicked over his face as if searching for the answer to some unspoken question.

"I'm almost done here," she said, "and it sounds like the CD ran out. Why don't you go into the living room and find something else to listen to? The CD player's in the entertainment center."

At her words, he realized the speakers in the kitchen were silent. "If you wouldn't mind, there are a few stitches left in my leg that could be removed. I could use your help."

Her gaze flashed down to his denim-clad thigh, hovering momentarily on his growing erection. Her eyes widened slightly just before a blush crept over her cheeks. She turned quickly back to her dishes. "Oh, yeah. Sure. I'll, um, grab some supplies and meet you in the living room."

A grin sliced across Theron's mouth as he headed for the stereo cabinet. His leg was growing stronger by the minute, and there really was no reason to remove the few stitches that were left, as they'd be gone by the following morning, but he wasn't above using any means he could to get his little human exactly where he wanted her.

She was, he decided as he opened the cabinet and glanced around the living room, a multitude of inconsistencies. When he'd asked how she found him behind that strip club, she'd told him she worked there. He'd tried to picture her in XScream but couldn't. She was tall for a woman, and she definitely had the body to strip, but there was an innocence to her eyes that other humans who worked in those places lacked. The way she'd taken care of him after the attack—a stranger who'd stumbled out of a strip club, no less—was in direct opposition to the tough woman she obviously had to be in such an establishment. He tried to reconcile the two parts of her but couldn't.

And then there was this house. Before he'd made his appearance in her kitchen, he'd taken a thorough tour and familiarized himself with both the interior and exterior. The house itself was old, the interior done mostly in white with bead-board walls and delicate crown moldings. The rooms were small, the ceiling only a foot or so above his head. The furnishings were antiques he couldn't picture her buying, because they didn't fit with what he'd seen in her bedroom: a red velvet club chair and fluffy gold pillows he could easily envision her sinking into. Modern art on the walls, a silver-framed mirror reflecting back into the room. Most of the house looked decorated by an elderly person. That one room didn't.

He made a mental note to ask her about the difference, and then changed his mind. In the long run her answer wouldn't matter. After tonight he'd never see her again.

He found the stereo equipment and was just opening the CD drawer when she walked into the room. A hint of lavender preceded her, signaling her arrival to his senses, setting off a heated reaction in his groin.

"Did you find anything worth listening to?"

He grabbed the first CD in the stack and read the cover. "Bing Crosby?"

Casey burst out laughing. He turned at the infectious sound, not entirely sure why she found his suggestion so amusing, but enjoying the reaction. If there was one thing he'd learned about humans over the last two hours, it was that they were wildly unpredictable and passionate in ways Argoleans never were.

"Is that wrong?" he asked hesitantly.

"Not if you're eighty, I suppose." She walked toward him and stopped so close he could feel the heat radiating from her skin. Her fingers brushed his as she flipped through the stack, sending a tingling along his nerve endings that, oddly, relaxed him. "Most of these were my grandmother's. She had a thing for good ol' Bing." She held up two CDs with Christmas trees on the front. He knew enough about human culture to recognize the holiday. "She'd listen to these year-round. Didn't matter if it was June or December."

She put Bing's CDs back and flipped a few more before she found one she liked. "Try this one. It's mine. I'll go grab my first-aid supplies while you do that."

He glanced at the CD cover. A man in a white shirt and big cowboy hat looked back at him. He didn't have a clue what kind of music it was, but he figured if she picked it, it had to be good. Music began filtering out of the speakers as he moved to the couch and sat down.

The seat wasn't large enough for his big body, but he stretched his legs out and relaxed back into the cushions anyway. He could hear Casey rummaging in the bathroom cabinet and smiled to himself. It had been a long time since he'd had to seduce a female. As an Argonaut, Argolean woman were his for the taking. If he wanted companionship, a crook of his finger was usually all it took.

She came back into the room and sat on the edge of the sofa just out of his reach, placing the first-aid kit on the low coffee table. "I love Kenny Chesney. He's got the best voice."

For a fleeting moment, he wondered just who the heck this Kenny person was and how he could find him and beat him to a pulp. Then when she started humming along to the music, he realized she was talking about the singer on the CD.

And wasn't that just the weirdest reaction to have? If he were human, he'd have defined the feeling as jealousy, but that was an unknown emotion for an Argonaut.

He managed a wan smile.

She glanced at his face with a look of skepticism; then her gaze ran down to his legs and back up again quickly. A blush crept across her cheeks, one that warmed his blood all over again.

"You"—she cleared her throat—"are going to have to take off the pants if you want me to, ah, look at your leg."

He fought to keep from grinning as he rose slowly from the couch, making sure to wince as if his leg was definitely hurting, and slid his hands to the top button of his jeans. Her eyes followed and froze, intent on watching what he was about to reveal.

A wicked thought occurred. And blood rushed to his groin.

Anything I want.

He popped the top button and hesitated. "I'm still a little weak, *meli*. I think I'm going to need your help with this. Give me your hand."

CHAPTER SIX

He wants you to take off his pants.

Casey caught Theron's meaning, but his words were muffled, almost as if from a dream. The blood roaring in her ears made it hard to hear his voice, but the sinful look in his eyes told her exactly what he wanted.

She wasn't sure what made her stand, but she thanked God her legs didn't give out. After swallowing hard, she wiped her sweaty palms on her thighs and stepped closer until she was heady from all that testosterone and sweet male scent.

She could already see from the bulge behind his zipper he was aroused, and she'd wanted to know just what he looked like erect, hadn't she? But if she did this, she'd be crossing a line from Florence Nightingale to Naughty Nurse that she wouldn't be able to retrace.

Oh, God. Was she actually going to do this?

Her gaze skimmed his hard body, from his growing erection up his toned abs to those impressive pecs and finally to his rugged face.

No, he wasn't classically handsome. His features were too prominent, his jaw too harsh, his cheekbones way too chiseled to be considered gorgeous. And there was a dangerous look to his dark eyes, to his entire being, that made her feel as if she were toying with a…god.

The thought hit her out of nowhere, but it fit. He looked like a large, dark, menacing biker god who'd ride her hard and put her away wet without a second thought.

No strings. No emotional entanglement. No regret.

She'd never bought into the whole one-night-stand thing before, but there was something about *this* man that pulled at her. Enticed her. Challenged her to take one small, sinful taste and say the hell with the rest of the world.

Her conversation with Dana flitted back through her mind.

I don't have a type.

And if you did, it definitely wouldn't be the bad-boy biker type.

Yeah. She was going to do this. Screw predictability and walking on the safe side. For tonight at least, she wanted to do something completely wild and totally out of character.

She eased closer and lifted her hand. Her fingers brushed his as she touched his waistband. His hands fell away and he sucked in a breath as she popped the second button. And the third. And finally the fourth. She felt steel beneath the black cotton boxers she'd bought for him. Watched as his dark, hypnotic eyes blazed with an erotic light. And was filled with a confidence that swept through her out of nowhere.

Her skin warmed. She savored each brush of her fingers, each scrape of skin against cotton. A sweet ache settled between her thighs as she slid her hands into the waistband of his jeans and settled them on his strong, lean hips. Gently, and with her eyes still locked on his, she pushed down.

"*Oraios,*" he rasped.

She didn't have a clue what he'd said, but she loved his husky voice, the lilt of his accent. She eased the denim down his hips and swallowed back a groan as it skimmed his impressive erection, which was very obviously struggling to be set free.

For a moment she wished she hadn't thought to buy him underwear at all, then realized it might be a blessing. It was like unwrapping a gift. One that kept getting better with each layer removed.

She was gentle as she pushed the jeans past his thighs, careful not to rub the denim over his injury. She knelt in front of him as she took the jeans to the floor and helped ease his legs free. The musky scent of his arousal flooded her senses as she worked, sending her libido into overdrive and shooting sparks between her thighs. Her body responded in turn, that sweet ache growing to explosive levels. She fought the urge to strip him naked right here and now and use him to extinguish the fire burning inside her.

When he was free of his jeans, she nodded toward the couch.
"Sit," she managed in a voice rough with her own arousal. She
coughed once to cover it, but knew he had to hear it too. "I'll, uh,
take a look at your wound."

She busied herself looking for supplies in the first-aid kit as he
eased back. He didn't speak as he sat on the couch beside her.
When she had what she thought she'd need, she turned to face him
and her eyes immediately ran to his hips. His legs shifted open, and
that massive erection pushed against his boxer briefs, just begging
for her attention.

Oh, God. Sweat broke out on her forehead. Her pulse kicked
up, and all the blood in her body rushed due south.

Focus, Casey.

She swallowed hard and zeroed in on the bandage on his thigh.
Her fingers shook slightly as she reached for the corner of the tape
and slowly peeled it away. He drew in a sharp breath, and for a
moment she thought she'd hurt him. But when she glanced up to
make sure he was all right, she saw pure, unadulterated lust tighten
the features of his chiseled face. Her gaze quickly swept back to his
hips, and the erection she'd thought was big before grew larger
before her eyes.

Oh, man. She was in trouble.

She refocused on what she was doing. Then gasped when she
had the bandage completely free.

There were no stitches. No evidence of a gaping wound. Just a
thin red scar that would, she suspected, eventually pale.

"Incredible," she whispered.

He glanced down at his leg. "It looks good, no?"

"It looks great. You're a medical miracle, you know that?" She
ran her fingers over the scar and marveled at the tiny ridge the
wound had left behind.

His breathing stopped.

Casey immediately pulled her hand back. "Oh. Did that hurt? I
guess I just assumed that since it looked so good, it had healed
complet—"

His fingers wrapped around her wrist, and he drew her hand
back to his thigh, back to his wound and the skin she'd been
stroking moments before. "No, *meli*. It doesn't hurt. It feels good.
Soothing. Don't stop."

She glanced from his leg to his face and back again.

She should stop. She was wading into uncharted waters. In her grandmother's living room, for crying out loud. In a matter of minutes she'd be in over her head. She ran her fingertip back up his thigh, hovered on the edge of his boxer briefs and licked her lips.

"Yes," he whispered. "More like that."

Feeling bolder, she traced the hem of his boxers, slid her fingers along the downy hair on his inner thigh. The muscles in his throat constricted and his cock twitched beneath the black cotton so close to her hand.

Point of no return.

"Your fingers are like *magikos*," he whispered. "You talk about how amazing my healing has been. Yet you seem to forget, without you, I wouldn't be sitting here now."

That was true, wasn't it? She slid her hand up his thigh to the junction of his leg and hip, felt the corded power beneath as his words sank in. Gently, she pressed her thumb into his pressure point and was rewarded with a small gasp that told her he enjoyed what she was doing to him.

"Your touch is more pleasing than any healer from my world," he rasped. "Each pass of your hand gives me strength."

A smile pulled at her mouth. She knew exactly what kind of strength he meant, and if anyone else had pulled that line on her she would have scoffed. But with him? Right now? For reasons she wasn't about to examine, instead of moving back, she shifted closer. And was rewarded as he reached out and brushed his knuckles across her abdomen.

Sparks shot to her center. Her pulse leaped, and she glanced up into his eyes.

Anything I want.

"You must be tired from all this...healing," she whispered. "You'll have to tell me what I can do to make it easier on you."

One side of his mouth curled at the corner as he caught the playful tone of her voice. Arousal darkened his eyes. His hand grazed her arm, slid up to her cheek and gently caressed her skin. She leaned into his touch and held her own breath while his thumb ran over her bottom lip. "You really are a fantasy *gynaíka*."

It crossed her mind to ask just what he meant, but before she could, he was pulling her face forward. And suddenly she forgot any questions she had and gave herself over to his touch.

His lips brushed hers, soft at first but with more ardor as the kiss deepened and his fingers tightened in her hair. On the second pass she opened to him without hesitation as his warm, wet tongue snaked into her mouth and stroked hers with long, seductive strokes.

He tasted like heaven. A hint of mint, of the dinner they'd shared, of sin served up on a golden platter. One of his large hands slid down her back and pulled her closer, until she was forced onto her knees, straddling his hips.

Her skin was on fire as he changed the angle of the kiss and his hands became more urgent. For a second she wondered if he was too weak for sex, then quickly dismissed the thought when he tugged her down and she settled on that monster erection she'd drooled over before. If he didn't have the strength for it, she'd do all the work. No way she was stopping now.

Her hands took on a life of their own as she examined his muscular torso and kissed him back. Her fingers ran down his black shirt to the hem, then up under so she could feel his chiseled abs and the silky smooth skin of his belly. His cock twitched against her, and she pressed against it in answer, wanting nothing more but to feel him deep inside her.

He growled his approval. His kiss turned frantic. Possessive. His hands rushed to the buttons on her jeans. "I need to touch you," he managed between breaths. "Need to feel if you're wet."

She was soaked, but she couldn't take the time away from kissing him to tell him that. As soon as his fingers found the button at her waistband, something inside her snapped. An urgent need she'd never experienced before. Suddenly she was wiggling against her jeans, helping him in any way she could.

He wrenched the zipper free, pushed her back just enough so he could slide one hand inside. He bypassed her underwear and went straight to her skin, and she gasped at the first touch.

His finger found her slick knot, already hard and aroused. He rubbed over and around until she broke free of his mouth, threw her head back and moaned in ecstasy.

His lips slid over her throat. He bit down, and a lick of pain shot through her. Then he suckled the spot until she was moaning all over again. "Oh, *meli*. You are so wet." His finger slid lower. Deeper. Inside. He groaned against her pulse. "And so tight."

Casey couldn't speak. Could barely move. Her release was coming and she was powerless to stop it. Gripping his shoulders with both hands, she tightened around his finger and let go.

But just as the wave was about to hit, his hand slid free and the pressure eased. He growled low in his throat and grasped the loose denim at her hips. "Need these off. Now." He pushed her quickly to her feet and stripped her free of her jeans in one quick swoop.

She didn't have time to protest, and should have been embarrassed, standing in front of him in only her sweater and low-rise boy shorts, but she wasn't. As he lowered his head and kissed her again, she gave herself over to him and kissed him back while he pulled her close and that erection stabbed into her belly.

"I want to touch you," she whispered.

He drew her bottom lip into his mouth in approval. While he took his fill, she reveled in his kiss, brushed her hand down his torso and slid it palm up into his boxer briefs. He groaned long and deep against her mouth as her fingers wrapped around his arousal. Velvet and steel filled her hand, raw power and the promise of mindless pleasure. She stroked up the shaft, circled the head, and marveled at the control she held over him as his big body shuddered against her.

His hands brushed her breasts, slid under her sweater and into her bra. Her nipples tightened as one rough finger grazed the tip. His mouth nipped her jaw, kissed its way across her skin and settled on the soft skin beneath her ear as he played with her breasts and brought her to new heights of sexual arousal.

Her strokes grew longer, bolder with every touch from his hands. On the downstroke she slid her fingers lower to grasp the twin weights beneath.

He groaned against her neck. "You're playing with fire. In a moment I won't be able to stop."

"I don't want you to stop. I want to know what you feel like when you come."

Whatever restraint he'd been exercising broke with her words. Her sweater was quickly wrenched over her head, her bra ripped free of her breasts as if it were paper. He bent, and his mouth captured first the right nipple and then the left, until she thought she would explode from just that attention.

Just as she was about to beg him to finish her, he turned her quickly and pushed her to her knees on the seat of the couch. One big hand pressed her torso into the cushions so she was leaning over the back of her grandmother's blue-and-orange-checked afghan.

"Gods, you're beautiful," he growled at her back. His weight depressed the sofa as he braced one knee on the cushions between her legs and nudged her thighs wider. "I can't wait to find out if you're as tight as you were in my dream."

His dream? *Oooooooh, yes.*

It struck her then that she should probably be a little afraid. She was with a massive man she didn't know, in a submissive position where he could do just about anything he wanted to her and she'd be hard-pressed to fight back. Considering what those two guys had tried to do to her outside XScream a few months ago, she should have been scared out of her mind. But she wasn't. Somehow, she knew instinctively Theron wouldn't hurt her. And his erotic words were sending her into a complete mind-melting frenzy.

One of his rough hands wrapped around her torso to cup her breast, the other clamped onto her hip. His mouth found her ear and nibbled her lobe until she wanted to scream. And when he pushed his hips into her from behind and rubbed back and forth, white light erupted behind her eyes.

The pleasure was swift and electric and not nearly enough. She didn't realize until moments later that they were both still clothed—he in his boxers and she in her underwear. He pressed forward again, retreated, teasing them both, mimicking what he would, in a moment, do to her naked flesh.

"Theron," she rasped.

His lips slid to the nape of her neck. Trailed lower. He drew his hand down her spine as he rubbed against her again. Both hands found the sides of her underwear as his lips kissed the base of her spine. He lifted his head slightly and pulled the edge down.

"Oh, yes." Casey arched her back and closed her eyes.

She was so swept up in the moment, she didn't realize Theron had gone still behind her until she pressed back and met only air.

She turned slightly to find him staring at her skin with wide eyes.

"What's wrong?"

His finger brushed over the lower left side of her back, just above her buttock. "This marking. Is it a tattoo?"

She knew what he was looking at. And he wasn't the first person to comment on it.

She chuckled. "I'm too afraid of needles to get a tattoo."

When he didn't respond, only continued to stare at her skin, apprehension crept into her chest. "I was born with it. It's just a birthmark."

His eyes lifted to hers. Though he'd removed his hand, heat radiated from his fingers where they hovered over her skin. "This doesn't look like a birthmark. Tell me about your parents."

He wanted to talk? About her folks? *Now?*

Apprehension turned to wariness, and the skin near her birthmark began to tingle. She pushed up from the couch and turned slowly, sliding down onto the cushions until she sat and her mark was hidden from his view.

His jaw was tight, his eyebrows drawn together until a deep crease lined his forehead. One glance confirmed what she'd already suspected. That heavenly erection that had been pressed up against her moments before was gone.

Her skin prickled, and a blast of self-doubt at her near nakedness washed over her. She reached for her sweater, dangling from the arm of the sofa. "My...my parents?"

"Your mother and father. Where are they?"

Unease knotted her stomach. She pulled the sweater over her head and, by the time it was once again shielding her breasts, discovered he was back in his jeans, staring at her with an intense expression she couldn't define.

This was what she'd wanted to avoid, right? This awkwardness. Things had gone too far, and now he regretted it. Just what had happened to change his mind? He'd been all over her before—

"Casey," he said sharply. "Focus. Your mother and father."

She gave her head a sharp shake, unsure why her brain seemed so muddled. "My mother died just after I was born. My father... I never knew him. They had a brief affair years ago when my mother was studying in Europe. She came home after she found out she was pregnant. I...I never met him." She glanced up. "Why do you want to know this now?"

He ignored her question. "Who raised you?"

"My grandmother. This is her house. Was," she amended as she looked around the living room and a sick feeling settled in her stomach. She could actually hear Gigia's disapproving voice in her head over what she'd almost done. "She passed a few months ago. Cancer."

His jaw clenched as he studied her with narrowed eyes. Then he uttered one word.

"Skata."

She knew enough Greek to recognize a few choice swear words. And at that moment, Casey was reminded that he was a complete stranger. She didn't know anything about him besides his name. Why had she helped him? What had actually happened to him? And what was he *really* doing in her house right now?

She pushed up slowly from the couch as questions pinged around in her brain again. Ones she'd somehow—and foolishly— brushed aside earlier. "What's going on here? Why the sudden interest in my genealogy? Just who are you anyway?"

His expression softened. Just a touch. Just enough so those black-as-sin eyes engulfed her attention.

Or maybe she only imagined they did. But for a moment, for a split second, he was the sensuous almost-lover she'd kissed and fondled wildly just a few minutes before.

"No one," he whispered, as he reached for her hand. "No one important." His fingers wrapped around her wrist and pressed into her skin ever so slightly, right over her vein, and though she knew it couldn't be, she thought she heard a note of regret in his voice. "No one you will remember. Close your eyes now, *meli.*"

And like a lamb being lead to slaughter, she did.

CHAPTER SEVEN

Isadora smoothed the covers over her legs and plastered on a smile as fake as the cubic zirconium some human women went gaga over as she looked up at her father's personal physician.

The crease between Callia's perfect eyebrows wasn't a sign of optimism.

Not that Isadora needed confirmation from the race's greatest healer. She was growing weaker by the day. She knew it in her head, felt it in her bones. She just didn't understand why.

Callia replaced the tools in her bag with quiet care. "No visible injuries. Your vitals are strong. Whatever agents you encountered in the human world shouldn't be affecting you like this. Is there something you aren't telling me?"

Now, there's a question. How in the name of Hades to answer that one?

Isadora twisted her hands in her lap to give her time to think of an answer, pushed her long hair over her shoulder and wished for scissors so she could cut the heavy mass. Tradition forbade it though. Females of the royal family were to remain untouched until matrimony. In every sense of the word.

And wasn't that just a kick in the pants? Not to mention, one of the many things she planned to change about the monarchy as soon as she was queen.

If, that is, she lived long enough to assume her crown.

"Of course not," she said under Callia's ruthless stare. "I've told you everything."

Callia's expression remained stoic. Her pale violet eyes narrowed. It was obvious she knew Isadora was lying, but the healer wasn't willing to challenge her.

At least not yet.

One check in the plus column.

Only problem was, it didn't do much to boost Isadora's mood. It was foolish to feel inferior, considering she was destined to command more power than any other Argolean, but at that moment, in front of this *gynaíka*, Isadora felt like a speck on the floor beneath a dirty boot. As a healer, Callia had powers most Argoleans only dreamed of, and Isadora's father loved to rave about the brains beneath Callia's startling beauty. To the extent that Isadora was often of the opinion he'd rather have Callia for a daughter than the one fate had saddled him with.

Her father's greatest disappointment was that in the almost seven hundred years of his life, his only heir had been female. Female and weak.

Callia finally broke the stare-down and finished gathering her things. Her long, auburn hair spilled down her back as she moved. She wore slim, tailored slacks and a fitted blue jacket that looked stylish and bold. As most Argoleans were at least half human, and fascinated with human culture as a whole, their dress and mannerisms often mimicked those from the human world. The exception was the royal family, and Isadora in particular. Sheltered. Cloistered. Forbidden from crossing the portal or even looking through to the other side. All in the name of tradition and of upholding that which had been established over three thousand years ago.

Callia represented everything Isadora wanted to be. She was the consummate professional with enough sex appeal charging the air around her to light an entire village. And confident without fault. Another reason—among many—Isadora wasn't fond of her.

"I'm going to return to the clinic and research your symptoms in more depth." Callia lifted the bag from the side of Isadora's bed. "Then I'm going to speak with your father."

"You don't need to burden him with my situation," Isadora said quickly.

"He's still king. And I greatly suspect the health of his heir is of monumental concern to him."

Right. His heir. Not his daughter. Not because he cared or anything.

Isadora didn't bother to answer. What could she say anyway?

Callia swept out of the bedroom suite as gracefully as she'd entered. From beyond the double oak doors, a trio of mumbled voices drifted into the room. Callia's, Isadora's handmaiden Saphira's, and the unmistakable sounds of a male voice.

Isadora tensed.

For two days she'd been wondering what had happened to Theron. She remembered his coming for her in the human strip club and carrying her outside. But everything after that was a blur. She'd awoken in the castle. In this same four-poster monstrosity that could sleep six comfortably and threatened to swallow her whole each day of her pathetic life beneath the heavy brocade covers she hated, with the morning light from Tiyrns—a city she only saw from her veranda—shining in the cathedral windows across her room.

No one had heard from him. When she'd inquired, her father's nurse said simply that the king had relayed a message to Isadora stating that Theron was attending to Argonaut business.

Which meant none-of-her-business business.

But Isadora knew that wasn't true. Theron had gone looking for her because she'd run off. And something had happened to him.

Heavy footsteps crossed the sitting-room floor outside her door, followed by the loud rap of knuckles against wood and Saphira's strained voice, urging the visitor to leave and let the princess sleep.

Isadora swallowed and pulled the covers up to her chest. She hated feeling weak and timid in front of the Argonauts, especially in front of Theron, because he was so big and strong and...robust. Hated, even more, being stuck in this blasted bed and *looking* like the weakling she really was inside.

"Y-Yes?" she managed in what even she knew was a pathetic voice.

Great commanding presence for the future Queen of Argolea to present to her loyal subjects, Isa.

She cleared her throat.

"My lady," Saphira said from the other room. "The Argonaut Demetrius is here to see you. Are you receiving?"

Demetrius? Here? *Now?*

Of all the Argonauts, Demetrius hated her the most, more so even than the rest of the Argonauts put together, though she didn't know why. And that was saying a lot, considering the Argonauts had a real chip on their shoulders about anything dealing with politics. All of them except Theron. He was the only one who never seemed put out about having to set foot on royal ground when summoned.

"M'lady?"

The hair on the back of Isadora's neck stood up straight as she thought of Theron again. What if Demetrius had come here to relay bad news?

Oh, gods. This couldn't be good.

"C-Come in."

Both heavy doors swung open as if they weighed nothing. And the guardian who stepped through the opening was as startling as the crash of wood hitting wall.

Demetrius was the biggest of the Argonauts, at just over six seven and close to three hundred pounds of pure steel. His features seemed carved out of marble—square jaw, straight nose, striking dimple in his chin and deep-set mocha eyes. Short dark hair framed his face, and the body beneath the black leather duster and skin-tight black pants was as impenetrable as any castle keep. So were his thoughts. He had a don't-mess-with-me air that permeated every room he stepped into, and never had Isadora seen him smile.

Sometimes she wondered if he even could.

"Your Highness," Saphira said in a frantic voice, "I apologize. He wouldn't be deterred. I told him you weren't well enough for visitors today. But he—"

"It's all right, Saphira." Isadora pushed herself higher into the pillows. "I'll see him."

Don't back down. Don't look weak. Stand your ground.

Or lay on it, as the case may be.

Demetrius didn't bow or nod or acknowledge the heir to the throne in any way, not that Isadora expected him to. The Argonauts were, collectively, the black sheep of the race. And Demetrius, even blacker.

Though they'd been chosen by Zeus and appointed as protectors of the race when it was established over three thousand years ago, few in the kingdom today understood or approved of their role. They saw the Argonauts as violent warriors given too much power by the king. Rogue individuals who spent most of their time in the human world hunting daemons, which were really no threat to their society.

Truth be told, up until last week, Isadora had feared the Argonauts like everyone else. She'd regarded them as dangerous rebels who reveled in their power and lived for the killing. She'd even found herself agreeing of late with the Council's anti-Argonaut propaganda campaign, which preached that so long as the portal was protected, Argolea was safe and the Argonauts weren't needed. Those who applied for permission from the Council to cross over into the human world to satisfy their curiosity did so at their own risk. Therefore, what was the big threat?

But then Isadora had found her father's letters. And she'd realized just why the Argonauts were so important. And so dangerous. Right then, she'd discovered the entire truth.

"To what do I owe this unexpected encounter, Argonaut?" She tried to command an air of authority from her regal bed but knew she did a half-assed job. She was in no position—physically or mentally—to command even an ounce of authority.

A snarl curled one side of Demetrius's mouth. "No one's heard from Theron since he went looking for you six days ago. I know you think your own asinine reasons for going to the human realm were warranted, but I disagree, *Highness*."

His last word was spoken with such distaste, he might have punched her in the stomach. The effect was the same. Had she thought she held any authority over him?

Think again.

"Because of you," he went on, "we may have lost one of our own. I want to know *exactly* where you went and what you saw."

She was still reeling from his lack of social grace, but one thing got through loud and clear: the hint of gloating in his voice.

For a horrifying moment, she wondered if Demetrius *wanted* Theron dead.

But that was ludicrous, right? They were kin, born of the same guardian class.

Her spine stiffened. "You would be wise to watch your tongue, Argonaut."

The look he sent her chilled her to the bone, but she lifted her chin anyway, straightened her shoulders and remembered she was royalty. It wasn't wise to test an Argonaut, especially a righteously ticked off one, but at some point she needed to stop being the weakling everyone expected her to be and stand up for herself. If, gods forbid, something had happened to Theron in the human realm, then as soon as her father passed, she was on her own. And the command of this ragtag group would fall to her.

Gods help her.

"You are not my queen," he snarled, his gaze roving over her as if he could see through the sheets and her night dress below all the way to her naked flesh. And the contempt brewing there said he wasn't impressed. "Not yet, anyway, and not likely, from the looks of things here. I answer only to the king. And to my kinsmen. You, Princess, would be wise to watch *your* tongue with *me*."

Isadora refused to swallow or show an ounce of intimidation. Theron frightened her at times, but she knew he'd never do anything to harm her. The others—especially Demetrius—were a completely different story.

"I told the servant your *kin* sent here yesterday everything I knew," she said in a voice she hoped like Hades didn't shake. "When I left Theron, he was fine. You ask the wrong person."

He stepped closer to the bed, his eyes narrowing on her face like a cobra ready to strike. "Oh, I think not, Highness."

Isadora stiffened.

"Do not think it has escaped my attention that you still refrain from declaring what was so damn important in the human realm in the first place. If Theron is dead because of you, my kinsmen will find out what you are hiding. And royalty or not, we will seek vengeance."

He would. That was certain. But not over his grief for Theron.

No, Demetrius would seek vengeance for the simple pleasure of doing so and the promise of a kill.

He towered over her, mere feet from her bed. It was clear to both of them he could do whatever he wanted to her before anyone outside would hear her scream.

She closed her mouth tight.

Seconds passed between them, a virtual stare-down which left her as cold as she imagined the blood pumping in his veins to be. Finally, she gathered her courage and swung her legs over the side of the mattress.

Though it took every ounce of strength she had in her, she slowly pushed to her feet. Even when she stood, he was still nearly a foot and a half taller than her, but she refused to show an ounce of weakness. The crimson robe she wore fell open, revealing the white nightgown beneath, but his eyes didn't stray downward. To him she was nothing.

"Twice you have challenged me, Argonaut. There will not be a third. You are dismissed."

"Princess," he sneered, "you shake." He stepped so close, she had to crane her neck to look up at him, and still they didn't touch. A malevolent, knowing smile cut across his lips. One that seriously made her want to step back.

She fought the urge.

"Tell me, *Princess*. Do I frighten you?"

Perspiration slid down her skin and pooled at the base of her spine. "I'm not afraid of you."

He leaned down so his lips were a breath from her ear. And for a moment, she wanted him to touch her. Just once. So she could have the connection and see into his future and what he was planning, as she'd been able to do so often in the past.

The only problem was, she wasn't sure her powers would work this time.

"You should be," he whispered in a chilling tone. "You would be wise to be very afraid."

"Demetrius. Enough."

They both turned at the harsh command and looked toward the doorway. Theron stood just inside the room, every bit as dark and brooding and dangerous as the commander he was.

Relief swept through Isadora's frail body. She braced a hand on the mattress to steady herself as Demetrius stepped away. One quick glance up confirmed what she suspected. Contempt slid across Demetrius's features before he masked it quickly with indifference.

The kinsmen shared quiet words at the door that Isadora couldn't hear. Demetrius cast her one last withering glare before stalking out of the room.

All her energy flagged. She wanted to flop back onto the bed she detested, but she still hated to show weakness.

Theron walked toward the bed as if he owned the room, those massive boots clomping across the tile floor, the sound echoing in her head. And for a moment it struck her as odd he was wearing denim jeans—something she'd never seen him wear before—but then she looked back up at his face, saw the harsh, disapproving lines there, and her interest in his state of dress left her. "You're pale again, Isadora."

His voice was direct and firm. Not the voice of a concerned fiancé but of a general, commanding his troops. Without meaning to, she backed up until her legs hit the mattress.

Good gods, this was the *ándras* who would soon be her husband. There was no reason for her to be afraid of him. She'd just been reminded her father could have chosen any of the other Argonauts—much more to her distaste—and all of them would have been ten times worse than Theron. So why did the thought suddenly terrify her?

Stop looking at him like he's a leper, and buck up.

She drew in a calming breath and shored up her courage. The situation sucked, but she needed to make the best of it. For both their sakes. "Your kinsmen have been worried. I think they were afraid something had happened to you."

"Did Demetrius hurt you?"

His big body seemed to suck up all the air around him as he drew close. She craned her neck back to look up at his face and was struck by the harsh lines and unfriendly features. "Heavens, no. Why would you think that?"

"Because you look like you're about ready to mop the floor with that gown of yours."

"Gown? I—"

He swept her off her feet before the protest reached her lips, then laid her back in her godforsaken bed. "Hades, Isadora. You look no better than when I saw you last."

His touch was warm against her clothing. Warm, and gone so fast she barely had time to register the sensation. He drew the thick, oppressive covers over her again and tugged them up to her chin.

She immediately pushed them down to her waist. What was that smell? She drew a deep breath. Lavender. Had he been injured?

She quickly pushed the question aside because it didn't matter. He was here, and he was healthy, and he'd never liked females worrying over him.

"Theron, I'm fine."

If he heard her, he didn't respond. Instead, he strode across the room, jerked the door open and barked orders at Saphira in the sitting room. Isadora heard Saphira's shocked response, then *gynaika* footsteps scattering away.

He closed the door and strode back to her, his dark hair swaying as he moved. He made it as far as the end of the bed and stopped. "Tell me what you were doing in that club."

Oh, Hades. Had she really expected him to let that one pass? Gods, she'd been fooling herself.

"I—I was curious."

"Don't lie to me, Isadora. I'm not Demetrius or your father or your humble maidservant."

"Handmaiden."

"Semantics." His jaw tightened. "I haven't told anyone where you were, but as your future husband, I think I have a right to know about the tendencies of my soon-to-be wife. How did you get by my guards into the human world? And why did you go there, specifically?"

Oh, boy. Isadora pursed her lips, glanced down at the heavy covers. She couldn't tell him about Orpheus and how he'd helped her. That would just cause too many problems. But could she tell him the rest? Indecision warred inside her. Did he already know about the half-breeds? About her father? About the reason her father and every king before him continued to send the Argonauts into the human world amid growing disapproval of the race?

She wasn't sure. And it wasn't her place to tell him. Not yet. Not until her father was dead and she ruled Argolea.

If she ruled Argolea.

"I was just curious, Theron." When he huffed in exasperation, she added quickly, "After my father announced our...engagement...I became nervous. You know the rules of the aristocracy. You know I'm...intact." Though it shamed her to admit her virginity to him, she knew he suspected it, and he'd discover the truth as soon as they were married anyway, so she buried the embarrassment and went on. "I heard talk about human skin clubs such as that one. I went to see what every other *gynaika* in the kingdom probably already knows. I didn't want to displease you with my inexperience."

It wasn't *exactly* a lie. At least not completely. She just chose to omit the fact that the idea of sex with him scared the crap out of her.

She held her breath and waited for his response, but he only studied her with unreadable eyes. Just about the time she was sure he wasn't going to say anything, he let out a long, frustrated breath.

"Isadora, you cannot displease me. If anything, I'm the one who is inexperienced. This royalty, protocol, procedure, *skata*, I don't know what to call it. All of it is beyond my comprehension. I know this situation isn't what either of us expected, but it's our responsibility to make it work."

His words should have comforted her. Except they were spoken in that same hard, flat, commanding voice he always used with her. The one that made her think he was ordering her to feel at ease.

It didn't work that way for her.

Resentment brewed in her veins as she studied him—those dark eyes, the stubble on his jaw, the tumble of black hair around his face. She guessed to other *gynaika* he was attractive. To her he was everything she didn't want.

And looking closer, she saw the same thing reflected back at her.

He didn't want to bind himself to her any more than she wanted to be bound. He was giving up just as much as she was. More, maybe.

She took a deep breath and eased back against the pillows, suddenly more tired than she ever remembered being.

"You need rest, Isadora. I have business to attend to with the Argonauts, but I'll be back for the binding ceremony in a few days. If you need me between now and then, you know how to get in touch with me."

Isadora nodded. Through his servant, at Lerna, his estate in the forests outside Tiyrns. She'd never seen it, but imagined it often— soaring ceilings, walls of glass, as massive and grand as he was. Would he take her there after they were married? Would she even want to go?

Probably not, and no. Sickness pooled in her stomach as she faced the grim reality that in a matter of days they would be married. Bound together. Permanently. That part of her soul that had never been at ease clawed to be set free.

"Good night, Isadora."

She had no words to offer in response.

As if he knew, he nodded and disappeared.

Alone and spent, Isadora slid down into the pillows and stared up at the vaulted ceiling above with its intricate wood beams. She tried to clear her mind of everything so she could sleep, but one thought kept pinging around in her brain.

Acacia.

If only there had been a way…

Theron turned at the base of the grand staircase and headed for the king's suite of rooms on the fourth floor of the castle. Enormous Grecian columns flanked the massive hallway. Plush furnishings, gilded mirrors, statuary and fresh flowers atop pedestals and marble tables filled the space around him as he moved. Wealth dripped from every trinket, from the velvet curtains at the enormous windows to the gold-dusted doors he passed along his way.

The place so totally wasn't him, his shoulders tightened with every step he took. How could the king or Isadora stand it? How in Hades would *he* manage living in this mausoleum? He could barely walk down the hall without feeling the overwhelming need to run for freedom.

Just as he reached the end of the hall, the king's door opened and Callia stepped out with her healer's bag in tow. He waited until she turned and saw him before speaking.

"Callia."

"Theron." She tossed her hair over her shoulder and gave him the once-over. "I see the rumors about you were true. I smell lavender. Is there anything you'd like me to look at?"

Always the same Callia. Direct and to the point.

"No, he said. "I'm well enough." Thanks to Casey.

He quickly pushed thoughts of the human out of his mind. "Tell me about Isadora. Her health concerns me."

Callia cast a quick glance over her shoulder toward the king's doorway, then motioned for Theron to join her across the hall, out of earshot.

"Yes," she said when they reached the staggering windows overlooking the stone courtyard below. "Theron, I'm not sure how to tell you this but, there's no other way to say it. Isadora's dying."

Her words should have elicited a reaction, but all Theron felt was…nothing.

No, that wasn't entirely true. A tiny part of him was relieved. And that emotion angered him more than the misery he knew he should be feeling.

"You're sure of this?" he asked. "How? She looks—"

"I've consulted every book I have, looking for something— anything—that's remotely similar. None of the traditional healing methods have worked. Something is broken inside her, only I can't figure out what. It's like…"

"What?"

She frowned. "You'll think I'm crazy."

"Nothing could be crazier than knowing our kingdom is about to lose both its king and its heir. Don't hold back from me, Callia. What?"

She let out a breath. "It's almost like she's losing that part of herself which is inherently Argolean. Her immune system, which is normally strong, is the weakest I've ever seen. It's as if her human half is taking over."

Theron glanced around the posh room but saw none of it. "Have you told anyone else this?

"No. You're the only one. I mentioned her fading health to the king, but I don't want to put more stress on him than necessary. He hasn't seen her since she was returned to the kingdom. I'm afraid her situation could push him over the edge."

Theron glanced toward the cathedral window and the view of Tiyrns down the hill below. A bird flew over the parapet, swooped low into the courtyard and landed on the fountain's edge. He followed the flap of its wings as the time line he'd been ticking off in his mind jumped to light speed. He'd spent precious hours with Casey, when he'd been needed here.

"How long?" he asked. "How long do you think she has left?"

"I'm not sure," Callia said softly at his side. "Could be days. Weeks. Possibly longer. But one thing's certain, Theron. She's not strong enough to produce an heir. A pregnancy would seal her death warrant."

No, he'd been wrong. He did feel something. A shred of impending loss for Isadora. And a low, searing ache at the bottom of his heart for their race. This changed everything.

His gaze snapped to Callia. "This goes no further. The Council cannot be told."

"You're the only one. As her future mate, it's your burden to bring this to the Council of Elders when you see fit."

He nodded, though it was a duty he didn't particularly look forward to. He was a fighter, a soldier who commanded an elite band of guardians against those who would destroy their world if they could. He cared little of politics and status and the bickerings of the Council. If Isadora died without producing an heir—even if he did marry her—the Council would never allow him to become king. And the direction of the Argonauts would shift forever.

He looked toward the king's bedroom door.

"Try not to stay longer than necessary," Callia said. "He's frail. If you have any other questions regarding the princess, come find me."

Callia stepped around him, leaving him alone in the deserted grand hall. When she disappeared from sight, he rubbed a hand over his face, and fleetingly thought of Casey. Staying with her would have been a helluva lot easier and way more pleasurable than coming back to all this.

The king's nurse rose from behind a large desk when he stepped into the outer sitting room. Theron waited while she checked to see if the king was up for a visitor.

When she returned, her lips were drawn down in a disapproving frown and lines creased the skin between her eyes. It was a look he'd seen often from her over the last few weeks. Not that he cared.

"Not long," she said. "He needs his rest."

He rapped on the bedroom door and waited. And told himself that somehow he'd find a way to save Isadora. It was his duty, not only as the leader of the Argonauts, but as her future husband.

"Come in, son," a weak voice called from the other side of the door. "I've been waiting for you."

CHAPTER EIGHT

From his chair near the window, King Leonidas gestured for Theron to join him with one frail, bony hand. "Come, come. Sit."

The elderly *ándras* had lost weight since Theron had seen him only a week ago. His red-checked pajamas and blue silk robe hung on thin shoulders. Hair becoming more and more silver captured the sunlight shining through the tall windows. Lines Theron hadn't noticed before deeply creased the king's sagging face.

As Argoleans only began to age during the last twenty-five years of their lives, the changes in Leonidas were amplified more each day. It was to be expected, yet each wrinkle and jutting bone seemed like a cruel death sentence to such a wise and boisterous male, and not for the first time, Theron cursed the gods who gave them such amazing powers but limited their existence to that of mere mortals.

"I've been waiting for you, my son." Leonidas nodded weakly toward the double doors Theron had closed at his back. "The old hag with the thermometer could rule the Argonauts with an iron fist and run Zeus himself into the ground if she wanted. Don't show fear, lad. She smells weakness." A mischievous glint lit his eyes as he glanced at Theron's jacket. "Did you bring me a gift?"

Theron reached into his coat. The king had few weaknesses, but among them was his well-known penchant for Irish whiskey. Whenever Theron went into the human world, he brought a bottle home with him just for the king.

It was one of the things Theron had always enjoyed most about Leonidas—his passion for life, so unlike other Argoleans who were, as a race, more reserved. He suspected the king had developed his desires during his time secretly spent among the humans, but the elder *ándras* never spoke of those days, and Theron had never bothered to ask.

Theron pulled the bottle from the inner pocket of his leather jacket and handed it to the king. "If she finds this contraband, I'm going to have to turn you in."

The king grabbed the bottle like a parched traveler in a dusty desert. "Pansy."

The human slang brought a smile to Theron's lips as he eased into a chair across from Leonidas.

The king broke the seal and took a long swallow of Jameson, then let out a contented sigh. "The damn Irish got one thing right. If you were half as smart as Zeus contends, you would have bought a bottle of this magic for yourself when you were there." His violet eyes narrowed with unseen knowledge. "But you didn't. Did you?"

"No."

The king took another long swallow and eased back into his seat. Though Leonidas's body had decided after six hundred and eighty-four years it was time to wind down, his mind was still sharp as a tack. And the cunning light shining in his eyes confirmed exactly what Theron suspected was on the old *ándras*'s mind. "Tell me, Theron. How do you find the human world?"

There it was. The same question he always asked whenever Theron came back.

How did he find it? Last night it had been steamy and sultry and nothing like what he'd experienced before. And he had a feeling the memory of that heat might haunt him long into his marriage.

Since that wasn't something he suspected his future father-in-law wanted to hear, he simply said, "Hot."

Leonidas chuckled. "It is that at times. But vibrant." He waved his gnarled hand around the room. "Oh, most would say nothing could compare to Argolea, and I would agree for the most part, but there's always been something intriguing about the human world…something we lack here. Olympus lacks it as well, which is one of the reasons the gods have always been so intrigued with humans, themselves."

"That and that they like to meddle," Theron muttered.

Leonidas grinned. "True. But Argoleans are fascinated as well. Look around you. Sometimes I have a hard time believing this is the same kingdom I was born into. Styles, speech, even our technology—though more advanced—are similar these days to what you find in the human realm."

Theron frowned. Yeah, he'd noticed that over the last two hundred years as well. Argoleans were applying for passage into the human realm more and more, even when it wasn't safe as the daemons grew ever bolder, bringing back popular culture as if it were treasure to be coveted, and the Council was letting them— though only the males. Didn't matter that most thought they were intellectually and physically superior to humans, they were still enthralled with what they didn't have. Theron couldn't see the fascination. And frankly, it disgusted him. Or at least it had. Before last night.

Leonidas took another swallow from the bottle. "Tell me, Theron. You've been all over the human realm. What's your favorite place there?"

"When I'm in the human world, I'm not paying much attention to the landscape."

"No, of course, you wouldn't be, now would you? You'd be hunting daemons, doing what you were bred to do."

Leonidas eyed Theron a long moment, as if debating what to say next, which was something new for the king, as he'd always seemed to know what to say and do. Theron's intrigue was piqued.

"You know, don't you," Leonidas finally said, "that you are probably the greatest Argonaut since Heracles. Your father was a great guardian, and a good friend of mine, but Solon was never as strong as you. He would be proud of what you've become."

Would his father be proud? Theron doubted it. Solon hadn't ever wanted to see the humans caught in the middle of their war. Theron thought differently. The only thing he enjoyed was the fighting. And since legally he couldn't unleash his anger on humans, he took that rage out on the daemons he encountered.

"You, of course," Leonidas went on, oblivious to his thoughts, "are smarter than Solon was. I like to think I had something to do with that, though I know it's probably more a testament to your genetics than it is to our friendship over the years."

The king was obviously feeling his age. Theron pushed aside the sting of the memory of his father's death and the revulsion it caused, and relaxed his shoulders. "You've taught me many things, Your Highness."

Leonidas waved his hand. "Bah. I took advantage, Theron. We both know that. If it were my choice, the kingdom would fall into your hands upon my passing. The Council—" He heaved out a breath. "The Council has different ideas."

"Tradition is to be upheld. It's fed our race for centuries."

The older *ándras* glanced out the window, a faraway look in his eyes. "Fed, but not nourished. Mark my words, boy. They will run this kingdom into the ground if they can. You are the only one who's strong enough to stop them."

He looked back at Theron, and whatever regret had shown in his eyes earlier was long gone. "I know you're not thrilled with the prospect of marrying my Isadora." When Theron opened his mouth to protest, Leonidas held up his knobby hand to stop him. "No, now let's not mince words. There are too many things I must tell you tonight, and I fear our time is coming to a close. Know this though, Theron. The sacrifices you make now and in the future are done for a reason. We may not see them at the time they are offered, but they are there nonetheless. You and I, we are both of Heracles's line, and therefore honor and duty rule us. Remember your blood when all is said and done. Remember the vows you took when you were inducted into the Argonauts."

Wariness crept over Theron as he listened to the king. There was something on the older *ándras*'s mind. Something more than the regrets of a long life and worry over his failing health.

The king took one last swig of whiskey, capped the bottle and handed it back to Theron. "You were absent these past few days. I take it you ran into trouble."

Theron replaced the bottle in his inner jacket pocket. "Four daemons converged just as I located Isadora."

The king nodded. "You sent her back here and dealt with them on your own. Your bravery is commendable. Four against one. Those are insurmountable odds, even for you."

Theron thought briefly of his knight in shining armor and the way she'd taken care of him in the aftermath. Strength, he knew, often came in unforeseeable packages, but he hadn't expected it of the human woman he'd stumbled across. "Not quite insurmountable."

The king eyed him a moment, then pushed himself out of his chair and hobbled toward the windows. Late-afternoon sunlight splashed over his wrinkled features and the weariness was evident in his withering body. "You are holding back. What's troubling you, Theron?"

Theron shifted his weight in his seat. Among the king's greatest powers was his ability to sense emotions in others. Some said he could read minds, but Theron had never known that to be the case. Leonidas did, however, have the ability to draw whatever you were thinking right out of your head, and in this case, though the king knew Theron didn't love Isadora, he didn't want the older *ándras* to know his thoughts kept running back to a human he had no right thinking about.

"The daemons' powers continue to grow," Theron said, hoping to distract the king. "Though the Argonauts have been successful in eliminating a large number of their army over the last few years, we aren't making the dent we should be."

The king showed no reaction, only continued to stare out at the city and the first twinkle of lights from houses far below. "That isn't what truly troubles you, though, is it?"

Theron thought back to the night he'd sent Isadora home. To the fact that the daemons hadn't killed Casey when they so easily could have. He chose his words carefully. "They're not hunting humans. The few we find dead seem more like random accidents than intentional murders."

"No," the king said without turning. "There's no benefit to them to kill humans outright. Not unless they kill the right one."

Theron's brow wrinkled at the strange comment, and while he waited for the king to go on, his spine tingled.

The king finally turned his way. "You know the story of Atalanta, Theron."

Yes, every Argonaut knew the story of Atalanta, who'd traded her soul for dominion over the daemons after Zeus refused to appoint her as one of the original seven Eternal Guardians. Even millennia later, she was still seeking revenge. Her goal was twofold: kill the Argonauts guarding the portal between Argolea and the human realm, and at the same time build her army of daemons.

"Each Argolean soul she sends to Hades makes her and her army that much stronger," Leonidas continued. "And that includes the souls of the half-breeds they kill as well."

"Half-breeds?" Theron asked. "I thought they were a myth."

"And humans think we're a myth. Half-breeds do indeed exist, though they are rare," Leonidas said with a sigh.

Theron thought back to the marking he'd seen on Casey's lower back—the Greek omega surrounded by wings. He'd convinced himself it was nothing more than a human tattoo. All Argoleans had the alpha marking—a brand from the gods themselves that signified the beginning of their race—but this was different.

The king gave him a searching look and nodded. "I can see your mind working, my son. If there's no benefit for daemons to kill humans, and they aren't intentionally hunting humans, what are they after? What are you and the Argonauts really protecting? The answer to both of those questions is simple: the key to the prophesy."

"What prophesy?" Theron asked cautiously.

"The one that will change this war forever."

Theron watched as the king crossed to the large hand-carved desk in the sitting area of his suite. The older *ándras* pulled a leather-bound book from a shelf against the wall and laid it out on the shiny wood surface. After flipping the book open, he sat in his regal chair, looking every inch his six-hundred-plus years, and very royal.

"When Atalanta was passed over as an Argonaut and she made her pact with Hades for immortality, Zeus was very concerned she would wreak havoc on humans in retaliation, since the Argonauts were guarding the portal and she couldn't get into Argolea to extract her vengeance on us. It's no secret Zeus and Hades have a long-running feud, or that Hades found humor in unleashing Atalanta on the humans Zeus has long been so fascinated with. In payment for creating Argolea, Zeus commanded the Argonauts to protect not only our race, but humans as well—some would say to right the wrong of what was once one of our own. And the Argonauts have done so, for nearly three thousand years. But as you pointed out earlier, Atalanta continues to grow in strength, regardless of your efforts."

His hand paused on the book. "Soon she and her army will be strong enough to overpower the Argonauts, leaving the portal unprotected. Then she can slaughter our people at will. That's where the prophecy comes in."

He turned the book so Theron could see it. Tentatively, Theron stepped forward and looked down at the handwritten page before him. The script was old, but he instantly recognized the native Argolean language.

"Loosely translated," the king said, "it speaks of a—"

"Loophole in Atalanta's agreement with Hades," Theron cut in, as his eyes scanned the page. The chronicle he was reading was three thousand years old and bore the seal of Heracles himself.

Leonidas nodded. "Yes. Hades loves a good joke, and as you know, there's always a catch to his bargains. Basically, this outlines the end to Atalanta's immortality. In every generation there are to be two halves of the same whole that, when joined, will render Atalanta mortal once again."

Theron's eyes narrowed with understanding. "She's hunting for the prophesied. To ensure her immortality."

"Yes."

"And the halves are human?"

"No, my son. One is a half-breed. And one is an Argolean."

Theron lifted his eyes to Leonidas. "Why have you never acknowledged the existence of half-breeds?"

The king sighed. "Because there aren't enough to warrant our concern. They learned early on to keep shielded from humans, and from us as well. The earliest kings believed, unwisely, that Argoleans were superior to humans, and that included the offspring of an Argolean and a human, as well. You see, half-breeds tend to live longer than the average human, but they don't possess the powers we do. The few half-breeds who popped up were…strongly encouraged to remain with their human parents."

"Why weren't the Argonauts told?"

"It's been the burden of every king to decide how much to tell his guardians. I decided long ago, the fewer who knew of the prophecy, the safer we would all be. We have had, as you know, some Argonauts who have not been as dedicated to our cause as you and I. Some who have ignored the rules and let our people pass through the portal unchecked. And usually with terrible consequences."

Theron knew that to be true. He thought briefly of Demetrius.

"Unfortunately," the king went on, "I've changed my thinking on this point."

"Why?" Theron asked with narrowed eyes. "What's changed?"

"My daughter is dying." The king moved around the desk to stand in front of Theron, wincing at the pain in his legs. "Callia has informed me of Isadora's dwindling health. I had hoped we'd have more time, but I see now that's a dream."

The king stiffened his spine, and the regality he'd once commanded seemed to flood his shoulders and prop him up a good three inches. "I'm left without a choice, Theron. In her current state, Isadora will never rule, and without another heir, the Council will override everything I and the kings before me have fought to contain. Your marrying her will not solve this problem, not unless she is well enough to bear an heir, which we both know she is not.

"The Council does not understand Atalanta's thirst for vengeance. Over the years and with the buffer the portal maintains, they've forgotten how vicious she can be. They want the Argonauts disbanded, seeing no need for the services you and your kin provide, aside from protecting the portal. Which, foolishly, they feel they can do themselves. If that happens, our race will be slaughtered.

"I've thought long and hard on this, and I want you to know now this is a heavy burden, one I would not place on your shoulders unless it were ultimately unavoidable. Isadora bears the marking of the One. I'm fairly certain my other daughter bears the other mark."

Seconds passed as the king's words sank it. If Theron had thought the king's admission of the existence of the half-breeds was a shocker, he'd been wrong. Nothing compared to what had just been revealed.

"Yes," the king said quietly. "There is another heir, though she will never rule, because she is a half-breed. Odds are good she doesn't even know what she is or that her fate is about to change forever."

"How...?" Theron had trouble grasping what he'd just been told. "How long have you known about her?"

"Since she was born. Her mother was human, a student I met when I ventured to Athens. Gaia was..." Something soft passed over his eyes as he looked off into space. "Kind. Isadora's mother had passed not long before I met the woman, and Gaia provided the comfort I needed at the time. Our affair was brief, but she meant a great deal to me. I arranged for her and her daughter to be well cared for, and I was careful not to reveal who or what I was, but I think Gaia knew. She was a very bright girl. Passionate. Full of life, and very interested in her heritage and the myths of the gods. She disappeared with the baby shortly after the birth, and though I have often wondered what happened to them, I never saw them again."

Unease rolled through Theron's stomach. "Then how do you know this child bears the marking?"

"I don't. But I suspect, primarily because Isadora and this young woman are of the same strong bloodline, and because Isadora went looking for her after she found the passage of the prophecy in the chronicles days ago."

That explained what Isadora had been doing in the human world. She'd gone to find her other half. His mind ran back once more to what he'd seen on Casey's skin last night. To the marking he feared was more than just a tattoo.

"The only way to ensure the race's safety is to find this marked half-breed and bring her here to Argolea before the daemons find her and kill her first," Leonidas said firmly.

"And then what?" Theron asked. "If the prophesy is fulfilled and Atalanta becomes mortal, she'll be more violent in her quest for revenge."

"True, but her powers will be limited. And then, Theron," the king said quietly, "the war truly begins. The one that will eventually give us our freedom."

Theron thought back to everything his father had believed in. Everything Theron despised. "And what of the humans? Will she not use them to get to us?"

The king stiffened. "We are running out of options. Every king has had to balance the directive of Zeus with what is best for our people. In the end, I must think about our world first. Yes, there may be more human casualties if the prophecy is fulfilled, but it's a small price to pay for the safety of our realm. Ultimately, I have faith that you and your kin can mount a defense. And in doing so, Theron, you will save Zeus's precious humans. You will also save your queen. You save our monarchy and our way of life. And you ensure the Council will not rule in my stead.

"Your destiny has called you, my son," the king said more softly. "You are the one I trust to finish what was started centuries ago. It's what you were born to do."

Theron considered all that the king had told him. Though the hurt of betrayal ran through his veins at the secrets kept from him and his kinsmen, he understood that knowledge of the prophesy could have caused pandemonium in the race, especially among the Council.

No matter how Theron looked at it, every choice in front of him was riddled with the probability of failure. A great many would die before the end—humans, half-breeds and Argoleans—and if he lived through it, he'd have to look back and know his decisions were made at the expense of many lives.

"What happens to this half-breed woman if I find her and bring her to Isadora?"

For the first time, the king avoided Theron's eyes. He dropped his arm and seemed to study his slippers with great interest. "One can't be certain."

"But you are," Theron said, sensing the king's lie. "You know exactly what will happen to her. Don't hold your tongue now, not when so much is at stake."

The king looked up. "She'll die. Her Argolean essence, that part of her that Isadora is losing, will be recycled by Isadora."

"And you know this for a fact?"

"Yes."

"How do you know it won't be the other way around?"

"Because weak as she may be, Isadora's Argolean heritage is stronger than the half-breed's. She'll take what she's missing and she'll be healed." The king reached out and laid a hand on Theron's shoulder, and in his touch there was compassion, though Theron couldn't tell if it was directed at him, at Isadora or at the daughter he'd never known. "It's not a question of how, Theron, it's a question of when. You have to find this woman and bring her to Isadora. Before it's too late."

This woman. Theron didn't miss the fact the king refused to call her by name. If she was indeed the Chosen One, and Theron was sent to find her, his presence in her life would lead her right to her death.

He'd killed many. Death was a part of who and what he was. But rarely a human, and only when it was unavoidable. And never a female.

What if Casey was this Chosen One? Could he do it?

As quickly as the thought struck, he dismissed it. The marking he'd seen on her back wasn't proof. There was still a chance it had been nothing more than a normal tattoo. Or a simple birthmark.

He'd been tired and injured and spiked up on lust when he'd been with her. He hadn't been thinking clearly last night.

"How will I know her?" he asked.

"Because she bears the marking of the Chosen, just like Isadora." The king's voice softened as Theron's mind spun. "Sometimes, my son, a great sacrifice by one must be made for the survival of many. Find her, Theron. And bring her to Isadora. You are the only one who can."

CHAPTER NINE

Casey clenched her hands in her lap, released her fingers and fought the urge to pop her knuckles. What the hell was taking so long?

She glanced at the wall clock in Dr. Carrow's exam room Monday afternoon and took a deep breath to steady her nerves. Ten minutes she'd been waiting. *Only* ten minutes. She needed to get a grip and settle down.

Two more minutes passed. Two minutes in which Casey felt like crawling out of her skin.

Okay, so sitting still wasn't going to do it for her. The paper crinkled as she hopped off the table and held the pink cotton gown together at her back. Coming here was a smart thing. Playing the what-if game over her exhaustion and nausea wasn't doing her any good. There was a logical explanation for the way she'd been feeling lately. It didn't mean she was going to end up like her grandmother.

A crisp knock sounded at the door, and Casey whipped around at the sound. "Come in," she said quickly, moving back to the exam table.

Dr. Jill Carrow walked into the room dressed in slacks and a navy blouse. Her auburn hair was pulled into a ponytail, a stethoscope was looped around her neck and she held a medical chart in her hand. She was, Casey thought, probably not much older than herself, but she exuded a confidence Casey had never known. And that put Casey at ease. At least a bit.

Jill smiled. "It's good to see you, Casey. It's been a while."

"Yeah." Casey shrugged, feeling stupid for not calling the woman who'd taken care of her grandmother up until the end. She balled her hands into fists at her sides against the vinyl cushion and thought of the thousand excuses she'd conjured up for why she hadn't scheduled that lunch date as she'd promised six months ago at her grandmother's funeral. They all sounded lame now. She settled on the truth instead. "Doctor's offices aren't my favorite places to hang out."

Jill chuckled. "Trust me, I know. No harm done." She sat on the swivel stool, opened her folder to study her last notes and then looked up. "So tell me what's going on."

Casey took a deep breath. "Nothing much. I mean, well…" Here's where she sounded like a hypochondriac. She crossed her dangling stocking feet at the ankles, twisted her hands together in her lap again. "I've been having some symptoms. Nothing major, but…" She bit her lip.

Jill immediately nodded in understanding. "But you just thought you'd get them checked out to be safe." She rose from her seat and set the folder on the counter along the far wall. With one hand she pulled a penlight from her pocket and flashed the beam over Casey's eyes. "Let's take a look."

"It's probably nothing," Casey said quickly. "I mean, a little insomnia's not a big deal, really. I—"

"Casey." Jill put her hand on Casey's arm. "A smart woman takes cues from her body. If she notices something out of the ordinary, she gets it checked out. You did the right thing by coming in. I'm sure it's probably nothing, but it's worth a quick check. And considering your family history, it's a smart one."

Casey released the breath she'd been holding. Of course Dr. Jill got it. She'd been foolish to think the woman wouldn't. She managed a weak smile. "Thanks."

Jill smiled. "Okay then. Now tell me what's going on."

Casey described her symptoms—insomnia, nausea, loss of appetite. She tried to downplay the bits of memory loss she'd experienced over the weekend because it hadn't been anything her grandmother had gone through, but one scathing look from Dr. Jill and she threw them out there anyway. Might as well be completely honest.

A small furrow creased between Jill's eyes as she felt behind Casey's ears and down her neck. "So they're not exactly blackouts but—"

"More like lapses," Casey said quickly. "And only the past couple of days." She decided not to mention her weird dreams for fear the good doctor might send her to a shrink. Instead she added, "I remember going home from the club but not how I got into my car or why I left."

"Hm," Jill said. "Could just be exhaustion. You've got some marks here on your neck." She moved to study the side of Casey's throat closer. "They look like—"

Heat crept up into Casey's cheeks. "Oh, yeah. That." She reached a hand up to rub the mystery hickey from the mystery man she'd very nearly had a one-night stand with.

Theron. That was his name. Another of her *lapses*. She remembered his name, but not much else about him, other than that he seemed to be a walking sex god who had a strange way of speaking. Oh, that and the fact that there was something oddly familiar about him, and that she'd wanted to jump his bones the moment she met him.

But the important stuff—like how he'd ended up at her house and where he'd gone when he vanished after their impromptu make-out session—were still a mystery to her.

"Casey?" Casey's eyes snapped up to Jill's curious face. "Something you want to tell me?"

Yeah, right. Casey gave her head a swift shake. "No. Ah, I mean, that was from a date."

Sort of.

A sly smile spread across Jill's face. "Well, at least I know you aren't so sick or tired that you've given up your social life. That's a good sign."

Casey frowned. She wished that were the case. Her evening with Theron the Mystery Hunk had been a definite exception to her measly love life. Or lack thereof.

"You've got a couple swollen lymph nodes," Dr. Jill said. "Nothing major, so my guess is your body's fighting off the flu, which is why you're not feeling so hot right now. Just to be safe though and to rule everything out, let's do a complete physical, okay? I see from your chart you're due for one anyway."

Casey blindly nodded. Knowing she wasn't doomed to the same fate her grandmother had been dealt was worth suffering through a half hour of poking and prodding. "Okay."

Jill smiled. "I'll get the nurse and be right back."

As Jill moved out of the room, Casey leaned back on the angled table and rested her head on the pillow. The paper crinkled beneath her. She stared up at a tiny fairy hanging from a strand of fishing line from the ceiling, crossed her hands over her belly and breathed out a sigh of relief.

She was good. All was well. When she left here she could go back to doing exactly what she'd been doing before her crazy weekend rendezvous with Theron. Mainly, figuring out a way to keep her grandmother's bookstore afloat. She really didn't have a choice, did she? If she couldn't make this work...where else would she go?

At some point she had to stop wandering and settle in. Quit looking for that elusive paradise where she'd fit in and grow roots. She was twenty-seven years old, for crying out loud. It was way past time. Her grandmother had loved this town, had loved the bookstore. Casey was determined to make this last move work.

As she relaxed farther into the pillow, she thought briefly of her almost one-night stand again. Her cheeks heated. Not the smartest thing she'd ever done, but at least one of them had come to their senses before it was too late. She'd just chalk the whole experience up to bad choices. And being overworked. And exhausted. But one thing was certain. It definitely wouldn't happen again.

"Casey?" Dr. Jill called from the other side of the door with a soft knock. "Are you ready?"

"Yes," Casey said. "Ready as I'll ever be."

Nick sensed the air change just as he had two days before. He lifted his mouth from the breast he'd been laving and went completely still.

"Jesus, don't stop now," Dana groaned beneath him as she arched her back to offer more. "Not yet."

"Shh." He planted a hand on the crisp sheets of her bed and tuned his hearing toward the disturbance he'd felt.

Her eyes narrowed in concentration as if she were listening as closely as he was. Of course she couldn't, but it didn't make her try any less.

"I don't feel anything," she whispered moments later. Her breath fanned across his cheek, remnants of the vodka and cranberry juice she'd inhaled to celebrate the end of her shift at

XScream wafting toward his nose. Outside, a car whooshed by on the rain-slicked streets, the only sound drifting up to the second-floor apartment she kept above the Wash-n-Go Laundromat on Third Street in downtown Silver Hills.

He knew why she kept the apartment and didn't live with the others, but it bothered him. Their kind should stick together. Especially now. Especially when he sensed there was a change coming. His scars had been tingling for days now.

"Nick?"

Her voice held an edge of impatience, a hint of unease and a whole lot of lust. It took less than two seconds to make up his mind.

He pushed off her and snapped his jeans. "I gotta go."

Her brow knit in disbelief just before her famous temper reared its ugly head. She sat up, not caring in the least she was naked as the day she was born. Dana Sampson was built like a siren and knew it. "No way. Not again. I swear to every one of the *fucking* gods if you walk out this time, it's the last."

He tugged his black T-shirt back over his head. "Don't be so damn dramatic, Dana. It's unbecoming."

"Unbecoming?" she scoffed. "Unbecoming is leading me on like this. Especially after the night I had. Karl was a complete ass at the club. I nearly laid him out flat when he groped me behind the bar for the tenth time and you *know* I can't get caught doing that shit again. I need a release as bad as you do. But no, you gotta get me all heated up and leave. Is this a game to you?" She bolted off the bed and shoved a finger in his chest. "If you go, I'm not letting you back in."

He sensed she was serious and that she was holding ground she felt sacred in Danaland. He also knew he could bend her will with just one push if he really wanted. But whatever want he'd had had fizzled as soon as he'd felt the change. He shrugged and reached for his leather jacket from the purple velvet chair she'd gotten from some hippie shop in Eugene. "You gotta do what you gotta do, babe."

She crossed her arms over her very natural, very well-endowed chest and glared hard in his direction. "I mean it this time, Nick. You're not the savior of the goddamn world. When are you going to figure out no one gives a fuck what you do? Those kids—all of them—you can't save them."

There was just enough truth in that statement to draw his jaw together hard. He turned his back on her and shrugged into his coat.

"The sooner you tell them all to cut and run, the safer they'll all be. Why the hell won't you do that? It's like you're just waiting for something apocalyptic to happen. If I didn't know better, I'd say you were inviting it so you could swoop in and save the day like your brother."

He whirled back at her so fast she didn't have time to brace herself. He caught her by the throat and pressed his fingers into her skin hard enough to get her attention. She gasped, her hands flying to his to try to get him to let go. In her wide eyes he saw surprise, then disbelief, then the edge of bone-melting fear.

And though it sickened him, her reaction fed the hatred he normally kept locked deep in the recesses of his soul. That part of him that was linked to the darkest evil. That part he fought every day of his unending life.

"You do not know of what you speak."

She rose on her tiptoes, her mouth opened to draw air into her shrinking windpipe. In her wide cobalt eyes he saw the reflection of what he was at that moment: a black stain, the scarred remnants of what passed for a man, the thing of nightmares. And he still didn't let go.

His lip curled in a snarl as he watched her grapple for control. Somewhere inside he registered he should feel something for her, for the twisted relationship they had, but he couldn't muster anything more than disgust.

He was just about to release her when a tingling ran over each of the scars on his back. And he knew.

She would die.

Not tonight. Not by his hand.

But soon.

He eased his grip. She dropped to the floor and sucked in a large breath. With steady hands she massaged her tender throat. He'd probably left marks, but that was nothing new for Dana.

"You bastard," she choked out.

No argument there. He didn't have enough emotion to muster a response, so he zipped his jacket instead and regarded her with steely eyes. "Go to the colony, Dana."

"Why?" she snapped, angry waves radiating off her naked flesh as if from a coal-burning furnace. "So you can put on a repeat performance? No thanks."

"No, so you can live. Something's coming."

He didn't know what, exactly, but the only other time his messed-up skin had buzzed like this, his half brother had been sworn into the Argonauts. Ever since then there'd been small bursts of electricity, a hum occasionally when the hunters were out, but nothing as big as what he'd felt the last few days. He knew now, of course, that the change had started back then, with Demetrius's induction, just as he knew it was now growing, rising like a swell of water on the open ocean, waiting to crash in a tidal wave over everything his people knew.

And how fucked was it that he was the only one that could see it coming?

He turned for the door, more intent than ever to figure out what the hell had just come through the portal again, and why only two days after the last crossing.

"Wait."

He halted but didn't turn.

"You're serious, aren't you?" she asked in a small voice.

He looked over his shoulder and watched as she pulled up the sheet to cover her naked flesh. The twin Fury tattoos on her breasts flashed as she moved. The third one, he knew, hovered at the small of her back. Modesty wasn't something she worried herself with, which meant she was right and truly scared.

Finally.

"Get to the colony and stay there," he said sternly. "I promise you'll be safe. I won't bother you there."

"Nick." Regret rushed over her features as she reached a hand out.

Yeah. Their sicko relationship was right and truly fucked. She liked it rough and he liked to give it to her, but what had just happened had crossed the line. And the fact she didn't see that flipped a trigger in his brain that screamed, *Get the hell out now. Fast.*

He was out the apartment's front door before she even took a step his direction, and headed for the back stairs that ran down to the alley at the rear of her old building. His hearing was still in tune with what was happening around him, searching for what he'd sensed inside, which is why he heard her sniffle one floor up and from behind supposedly soundproof walls.

And shit, like he needed to hear that tonight.

He slung a leg over his Harley, parked near the Dumpster, and snapped on his helmet, not because he was worried about cracking his skull open but because it was the law. A hell-on-wheels, no-helmet biker attracted cops. And cops attracted trouble.

The bike roared to life beneath his fingers. As he tore out of the alley and onto the four A.M. deserted streets of Silver Hills, the raw power of the machine beneath him rumbled through his body.

As did the tingles. All over his skin. Stronger this time. Vibrating electric energy against his clothing so much that he was sure he had to be glowing beneath his denim and leather.

The portal had opened again. And this time what came through was no match for the darkness inside him. It was a thousand times worse.

CHAPTER TEN

"Are you sure there's no sex in here, dearie? Because you know how I feel about all that humping and bumping."

Casey plastered on her most pleasant yes-ma'am smile as the bell above the door jangled. A blast of crisp air rushed into the store just before Dana stepped in, wearing chic jeans, her favorite chunky boots and a bloodred leather jacket with shiny silver grommets running up and down the sleeves. In her hands she held two steaming paper cups, one of which Casey desperately hoped was filled with mocha Valencia.

Casey held up a finger to tell Dana she'd be right with her and turned the book in the sixtyish woman's hands so she could see the author's photo on the back jacket. "None at all, Mrs. Colbert. Joan Swan strictly writes mysteries. A little murder and mayhem doesn't bother you, does it?"

Adelaide Colbert glanced over her reading glasses at Casey and lifted her badly red-tinted eyebrows. "Of course not. Do I look like a prude? Just so long as we're clear on the sex thing." She flipped the book back to examine the cover, then lifted her voice just loud enough so anyone else browsing the stacks in Casey's corner bookstore could hear her. "I run the women's league at Saint Michael's First Episcopalian. I have a reputation to live up to, you know. No humping and bumping." She winked at Casey.

Casey reached for the end aisle display and added another Swan book to Mrs. Colbert's arms. "Then might I suggest this one as well. Definitely no sex here."

Mrs. Colbert harrumphed, then took the books Casey had suggested toward the register at the rear of the store where Mandy,

Casey's part-time employee, rang her up with a smile and chatter about the local high-school football team.

Amused, Dana sauntered in Casey's direction and handed her the Java House cup she'd picked up across the street. "I thought Swan wrote steamy fireman romances."

Casey lifted the cup and took a slow sip. Ah, just like those chocolate oranges Gigia used to send her at Christmas. Life was already better. She licked her lips. "She does."

"Uh-huh," Dana said. "Say no more."

Casey waited as the older woman finished her purchase and headed for the exit. Warmth spread from the cup in Casey's hand to her fingers and then into her arms, and she hoped it would continue its journey through her chilled body. She was colder today than she had been yesterday. Colder and more tired. It had taken all her energy just to get out of bed and haul herself to the bookstore.

"Stay warm, Mrs. Colbert. Weather report said we're in for a windstorm."

"I'll believe it when I see it," the old woman muttered as she pulled the heavy glass door open. "Good day, Casey."

"Speaking of the storm…" Casey handed Mandy a checkbook and the list of supplies she'd made out earlier. "Why don't you head over to Staples now before the weather hits? I can handle things here."

"You sure?" Mandy asked, already reaching for her coat from the hook along the back wall.

"Yeah," Casey said. "Go ahead and grab an early lunch while you're out."

"Want me to pick up any for you?" Mandy looped her scarf around her neck.

"No. I'm fine."

"You dieting?"

The question caught Casey off guard. She knew she'd lost some weight—she could feel it in her clothing—but not so much she thought anyone else would notice. "No," she said, in what she hoped was a calm voice. "Just not hungry."

"'Kay. I'll catch you later." Mandy smiled at both of them, then left the store.

Unfortunately, Dana wasn't so inclined to buy Casey's "not hungry" line. She studied Casey with scrutinizing eyes. Which only unnerved Casey more. Like she didn't have enough to deal with today?

"Thanks for the coffee," Casey said quickly to fill the lull in conversation.

"No problem." Dana glanced down at the book on the counter and lifted her eyebrows. "Something I should know?"

Shit. Casey's eyes cut to the title she'd pulled from the stacks before opening and then had been too distracted to set aside: *Healthy is a State of Mind.* She quickly stuck the book under the counter, out of sight. "A customer requested it. Hey. What are you doing here so early anyway?" She looked at the clock—ten forty-five A.M.—then back at Dana. "Didn't you close last night?"

"Yeah." Dana shrugged, following the change in topic as she leaned a hip against the counter. "Couldn't sleep."

Though they didn't get together often, over the past few months, Dana had developed a knack for dropping in unexpectedly, and she was the only person at XScream Casey felt even remotely close to. But her friend was a creature of the night and rarely ventured out before midday, so the fact she was here now brought Casey's instincts on alert. For reasons Casey couldn't explain, there was a bond between the two of them. Had been from the moment they'd met. She'd stopped questioning it about two months ago and had finally just given in to the strange sensation of having a friend around, albeit an unpredictable one. "Uh-oh. Rough shift?"

"No worse than normal."

Casey nodded in understanding. And cursed Karl, as she did every time he made a play for Dana. The guy was a slime, and he ran XScream as if it were his own private Playboy Mansion. Dana wasn't the only girl who'd mentioned he liked to get rough, but she was one of the only ones who routinely put up with it. Why, Casey didn't know, but she'd given up bugging Dana about it because the answer was always the same: *I have my reasons.*

Thank God Karl had never tried anything on her, Casey thought. But hell if she could see what Dana's reasons were now. "I guess that explains the marks on your neck."

"I guess so. Doesn't explain yours though."

Damn. She thought the collar and makeup she'd applied this morning had hidden her fading hickey.

Casey adjusted her collar while Dana grinned like an idiot and didn't do a thing to hide her own make-out marks. "Wanna kiss and tell?"

"No."

Dana pursed her lips. "Party pooper."

"Whatever." Casey tipped her head and tried one last time to get through to her friend. "Just please tell me it wasn't Karl who did that."

"It wasn't Karl." Dana pushed away from the counter, and whatever teasing mood she'd been in suddenly vanished. "Look, I only stopped by to let you know I'm taking off for a while."

"You are? Where to?"

"Don't know. Was thinking maybe I'd head north, up to Canada. Maybe into Vancouver. You could go with me if you want." A smile tugged at her mouth. "State-of-mind thing and all that. We could hit Robson, do some shopping, hook up with some Canucks. You know what they say about Canadian men. Everything's bigger up north."

Casey cringed and held up a hand. "Ew. It's too early in the morning to think about that." Especially now. Especially when all it would do was get her worked up over the naked mystery man she'd had in her bed two nights ago. The one who'd left his mark on her neck, who'd branded her skin with his heat, then vanished like a thief in the night without so much as a flippin' word.

And she wouldn't *even* let herself think about the size of his…yeah.

"It's *never* too early to think about sex, as the innocent Mrs. Colbert just pointed out." Dana glanced over her shoulder. "Speaking of which, why don't you ring me up one of those Swan books for the road."

"You're incorrigible."

"I'm something," Dana agreed.

When she had her new book and the coffee was gone, Dana headed for the exit. She stopped two steps from the door and turned to study Casey for a long moment. "You know, I don't get along with most women."

"Really?" Casey mocked. "I never would have guessed." Though she was a good five inches shorter than Casey, Dana had always seemed bigger, more vibrant, more alive than anyone Casey knew. If Dana was in a room, people took notice. She just had that kind of personality that filled up the space around her.

"I didn't like you at first, you know. There was something about you that I found odd. Funny, huh? Most people say that about me."

"You are odd, Dana. Unexpected trip to Vancouver no exception."

Dana smiled. "Yeah, well. If we were all the same, how boring would that be?"

"Very."

"See? Different is good." As quickly as her smile had come, something dark crept into the edges of Dana's pretty blue eyes. "Do me a favor, Casey."

"Anything."

"Watch your back. People around here aren't what they seem."

"Meaning…?"

"Meaning, be careful. Ted Bundy was a good-looking guy and he turned out to be a serial killer. Don't buy things at face value. Not everyone's as sweet as I am." Before Casey could ask what that meant, she was being hugged. "And don't stress over what the doctor tells you."

"How did you—?"

"Gotta run. See you when I get back."

Dana left the store in a rush of wind. Dry leaves scattering the sidewalk outside blew into the store before the door snapped shut, bringing with them the smell of impending rain and gloom.

How had she known? Casey stared out at Dana rushing across the street, and tried to remember if she'd mentioned the appointment. Had she written it on something here in the store? Had she told Dana about her fears and then forgotten all about their conversation?

The answer to those questions was simple: she hadn't told anyone what she was afraid might be wrong with her, so there was no way Dana could know. She'd barely even admitted it to herself.

People around here aren't what they seem.

What the hell did that mean?

A strange sense of foreboding slid down Casey's spine as she stood rooted in place, watching Dana through the plate-glass windows as she walked briskly down Main Street and turned onto Halston.

They'd only known each other six months. What was Dana trying to tell her? What did she know?

Nothing, Casey decided. Dana was obviously just reading the signs. Mandy's comment, the book, feeling emotional about her trip… Maybe she'd even seen Casey's car parked outside the clinic yesterday.

Yeah, that had to be the answer.

Pushing the jumbled thoughts out of her mind, Casey scanned the street. Two cars were parked down the curb, but the sidewalks were empty. The coffee shop across the way was a virtual deserted island. Beyond the town square where no children played, dark clouds gathered, signaling the coming storm.

People obviously had heard the forecast of high winds and heavy rain and this time taken heed, hunkering down at home, ready to wait it out.

Everyone but her.

She turned for the checkout counter and considered the possibility of closing early. But what would she do at home alone for the rest of the day? She was on pins and needles waiting for that dreaded phone call from the doctor, unable to settle down because her brain kept pinging back and forth between what she suspected was wrong with her and what had happened the other night.

The phone rang just as she reached the stock-room door. She froze and glanced toward the counter. A strange vibration hummed along the base of her spine, near her birthmark.

Be careful. Don't buy things at face value.

She lifted the receiver and mustered up her courage. "Once Upon a Time."

"Casey? It's Jill Carrow."

Her doctor. Casey pulled in a breath. "Hi. I was hoping you'd call."

"I have your test results back."

No beating around the bush. This couldn't be good. "And…?"

Jill hesitated, and in the drawn out silence, Casey heard her answer before the words were even spoken. "And I think you'd better come in so we can talk about this in person. I'm afraid we found something."

* * *

It was dangerous to open the portal in the same place he'd exited only days before. To keep from drawing unwanted attention, Theron chose a location fifty miles from Silver Hills and hot-wired a car he lifted off an abandoned side street to drive himself back to the small town.

Man, it would just be easier if he could flash from place to place on earth like he could in Argolea. But no, that was an ability he and his Argolean kin enjoyed only in their homeland. And truth be told, if any humans saw him disappear into thin air, they'd probably freak out more than if they knew daemons roamed the lands around them.

Since he'd walked among humans most of his life, he had a fair working knowledge of their technology, so the mechanical aspects of driving weren't a big deal. He normally wasn't one to steal, but desperate times called for desperate measures, and he was anxious to get to Silver Hills and get this little job over with.

He slowed as he neared the town's city limits and turned onto Main Street. A series of shops lined both sides of the street, while little banners announcing the annual Autumn Harvest Festival flapped in the wind from old-fashioned-patina light posts every two hundred feet. A few leaves desperate to hang on to summer clung to branches above the road, but their days were numbered. Mother Nature was in a foul mood, judging from the swirling black sky above, and she looked nearly ready to unleash.

It was, Theron suspected, the quintessential American small town. When he'd passed through here only days before, he hadn't paid it much heed, but now he did. The gingerbread trim, the hand-painted signs, the dried hops strung around doors and wound into wreaths. Part of him wondered what the humans who lived here would do if they knew one of his kind lived among them.

His kind?

No. Not his kind. This time the woman he'd come to find was nothing more than a human with a little something extra. Something Isadora needed.

He parked the car halfway up Main Street and climbed out. Crisp air surrounded him as he headed down the sidewalk. The king had given him only a name—Acacia Simopolous—and told him of a store the woman's family had run for the last twenty-odd years. He figured it was the best place to start.

A few cars were parked along the street, but there were surprisingly few humans roaming around for this time of day. All things considered, it was fairly safe. Daemons didn't like to come out during the day, though that didn't mean they wouldn't. Scanning businesses he passed, Theron spotted his target.

A tingle ran over his spine, and he fleetingly thought of Casey again and wondered if he'd run into her on this trip.

He hoped not, for more reasons than the most obvious.

A "closed" sign swayed from a hook on the inside of the door. Theron peered into the shop and saw some of the lights were still on. Strange to be closing so early in the day, but what did he know of human behavior?

He decided to try the door. To his surprise, it pushed open.

A bell jingled above, and as he stepped inside he was immediately enveloped by warmth and scents of paper and vanilla wafting on the air.

"I'll be right with you," a female voice called.

Casey's voice hit him like a punch to the gut, stealing the air from his lungs and nearly buckling his knees. The wicked attraction he'd felt for her at first sight erupted in his chest as he stepped farther into the store and saw her at the far end of an aisle of books, standing three steps up on a ladder, replacing leather-bound tomes on a high shelf. His body hardened with just one look, an urge to touch her soft skin, to feel her flesh against his, to finish what they'd started, as strong as it had been the night they'd been together.

But now that desire was overshadowed by the reality that he'd been wrong. This human—whom he hadn't been able to stop thinking about for three long days—was the woman he'd been sent to find.

The king's long-lost daughter.

The lone woman who would save his race.

The one he would lead into certain death.

CHAPTER ELEVEN

She should have been shocked to see him again, but Casey was too numb to feel anything other than irritation at the interruption. "We're closed early due to the weather."

"I—" Theron cleared his throat. "I'm looking for Acacia Simopolous."

He didn't even know he was looking for her? Wonderful. Her day was *sooo* getting better.

"You found her." She refocused on her task and shoved a book on the shelf harder than it needed. "And for the record, the only person allowed to call me Acacia is my grandmother, who, thanks for reminding me, is dead. Now, if that takes care of the reason you're here, you can head right back out the way you came in."

He let out what sounded to her like a frustrated breath. As if she cared.

"I'd like a few minutes to speak with you—"

She turned to flick a withering look his direction from above. "My friends call me Casey. Since you are neither a friend nor relative, you can call me Ms. Simopolous. Assuming, that is, you can remember my frickin' name."

When he continued to stare up at her with a befuddled expression, her last shred of patience broke. "Oh, for heaven's sake. What the hell are you doing here, Theron? You made it perfectly clear the other night you didn't want to have anything to do with me."

"You remember that? I didn't—"

"Trust me, buddy. I'd like nothing more than to forget I ever met you."

"Acacia—"

She waved a hand and continued to roll right over him as the pressure in her chest intensified and every one of her worries hit full force like a Mack truck. "So there's really no reason for you to be here now, is there? Just turn around and go, because I don't want you to…be…here right…"

Oh, God. She was gonna lose it. The pressure built until it felt like a ten-ton bomb was sitting on her chest. Tears pushed at her eyes. She would not cry in front of this man. She wouldn't give him a single reason to think it was about the way he'd treated her, because it wasn't. It was about everything else. Everything Jill had just told her.

She climbed down off the ladder quickly and pressed a hand to her chest.

"Meli." He advanced on her.

"Don't!" She held up a hand to block him. There must have been enough panic in her voice to get through, because he stopped two steps away. She focused on taking several breaths, on clearing her head, and when she felt calmer, she opened her eyes and looked up.

His skin had healed so well, there were no remnants of the accident he'd been in. He was, she noticed now, just as rugged and dangerous and sexy as he'd seemed that night in XScream. The stubble on his jaw, the dark, silky hair brushed back from his face, the strong square chin and those deep-set black eyes. But he also looked tired. Worn. As if he carried the weight of something mighty heavy on his shoulders.

Well, that made two of them. And she didn't have the time or energy to worry about what the hell was up with him.

"I asked you to leave. I'd appreciate it if you'd do at least one thing I asked."

"Are you all right?"

Was she all right? What a joke. She wanted to scream, *No, I'm not all right. I'm never going to be all right again, you idiot!* But she knew it was useless and childish, and she had just enough self-respect left to keep from making a fool out of herself in front of him. She'd already done enough of that the other night, when she'd nearly gone to bed with a complete stranger.

"I'm fine," she snapped, jerking her hand away before he could touch her. Why wasn't he leaving?

He glanced around the store as if taking it all in. "How do you…?" He gestured to the stacks of books. "I thought you worked at that club."

Oh, that's right. She'd not only *almost* gone to bed with this guy. She'd almost gone to bed with him *after* meeting him at a strip club. Yeah. She got the gold star for brains this time around.

"I do," she huffed. "Part time. Not that it's any of your business anyway."

What could only be described as pity crept into his eyes. Pity that fueled her temper. "I'd really hoped I was wrong."

Wrong? Oh, now he was gonna get it. "Look, buddy. I'm not completely sure what the heck is going on here, but—"

His spine stiffened. "I have something very important I need to talk to you about, Acacia."

The clip to his voice stopped the argument on her lips. "What could you possibly have to talk to me about?" she asked hesitantly.

"Your father."

Okay, she'd been wrong. Seeing him again wasn't the biggest shock of her life. This virtual stranger had just dropped the f-bomb on her.

"My father?" she asked in stunned disbelief. "My father's dead."

"No, he's not. He's very much alive. At least for the moment."

Casey eased back against the shelf and steadied her hand on a stack of books. Paperback novels pressed into her spine, but she barely felt them. For the first time since Jill had told her of the test results and the extra battery of tests they wanted to run, she wasn't thinking of herself.

"Wh-Where is he?"

"Far away. But he's asked for you. He's a man of great importance where I come from. There isn't much time left." Theron held out his hand. "If you come with me, I'll take you to him."

Casey looked from his strong hand up to his intense, midnight eyes and back again. He could take her to her father. To the man who'd known her mother. To the man who should have been the one to raise her and love her and take care of her. To the one who could put together the broken pieces of her family and answer all her questions about who she really was.

Slowly she extended her hand. Warmth and electricity zipped along her skin even before their palms met. She looked up, surprised, and that's when she saw it. Just a flicker behind his hard eyes. A window into his thoughts. And what she saw there chilled her.

Lies.

She jerked her hand back before he could touch her, and closed her fingers into a fist. "Before I agree to anything, I want to know what's going on. Who are you?"

A menacing chuckle came from the doorway. "A hero who's about to die."

Theron whipped around at the growling voice, and what Casey saw standing in the middle of her store was straight out of a nightmare. A towering figure with horns and fangs and claws so big, it looked like something come to life from *Alien vs. Predator.*

The beast's eyes turned a blinding, glowing green. And from the periphery of her vision, she noticed two more just like the first, standing in the shadows, waiting to strike.

Her eyes flew open wide. She'd seen them before. In the parking lot behind XScream. With Theron.

The fuzzy memory she'd been fighting the last few days came back in a rush.

Theron's big body moved between her and the first beast. His muscles coiled tight as he sprang down into a fighter's stance. In a flash, he reached over his head and pulled a weapon that was a cross between a dagger and a sword and as long as his forearm from somewhere inside his jacket.

A momentary thought hit—that somehow she'd stumbled into some freaky sci-fi movie and none of this was real—and then she tracked nothing. Not the movements in front of her, around her or above her. All too fast for her eyes to follow. But she heard it. The clash of metal against flesh, of claws against skin, of teeth against bone.

And she screamed just as the beast to her right charged.

Isadora jolted awake in a cold sweat.

The sheets beneath her were wet and her heart was pumping as if she'd just competed in the modern-day Olympics. She focused on drawing air into her lungs as she glanced around the plush bedroom, with its heavy brocade drapes, antique furnishings, curved sitting area and soaring ceilings.

The castle. Her suite. A place these days she hated to call home.

It took her moments to realize she wasn't actually in a small corner bookstore in the human world, one lined with wooden shelves and trailing plants and smelling of smoldering vanilla and the stench of impending death.

But she knew, without a doubt, that Theron was there. She could see him as clearly as if he were beside her now.

She threw the covers back and bolted for the door, barely caring that she was wearing her sleeping gown, that her hair was a mess or even that her feet were bare. She needed to get to her father. To find Theron. To warn him before he walked into a trap.

Her bedroom door flew open and banged against the wall. She gathered the floor-length, flimsy white skirt of her gown in her hands and raced down the corridor. As it was night, candles lit by servants lined the stone hallway. For a fleeting moment as she ran, she found it ironic that in this day and age, with their technology, her father still insisted on burning candles in the castle. He was as old-school as they came.

She rounded the corner, her hair flying behind her, and reached one hand out to grab the stone balustrade. The muscles in her thighs burned as her feet landed on the marble steps and she skipped stairs to get to the fourth floor as quickly as possible. Breathing heavy, she palmed the last railing and sailed around the corner, only to slam into a wall of muscle.

A gasp rushed out of her. Her hands flew out to the side to steady herself as the floor gave beneath her feet. And for one illuminating moment, she had a horrible premonition she was going to fall to her death from a towering height.

Which was ironic, and just plain wrong, wasn't it? She could see into everyone else's future but her own, so she didn't know exactly how she was going to die. Though this would be a nasty way to go.

Strong fingers dug into the flesh of her upper arms, and before she could right herself, she was jerked forward and up against solid steel once more. She recognized the scent of the Argonaut holding her. And the wicked chuckle rumbling in his chest was one she'd never forget.

"Oh, Princess. What a precarious position we find ourselves in this night."

Demetrius.

She teetered dangerously close to the edge. All he had to do was let go and she'd tumble backward and crack her head wide open on the marble her father so loved.

"I find myself in a conundrum," he whispered in a menacing voice close to her ear. "To be the hero—or the villain, as you so peg me. Beg me to save you, Princess, so I can choose which one to be."

Isadora's adrenaline spiked. Every horrible sensation she'd ever had about Demetrius rushed through her. She knew he would let her go just to watch her suffer.

"Demetrius!"

Heavy footsteps echoed at Demetrius's back. Isadora gasped again as those bruising hands yanked her against that unforgiving chest and Demetrius turned them both.

"What's happening here?"

She recognized the other voice. Zander. One of Theron's Argonauts. The most unpredictable, and rumor had it, the only one who couldn't be killed.

Right now, teetering on the edge of this precipice, with Demetrius the only thing between her and death, she'd have loved to be immortal.

"Just saving the day," Demetrius said, pulling her even closer until she felt like gagging. "It seems the night has drawn out all kinds."

As quickly as Demetrius had captured her, he let go, and she found herself swaying on her own feet. Zander grasped her arm to steady her. "You don't look well, Princess."

"I—I'm fine." Isadora wiped a hand over her brow, swallowed hard to get her composure. And remembered why she'd flown out of her bed in the first place. "I need to see my father."

The two Argonauts exchanged looks, and as always, Demetrius was a like a solid, stone, unyielding presence beside her, one she couldn't get away from fast enough.

"I'm afraid that's not possible," Zander said. "Your father's resting.

"You don't understand. I have to—"

Zander turned her toward the stairs. "We'll take you back to your suite."

"No. I—"

"These are dangerous times, Princess. And you're not well. Your father's asked that we ensure your safety."

Dangerous times? What in Hades did that mean?

Isadora found herself being led down the stairs away from her goal, while questions and disbelief whirled through her mind. Demetrius's heavy footsteps echoed closely at her back.

When they reached the second floor her brain finally kicked back into gear and she jerked to a stop. "No. Wait. I need to find Theron. I need to talk to him. I need—"

"Theron's on business for the king. He'll contact you when he returns. Now, Princess—"

Screw that. Isadora's jaw flexed and she dug her bare heels into the marble. She was going to be queen. These two Argonauts couldn't tell her what to do.

And just as she was about to lay into Zander with that, those sickeningly familiar hard arms swept her off the floor from behind, and she found herself cradled, not so gently, against Demetrius.

"Enough argument. You're to remain in your suite until the king deems you're well enough to venture out. End of story, *Princess.*"

The last word was sneered, and she struggled against his hold, but it was useless. Moments later she was dumped on her bed, the covers pulled up to her chin, with the echo of resounding footsteps swirling in the room as the Argonauts swept out. Then she was alone, the only sound the click of a key turning in the double doors from the outside.

And she knew then she wasn't being protected. Not from any outside threat or for the sake of her health. She was a prisoner. And her father had just issued her death sentence.

CHAPTER TWELVE

Acacia's scream brought Theron's head around. The daemon he'd been fighting clocked him in the jaw. Theron roared and lashed out with his blade, slicing the beast across the chest. A rush of liquid sprayed over his skin, but in the chaos he didn't know if it was his blood or the daemon's.

He whirled around and kicked the second creature in the chest, then plunged his parazonium, the ancient Greek dagger he'd gotten from his father, deep into the unholy's side. The beast went down with a howl, all twelve inches of the blade disappearing inside the daemon's flesh, but Theron knew neither one was dead, just dazed and seconds from pouncing again.

He didn't have time to finish either of them off, though. He turned to look for Acacia, only to see she'd scrambled behind the counter and was throwing books and office supplies at the third daemon, who kept advancing on her, as if that would keep him back. When that didn't work, she jumped to her feet and yanked the fire extinguisher from the wall, pointed it at the daemon and turned it on full blast.

The daemon was temporarily blinded by the gush of white foam, but with a roar he charged again. Theron raced across the room and reached the counter just as Acacia swung the canister and nailed the daemon in the side of the head. She climbed to the top of the counter and did it again, this time using her leverage from above to nail him hard.

The beast went down. Theron drew his blade. And was kidney-punched from behind as one of the other two found its footing again.

Claws flashed, Theron whipped around, his blade slicing through flesh and air, but still the daemon came, seven feet and three hundred pounds of unending muscle. From behind him he could hear Acacia swinging the fire extinguisher at the other beast. A growl from the front of the store indicated the third was back on his feet.

Skata. They were in serious trouble.

Two he could handle easily. Three if he were by himself. But not with Acacia. And even if he could manage to figure a way out of this one and get her far enough away to concentrate and open the portal, she had to willingly go with him. Because she was human, he couldn't force her across the threshold.

And in her current state of hysteria? Wasn't gonna happen. Which meant they were well and truly screwed.

The daemon flipped him to the ground and lunged. Theron cracked his head against the daemon and threw the beast off him as if it weighed nothing. The daemon crashed into a shelving unit. Books rained down on top of him, but the monster scrambled to its feet and charged as if he hadn't even felt the blow. Theron jumped to his feet as well, and in one mighty sweep his blade ripped through flesh and bone. With a sickening crack, the head was severed from the daemon's body and rolled across the blood-soaked carpet.

A horrendous roar echoed through the store. The daemon Theron had left bloodied by the door plowed into him and took him down to the carpet. His blade flew out of his hand and clanged against the counter. Theron's face was pressed into the carpet as claws ripped across the jacket on at his back.

Fuck. Now they were really screwed.

Then he heard a thud, and a swoosh. Felt a gush of something warm across his back and heard a mighty howl as the daemon fell off him.

Theron was on his feet in a flash, only to realize Acacia had his blade plunged deep into the daemon's chest.

She pulled the weapon out. The daemon fell back, shook himself and seemed to regather his strength.

Theron quickly took the weapon from Acacia and pushed her behind him. Out of the corner of his eye he saw the second daemon, covered in foam, rising slowly to his feet. "Get back!"

"Oh, shit," she muttered.

He crouched down in his fighter's stance, lunged toward the first and sensed the second circling around to advance on Acacia. He had microseconds to decide his next move, and then suddenly the tide shifted.

Glass shattered at the front of the store, and a man flew through the broken glass and charged the second daemon.

Weapons clashed. Jaws snapped. Metal met flesh and bone. Heads rolled, and then there was nothing but blood and severed body parts and the aftermath of a fight that ended as quickly as it had started.

Breathing heavy and having trouble seeing through what he hoped was sweat, and not his own blood, Theron straightened and studied the newcomer—human, but not totally. And an Argonaut.

Which made *noooo* fucking sense whatsoever.

The man turned toward Acacia, who'd somehow managed to scramble back onto the counter. "Casey, come down."

"Oh, my God. Nick. Jesus Christ, what the hell—?"

The blond's big hands plucked Acacia right off the counter before Theron had a chance to stop him, and he set her on her feet in the middle of the store. The man grasped her shoulders and held firm. "Take a breath, Casey. More will be coming."

"More? What do you—?"

Then, almost as if she'd just realized the two of them weren't alone, her eyes flashed to Theron, understanding dawning in their violet depths. And for the first time since he'd met her, he realized how similar those eyes were to the king's.

"Those things," she said. "I saw them that night with you. Outside XScream."

The man she'd called Nick glanced up sharply. "You brought them here? To her?"

"No," Theron said, shoving his weapon back into its scabbard at his back. Now he was the bad guy? Fuck that. "I was sent to protect her."

Nick's eyebrows lowered. "Sent? By whom?"

He hesitated, then figured if this guy knew about the daemons, he had to know about the rest of it. "King Leonidas."

And oh, yeah, this guy definitely had some link to Argolea and didn't like it, because his eyes flashed at the name and his jaw hardened until it was a slice of steel beneath flesh.

Acacia looked from one to the other, a little crease between her eyebrows as she tried to make sense of their conversation. "Who's Leonidas? What were those things? And where did they go? Will someone please tell me what's going on here?"

The hysteria was edging its way back into her voice, and Theron knew he had only seconds to get her away and through the portal before she was too far gone to cooperate. He held out his hand. "Come with me and I'll explain it all to you."

Nick grasped her arm before she even lifted it, and those amber eyes of his flashed black. "She stays. I know exactly what you are, Argonaut, and if you think I'm letting her go anywhere with you, you're higher than a kite."

Theron sensed the portal opening just outside the city limits and knew in a matter of minutes they were going to be surrounded and outnumbered again. And this time odds were good they wouldn't get out of it so easily. Nick obviously sensed it as well, because his hand tightened around Acacia's upper arm and urgency rushed through his words. "Do you have matches?"

Perplexed, she looked up. "In the drawer. But what for?"

Nick let go of her and marched around the counter. He yanked draws open until he drew out a large box, then flipped open the cupboard door and rummaged around, finally emerging with a metal canister of some kind. "Rip the spines off some books and throw them on the bodies."

"Wait. Rip the *what* off my books? Hold on a minute."

Theron didn't need to ask, and he didn't have time to clarify to Acacia. He reached for the closest display of paperbacks and began tearing pages until he had a mound of papers wadded up and covering the closest daemon. Nick did the same, then sprayed liquid over the whole mass.

Acacia's eyes flew open. "What do you think you're doing? You're gonna have to pay for that. You can't just—oooh!"

She screamed and jumped back as the body went up in flames. Nick ignited the second and the third and threw the box of matches and the bottle of alcohol into the fires. Flames licked the ground and rose to the ceiling, forming a black cloud, which was already spreading. "Let's go."

Theron met them at the door and stopped Nick from leaving with Acacia. "She goes nowhere without me."

In the split second of silence between them, Nick obviously knew he was out of time and options. He nodded. "So be it. But you so much as harm one hair on her head and I'll kill you myself. The leader of the Argonauts means nothing to me and mine."

Theron glanced at Acacia while flames roared to life behind him, oddly reminiscent of the fires of hell. "So be it."

They'd set her store on fire.

Casey found herself being pushed into the back of an enormous SUV while she struggled to look back at the destruction that had once been her grandmother's pride and joy. Her chest tightened until it was hard to get air, and she knew it wasn't just from adrenaline or smoke.

The one place she thought she had fit in was gone. Now engulfed in flames.

Nick slid into the driver's seat, while Theron wedged himself in the back with her. Both men were so big they seemed to suck up all the air in the vehicle, and had she not already been on the edge of freaking out, just that alone would have been enough to send her into a tailspin.

All four door locks clicked at the same time as Casey turned to watch the building burn.

Oh my God. They set my building on fire.

"Hurry," Theron exclaimed, grasping the front passenger seat and turning around to look behind them. "They're coming."

Fury erupted in Casey's chest as the SUV's engine roared. She slammed her fist into Theron's shoulder. "You son of a bitch! You burned down my store!"

The SUV jerked away from the curb with a force that sent Casey sprawling against Theron's massive chest. He grabbed her by the wrists and easily subdued her with one hand, holding her with the other to make sure she didn't fall to the floorboards. "Assuming we get out of here, you'll thank us later. Only a fire can destroy a daemon's body."

Like she cared about that now? Everything she'd worked so hard for the last few months was gone.

The sky chose that moment to unleash its misery on the small town of Silver Hills, and a torrent of rain pummeled the vehicle, slashing against the SUV as if Mother Nature were good and pissed as they rocketed down the empty street. Casey clawed at Theron to let her go, but he just held on tighter.

Nick drove like a bat out of hell. He shouted something at Theron Casey didn't catch. Then Theron shifted her to his side and reached into his pocket. Before she saw what was in his hand, he rolled down the window and tossed the object behind them. A fireball erupted on the road at their backs, followed by howls and shouts, the kind Casey only imagined could come from hell. And that's when she realized those things back at her store were still following them. Or rather, that new ones had joined the fight. They weren't out of trouble yet. Not by a long shot.

She gave up struggling, and instead clamped on to Theron's shirt, drawing the cotton between her fists as Nick drove at breakneck speed out of town and into the forest beyond. Her adrenaline spiked as the reality of the situation sank in. Then she closed her eyes and said every prayer she knew that they'd get out of this alive.

She didn't let go of Theron's shirt even when he shifted back to lean against the seat again. And she didn't fight his hand on her spine or his arms gathering her close, when any sane person would have.

Okay, it made her out to be a weakling, but she didn't care. Her store was gone and some freaky monsters were following them. Considering everything she'd been through with Jill that morning, her nerves were at the end of the line. All things considered, she'd take a moment of comfort wherever she could get it, even from him.

"I think we lost them," Theron said, glancing over his shoulder.

Nick harrumphed from the front seat.

"Where are you taking us?" Theron asked into the silence, after they'd been driving for a while.

"To her home," Nick said.

"They'll find her there."

"How?"

"Because they're here for her."

Casey didn't imagine the silence that followed, or the tension between the two men in the car with her. And though she didn't know how, she understood these two knew each other from somewhere. Or knew *of* each other. And neither was happy with that knowledge. Nick jerked the car to the side of the road and slammed on the brakes.

She was thrown forward and back, but Theron held on to her tight. "She goes nowhere without me," Theron reiterated as the car idled. "I was sent here to protect her. I want nothing to do with you or the others."

Others?

"So help me gods," Nick bit out, "if you're lying—"

"I'm not."

Silence hung like a dark, thick cloud in the car. Casey didn't dare move. She sensed these two were at a virtual standoff, and if she wasn't careful, she'd get caught in the middle. What could go down between them would put that battle back at her store to shame.

Finally Nick swore in a language Casey didn't recognize, and then the car whipped a U-ie in the middle of the road. Theron braced a hand on the seat in front of him to steady them both as they rocketed back down the road and made a sharp ninety-degree turn onto a dirt road leading off into the trees. A road Casey'd never noticed before.

"This doesn't change anything, Argonaut," Nick ground out.

"I wouldn't want it to."

Nick huffed and accelerated. Dust kicked up behind them. "In a few minutes you may be wishing you'd never set eyes on her."

A strong hand shook Casey from sleep. She wasn't sure how long she'd been out or how far they'd driven, but when she pried her eyelids open and pushed off Theron's chest, she didn't recognize her surroundings.

Nick was already out of the SUV and opening her door. She eased out of the vehicle and stumbled on the battered road. Theron caught her from behind before she went down.

"Easy."

She may have been weak and tired from everything that had happened, but she didn't want to look it in front of him. While she'd accepted Theron's comfort in the car, her brain was starting to function again, and until she got some answers, she didn't want or need his help.

She tugged her arm from Theron's grasp and glanced around. The road, if it could be called that, was nothing more than a section of dirt that came to an abrupt end. Towering trees and dense underbrush surrounded them from nearly every side. In a brusque tone, Nick said, "Wait here," then climbed into the car and backed it into the shrubs until it disappeared from sight. A few moments later he reappeared, gesturing with his shoulder. "From here we walk."

Nick took the lead, blazing a trail through the forest, and Casey followed close behind, watching where he stepped, careful not to look anywhere but where she was walking. She was still shaky, a little unsure on her feet, and the last thing she needed was to fall on her ass in front of these two.

Theron was a commanding presence at her back, close enough to touch and smell. Why wouldn't he back off? And why did he unnerve her so much? Especially now?

In her mind, she was still working through everything that had happened, but one thing was glaringly clear: Theron had come back for her. He'd said those daemons were looking for *her*. Which meant he knew what they wanted. It also meant he hadn't come looking for her because he wanted to pick up where they'd left off. Namely, the hot, wicked sex she'd been fantasizing about since he'd ditched her ass for greener pastures.

Bastard.

The path rose in elevation until Casey's breath came fast and shallow. Sweat trickled down her chest between her breasts. She wiped a hand across her brow and wished desperately they could stop. Just for a minute, long enough so she could catch her breath. But she wasn't about to ask. She had a strange sense Nick was intent on getting them to their destination fast. And that thought made her brain work itself right back around to what they were running from in the first place.

She lifted her head once to glance around, and in the process stumbled on a stone that was in the way. Her hand darted out to grasp the base of a tree to her right, but she never made contact. In one fell swoop she was lifted off her feet and cradled against Theron's massive chest.

"Let me down," she snapped. "I can walk just fine."

"Not like that, you can't. You are pale as snow." When she wriggled against him, his grip only tightened under her arms and beneath the backs of her knees. "Stop fighting me or we'll both go down."

"If you think I'm going to let you touch me after what you
did—"

The rest of her protest rushed out of her mouth on a screech
when he tossed her over his shoulder so her hands were shooting
down his muscular back for balance and her ass was sticking
straight up in the air. "This works better for me as well, *meli*." Both
of his arms held her legs locked together against his chest in a vise.
"And the view is more appealing."

Heat rushed to Casey's cheeks, followed by disbelief at his gall.
"Why you—"

"What's the problem back there?" Nick asked from ahead of
them.

"No problem," Theron called. "Acacia's just a little wobbly.
We've got it covered."

Traumatic experience or not, this guy didn't speak for her.
Casey opened her mouth to lay into him, only to be cut off by a
warning rumble from the man holding her captive. "It would be
wise to do as I say right now, *meli*. I don't know where we're
headed, and wrestling with you, while stimulating in its own right,
is too much of a distraction."

"The blood is rushing to my head, you jerk."

"Good. It'll bring your color back."

"Of all the—"

He chuckled and picked up his pace.

With a huff, Casey blew the hair out of her eyes. Tossing insults
with him wasn't getting her anywhere, and part of her was happy to
be off her aching feet. Though she'd never have admitted that to
him in a million years.

Frowning, she relaxed against him, only to tense once more
when his hand drifted up the back of her hamstring. She braced her
hands on his lower back and pushed herself up. "Watch it, buddy."

"Just getting a better grip."

Oh, she just bet.

Before she could tell him just what he could do with his hands,
darkness overtook her, and she realized they'd stepped into some
kind of cave or tunnel.

Theron eased her down to the ground. Behind her Nick said,
"Not far now. Stay close and keep me in sight. Tunnels branch off
in various directions. You'll be lost forever if you choose the wrong
one."

That didn't sound so appealing to Casey right now, who wanted nothing more than a warm bed, a stiff drink and a chance to sleep this nightmarish day right out of her mind. She followed closely behind Nick and knew after the first turn that if he weren't leading her, she'd be lost in an instant.

What little light shone in from the opening quickly went out, and darkness pressed in as they made turn after turn. Casey reached out a hand to steady herself on the rock walls, the scents of earth tingling heavy in her nose. From ahead she saw a pinpoint beam of light and realized Nick had pulled a flashlight from his pocket. Though the tunnel was tall enough for all three of them to stand in, the walls were close, and both men had to turn sideways to fit their broad shoulders through the space.

After what seemed like an eternity of hairpin turns and rapid elevation changes that stole Casey's breath all over again, the tunnel finally opened into a massive cavern illuminated by hundreds of torches. Casey gasped as she blinked rapidly at the increase in light. Three-story wooden structures were built into the rock lining both sides of the cavern. Doors and windows and balconies looked out to a central pool of water, fed by a massive waterfall that fell from the ceiling of the cave, nearly a hundred feet above.

"Oh, my," she whispered. People milling around the central pool stopped to look their way as wary eyes peered down from the structures on both sides.

She took a cautious step backward and ran smack into Theron's chest, but he didn't move. Those eyes staring down at her weren't the least bit friendly, and she had a wild impression that she'd just been thrown into the lion's den.

A small child, no more than five, broke free from a woman standing off to the side and raced toward them, yelling, "Nick! Nick!"

Nick dropped to his knees to catch the child as she threw herself into his arms. Their hug was brief, but it was clear even to Casey that the two shared a special bond.

"I knew you'd come back okay," the girl said to him. In her hands she held a doll cradled to her chest. "Minnie told me."

"Minnie's a smart girl," Nick said, chucking her under the chin and rising to his feet.

The girl glanced briefly up at Theron, standing at Casey's back, then turned her attention to Casey. And it was then Casey noticed the marks.

The entire right side of the girl's face was covered in puckered scars, as though she'd been in some terrible car accident and then burned. Her right eye was covered by a patch, and hair that should have been long and thick was sparse on that side of her head.

But it wasn't the girl's appearance that made Casey catch her breath as she looked down at the small child. It was the look in the girl's good eye. Like she'd seen the world and beyond. Like she'd already lived a lifetime and aged eons beyond her years. Like she was looking straight through Casey and into a future no one knew but her.

"I knew you'd come," the girl said. "Minnie told me."

"Who's Minnie?" Casey found herself asking.

The girl held up her doll. "Minnie knows everything. She knew that Nick would battle the monsters today and win, and that he'd come home safe. And she knew he'd bring you here to save us."

Casey glanced at Nick, who was staring at the girl with a perplexed expression.

A chill of foreboding slid down Casey's spine. She returned her attention to the girl. "What do you mean, 'save us'?"

"All of us." The girl held up her free hand and gestured behind her. "The whole colony. Minnie said that's why you've come."

Though it was completely insane and made no sense whatsoever, considering everything else, two words pinged around in Casey's brain. *My people.*

She dropped to her knees in front of the girl without hesitation. "What's your name?"

"Marissa."

"Marissa," Casey repeated, eyes running over the small child. "What else did Minnie tell you about me, Marissa?"

"That you would come with him." She nodded toward Theron, standing close at Casey's back. "And not to be afraid of him." She leaned in close to Casey's ear. "The others don't understand that. Not even Nick. But he's here to protect you, and you need him as much as we need you."

"Why?" Casey whispered.

Marissa pushed the doll into Casey's hands. "Let Minnie show you."

Elisabeth Naughton   119

The moment Casey's fingers touched the girl's hand, a jolt shot through her, and suddenly she was soaring through time and space, then standing on the edge of a great cliff, looking down at a horrific scene.

Flames shot to the heavens. Screams echoed above and beyond, and a great roar rose from a scuffle just beyond the fire. The youngster—Marissa—was hurt and bleeding, flames engulfing her dress and searing her flesh. A woman was working to smother them but couldn't get them out fast enough to save the child's delicate skin. Beyond them, the same monsters that had converged on Casey's store earlier in the day were devouring a man.

Then Nick appeared on the scene and began battling the creatures, just as he had in her store.

He was swift and efficient, and his strength and skill were mind-boggling. He saved the young girl and her mother, but the man was devoured before the child's eyes, and in horror Casey watched as the monster reached into the screaming man's chest and ripped out his heart.

The girl's hand on Casey's arm pulled her from the vision and back to the present. But the pain was still fresh and real in the youngster's good eye, and Casey felt it too. Her voice dropped to a whisper. "What they'll do to you will be worse."

"Marissa!"

At the sound of the sharp female voice, Casey eased to her feet, more shaken than she wanted to admit. The woman who came running at breakneck speed was also burned and scarred, and she scooped Marissa up into her arms just before shooting Theron a scorching look and hurrying off into the village, speaking in a language Casey didn't understand.

Casey's heart was beating a mile a minute as she looked up at Nick, but if she'd expected answers on his hard face, it was clear she was on her own. His amber eyes were narrowed, and focused directly on her as if he were seeing her for the first time.

"Marissa is a soothsayer," Nick mumbled. "A seer. She uses Minnie, her doll, as her medium, but she senses happenings in the future without her."

Ooookay. That didn't help any. Because somehow Casey knew that what she'd seen hadn't been the future, but the past.

Casey let out a nervous laugh that held absolutely no humor. "Well, this time she's wrong. She's obviously mistaken about me. I can barely save myself, let alone anyone else."

Theron and Nick exchanged confused glances, and weird clairvoyant child or not, Casey decided it was time for some answers.

She squared her shoulders. "Just what's going on here, Nick? What were those things back there, and where the hell are we?" She looked Theron's way. "And where on earth did you really come from?" She glanced between the two mammoth men again as panic edged its way back into her voice. "It's about time someone started talking, or I'm walking."

Nick's eyes settled on Theron. "I think it's about time we all got some answers. But not here in front of the others. We'll do this in the lodge."

CHAPTER THIRTEEN

The lodge was a massive expanse of wood built at the far end of the enormous cavern. As they walked through the central courtyard and passed the waterfall, Theron stayed close to Acacia's side. Though he sensed the villagers' unease was solely due to his presence, he didn't put it past them to take a swipe at her because of him.

Gods, there were so many. He scanned the crowd that parted for them. So many worn and battered and bearing marks of battles past. How could so many have been kept secret from the Argonauts for so long?

It was clear Nick was the band of half-breeds' leader. He exuded an air of authority over the entire colony, and heads bowed slightly as he passed. Not for the first time, Theron wondered who this rogue warrior was. He'd noticed the fingerless leather gloves Nick wore, and that strange sense that had struck Theron at Acacia's store hit him again as they walked—the feeling that this man was both human and Argonaut.

But how could that be possible?

They reached the steps of the lodge, and Nick led the way into what appeared to be a gathering area. A giant iron chandelier lit with candles showered golden light over the space. The ceiling featured beams carved from massive trees and the floor was a rich honey-colored wood. A giant staircase directly ahead led to the second floor. To the right a living area, complete with leather chairs and rustic tabletops set in various groupings, littered the space. Double doors opened to the left.

Nick led them into the office. Once inside he closed the doors and pulled the blinds, blocking out the view and the curious eyes from the village below.

Acacia didn't wait for an invitation to sit. She dropped onto one of the green leather couches in the corner of the room on a long sigh. She didn't look good, and as he had back in her store, Theron sensed the illness racking her body. The same illness that plagued Isadora.

Skata, he needed to get her back to the castle. Like, *now*.

The guilt he felt over what he'd been sent to do was swift and useless, so he pushed it aside and decided to dwell on the facts. "What is this place?"

Nick eased into the chair behind a large oak desk, leather creaking beneath his big body. "Refuge. Or the best we can get. The caves allow us protection. Any daemon who ventures inside will be lost in the tunnels and picked off by our sentries. This colony's been in existence for nearly five hundred years, and not once has it been breached."

Five hundred years. Dear gods.

"How many are there?" Theron asked.

"In this colony?" Nick's brow lifted, and though he volunteered answers, the challenge in his eyes was evidently clear. "Two hundred and forty-seven. On a good day. But our numbers rise and fall as our people move from colony to colony."

Two hundred and forty-seven? Holy *skata*. And there were other colonies? That the king knew about?

When he could speak after the shock that brought, he asked, "They don't remain?" If the fortress was as impenetrable as Nick claimed, why on earth would any of these half-breeds risk venturing out into the human world, where they could be identified and killed on sight?

"We have to live, Argonaut. Although I'm sure you'd like it if we didn't."

Theron sensed the aggression, and didn't respond. Nick's eyes narrowed to thin pinpoints. "No comeback for me? Yeah. I didn't think so."

In the silent tension between them, Nick lifted a pencil and tapped it against the edge of the desk.

"What do you mean, colony?" Acacia asked in a small voice from the couch.

Nick turned her way, and his voice gentled. "What do you think I mean, Casey?"

Theron's eyes narrowed as he looked between the two. There was a connection between them, a bond that set off a strange tingling in Theron's chest.

Wary, Acacia eyed Nick. "I—I'm not sure. But I have the strangest feeling those people out there aren't..."

"Aren't what, Casey?" Nick asked. "Aren't...human?"

Her eyes flicked to his, and whatever she saw there made her catch her breath.

Nick nodded Theron's way. "Show her."

The command wasn't just startling, it was inconceivable. You didn't order an Argonaut, especially its leader, to do anything, because doing so was as good as inviting a death sentence. But Nick obviously didn't give a flying fuck about protocol and threats. And that made him the most dangerous kind of adversary.

Common sense told Theron he was basically SOL here. The half-breeds already knew who he was. Acacia would never believe until she saw for herself. And until he won her trust, she wasn't going anywhere with him anytime soon. Ever since the incident at the store, she'd been looking at him like he might be a daemon himself.

Reluctantly, he held up his hands, flashing the markings on his skin. Because he was an Argonaut, he could open the portal from wherever he was. When his pinkie fingers touched, a burst of energy flooded the room. His hands glowed white light that shimmered and backlit the markings. And in the light, the portal opened, casting a vision of the kingdom of Argolea over the walls and floor and ceiling, filling every inch of space in the office with its presence.

Acacia gasped. And Theron tried to view it from her perspective—as an outsider looking in. He'd opened the portal countless times with barely a thought, the beauty and regality of his home lost on him over the years. But now, looking at it through her eyes, at the blue-green mountains and the white marble buildings with their bronze-topped spires, for the first time he saw secrets. Lies. Half-truths that had possibly left an entire section of their race in peril.

He separated his hands, and the portal closed in a rush, the light and vision fading as quickly as they'd appeared.

Wide-eyed, Acacia looked up to his face. "Okay, that was a little freaky. *Chriss Angel Mindfreak* freaky. Wh-What the hell was that?"

Theron glanced toward Nick. "Chriss Angel?"

"An illusionist. Human. No doubt you wouldn't know him." He refocused on Acacia. "That was Argolea, Casey."

"Argo*what*?"

"Argolea," Theron repeated. "My home and the home of your father."

Her wide eyes slid to Nick for reassurance in a way that made Theron want to pull her eyes right back to him and punch Nick smack in the face.

Nick rose from his chair and moved around the front of his desk. "Theron's a hero, Casey."

"A what?"

"A hero," Nick repeated. "Your grandmother was Greek, right?" Acacia nodded. "In Greek mythology, the heroes were mortals of great strength and ability, spawned from the union of a mortal and a god."

Acacia's eyes shot to Theron's face, and as unexpected as she was that first night he'd met her, the connection they'd shared flared hot and bright. A connection that made absolutely no sense, considering who and what she was. "You're telling me he's a god?"

"No," Theron said quickly, refocusing. "A descendant. The first heroes were half human, half god. Over time, as they reproduced, our race was born and the lines were blurred. My people are the offspring of those original heroes."

"What race?" she asked hesitantly.

"We are called Argoleans. Our home is in another realm, established outside the human world."

Her brow shot up in a "what the hell have you been smoking?" look. "You mean like Olympus?"

"No." Theron shook his head. "Olympus is home to the gods. Argolea was a land established specifically for our race, a place where we could flourish and remain free."

Nick huffed. "You mean where your kind could hide."

Theron ignored the barb. He'd deal with Nick and his colony of half-breeds later. Right now he could see that Acacia wasn't buying any of what he'd just told her, and making her understand her lineage was important if he was going to get her to go back with him. "Your father is of my kind."

"What he's neglecting to tell you, Casey," Nick said, straightening, "is that he's not just an Argolean. He's an Argonaut. One of his race's so called Eternal Guardians. The leader, if I'm not mistaken. And aside from the obvious—why he's in our world now—I'm just a little curious why he's zeroed in on you." Nick crossed his arms over his chest and glared at Theron.

Moment of truth. The hair on the back of Theron's neck stood up as he looked from Acacia to Nick and back again. He hoped to Hades this gamble paid off. "Your father's name is Leonidas. King Leonidas. The ruler of my kingdom."

Nick swore and dropped his arms.

Casey's eyes grew even larger. "My father's a king?"

Theron nodded.

"As in red robe, pointy crown and a jester at his feet king?"

Theron lifted one brow, amused at her wit. "The gods were never fond of jesters. Didn't get passed down to us."

She only continued to stare at him with that same wide-eyed, you-are-higher-than-a-hot-air-balloon look on her face. She turned to Nick, the candles on the walls casting warm light across her face. "Explain to me what this place is. And who are all those people outside?"

Theron's humor faded. What was that pinch in his chest he experienced whenever she looked to Nick for answers?

Nick's scarred features softened in a way that kicked up that pinch to a stab. "They're like us, Casey. Half-breeds, or so his race calls us. Half Argolean, half human."

"What do you call them?" she asked quietly.

A frown pulled his eyebrows together. "Really fucking unlucky."

Theron gritted his teeth as Nick moved to sit beside her on the couch.

"Misos, Casey," Nick said. "It means half, which is what we are. I know this is confusing, but do me a favor. Just tell me if I'm wrong. You're twenty-seven years old, yet you feel like you've never belonged anywhere. You've flitted from job to job, never passionate about anything in particular. You loved your grandmother, but you always sensed she didn't understand you because you were different, and you never felt bound to stay with her after you were grown. Your friends never truly accepted you, and you didn't fit in with the people you interacted with. When you started working at XScream and you met Dana, as much as the club sickened you, it was the first time you'd ever felt a connection with another person that went deeper than the superfluous. And though I scared you and gave you every reason to be afraid of me, you trusted me with your life and didn't once question who or what I was. At least not out loud."

Acacia's chest rose and fell as she took long, steady breaths, but her eyes were locked on Nick's. "How do you know all that?" she whispered.

"Because I've been there. Because I was once like you, wondering where I fit in. I found it here. With my people. With *our* people, Casey."

"I—I don't understand this. How...?" She glanced toward Theron. And his chest grew tight at the questions in her eyes. At the way she looked to *him* for answers. "If you live in a different"— she swallowed—"world, then how did my mother...? Was my mother one of you?"

Theron shook his head. "From what I know, your father met her when he was in the human world. Many from our race do cross over from time to time, but it can be dangerous and it isn't encouraged."

Nick frowned. "Obviously it happens more than the Argonauts would like to admit."

"Dangerous," Acacia said, missing the barb as her eyes flicked back to Nick. "Because of those beasts. What were they?"

"Daemons," Nick said matter-of-factly. "Beasts of the underworld spawned by Hades and given power by a demigod. They hunt us."

Her eyebrows drew together, forming a crease in the middle of her forehead that was so damn sexy, Theron's legs itched to cross to her and kiss it from her skin.

"Why? I don't understand that. I mean, I've never heard of them. Do they hunt humans, too? Is this some big conspiracy theory the government's not telling us?"

Nick placed a hand on her arm. And that stab in Theron's chest shot up to a warning roar. He fought the urge to throw himself at Nick and pry the man's hand off Acacia's arm, then break every bone in the half-breed's body.

"You have to stop thinking of yourself as human, Casey," Nick said. "I know it's hard to understand, but you're one of us, and as such your life is vulnerable in different ways. The goal of the daemons is to eradicate the Argoleans and everything associated with them. And that, unfortunately for us, means our people as well."

"But why? What did we ever do to them?"

"Nothing," Theron said, drawing her attention his way. Her violet eyes flicked up to his, and when their gazes met, the roar in his head quickly morphed from one of protection to white-hot desire, just as it had that night up at her house by the lake.

And that's when it hit him. All of it at once. The real reason he hadn't recognized who and what she was the first night he'd met her. It wasn't because he'd been hurt. It was because she was *his* One.

He swallowed hard at what he hoped couldn't possibly be the real explanation. She was just a woman. She was *human*, something he couldn't stomach even on a good day, which this most definitely was not. And she was going to save his race, whether she knew it or not. He had to focus on that. And not the…other possibility.

"It goes back centuries," he said, harsher than necessary. "To a disgruntled hero who sold her soul to Hades in exchange for immortality. She seeks to destroy that which shunned her. And she's unleashed her daemons on the world to extinguish a race she hates."

"And that's why you're here," she said plainly, those mesmerizing eyes of hers still locked on his. "To protect the race."

"To protect *his* race," Nick cut in, shooting Theron a contemptuous look. "Make no mistake, Casey. Theron isn't here to protect the Misos. Your father the king hasn't tried to contact you once in twenty-seven years, and now suddenly he wants to see you? Before you agree to anything, ask yourself just what the heck he or this guardian could possibly want from you."

Acacia looked from Nick to Theron and back again. And then, as if someone had turned off a light inside her, she closed her eyes and leaned her head back against the couch. The color drained from her face, leaving her weak and spent, reminding Theron that even though her mind was strong, her body was not. "I don't know what to think of any of this."

Nick rose from the couch and moved toward the door. On the wall he pushed some kind of button connected to a wire that disappeared into the rock. "You don't have to think about it yet. I want you to get some rest. You don't look well."

Acacia's eyes flipped open just as the door creaked. A female who looked to be no more than twenty-five edged into the room. "Yes, Nick."

Nick helped Acacia from the couch. "Helene, this is Casey. I want you to get her settled in a room upstairs. She's had quite a day and needs to rest. Bring her anything she needs."

Helene smiled at Nick, her dark eyes sparking, and only when she came more fully inside did Theron realize the half-breed female walked with an obvious limp.

"Of course. Hi, Casey. We're glad to have you with us."

Acacia glanced from Helene to Nick. "But—"

"It's okay," Nick said. "Theron and I have things to discuss, and you need to sleep before you fall over. You're completely safe here. Rest, and when you wake, I'll answer your questions."

Acacia glanced around the room again in indecision, then finally turned her attention to the dark-haired woman. "I guess I am a little tired."

Helene's grin widened. "Come on then. I know just which room to give you."

Theron watched the two women exit the office, consumed by a dark desire to follow Acacia out and up those grand stairs—which was suddenly starting to make a sickening sort of sense.

No, no, no. He had to be wrong.

"Enough with the crap, hero."

Slowly, Theron pulled his gaze from the closed door to look toward the suddenly aggressive half-breed in his presence, ready to do battle to the bitter end. Whatever questions he had about Acacia would have to wait.

Nick's scarred face twisted into a scowl. "I'm done playing games. It's time you tell me just what you're doing here and what the hell you really want with Casey."

Casey couldn't remember ever being so tired. She was sore from the attack in her bookstore, emotionally spent and mentally whacked out. As she followed Helene up the wide staircase, she tried not to think about everything Nick and Theron had just told her. It was ludicrous, wasn't it? Other races didn't exist. And mythological heroes were just that...*mythological*, for crap's sake.

But even as she fought what they'd told her, she had the strangest sense she was wrong. It explained so much about who she was and where she'd come from and why she'd never connected with anyone in this world.

And holy cow, she needed a lobotomy if she was so easily buying into all this.

They reached the top of the staircase, and Helene gestured down a long hallway lined with closed doors and lit with candles every ten feet. "I think you'll like the blue room. It's very peaceful."

For the first time, Casey noticed the girl's limp and wondered if she'd recently been hurt, possibly by those beasts they'd encountered earlier. "Are you all right?"

Helene smiled. "I'm fine."

"But your leg—"

Helene stopped and lifted one pant leg. A metal bar was anchored in a Nike running shoe. "Titanium. It's new and I'm still getting used to it. My last prosthesis bugged me to no end. This one's lighter."

Casey tried not to stare as the girl dropped her pant leg and kept moving down the long hallway. "I'm sorry. I didn't know. I—"

"It's okay," Helene said. "I've been without my leg for a hundred years."

Casey's jaw nearly hit the floor. "You're a hundred years old?"

"One hundred and thirty-six, to be exact."

The hallway spun. Casey reached a hand out to steady herself. "How is that possible?"

Helene's arms were suddenly around her, supporting her, as she helped Casey inside the room. "Whoa there. I take it Nick hasn't explained that part to you yet." She eased Casey into a chair Casey vaguely registered as being white and incredibly soft. "Our lifespans are relatively long. Not as long as an Argolean's, of course, but it's one of the reasons we live here in the colony and not with humans." A wry smile slid across her pretty face as she crossed the room to an armoire. She opened the double doors, fiddled inside for a few moments and came back with a mug of steaming tea, which she handed to Casey. "A one-hundred-and-thirty-six-year-old woman who looks like she's thirty? That might garner a little attention in the human world, don't you think?"

Casey took the tea and brought it to her lips. A familiar scent surrounded her as she took a deep drink. "I smell lavender."

"Yes," Helene said. "It'll help you rest."

"You use it for healing," she said, as images of her night with Theron flickered through her mind.

"Among other things." Helene crossed to a gigantic four-poster bed done all in light blue fabrics and folded back the plump covers. Crisp white sheets beckoned, promising respite. "There's a small button on the wall next to the door. If you need anything, just push it and someone will come running."

"So modern?" Casey asked, remembering the candles.

Helene smiled. "Yes. It's not the Ritz, but we do have electricity and indoor plumbing. A main generator powers the colony, but because we're not self-sufficient and everything costs money, we try not to overburden it. Candles are cheap and soothing, so we use those quite a bit. Up near the surface we have a lookout station complete with surveillance equipment, satellite phones and everything we need to connect with civilization."

At Casey's perplexed expression, Helene came around the bed. "I imagine you have a thousand other questions, but for now, try to rest. When you wake, Nick will tell you anything you want to know. Now sleep, Casey. And don't worry. Tonight nothing will harm you."

"Thank you, Helene."

Alone, Casey leaned back in the plush chair and studied the room she'd been given. Pale blue walls on three sides matched the comforter on the bed. Two club chairs separated by a small side table occupied the corner. An enormous stone fireplace, already burning, took up nearly one whole wall. But the far wall held the most interest. It was made entirely of stone, and a small, naturally occurring opening formed a porthole-type window that had somehow been sealed with glass and covered by a variety of branches which, she imagined, camouflaged the opening from the outside. One look out into utter darkness signaled that this part of the cavern must form the edge of some massive cliff.

So strange to be in a room in a cave. Kind of like the Anasazi tribes in the Southwest. Big villages built deep into the rocks for protection.

Tired to her bones, she rose and pulled the small blue drapes to block out the darkness, blew out the candles on the walls, then tumbled into bed, not wanting to think about what had happened to the Anasazi. Or about hiding places or predators. Or kings or countries or gods or heroes. She just wanted to think about...nothing.

But it didn't work. As soon as she closed her eyes she saw the fight in her grandmother's store. The fire. And...Theron.

Why had he really come back for her?

Not to finish what they'd started in her house, that was for sure. Not that she even wanted to anymore.

Liar.

Casey rolled to her side and closed her eyes tight. Stupid thoughts. Where Theron the Wonder Hero was concerned, she needed to watch her back, be on guard, not let him get to her the way he had the first time they met. The way he'd manhandled her on the hike up here was proof of that, wasn't it? If he was his race's idea of a hero, she wasn't so sure she wanted to know more about her lineage.

She let out a long breath as her muscles relaxed one by one and sleep tugged at her. And though she fought it, she pictured Theron's face. His dark eyes. His lush lips. The perfectly shaped nose and the small scars from battles fought and won. Saw, clearly, the smoldering look across those chiseled features when he'd bent and kissed her with the slightest brush of skin against skin that night at her house. And felt the rush of arousal in response that heated her blood.

Damn, but for all her posturing she was in deep trouble. Even with all that she'd lost today, she had a sinking suspicion events hadn't turned her world upside down. *He* had. And that feeling had nothing to do with daemons and heroes and kings and half-breeds. It had to do with one man who, somehow, had wormed his way into her soul from the very moment she'd laid eyes on him.

CHAPTER FOURTEEN

Dana was in a foul mood and it was getting fouler by the minute. As she drove back into Silver Hills—a town she *thought* she'd left behind nearly an hour ago—turned onto Old Cornell Road and passed XScream, she flipped the building the bird just for the heck of it.

She hadn't bothered to tell Karl she wasn't coming back—*ever*—and she didn't feel an ounce of guilt over that decision. As far as she was concerned, he could go in the back room and fuck himself for all the nasty things he'd said and tried to do to her.

And who the hell was Nick to *order* her to go to the colony anyway? He might be a good lay now and then, but that didn't give him the right to tell her what to do.

Her blood pressure shot up a level as she neared the lake and thought about the stupid-ass men in her life. Had she seriously thought Nick was forever material? Man, she really was delusional. She needed to get out of this town and away from the Misos before she did something stupid, like murdered Karl, and outed the colony to the humans once and for all.

As if *that* would improve things for her.

Dana blew her bangs out of her eyes as she pulled into Casey's driveway. She knew Casey wouldn't be home yet from the store and figured that was a good thing. She wasn't in the mood to chat, and she hated drawn-out good-byes. The one at the store had been bad enough. She'd only come back here because she realized too late that she'd left her cell phone at Casey's house the other night, and she needed it back if she was going to keep tabs on the colony. Even *she* wasn't stupid enough to cut all ties. The GPS Nick had put inside everyone's phones was her one link back if things got hot for her out in the *real* world.

As she killed the engine and stared at the front of Casey's cute one-story, she couldn't help thinking back to the way Casey had looked today, standing behind the counter in her store, surrounded by all those books.

And she couldn't help but think of the way she'd smelled either. The scent of death was growing around her. When Dana first picked it up at the club, she'd hoped she was wrong, but every time she'd seen Casey since that night a few weeks ago, that wretched scent was getting stronger.

A wave of despair washed over her, and for once she wished she was full Argolean and not prone to stupid human emotions. Misos were supposed to be stronger than the average human, but in Casey's case, that wasn't true. And dammit, it wasn't fair. Especially because Casey was one of the sweetest people—Misos or human—Dana had ever met. The only bright spot was that Casey didn't know what she really was.

Man, Dana, your powers truly suck. Of all the gifts a Misos could have, she'd been saddled with the worst one of all. She could sense disease, but she couldn't do a damn thing about it. She wasn't a healer. She wasn't anything important. She was simply…a sensor. The prelude to the Grim fucking Reaper.

With a scowl, she pushed the useless thought out of her head as she popped the door and eased out of her red Saturn. She was ninety-eight years old and she had a couple hundred years to go before she made it to the Isles of the Blessed. *If* she made it to that elusive plane where the favored heroes dwelt. Knowing her dumbass luck, she'd wind up stuck in Tartarus for all the bad shit she'd done in this world.

And since that was just the king of all depressing thoughts, she wasn't going *there*, either.

She trudged up the three porch steps and dug around in the potted yellow chrysanthemums Casey'd planted until she found the hide-a-key. Shaking her head, she told herself to convince Casey to find a better hiding spot. Any two-bit thug would find this in a heartbeat. That despair came back full force when she realized neither of them would be around for that conversation.

Don't dwell on it. Not your problem anymore anyway.

The house was cold and empty when she stepped inside. She flipped on a light in the living room and glanced at the coffee table where she was pretty sure she'd set her phone the night she and Casey had watched *National Treasure* and polished off a bottle of wine.

No phone.

Deciding that maybe Casey had moved it to the kitchen, she headed for the back of the house, twirling her key ring around her fingers as she moved while humming a few bars from Linkin Park's "In the End."

She was so preoccupied, she didn't notice the change in temperature until it was too late. Until she was already stepping into the room and her breath was curling in wisps of white around her in the suddenly frigid air.

The first daemon stepped out of the laundry room, green eyes glowing, and studied her from head to toe. "You are not the One," he growled.

Oh, shit.

Panic clawed up Dana's throat. She didn't think, just let instinct rule as she turned to run. And made it as far as the couch in the living room before the second daemon emerged from Casey's bedroom, blocking her path to the front door. This one drew in a long whiff and uttered only one word.

"Misos."

Oh shit, oh shit, oh shit.

Dana's adrenaline spiked. The daemon from the kitchen had followed her and effectively cut off her only other means of escape.

"Where is the One?" the second growled.

Dana backed up against the TV cabinet. She opened her mouth, but fear rendered her speechless. She started to shake.

"She doesn't know," the first said.

"She knows," the second growled, moving closer. "Where would she go?"

Dana's trembling intensified.

"To the colony," the first said, easing forward. "If you want to live, tell us how to find her."

"I—" Dana choked back a sob. "Please," she whispered. "I can't."

A look passed between the two just before they lunged.

Dana never had the chance to scream.

* * *

Theron was not in a mood to go a round with this half-breed. He suddenly wanted answers that had nothing to do with Nick or the colony.

"I asked you a question, hero," Nick snapped. "Of what interest is Casey to you?"

Theron's jaw clenched, and impatience bubbled through him. He needed to find Acacia and figure out what in Hades she was up to, but the aggression flashing across Nick's face held him up. The half-breed was itching for a fight, and from the looks of it, he wasn't about to let Theron out of his sight until he got his answers.

Theron decided that being honest—to a point—was the best way to handle Nick so he could get the hell out of here and go find Acacia. "The king's health is failing. He wants to meet his daughter before his time is up. I'm to take her to Argolea unharmed."

Nick's amber eyes grew wary. "Just like that?"

"Just like that."

"Bullshit." Those amber eyes flashed. "Either tell me the truth or I'll have my soldiers throw you out by the scruff of the neck and beat you to a pulp in the process."

Theron's muscles flexed. "Try it."

Nick's upper lip peeled off his teeth. "Argonaut or not, you don't scare me. We've existed for hundreds of years without your help. I doubt there's anything good ol' King Leonidas wants that Casey could provide. And I don't for a second buy your load of bull."

Theron didn't answer.

Nick crossed the room in two long strides and got right up in Theron's face. They were roughly the same height, close to the same size, and as the man got close, once again Theron had that strange recognition he'd had back in Acacia's store.

"You're dangerously close to death, half-breed," Theron warned in a low voice. "I'd rethink what you're about to do."

"I don't know what the hell is going on here or what you really want with Casey," Nick said, his face inches from Theron's, "but I intend to find out. And that means she's not leaving here with you or anyone else until I'm satisfied with the answer."

"Nick!" The door to the study burst open and two women spilled into the room, saving Nick from dismemberment.

The first Theron recognized from earlier—Helene, the one who'd taken Acacia to her room. The other was of average height but thick around the middle, with dark hair pulled into a braid at the back of her head. Both looked upset, but the dark-haired one was frantic.

Nick's gazed snapped to them. "What's happened?"

"It's Dana," Helene said. "No one's heard from her or seen her since yesterday."

Nick's focus shifted to the dark-haired woman. "Leila, when did you talk to your sister last?"

"Yesterday morning." She ran a nervous hand over her hair, unknowingly pulling strands from her braid. "She called from town. I thought she'd stayed over at her blasted apartment, but now I'm not so sure. Something was wrong. She didn't sound like herself, was talking about new starts and making changes. She said to call her on her cell if I need her. I've been trying all afternoon and can't get through to her. Nick, something's happened to her. I feel it."

Nick moved behind his desk and flipped open a laptop Theron hadn't noticed earlier. Beneath all this rock, it had to be wired to a satellite somewhere on the surface. Nick's fingers ran over keys and his eyes scanned the screen as he searched. His brow lowered. "Her phone's at Casey's house."

"Whose house?" Leila asked.

"The woman who came in with Nick today," Helene volunteered.

Leila's frantic eyes flicked between Nick and Theron, as if she'd just realized Theron was there. "What is Dana doing there? She knows she has to check in."

Nick closed the laptop with a snap and jerked his jacket from the desk chair. "I didn't say she was there. I said her phone was there. I'm heading over to take a look."

For the first time, Theron noticed the dread darkening Nick's features. Whoever this Dana woman was, she was out there alone, and if she'd gone to Acacia's house, odds were good she could have run into daemons.

He grasped Nick's arm as the half-breed brushed by. "I'll go with you."

"I don't think so."

His grip tightened. "Don't be an idiot. You'll need my help."

"I fucking doubt it."

When Theron's grip didn't lessen, Nick turned his fiery eyes Theron's way, and in them Theron saw disgust and a hatred bred for hundreds of years. "I know your kind, Argonaut. And I've seen your help." He pointed toward the door. "Every Misos in this colony has seen the way your kin *helped* us. They have the scars to prove it."

The mutilated faces Theron had seen in the colony outside flashed in his mind. Followed by the king's admission that the half-breeds' existence had been kept secret because there weren't enough of them to make a difference.

He looked deep into Nick's eyes. "I knew nothing of this colony or ones like it until I came here to find Acacia. When I return to Argolea, the Argonauts will look into this matter fully."

"How do I know you won't send your kin to kill us all?"

It occurred to Theron then that Nick's hatred for the Argonauts and Argolea as a whole ran much deeper than what was evident on the surface. Somehow, this Misos was connected to Theron's world in ways no one in this colony could begin to understand. And Theron intended to find out what that connection was.

But not now.

"You have my word as leader of the Argonauts. No harm will come to you and your people by our hands."

Nick searched Theron's face for some sign he was lying. Both women in the room were silent as the seconds ticked by on a clock somewhere on the wall. Theron released Nick's arm, but he didn't avert his eyes. And neither did Nick.

"You'll stay here, hero," Nick finally said. "But only because I don't want to have to watch my back with you around." He pulled on his jacket. "Casey has to willingly go across the portal, and considering everything that happened to her earlier today because of you, I think it's safe to say she's not going anywhere with you right now. You sit tight until I get back." His eyes flared again as he stepped around the women. "And you better fucking believe we're going to finish this then."

He glanced toward Leila. "I'll call when I find her."

When he was gone, the woman called Leila finally turned her attention Theron's way. "Are you really…?" Her gaze swept to Helene. "Is he really…an Argonaut?"

Helene nodded slowly. "It looks that way, doesn't it?"

Leila seemed stunned stupid. Both continued to stare at him as if he had a third eyeball stuck smack in the middle of his forehead. Neither appeared to know what to say.

And then Leila stepped toward him, spat in his face and rushed from the room.

Theron wiped a hand slowly down his cheek and looked toward the one woman who had the stupid sense to remain in the room with him. "Where is Acacia?" he asked as calmly as he could.

Helene regarded him with flat eyes. And he saw then it wasn't stupidity but strength born of circumstance. "Upstairs. Sleeping."

He headed for the door and paused only when he realized she wasn't about to stop him. "Why are you not afraid of me?"

"I've seen too much to be afraid of someone like you."

"I sense your hatred for me and my kind. You could have kept me from her."

"Could anything keep you from her?"

She knows. He turned and stared at her. Then slowly shook his head.

"Then my helping you is irrelevant," Helene said. "But you'd be wise to remember one thing, Argonaut. Even the original heroes were part human like us. Misos from the very beginning. She's not all that different from you. And neither are we."

The woman brushed past, leaving him standing alone in the doorway to contemplate her words, a strange sense of unease and foreboding mixing in his veins.

Half-human. Like me.

He glanced toward the stairs. His human side had been repressed for over two hundred years. Could that be what he was tapping into? And if he was, did that mean Acacia was the cause?

As he climbed the stairs two by two, he rubbed the heel of his hand against his sternum. And felt that pinch all over again.

After mere minutes of searching, Theron found Acacia in a room near the end of the hall. Helene had been right. He'd have found her without the woman's help. He could have located her simply by breathing deep and focusing.

As soon as he stepped in the room and smelled the familiar scents of lavender and vanilla, his blood heated, and the dream that had become an unfinished reality back in her small house by the lake flared bright.

A warm glow from the dying embers in the fireplace fell over her body. She lay on her side, snuggled into her pillow, the thick blankets twisted in her long legs. Her shirt had ridden up, and the slightest hint of flesh was visible between the low waistband of her jeans and the edge of her blue cotton tee. His eyes ran over her bare skin, lower to her hip and over to the soft sweet mound of her ass. Thanks to their sultry night together, he knew exactly what that ass looked like...bare and beautiful and marked. His blood pulsed low and hot in response.

She is the One.

He frowned at the strange voice in his head. Yeah, well, he knew that already, didn't he?

Forcing his gaze away from her beautiful backside, he ran his eyes slowly up her body, across her abdomen, over the swell of her breasts to her face, trying to tamp down the arousal turning him into a rocket launcher. Exhaustion lines marred her perfect skin, and blue smudges had formed beneath her lashes, but to him she was just as stunning as she'd been the night she rescued him from the daemons outside that club.

Just as beautiful, but thinner.

For the first time, he noticed Nick had been right. She looked exhausted. Her skin had lost its rosy color and she'd dropped several pounds in just the past few days.

She's the One.

The voice grew stronger as he stood there staring at her. Would the Fates really be so cruel as to give him a half-breed destined to save his race as a soul mate?

His heart pounded in his chest as he turned for the bathroom and took a cold shower that did nothing to cool him down. Of course the Fates would curse him. Because he was of Heracles's line. The one hero that was still, to this day, revered by some and reviled by most others. Heracles's indiscretions were as numerous as his accomplishments, and every Argonaut of his line had been dealt a blow because of his selfishness. Why would Theron think he'd be any different?

Of course, it was still possible he was only attracted to Acacia because of the way they'd met and who he knew she was. And the fact she was a forbidden and tempting treat he'd never sampled. If she was *his* One, however, there was a sure way to find out.

He grew hard and hot at just the thought. As he toweled off, he debated his options. The one that stood out strongest wasn't ideal, but he had to know, didn't he? Once he got this absurd thought out of his mind, he could refocus on the real reason he was here.

Decision made, he pulled on his pants and quietly walked back into the bedroom. Acacia was still out, having shifted only slightly since he'd first stepped into the room. Tired to his bones, he slid into the big bed beside her and gently pulled the covers up around her waist. As he rolled to his side, he fingered a lock of hair falling over her shoulder and brought it to his nose.

He smelled grapefruit and remembered the shampoo in her shower. Her hair was soft and silky between his fingers. As silky as that between her thighs. The roar returned to his head. His erection responded to the visual in his mind, and he hissed in a long breath to tamp down the renewed arousal zinging along his nerve endings.

Even if she is your *One, she's sick. And she's the king's daughter. It won't make a difference.*

Yeah. There was that. And the fact that honor and duty came first with him, no matter what.

Though it nearly killed him, he forced himself to let go of her hair, and in the process brushed her shoulder with the slightest touch. In sleep, she groaned and inched his way, as if searching for more contact. And before he knew it, her beautiful backside came into full contact with his hips, and the erection he'd been trying so hard to keep in check grew rock hard.

The blood rushed out of his head with a screaming roar and went due south.

Take her. Now. Find out, right here.

His cock wedged its way into the crease of her behind as if it had a mind of its own, where it pulsed and pounded and begged for release. A moan slipped from her lips, a mindless act of approval. His lust for her grew to explosive levels. He slid one of his arms around her belly and tugged her back into his bare chest. It was all he could do not to tear off her jeans, flip her to her stomach, lift her hips and plunge hard and deep to discover just what it was about her that left him in such a frenzy.

And oh, he was ready. He wanted. Needed. But just as he shifted to turn her, her scent drifted into his nose, that sweet and familiar combination traveling through every nerve in his body and all the way into his soul.

Where, oddly, it calmed him. The way it had in her little house. Enough that his brain kicked into gear and common sense came flooding back. His cock still jerked with a rabid desire to explode inside her, but he found he could control the urge. That he could lie here next to her and enjoy the warmth of her body against his without the burning need to overpower and take what he wanted by force.

He wanted her to come to him as she had in her house.

His heart rate slowed. He closed his eyes and drew in long, deep breaths, more tired than he remembered being in…ages. And that's when he heard the voice. Again.

She's the One.

CHAPTER FIFTEEN

Casey knew she wasn't alone even before her eyes drifted open. The rhythmic breathing at her back was a dead giveaway. As was the hard arousal nestled against her backside.

Any normal woman would have panicked, especially considering the circumstances. But she wasn't normal—not anymore—and even before she looked she knew it was Theron up tight against her back. His dark, spicy scent flooded her senses. In the stillness, the solid weight of his arm across her hip became as real as her pulse pounding in her brain.

What the hell was he doing in her bed?

Carefully, so as not to wake him, she rolled to her back. The movement made his arm slide across her belly, sending sparks along her nerve endings. She sat up slowly and reached for his hand to free herself from his gasp, only to falter when their fingers touched.

A jolt of electricity shimmied through her. The room spun. And suddenly she wasn't in a bedroom anymore, but in a dark and cold forest, surrounded by the undeniable sights and smells of death.

She gasped. Turned a slow circle. Wondered how she'd gotten here and where Theron had gone. Cannons exploded behind her, the loud sounds making her jump and whip around. Dried leaves crunched beneath her feet. Shouts and curses and bloodcurdling screams came from far off in the distance.

Dear God, she was in the middle of a war zone. Her adrenaline spiked. She looked right and left as her heart kicked up to rival the roar of a 747 on takeoff. Where was Theron?

Gunfire echoed. Followed by a voice Casey knew intimately, booming from the trees no more than twenty yards away.

"Patéras!"

Without questioning her common sense, Casey tore off in that direction. Then pulled up short when she reached the small clearing and the scene laid out before her.

Two daemons lay mauled and incapacitated on the hard earth near a small bubbling brook. Fresh blood oozed from their wounds to run down their grotesque faces, staining the ground with the vileness in their veins. A man—the one from Casey's dream the night she'd met Theron—lay on the ground mere feet away. More blood gushed from a gaping wound in his chest, his eyes and mouth open as if he was in shock. Across the small stream, a boy who looked no more than fourteen, wearing a ratty gray coat, stood slack-jawed, with eyes as wide as saucers. In his arms he cradled a smoking rifle.

Theron bolted through the trees at Casey's right and dropped to the ground beside the older man, his own features twisted in disbelief. *"Patéras.* No."

"Theron," the man gasped, reaching a shaky, bloody hand up to grip Theron's shirt. "You must finish them."

"I will. I... *Patéras.*" He placed both hands over the wound in the other man's chest. "We have to get you back. Now. We—"

"Ochi," the older man barked in a weak voice.

Theron's muscles froze as if he hadn't heard right.

"Ochi," the older man said again, softer this time. "My time has already come and gone. You must"—he cringed in pain—"finish them."

Theron lifted grief-stricken eyes to look toward the daemons, who, Casey realized in horror, were starting to revive, bloody stumps and all.

"This is what you were born for," the older man said, pulling Theron's attention back to him. "You will take my spot—"

"No."

"You will do as the king commands. You won't question his authority. Trust him as you trust me. Remember we are"—the older man took a shuddering breath—"of the same line."

"Patéras," Theron whispered.

The older man's hand fell against the dirt. His eyes flickered, and his voice dropped to a whisper. *"To peprōmenon phugein adunaton, gios mou."*

Then his head rolled to the side, and in the silence that followed, Casey watched a single tear slide down Theron's cheek, roll across his chin and drip onto the older man's face.

Though the daemons were now growling low in their throats and groaning as they righted themselves, Theron's motions were slow and methodical. He carefully closed the older man's eyes, then looked up across the river to where the young boy, still frozen in place with the whites of his eyes showing all around his dark irises, stood immobilized, staring at the scene.

And though Casey couldn't see Theron's face, she knew there was murder in his eyes. The boy knew it too. He wet himself, dropped the gun and ran as hard and as fast as his small legs could carry him.

Casey screamed a warning just as the first daemon lunged. But she needn't have bothered. Theron was on the beast in an instant, pulling a blade as long as his forearm from somewhere deep in his coat and decapitating the staggering daemon with one vicious slice.

The other daemon rose to his towering height of seven feet and, though visibly wounded, growled low in his throat. "You will pay for that, Argolean."

"I'm no common Argolean," Theron snarled. "And you are about to meet Hades up close and personal."

Casey gasped at the malicious intent she saw in Theron's face, took two steps back until her spine hit a tree trunk, then covered her eyes to block out the vision of death in front of her. This one Theron did not send back to Hades quickly. No, he slaughtered the beast one limb at a time, taking out on him every ounce of hatred and grief he had in him.

When it was over, when he was exhausted and dripping with a combination of his own sweat and blood and that of the daemon that lay mutilated in front of him, he rose and stared down at what he'd done.

Horrified, Casey slid the fingers covering her eyes open to stare at him, too afraid to move or speak for fear he'd turn his vengeance on her. But what she saw shocked her. Though the homicidal glint was gone from his eyes, there was not an inkling of remorse. She watched as another lone tear tracked down his cheek. Oblivious to it, he decapitated the daemon as he'd done the other.

And then, as if he'd finally realized something was on his face, he reached a grimy hand up to his cheek, wiped at the tear and stared at the liquid on his finger with a perplexed expression, as though he'd never cried before.

And Casey knew in that moment, he never had.

Her skin was cold all over as she blinked and came back to herself. She wasn't in a dark forest surrounded by war, but in the same bed she'd fallen asleep in hours ago.

She stared at Theron, still asleep beside her, his hand clutched tightly in hers. And knew, without even asking, that what she'd just seen had been real. Just like the vision she'd had of the little girl in the middle of the village when she'd first arrived.

Okaaaaaaaaay. That little bit of news on top of everything else was enough to seriously wig her out. Heart pounding, she gently eased out from under his arm and slid out of bed. Though it was still dark, she had an uncontrollable urge to see the sun, to feel its warmth, to put the cold far, far behind her.

She crossed to the small porthole window and opened the curtains. The moon had set, and the first rays of dawn were already spilling over the horizon.

She took slow breaths, and when she felt better, looked back toward the bed.

How long had she been out? And when had Theron come to her room?

Her so-called hero had rolled to his back, one hand at his side, the other fanned across his broad, bare chest. He wore only low-riding black pants that showcased his hard abs and the thin line of dark hair that drew her attention downward. Looking up and away from that temptation, she focused on his muscular arms. In the dim light she could just make out the markings across the backs of his hands and remembered the show he'd put on in Nick's office.

She quickly turned back to the window. Um. Okay. Yeah. Remembering *that* whole spectacle didn't settle her nerves any either.

"It's a three-hundred-foot drop."

Her heart rate kicked up at the velvet sound of his voice, but she didn't look back. He might be a sex god she hadn't been able to get out of her head since their night together back at her house, but he was also the man...Argonaut...*whatever*...who'd kidnapped her. She wanted answers. And she wanted them now. "Excuse me?"

MARKED

The bed creaked behind her. "Out the window. Three hundred feet. At least. I already looked. If you're searching for an escape route, that's not it."

She flicked a look over her shoulder. "If I wanted to leave, you couldn't stop me."

"Who told you such a lie?"

She glared at him. His eyebrows lifted in challenge. Aggravated beyond belief, she finally dropped her arms and turned his way. "Why you pompous piece of—"

He chuckled as he swung his massive legs over the side of the bed. "I see we have both feet back on solid ground. Your rest did you good."

Her mouth snapped shut.

"I can also see your little brain's filled to the brim. Go ahead and ask me whatever you want."

Her "little brain" was nearly at a breaking point. "Are you not bothered at all by the fact you kidnapped me and destroyed my store? Not to mention taking advantage of me that night at my house when I was only trying to help you?"

He let out a weary sigh. "I didn't kidnap you, I rescued you. And if it makes you feel any better, I regret that your store was destroyed. The less the humans in your town know of the daemons and our war, the safer they'll be. And for the record, I wasn't the one taking advantage the other night. I seem to remember someone else making the first move."

Her cheeks heated. But just as quickly her temper reared. "'Anything I want,'" she mocked.

A sheepish one-sided grin pulled at his mouth. "You remember that, hm?"

"Of course I remember it," she snapped. "In fact, it's a lot clearer now than it was then. You tricked me."

He leaned forward to brace his forearms on his knees. "It's called *élencho*. And it's more of a mind-bending technique than a trick. Though as you've proved, *meli*, it doesn't work so well on half-breeds."

She ignored that fact because it seemed to be true and because it put the blame of what had happened between them back on her. "You say that word, *half-breed*, like it's dirty."

"I don't mean to."

"Then watch how you say it. And for the record, I think they prefer to be called Misos."

He looked up at her without responding. And the hint of regret in his eyes softened her.

Dammit, she wanted to stay mad at him. But when he gazed at her like that, all she could think about was the way he'd looked in the candlelight of her kitchen, the way he'd tasted and felt on her couch. The way she knew he could make her feel now if she crossed the floor right this minute.

"Is there something you want from me, *meli*?" he asked in a low voice.

Her eyes flicked up to his. And she saw her own desire mirrored in those pools of obsidian.

Sex as a distraction from all the crazy stuff happening had its advantages. But not with him. She'd learned her lesson where this hero was concerned.

"Not a single thing."

He smiled then, as if he knew she was lying. "When you're ready, just tell me."

She glared at him again. "I don't think so."

A chuckle bubbled through him. "Oh, *meli*. I do like you. You weren't nearly so spirited that night at your house."

She sent him a bored look. "I was a little distracted. I thought you were dying. And what does that word mean? You keep using it. *Meli*. My grandmother used it now and then."

"She did?"

She nodded as a thought occurred. "She told me once it was my mother's nickname."

He looked thoughtful for a moment and then said, "It's Argolean. Loosely translated, it means beloved."

"Then how would my mother have known it?"

"Maybe it was a nickname from your father."

She lifted her brow. "My father the king? Uh-huh. Right. So how does this work? There aren't enough Argolean women in your world? The men have to come hunting for human women?"

He laughed again and ran a hand across the nape of his neck, very much amused at something she didn't find the least bit funny. "No, there are plenty of females in our world. We call them *gynaikes*."

"That's Greek."

He nodded. "A lot of our words come from the Greek root. As for your father, I told you some of our people cross over, though it's not encouraged."

"You can't stop them?"

"It's not my job to stop them. Your father…liked to visit. He's always been fascinated by humans."

"But you're not."

His jaw clenched, but he didn't answer.

The visions she'd glimpsed earlier flashed in her brain, but she knew instinctively, if she brought it up he wouldn't talk about it. And she wasn't sure she wanted to know what made him tick either.

She snorted and turned her attention back to the sunrise. "Then definitely don't call me *meli*. We both know you don't mean it."

"Acacia—"

"And before I forget, just what do you think you're doing in my bed?"

"Do you like having me in your bed?" he asked quietly.

A tingling ignited in Casey's chest. She glanced briefly over her shoulder and regretted it immediately. The same carnal desire that was suddenly careening through her veins all over again was carved into each hollow and plane of his handsome face.

Oh, yeah, this guy was a sex god all right. And he was playing her good.

"I like your eyes on me, *meli*. It makes the blood pound in my veins. But more than your eyes, I would much rather have your hands caressing me the way they were that night on your couch."

Her heart rate kicked up at the memory. Arousal colored her cheeks and spread warmth between her thighs. She sensed herself falling into the same trance she'd been in with him once before. The heat from his body, the scent of his skin, the sultry sound of his accent all coalesced to turn her to mush right in front of him.

He held out a hand, beckoning her forward. "Come here, *meli*. Let me remind you."

Her gaze dropped to his hand, and she remembered the way he'd held his hand out to her in the store like that just yesterday. Then remembered the flash of uncertainty she'd seen in his eyes.

A hero who knew what he wanted would never be nervous. Which meant only one thing: he wasn't being honest.

The sexual fuzz cleared from her brain, and she brought her chin up in defiance. "Nice try. Fortunately, I'm not stupid enough to fall for that twice in this lifetime." She crossed her arms over her chest. "Now, I think it's time you answered some of my questions."

He let out a long, weary sigh and dropped his arm. "What else do you want to know?"

That was easy. Careful. She tipped her head. "What exactly is an Argonaut? Nick said you were a guardian. Is that like a general?"

"Do you know the story of the original Argonauts?"

"From Greek mythology? Sure. They were the band of heroes who sailed with Jason on the *Argo* in search of the Golden Fleece. There were fifty, if I remember correctly."

"Fifty-five. They are, technically, the founders of our race. Mostly men. Some women, though there were other heroes who didn't sail with Jason but who also fell into that category. Their offspring became known as Argoleans, named after the realm the gods granted us when it became evident the heroes were reproducing." Casey eased down into a chair as he spoke. "The original strongest seven—Heracles, Achilles, Theseus, Odysseus, Perseus, Jason, and Bellerophon—were chosen as the race's guardians and were therefore granted the title Argonaut. In every generation, one from the original seven bloodlines is chosen to continue the guardian tradition. My line goes back to Heracles." A wry smile curled his mouth. "Or as you Americans prefer to call him, Hercules."

"The greatest of the heroes," she said, thinking back to what she knew of them. "That's why you're the leader?"

"Yes."

"Wasn't the ship Jason's?"

He shrugged. "Minor technicality."

A look she couldn't define passed over his eyes, making her suspect there was more he wasn't saying, but other questions burned. "So there are seven of you now?"

"Yes. My kin. Brothers in battle. We each have a different power, which is generally linked back to our ancestors. Mine is great strength. All Argoleans have powers of some type, but those of the Argonauts are magnified."

She chewed over that answer as she said, "And what do you do…you and your brothers?"

"We protect the race," he said flatly.

"By hunting daemons?"

"Among other things."

"But you do more than that, don't you? Otherwise you wouldn't be here now."

"Yes," he said hesitantly. "We do."

She waited for him to explain, and when seconds passed and he didn't, she realized she'd hit a dead end. Tucking her feet under her, she tried another tactic. "So how old are you?"

"Two hundred and two."

Her mouth fell open, and only when she realized how stupid she must look did she close it. "Oh, my God. Are you serious?"

He nodded.

"How long do you live?"

He shrugged. "Argonauts and those of the royal family live roughly seven hundred years. Some a bit longer. We are the strongest of the race."

"Wow." Casey couldn't think of anything else to say. Her brow wrinkled. Or wait…maybe she could. "How long will I live?"

"Most Argoleans live about five hundred years. I would guess the half-breeds—Misos," he corrected before she could do it for him, "live about the same."

Okay, there was definite disgust in that answer. Did he think he was superior to humans? That was just…bigoted. Not that she cared. He could believe whatever he wanted. She still needed answers.

She refocused on what he'd told her. And thought of Jill's phone call yesterday and the battery of tests awaiting her. Five hundred years. She was only twenty-seven. If she had the same cancer as her grandmother…

A lump formed in her throat. "Can you die before then?"

"Do you mean are we mortal?"

She nodded.

"Yes," he said. "We are mortal. We can be killed just like humans. But our resistance to disease and our ability to heal are amplified."

Thank God. She let out a relieved breath.

"I'd venture to guess that's not the case for the Misos though."

And there went her relief. No, she wouldn't be that lucky, would she?

"Well," she said with a frown, "I guess that explains your miraculous healing back at my house." But it didn't explain the vision he'd projected to her when he'd been asleep.

Brow creased, she said, "If that's true, then why couldn't your father be healed?"

"What?" For the first time since he'd opened his eyes and shot sparks across the room that had been lighting her up like a Christmas tree ever since, he looked dazed.

"Your father. Why couldn't he heal from that gunshot wound? I watched you heal from something almost as bad. Was he too old?"

His dark eyebrows drew together in confusion. "How…do you know about his death?"

"You showed me." When he only stared at her like she'd sprouted snakes in her hair, she added, "When you were asleep. I saw the daemons you were hunting and the boy across the river. He didn't mean to shoot your father, did he? He'd tried to shoot the beast you both were fighting."

The color drained from Theron's face, and in a quiet voice he asked, "Acacia. Have you had dreams like this before?"

"I wouldn't call them dreams. More like, I don't know, visions. But yeah, I guess I have."

"When?"

His change in tone sent alarm bells off in her head. The skin on her lower back near her birthmark tingled. "The first night we met. After I stitched you up and you were sleeping. I laid down on the couch and had a vision of you and your father standing in a field overlooking a battlefield." Her gaze locked on his. "Oh, my God. That was the Civil War, wasn't it? I saw blue and gray coats."

He nodded slowly and rose to his feet. "Yes. When else? What other times did you have these visions?"

Okay, the crazed look in his eye wasn't doing anything to ease her nerves. In fact, it was kind of freaking her out. She knew he had some kind of superhuman strength, she'd seen it in action, which meant the Argonauts had powers humans could only envy. But if she was reading him right, he hadn't projected those images onto her the way she thought at all. And that meant somehow she'd conjured them herself.

That tingling intensified. "Yesterday. When we got here. That little girl who came running up to us? I…when I held her hand I had a flash of her family and the daemons attacking her home."

Theron stiffened. Apprehensive, Casey dropped her feet to the floor. "I figured I was just hallucinating. What with everything that had happened yesterday, you know?"

He stared at her with wide and very focused eyes, but didn't speak.

"What?" she finally asked, easing out of her chair.

"You have the gift of hindsight."

Hindsight? Well, that didn't sound so bad. "That's a good thing, right?"

He didn't answer. But a look of great confusion passed over his features before he turned and surveyed the room as if seeing it for the first time. "I need to find Nick."

Nick, the half-breed he couldn't stand? Oh, this wasn't sounding good at all.

He grabbed his shirt from the back of a chair and tugged it on, then his boots from the floor, and sat on the bed as he bent to lace them with swift fingers.

"Theron, what's going on?"

A ruckus out in the hall brought both their heads up. Their eyes met briefly before he rose and jerked the door open, careful to keep her shielded from sight.

Helene rushed by. Theron grabbed her by the arm to stop her. "What happened?"

Helene looked through the doorway toward Casey. "Marissa's missing. No one can find her. They're talking about sending out a search party—"

"No," Theron said fiercely.

Casey pushed past Theron to grip Helene's hand. "Where was she last seen?"

"In her bedroom." Fear rushed over Helene's delicate features. "Her mother put her to bed last night, and when she got up this morning, Marissa was gone."

Casey thought of the young girl she'd met yesterday, then of the young girl's words: *Minnie knew he'd bring you here to save us.*

She squeezed Helene's hand. "I'll get my coat."

She swept back into the room, slid her feet into her shoes and grabbed her jacket, not caring that she hadn't brushed her teeth or combed her hair or even had her morning cup of coffee. But when she turned she was very aware of the mammoth body blocking her exit.

"You're not going anywhere, Acacia. This is none of your concern."

None of her concern? Oh, screw that. She set her jaw. "Those are my people. That girl is one of *my* race. So don't you dare tell me this is none of my business." Her eyes narrowed, and the air crackled between them, but she didn't back down. For the first time in her life, she had something to fight for.

"You can't keep me here, Theron. One way or the other, I'm going to help find Marissa. So either move your ass out of my way, or make yourself useful and do something to help me."

CHAPTER SIXTEEN

She was seriously losing it.

Isadora paced to the windows, turned and wrung her hands together as she passed the settee. Four more steps and she was near the closet door, moving by the high-backed dresser and looping around the canopy bed again. This room had always been a place of comfort and solitude for her, but not now. Not when she was ready to claw her way through stone and mortar just to get free.

She jumped at the soft knock on her door. "Yes?"

"It's just I, my lady." Saphira poked her head around the door. "May I come in?"

Isadora breathed a sigh of relief. She'd half expected it to be Demetrius, or one of the other Argonauts. For a group of *ándres* who couldn't stomach the castle, they'd sure been hanging around a lot lately. Which couldn't be good on any level. "Yes, yes, come in."

As the door opened she caught a glimpse of her latest sentry, Cerek, his short dark hair and broad shoulders easily discernible in the sitting room to her chambers.

Resentment burned hot in her, but she tamped it down as Saphira closed the door with a soft click. The younger woman held a tray of food—soup, crackers, a bowl of fresh fruit. The scent of stewed chicken and vegetables made Isadora's stomach roll. She placed a hand on her abdomen, waving away the tray and its contents with the other. "I'm not hungry."

Saphira set the tray on a low table near the fireplace. "You must eat, my lady."

Eating was the last thing on Isadora's mind. And she knew it would just come right back up if she tried. "Has Theron been back to the castle?"

Saphira glanced toward the door as if she was afraid to speak too loud. She moved closer and in a low voice said, "No, my lady. Not yet."

Damn. Though being shackled to Theron wasn't Isadora's first choice, at least she knew he wouldn't shut her in a room and forget about her, which was what her father and the rest of those mercenaries were doing to her now. "What about the king?"

"The same. Callia's been to see him several times, but there's no improvement."

Isadora placed her finger to her lips and walked to the windows. The gown she wore weighed heavy on her shoulders, and not for the first time, she vowed to change the monarchy's archaic traditions—clothing being the first—as soon as she became queen.

"Do you know where Theron is?" she asked.

Saphira's voice held an edge of pity that gnawed on Isadora's last nerve. "Word is he's on an important assignment for your father. No one seems to know where he's gone, though. And with one of the Argonauts outside your room every minute, few in the castle are speaking, let alone gossiping about what they know."

Isadora closed her eyes. A personal favor for her father. That could only mean one thing. She had a pretty good idea where Theron had gone. And whom he was with. The question was, would he be able to convince her to come to Argolea with him? And if he did, would it be too late?

Isadora lifted bony hands and looked down at her pale skin. Even she knew she was wasting away. The way her energy was lagging lately, she guessed she had a week, maybe two, tops, before she lost the battle completely.

The prophecy flashed in her mind as she stood there. The one she'd stumbled across in her father's books when she'd gone to sit by his side in his illness.

There shall be two in every era,
Born of god and earth and men.
One of strength and one of courage,
Two separate halves to bring the end.

And they shall be known by the markings they bear,
United in the twenty-seventh year.
Only joined will the strong survive,
To dissolve the pact and bring the end to life.

A shiver ran through Isadora at what her father was doing. But how could he know for sure what would happen? And how could he sacrifice one daughter for another?

Not for the first time, she thought about the half-breed sister she'd not known about until only days before. Would they have anything in common? If they met on the street, would they recognize each other? Would there be a connection?

She didn't know. But one thing was clear. The ease with which her father and the Argonauts had locked her in this room made it clear they regarded her as nothing more than a pawn. Nothing but a pet to keep fed and quiet and well-groomed.

The tightness in her chest she'd been fighting the last few days came back with a vengeance. And as she eyed the courtyard below, she knew what she had to do. "Saphira, I need your help."

"Anything, my lady."

Isadora crossed the floor and reached for a piece of paper from the top drawer of her desk. Scribbling quickly, she said, "Find Orpheus and give him this letter."

"Orpheus?" Saphira asked, bewildered. "But why? He's Lucian's nephew."

As Lucian was the top ranking member of the Council, and very much *not* her friend, the question was warranted. But what Saphira didn't understand was that Isadora knew Orpheus's darkest secrets. And he would do just about anything to make sure they never came to light.

"Because he owes me." She reread the note quickly and, satisfied it would set the wheels in motion, signed her name, slipped the paper into an envelope and affixed her royal seal. She handed the paper to Saphira. "Deliver it right away. But take care. It goes only to Orpheus. No one else."

Saphira nodded and slipped the envelope inside her jacket. "It will be done."

Alone, Isadora looked out over the courtyard once more and drew a deep breath. Then thought of her sister.

Two weeks. Max. She had two weeks to put her plan in motion before they both died.

She only prayed she was doing the right thing.

CHAPTER SEVENTEEN

The woman was as prickly as the tree she was named for.

Theron scowled as he followed behind Acacia on the narrow path. He hadn't been able to talk her out of her crazy plan to search for the youngling. Though Theron was loath to have her anywhere out in the open, he knew when he was up against a rock wall of stubbornness, and he was quickly discovering Acacia could dig her heels in with the best of them.

Since there was no way he could trust her safety to anyone but himself, he'd had to come along. They'd separated from the others more than an hour ago, and he scanned the forest on both sides as they moved. Odds were good the child was already dead, though why that bothered him so much was as foreign as why he couldn't stop thinking about getting between Acacia's thighs right this very minute.

Focus, dammit.

There were a thousand things he should be concentrating on, namely how in Hades it was possible a half-breed had the gift of hindsight. But the only thing he could think about right now was how soft her skin had been last night, how lush her body, how perfectly she'd fit against him.

"You're doing it again," she said from ahead.

He lifted his head. "Doing what?"

"That muttering thing in another language. Didn't anyone ever teach you that's rude?"

He glanced at the soft sway of her hips as she moved and the way she filled out the backside of her jeans. "Would you prefer I spoke my thoughts in English?"

The husky timbre of his voice must have registered, because she stopped abruptly and turned on him. Her cheeks were pink from the cool morning air, but there was a heat in her that had nothing to do with the temperature. Her gaze raked his face, slid down to his chest and hovered there until his blood warmed with arousal.

"Look your fill, *meli*," he whispered.

Her eyes snapped to his just before she swiveled on her heels and resumed walking. "I don't like you."

One side of his mouth curved in amusement as he followed. She was a terrible liar, something he'd discovered early on. The knowledge thrilled him. "Yes, you do. You like me a lot."

"I may have. Once." She lifted a branch so she could move under it, then released it with perfect timing so it smacked him in the face.

He chuckled even as he rubbed at the sting on his cheek. He liked that she stood up to him. There wasn't a *gynaíka* in Argolea who would dare try to tell him what to do. If he had to be stuck out here, he couldn't think of anyone he'd rather be stuck with. The woman had to be exhausted, they'd been walking for nearly an hour, but she was determined, and she wasn't letting it affect her mood. Every time he suggested they look in a different direction and that it was inconceivable for a child to walk this far, she'd flicked him a look and kept going.

"That is," she added, cutting through his thoughts, "I may have liked you before you set out to seduce me and then walked out without a word."

Ouch. "Acacia." He stopped her with a firm hand on her arm. This wasn't the time or place to get into it, but he had an overwhelming urge to explain what had happened that night and why he'd left.

Though why he thought he could make her understand when he was still having trouble rationalizing the whole thing was beyond him.

"What happened between us had nothing to do with why I'm here now. I didn't know who you were then. I only learned of your identity when I went to the store to find you."

"You expect me to believe that?"

"It's the truth. Look in my eyes. You'll see that I'm not lying."

She did. And their eyes met. Then a blush crept up her cheeks, one that told him she was remembering exactly what had happened between them.

That warmth went white-hot. Urgent and needy. So demanding it blocked out the rational side of his brain, which warned this was a bad idea.

Before he thought better of it, he reached for her other arm. "Do you believe in fate?"

"You mean like destiny?" He nodded, and she shook her head. "No. Everyone makes their own decisions."

"But do you believe fate gives us choices, and where we go is up to us?"

Her violet eyes narrowed. "Why are you asking me this?"

What exactly could he tell her? How much did he *want* her to know? That her lifespan could probably be counted in days, not years? That she was pegged to bring about the beginning of a war that would hopefully free his people? That he was starting to suspect she was his soul mate, and aside from the sexual benefits that conjured in his mind, the idea pretty much creeped him out?

None of that sounded like anything she would believe, or understand, so he opted for what was most pressing. And figured a little bit of honesty couldn't hurt at this point. "I think fate's playing a trick on us. I've had these…strange feelings…that you and I were brought together for a reason that has nothing to do with your father."

She leveled him with a look that was so damn sexy, he itched to kiss it from her face. "Hearing voices, are you?"

Yes. "Not exactly. It's hard to explain."

"Schizophrenia's not that uncommon. Try medication."

Smartass. "I don't think—"

"Me either." The humor in her eyes faded. "My so-called *father* brought us together because he wants something from me. That's not fate, Theron. That's manipulation."

"And what do you call this…this attraction between us?"

She cocked her head. "Your problem?"

"I call it opportunity. A chance to see if fate is really pushing us toward a combined destiny. And there's one way to know for sure."

Her eyes narrowed. "How?"

He moved closer, barely brushing his body against hers, and felt her shudder. And oh, yeah, as far as gambles went, this was the big one. "All it takes is one night."

She blinked twice. "Are you for real?"

"In my world, an *ándras* can tell if a *gynaíka* is his soul mate by sharing a bed."

"Soul mate. I see. And I'm assuming the whole 'sharing a bed' thing would be done in the biblical sense?"

"Is there any other sense?"

She stared at him so long, his blood heated at the knowledge she was considering the offer. He imagined taking her back to the colony, peeling her clothing off one piece at a time, unwrapping the gift of her gorgeous body, then pressing her back on that soft bed and joining them in a way that would tell him for sure if she was his or merely an infatuation he'd soon get over.

The vision was so real, his pants grew tight and his heart rate kicked up in time to the beat of a snare drum. He waited for her to step to him, to ease up on her toes. To bring their mouths together and their bodies into much-needed contact.

But then she laughed. A rolling, rich sound that came from her belly and jerked him right out of the fantasy and dropped him firmly back in reality.

Her laughter went on and on, to the point a frown worked its way between his eyebrows. When she finally paused to breathe, tears were streaming down her face. She reached up to wipe her cheek. "Oh, my God. That was the best line I've ever heard. 'Here, sleep with me and I'll tell you if you're my destiny.' Nice one, Theron." Still chuckling to herself, she eased out of his grip and resumed walking.

"I didn't think it was so funny," Theron mumbled at her back.

"You can't be serious," she said, waving her hands out to the sides as she walked. "That's like the lamest thing I've ever heard. And I worked in a strip club, for crying out loud. I've heard some pretty sad come-ons!"

"Why were you there?" he asked, her comment bringing up a question he'd wondered about several times.

"Why does anyone work in a strip club? The money's good."

"I thought your family owned that bookstore?"

A sigh of regret slipped from her mouth, and he knew she was remembering the fire and what she'd lost. "My grandmother's hospital bills were pretty nasty. I had to work two jobs to make ends meet."

"About that club. Did you…? Were you…?"

"Was I what, Theron?"

The humor in her voice only aggravated him more. He stopped on the path, unsure how to voice his question. "How much money did you make?"

She stopped as well, turned his way and tapped her finger against her cheek in a thoughtful move. "Well, that depends. You know, in a place like XScream, a woman's pay is based on job performance, and I was good. Very, *very* good at what I did." A wicked smile slid across her tempting lips. "Just ask Nick."

A spear of jealousy stabbed him in the gut.

But Argonauts didn't get jealous. Only humans did.

And then she smiled. A grin laced with pure victory and female delight. She was playing him. And *enjoying* it.

"You weren't a dancer." His eyes ran over her svelte body, and the relief that rushed through him was swift and consuming. "I can't see you taking your clothes off for strange men for any amount of money."

She only rolled her eyes and resumed walking. "I did it for you, didn't I? And for free, no less. And you're the biggest stranger of them all."

"Acacia." He gripped her arm again, stopping her. As he turned her his way, a voice in his head screamed, *Keep your mouth shut,* but he couldn't. "Three thousand years ago, when Zeus set aside Argolea for our race, Hera played her cruelest practical joke."

"Zeus's wife? Why would she care about you and your race?"

"She hated Heracles. For a variety of reasons, but mostly because he was one more of Zeus's blatant infidelities. And because of Zeus's affection for the heroes as a whole, she likewise hated the Argonauts. What better way to get back at all of us than by convincing the Fates to make sure we are never happy?"

"What do you mean?"

"The Argonauts, every one of them, me included, were given one soul mate. Just one. And it's always the last person they would ever choose. Most Argonauts go their entire lives without finding theirs. Since I met you, all the signs point to you being mine."

"What signs?"

Don't tell her.

He glanced around the forest again, remembering that being out in the open like this wasn't safe, but unable to let this subject drop. "The attraction between us, for one. The sexual heat." Her cheeks blushed again, encouraging him. "The fact that even when I thought you were human, I recognized something unique and alluring in you I'd not recognized in another."

"You're not wild about my being human, are you?"

He didn't answer. Couldn't.

She looked at his chest, then up to his eyes, and if he thought he saw a flicker of disappointment, she masked it well. "Just how many women do you have to sleep with to find this soul mate?"

He recognized her sarcasm, and knew he was dancing perilously close to the edge with her. "It's not like that."

"Oh, it's not?" she asked innocently. "Then that means you don't want to have sex with me?"

He eased closer and dropped his voice. "I want very much to be with you, you know that. You can see it in my eyes."

"To see if I'm your soul mate," she said plainly.

"Yes." Her eyes flashed. "No," he corrected. Good gods, she was trying to trap him in a lie. "I want to lay with you because I haven't been able to stop thinking about the way you feel and taste since that night in your house."

She tipped her head. "And an eager and willing captive is so much more appealing than a combative one."

"Acacia—"

"You know what, Theron? Don't even try to dig yourself out of this one." She patted him on the shoulder. "Nice try, though. I'm sure it works on some women. Just not me." She marched up the path with a smug sway of her hips.

As she moved away, Theron cursed under his breath and berated himself for being so stupid. Why in the name of Zeus had he told her about the soul mates? She'd never understand the importance or the fact the Argonauts as a whole were seemingly immune to tapping into their humanity, which was Hera's original plan. Even if they did, the fact the goddess had made sure their other half was the exact opposite of what they wanted was a guarantee of disaster. And an Argonaut who'd found his soul mate and then lost her? He might as well just open a vein and bleed out all over the floor. Because that's what it would be like. Nothing left inside him. Theron knew from watching his kinsman Zander these past ten years that was true. And it wasn't something he ever wanted to experience.

Of course, Acacia would never get that. Hell, she hadn't even fully accepted who and what she was. And then he'd gone and told her he'd know if they were destined to be together by screwing her? Yeah. All things considered, he was lucky she hadn't hauled back and nailed him in the nuts for that suggestion.

He was so caught up in his own thoughts, he didn't realize Acacia had picked up her pace until she rounded the bend and disappeared from sight. A tingle spread down his spine as he jogged to catch up with her. As he turned the corner, he discovered the forest opened into a clearing and what had once been a small settlement.

Had been, he realized, because all that was left now were a few burned-out buildings, half walls and foundations supporting blackened beams and broken windows.

Acacia stood at the edge of the village, her eyes taking in the entire scene as he stepped up to her. "This was where it happened," she said, lifting a thin arm and pointing toward what was left of a house, three buildings in. "That was hers."

The settlement was nestled into a valley. Mountains rose on three sides, and a creek meandered along the edge of town, bubbling and gurgling in the warming air. "They struck from the mountains. The villagers didn't even have time to react."

Theron turned in her direction only to falter at the pain he saw etched deeply into her face. Once again he was awed by her strength and resolve. By her loyalty to a people she'd just discovered and the ease with which she pitched in to help. And through all that, he realized if she turned out not to be his soul mate, he'd be hard-pressed to find another *gynaíka* who intrigued and mystified him the way she did.

He looked out over the burned homes and imagined what the half-breed families must have gone through during that vicious attack. Daemons were not known for mercy. And the king had been aware of their struggle for eons.

His chest tightened. Back at the colony, he'd been able to convince himself the problems of the Misos were not his to bear. But standing here, staring at the destruction, all he could think was *We could have done something.*

"Acacia, I—"

"Shh." She placed her hand against his chest, and the skin beneath his shirt tingled with awareness from just the slightest touch. "Did you hear that?"

He listened, hearing nothing but the wind whistling through the ominous Douglas fir. The air was warm, so he knew she couldn't have heard a pack of daemons. "I don't hear anything."

"That."

He turned his head to listen closely. And heard the slightest sound. "That's—"

"A voice," she said, excitement building in her words.

"Acacia, wait—"

But she didn't listen. She took off at a slow jog toward the only intact building in the settlement. An old barn that sat at the far end of town with a rope from the second-floor loft blowing gently in the breeze.

"Marissa?" Acacia called. "Honey, answer me if that's you. It's Casey. Marissa? We're all worried about you."

Silence.

Theron caught up with her just as she stepped inside the dark barn. He grasped her upper arm and leaned close to her ear. "Stay close to me. On this we don't negotiate."

She nodded and let him take the lead, but she continued to call out to Marissa, and he didn't stop her because he hoped the child would respond to her voice.

"Marissa?" she called again. "We've walked a long way to find you. There are a lot of people worried about you, honey. Don't be scared, sweetie. But you have to tell us where you are."

A shuffling sound echoed from above. Acacia put her hand on Theron to stop him. She nodded toward the ceiling and they both glanced up.

A ladder to the left looked as though it led to the second floor. Theron placed a hand and foot on the cracked rails and prayed they'd hold his weight. Just as he was about to step on the first rung, they heard a small voice from above.

"Casey, is that you?"

Acacia let out a long, relieved breath. "Yes, honey. It's me."

"Are you alone?"

The two shared a glance, and Theron shook his head, afraid if the youngling knew he was there, it might scare her into retreating again, but Acacia ignored his warning. "No, Marissa. I'm not alone. Theron's here with me."

"He is?"

"Yes."

Silence.

Theron looked up and listened closely for any movement that indicated Marissa was getting ready to bolt.

"In that case," Marissa said in that same soft voice, "you can both come up and have tea with me and Minnie."

Acacia's smile touched Theron somewhere deep in his chest, and as he climbed the rickety ladder, he felt lighter. More at peace than he'd been in...forever.

And he had a sinking suspicion it was because of Acacia.

It was brighter upstairs. Sunshine flooded the second floor from an opening at the end of the loft. Theron waited while Acacia climbed the ladder. Across the floor, Marissa smiled and waved to him as if they were two old friends meeting at the park. She was sitting on a bale of hay. Her doll, Minnie, was next to her. An overturned crate served as the table, and on the other side was another bale of hay. A tiny chipped tea set was set out in front of each place.

Acacia went to her knees in front of Marissa and pulled the girl into her arms. "That wasn't a smart thing to do, Marissa. Your mother's worried sick about you. So's everyone back at the colony."

"But I'm fine."

Acacia pushed the girl to arm's length. "Honey, you know it's dangerous to be out like this."

Marissa rolled her big brown eyes. "Nothing will happen to the others."

"How do you know? People are out looking for you right now."

"I know because Minnie showed me."

Acacia glanced up at Theron, standing off to the side, then over at Marissa's doll. "Showed you what?"

"The little woman in the long robes with the pretty thread. She said you'd both come to find me if I came here." At Acacia's perplexed expression, Marissa leaned in close and whispered none too quietly, "Don't you see? I had to do it so you two could have more time alone together."

Acacia's eyes grew wary. "What do you mean?"

Theron held his breath and sensed he knew the answer even before the words were spoken. Was this another sign? Or a child's overactive imagination?

Marissa smiled a beaming, child's grin. "You'll see."

The air chilled, and the hair on the back of Theron's neck stood up before he could question the child in depth. Destiny forgotten, he edged toward the opening of the loft that looked down over the burned village. Then cursed long and low.

"Marissa," Acacia said in a forceful voice. "Did Theron put you up to this?"

Theron moved as quickly and quietly as he could across the floor and grasped Acacia by the arm, pulling her up to his side. "We have a problem," he said quietly into her ear.

She looked over with irritated eyes. "What now?"

"Three daemons. They look to be on patrol." Acacia's face went ashen. "My guess is they watch this area for stragglers in the hopes they may lead them to the colony."

"Oh, shit," she whispered.

"Acacia," he said brusquely as he she trembled against him. "Stay with me." Wide violet eyes met his, but there was fear there—lots of it—as she obviously remembered their last run-in with Atalanta's henchmen.

Dammit, this was what he'd been afraid of the moment she set out on this stupid quest. "I can handle the daemons. But you have to get Marissa to safety."

She glanced right and left. "All three? You can't... Back at the store—"

"I can," he said quickly. "At the store I was worried about you. Trust me. I know what I'm doing. But only if we work together."

"Oh, God." When she sagged against him, he knew he was losing her.

He tightened his arm around her waist while listening intently to what was happening outside. The daemons were moving closer. He was running out of time. "You have to pull it together right now, because I want to hear all the other reasons you're not really attracted to me."

She looked up, swallowed hard. And as their eyes met, the connection they'd shared from the first flared deep in his soul. He knew she felt it too. Just as he knew if something happened to her here, he would never be the same.

She nodded once, twice, and pulled her courage up like a suit of armor. "I...I'm not attracted to you." But she gripped his shirt at the chest and didn't make any move to let go.

"Liar," he whispered, just before dipping his head and taking her mouth.

The kiss was fast, and not nearly as deep as he wanted. But they didn't have time for anything more.

He pulled the spiked dagger knife from his ankle, unsnapped the holster and attached it to her calf. Then he opened the weapon that was shaped like a bowie knife with menacing spikes sticking out of the underside of the handle. "Take this. Hold it here." He positioned her fingers. "If any get past me, this won't do you any good unless they get close. Swing like this. Away from your body." He moved her arm to show her what he meant. "The spikes tear up the flesh and the blade does the rest. It won't kill a daemon, but a good solid hit will incapacitate one long enough for you to get away."

"Theron, I—"

"We don't have time." He shoved a penlight into her pocket, then grabbed Marissa and pushed her toward Casey. "Wait until you see me out front, then take the back ladder and head for the mountain across the stream. Try to find a cave or shelter to hide in. I'll find you after."

Shaking, Acacia slid the knife into its holster, lifted a frightened Marissa into her arms and cradled the child against her chest. "But how will you know where we are?"

He crossed the floor and stopped at the edge of the shadows, just out of sight of the daemons below, and took one last look at her. "I'll always find you, Acacia. That is a promise."

"Theron—"

He didn't wait for her response. Instead he stepped off that second floor and landed against the cold earth one story down. All three daemons turned his direction with surprised glowing green eyes.

"Hello, boys," he said, reaching for the parazonium strapped to the small of his back. "You look a little lost. Let me direct you back to hell."

CHAPTER EIGHTEEN

"Run!" Casey set Marissa on her feet and pushed the girl toward the ladder at the back of the loft. She could feel Marissa's fear, but thankfully, the child didn't question her.

Casey went down the ladder first, reaching up to pull Marissa the rest of the way to the ground. Outside, the frenzied growls of the daemons mixed with Theron's grunts and the clash of weapon against flesh as they battled.

An instinct somewhere deep within urged Casey to go out front, to help Theron even though she knew that was pretty well useless. What could she do that he couldn't? But oh, God, what if he was killed because she'd insisted they come here?

Don't think like that. She flashed on the image of him battling the daemons in her store.

He knows what he's doing.

Gripping Marissa's hand tight in hers, she tiptoed to the back of the barn. One peek confirmed the area surrounding them was empty. She eyed the trees, thirty yards away, that turned into woods sprawling up the side of the mountain, then contemplated the chances of running and not being seen.

More grunts resonated from the front of the building. A sharp cracking sound echoed around them. Marissa screamed as a body was thrown through the front of the barn door and crashed to the ground in a pile of hay and dirt.

Casey grabbed the girl and pulled her tight to her stomach, drowning the child's cries as she jerked her into the shadows. One glimpse told her the body was Theron, but he bounded back up as if the blow hadn't even fazed him and tore from the barn, throwing himself back into the battle.

Her heart was in her throat, but Casey lifted Marissa into her arms. "Wrap yourself around me and hold on tight."

Marissa's small head nodded against Casey's neck. Casey took one deep breath, glanced back out the door to make sure the coast was clear and ran.

They tore across the back clearing at breakneck speed and made it almost as far as the trees before a daemon dropped out of nowhere in front of them.

Casey gasped and slammed on her brakes. The daemon's eyes flashed green as he moved forward. He drew in a long, deep breath and said only one word.

"You."

Casey pushed Marissa to the ground and stepped in front of the child, using her body as a shield. Wide-eyed, she reached for the knife at her lower leg with shaking hands.

The daemon chuckled, as if he found the entire scenario amusing. "You cannot stop me, half-breed. Atalanta is waiting for you."

At that moment, Marissa let out the mother of all screams. The pitch was so high and loud, both Casey and the monster flinched and were momentarily frozen. The sound went on and on until finally Casey gave her head a shake and drew the knife as Theron had shown her.

The beast tensed as if to lunge.

Casey's hand shook around the knife as the daemon charged. But before she felt impact, Theron leaped over her and slammed into the beast.

The two rolled, fists and fangs flying. The daemon got the upper hand and pinned Theron to the ground, pressing his massive leg into Theron's chest with a mighty growl. Casey quickly realized Theron had lost his dagger when he'd crashed into the beast as it had lunged for her.

"Theron!"

He looked over just as she threw the spiked knife. It stuck into the ground a foot from his shoulder. His hand snaked out like lightning, even pinned beneath the daemon as he was. Then all Casey saw was the blade flashing in the sunlight. Blood spurted out of the daemon. Theron quickly flipped the monster to the ground and used the knife to decapitate it.

Casey pulled Marissa against her body so the child couldn't see what was happening.

When it was over, Theron's body was covered in a mixture of blood and sweat, and he was breathing heavy, but didn't look injured. He took one step toward her just as a roar resounded from the front of the barn. Theron thrust the knife back into Casey's hand and pushed her hard toward the trees. "Run!"

Casey didn't hang around to ask questions. She grabbed Marissa and took off, heart rate thundering and adrenaline pumping.

Her legs burned and her lungs hurt like a bitch, but she didn't slow. When Marissa cried "Minnie!" against Casey's throat and threw out a hand, she only clutched the child tighter. She wasn't going back for anything, especially a silly doll the girl had left behind. She ran hard and fast, around boulders and between trees, and didn't slow until she couldn't hear the battle below anymore and the only smell was that of pine and moss and the damp forest around her.

Marissa's face was streaked with tears when Casey finally set her on the ground. The child crumpled into a ball against a rock. Comfort would come later. Right now all that mattered was finding a place to hide.

Still trying to draw air into her lungs, Casey surveyed the surroundings. The trees were thick, but ahead and to the left there appeared to be a rock formation that just might have enough space for them to hide.

She lifted Marissa into her arms again. "Come on, Marissa. We're almost there."

A grouping of boulders as tall as a man were lined up in a neat row. Between the first two, a small opening, big enough for someone to crawl through, looked like it led into the mountain.

Casey hated small spaces, but given the choice, she'd take a dank, dark cave over what was possibly hiding out here in the trees. She set Marissa at her feet and dropped to her knees. "In here, honey."

Marissa hesitated. "It's dark."

"I know. But I'm right here." Marissa glanced over her shoulder, clearly contemplating their options. Casey reached for her hand. "I won't let anything happen to you. I promise."

The answer seemed to satisfy Marissa. After one more quick look, she fell to her knees and crawled through the space after Casey.

The tunnel was no higher than about four feet, but luckily, it wasn't long. Ten yards in, Casey had the impression of soaring ceilings and a vast space. She pulled the small penlight Theron had given her earlier from her pocket and flicked it on. Then gasped at what she saw.

Stalactites hung from the ceiling in a rainbow of colors. The fifteen-foot round room was tall enough to stand in and avoid being stabbed at by those giant fanglike cave formations. Another smaller room opened off this one, but it didn't seem to have any outside access. And luckily, aside from a few bugs Casey didn't want to think about, both areas looked to be deserted.

Casey gripped Marissa's hand and led her as far back into the mountain as she could, into the smaller room and around the corner, so if something did come into the first room searching for them, they wouldn't be seen. After wrapping her jacket snuggly around Marissa, she settled back against the rocks with the child cradled in her arms.

Marissa sniffled and snuggled closer. "I miss Minnie," she whispered.

"I know, honey." Casey ran her hand down Marissa's hair.

"Can't we go back for her?"

"No, Marissa. It's not safe."

"Casey," Marissa whispered in the silence. "Are you scared?"

Casey hesitated, then nodded as tears burned behind her closed eyes. "Yes, honey. I am."

"Don't be. Theron will come back for you."

Casey drew a shaky breath. And thought about how quickly things could change. Hours ago she'd wanted only to get away from him. Now she prayed the child was right.

The scent of death hit Nick's senses the second he killed the bike's engine and pulled off his helmet.

Casey's house was dark, but he knew even before he stepped inside what he'd find.

With a sinking stomach, he walked around the house and found the back doorframe shattered, the door itself hanging from its hinges. The kitchen was neat and orderly, but even here he could smell what lay farther inside.

He made himself cross the hardwood floor, his boots clunking with each step. When he reached the arched doorway that led into the living room, he stopped and swallowed the bile sliding up his throat.

The couch was slashed and overturned, the coffee table nothing more than a pile of kindling. Books and broken trinkets littered the floor, and in the middle of the mess lay Dana's lifeless body.

"Ah, shit, Dana."

He knelt beside her, scanning what was left. Dana's wide, unfocused eyes stared up at the ceiling, and her face was bloody and bruised. One leg was cocked at an odd angle, the bone jutting through skin and denim alike, and bloodstained scratches marred most of her body. But the most disgusting thing—and that which Nick had suspected when he'd first come upon the house—was the gaping hole in the center of her chest where her heart used to be.

He ran a hand over his mouth, shut his eyes and cursed himself for walking out on her the other night. He'd sensed her death was coming, but he hadn't done enough to protect her. If he'd driven her back to the colony himself, if he'd been more insistent… Dammit, if he'd opened his eyes and tuned in to her, she'd be alive now.

If *is for shit. She's dead, no thanks to you.*

He opened his eyes and stared down at her. Their relationship had been warped on more than one front, but in his own way, he'd cared for her. More than maybe anyone else in his life. She'd understood him and his needs, and she'd never once said no, even when those needs had been pretty fucking twisted. And how had he repaid her? With this.

She'd accused him of having a god complex. He knew she was right. But even a god wouldn't fuck up this bad.

The cell in his pocket vibrated. "What?" he answered.

"Nick, it's Helene. We have a situation."

He rose slowly to his feet as those fucking scars on his back began to tingle. "What's happened now?"

"Marissa wandered off this morning. Search parties are out looking for her. But the woman you brought here yesterday? Casey? She and the Argonaut are out there now, too. And they're the only pair that hasn't checked in yet."

Nick's hand tightened around the phone. "Fuck me."

"I know. I'm sorry. I couldn't stop her from going."

"I'm on my way back."

"Did you find Dana?"

Nick glanced down at Dana once more and buried the pain deep inside as he did every time one from his colony was killed. The anguish from her death would last longer than the rest, but he was half Argonaut. His son-of-a-bitch side would get over it soon enough. "I found her."

"Is she—"

"Ready the fires, Helene."

He closed the phone just as Helene began weeping.

CHAPTER NINETEEN

The hours blurred together. Casey didn't know how long she and Marissa had been holed up in the cave, but she was sure it was dark outside by now. They must have been in this cave at least six hours, and still not a word from Theron.

She'd already envisioned all the horrible things that could have happened to him, knew he could be out there suffering as she sat here hiding, but she couldn't force herself to get up and look. He'd told her to stay put. And every time she'd thought about ignoring that order, Marissa's strange warning from yesterday lit off in her brain.

What they'll do to you will be worse.

Why her? When that daemon had dropped in her path as they'd been running from the barn, he'd acted as if he knew her. Come to think of it, the ones in her store and even the ones the night she'd met Theron had all acted as if they knew who she was. How was that possible? And what did it mean?

A scraping noise from out in the tunnel brought her head up. She reached for the flashlight on the ground by her thigh. Though she'd flipped it off hours ago to conserve battery life, she wanted to be able to see what was coming at her. Hands shaking all over again, she grappled for the knife as she inched her way around the corner and into the main room.

Whatever was coming through the tunnel was big. She could hear it grunting and scraping along the tight tube. She didn't dare flick on the flashlight now, so she prayed she was pointing the knife in the right direction.

The shuffling stopped. Her heart pounded so loud she was sure it was giving her away. Whoever, or *what*ever, had come through the space lifted to its feet and drew in a ragged breath.

"Don't cut me, Acacia."

"Theron!" Casey dropped the knife and flashlight and lunged for his voice.

His strong arms caught her and pulled her close. She choked back a sob, never so happy to see someone as she was at this moment.

A soft chuckle came from his chest, vibrating against her until she felt it in her toes. "Miss me, did you, *meli*?" he whispered into her hair.

Oh, God. The sound of his voice. Like music. Her hands closed into fists against his damp shirt. "It's been hours. Where have you—?"

"Where's the girl?"

"Sleeping. Finally. Theron. God. How did you know where to find us?"

One strong hand ran down the length of her hair. "I told you. I'll always be able to find you."

She didn't have a clue what he meant by that and didn't want to get into it now. She was just so thankful he was here. She pressed her forehead against his massive chest. "Theron. I was so…" She didn't want to say "worried," because that made her sound like a weakling. But she was. Out of her mind with worry over him. She gave her head a small shake. "What happened?"

"I told you. This is what I do."

What he did? And he expected her not to freak out over it when monsters from one of Stephen King's novels were coming after him? Yeah, right.

"It took so long. I thought—"

"They were sent back to Hades shortly after you and the girl left. There was nothing for you to worry about."

Shortly after. Casey pushed back from his chest and looked up, wishing she could see his face, but lucky for him, it was too dark. "Shortly after? What the hell have you been doing since then? Getting a pedicure?"

"Waiting," he said. "To make sure there weren't any stragglers."

Her adrenaline chose that moment to come crashing down. Screw worried. Now she was mad. "While I sat in here for the last six hours imagining you drawn and quartered and going out of my mind with fear?" Jackass! "Thanks a lot!" She hauled off and kicked him in the shin as hard as she could, then turned on her heel and headed for what she hoped was the archway into the next room. It'd be just her luck to run headfirst into a rock wall instead.

He caught her before she made it three steps, those beefy arms of his wrapping tight around her waist and picking her up off the floor until she was running on air.

"Put me down!" she hissed so as not to wake Marissa. "I've already been manhandled enough for one day."

"Hold on, *meli*." He shifted her so she couldn't kick him in the balls, repositioned his arms until he had both of hers pinned. She struggled, but even she knew it was useless. He was a thousand times stronger than her when she was healthy. Now, with the combination of fear, exhaustion and sickness coursing through her body, she was like a toothpick blowing in the breeze. "I'd have come for you sooner if I'd thought it was safe."

"Word to the wise. It's not safe for you here now, so just go back out the way you came in."

He gentled his hold but still held her firmly. *"Meli."*

Dammit, why did that one stupid word make her go all soft and gooey inside? Especially when he said it so tenderly?

The fight rushed out of her in a blur. She bit her lip hard so she wouldn't cry like a blubbering baby. "You have no idea what I've been through."

"Shhh." He eased his hold and turned her gently toward him. "And in the dark, too." He brushed her hair back from her face in a move that was so damn sweet, she was glad she couldn't see his eyes. He'd saved her life twice now, and though she didn't understand him in the least, she had a sinking suspicion he was right: some kind of fate or destiny she couldn't see and wasn't sure she believed in was pushing them together.

The only question was, why?

"It's over now, *meli*."

"For you," she whispered. Thank God there was anonymity in the dark. "But those things... Tell me the truth, Theron. They're looking for me, aren't they?"

When he wrapped his arms tight around her again and pulled her close without answering, she knew she was right. For some reason, those daemons were hunting her. And she suspected it had something to do with a father she'd never known and a world that was as foreign to her as China.

"What happened to the flashlight I gave you?" he asked.

Casey knew he was changing the subject, but was too exhausted to call him on it. She eased out of his arms when he loosened his hold—not because she wanted to but because it was either that or fall on her ass. "I dropped it somewhere."

His big boots shuffled along the rock floor. Seconds later, a single beam of light pierced the darkness. Theron shone it around, checking out the cave.

Casey pointed toward the smaller room and lowered her voice. "Marissa's sleeping in there. I gave her my coat."

Theron pointed the light in that direction. "That's good. It's dark out now. We'll let her sleep till morning, then head back to the colony." He turned and picked up something from the ground behind him. Minnie.

And the waterworks chose *that* moment to flood. Killing three monsters hell-bent on mutilating her wasn't heroic enough for him. Oh, no, Theron, leader of the Argonauts and descendent of Heracles, the greatest hero ever, had to rescue that stupid doll and bring it back for a little girl who was miserable without it.

Casey was sitting on the floor, leaning back against the wall of the cave, wiping her eyes like an idiot when he came back from returning Marissa's toy. She saw the alarm on his face and scowled, wishing she'd left that damn flashlight on earlier so the batteries would now be dead. She did *not* need to see concern from him. She already had a feeling she was dangerously close to falling for this guy without it.

A hero. Fabulous. Of all the stupid things she'd ever done, this would be the topper. Forget the fact they came from two completely different worlds. Forget the fact she was sick and didn't seem to be getting any better. Even if they were on even ground, she'd still never be enough for him. She'd seen the disgust on his face whenever he remembered she was human. And now that she'd glimpsed what had happened to his father, she understood why.

"Don't cry, *meli*." He sank down next to her and pulled her onto his lap. She thought about refusing, then figured, *What's the point? I'm too weak to fight him and odds are good I'll end up here anyway.* "I can't handle seeing you so upset."

"I'm not crying over you, you stupid jerk." She swiped at her eyes again and punched him in the shoulder with what little strength she had left. "I'm just...tired."

He clicked the light off and set the flashlight on the ground by his hip. In the silence she heard the strong beat of his heart. "You did good out there," he said. "Saved me again. Better not let my kinsmen see or they'll be firing my ass and inducting you into the Argonauts."

She let out a sigh, relaxed against him. God, his body felt good. Warm. Right. Even soaked with sweat and other things she didn't want to imagine. "I hate those things."

His hand ran over her hair, pressed gently against her head until she laid it on his shoulder. "We all do."

In the silence she asked a question that had been pinging around in her brain since the run-in at her store. "Why don't you use guns?"

"In battle?"

"Yeah."

"We've tried all kinds. So far the daemons have been able to throw off bullets with little effort. A blade to slice open their flesh works better, creates more damage. Titus, one of my Argonauts, is constantly experimenting with new weaponry in our fight, though."

Interesting. "Who's Atalanta?"

His hand stilled in her hair. "How do you know of her?"

"The daemon who cornered us mentioned her. He said, 'Atalanta is waiting for you.'"

His silence unnerved her, and just as she was about to lift her head and ask what he was hiding, he said, "She's the one who traded her soul to Hades for immortality and dominion over the daemons. She felt she was shunned from the Argonauts because she was female."

"She was one of the original fifty-five on the *Argo*?"

"By some accounts, yes."

"And was she? Shunned?"

"Probably. Three thousand years ago, females were looked at differently. And a female Argonaut is still not as strong as a male, which is why the guardians chosen from each line are generally males."

"A woman can be president and can serve in the military, but she still can't fight. I guess sexism crosses all cultural barriers, huh?"

He chuckled, and the vibrations zinged along her nerve endings. "Acacia, I think you're getting the wrong idea. *Gynaíkes* are the mothers, the wives, the daughters who keep our race flourishing. No *ándras* in his right mind would let his mate serve in the ranks of the Argonauts. And no Argonaut would ever consider letting his soul mate near battle."

"Did Atalanta have a soul mate?"

He shifted his big body beneath her, nestling her tighter against his groin. Though she couldn't be certain, she thought she felt the stirrings of his arousal pushing against her hip. But that couldn't be, could it? He had to be spent and exhausted from fighting, and they weren't even talking about anything even remotely suggestive.

"Some say she did. Her father wanted her to marry and she refused, so he set up a footrace to spite her. Any suitor who could beat her in speed would win her hand. Hippomenes was the only one to best her, and they eventually married. But many believe he wasn't her soul mate."

"Why not?"

"Because an Argonaut only gets one. A punishment, like I told you, cooked up by Hera and Lachesis, one of the Fates. It's no great secret Heracles had a ferocious sexual appetite. He seduced both men and women, god and mortal, never caring about the consequences. When Zeus granted Argolea to Heracles's and the other Argonauts' offspring, Hera made sure she had a hand in their destinies."

"By giving them a soul mate? That sounds like a blessing."

"By giving them *one* soul mate, *meli*. And by making sure each one is the exact opposite of what that Argonaut wants and needs. To make matters worse, Hera made sure the only way an Argonaut could even acknowledge his soul mate was to tap into his humanity, something we're trained not to do."

"Why? I don't understand."

He let out a long sigh. "Because doing so stirs emotions that tend to get in the way of our duties. Our god side is…let's just say, not overly concerned with right and wrong, having a conscience, being unselfish. The twelve gods of Olympus aren't entities we worship. They're nothing more than fallen angels who turned away from the Creator for their own selfish gain. True emotions—love, hate, sacrifice—those are things the gods don't understand, because they don't feel them. Not in their truest form, at least. Suppress those, and you suppress that side of our heritage that leaves us vulnerable and weak. Very few Argonauts are able to open themselves up to their humanity and continue to serve as guardians. Therefore, most never find their soul mate."

Casey's eyebrows drew together as she thought about what he'd told her. She was human, and very definitely something he despised. Would fate have saddled him with a human soul mate just to spite him?

The question sent her brain buzzing. She wasn't actually buying into this, was she? She gave her head a small shake and refocused on their conversation. "But Atalanta had one? And it wasn't Hippomenes?"

"No. Most believe her soul mate was Meleager, a Greek prince and fierce warrior who killed numerous times to win her attention. For reasons no one quite understands, she denied his love until it was too late and he was killed. After that she walked around in a fog for years, a great warrior herself, but without heart. Eventually her father tricked her into marrying Hippomenes, but she didn't love him, and he was later killed as well. Some say her despair over losing both men compounded her anger at being passed over for the Argonauts. And that spurred her on to make her pact with Hades."

"What if an Argonaut never finds his soul mate?"

"He exists as he always has. A living, breathing killing machine born of honor and duty."

His definition of himself was so mater-of-fact, it sent a chill down her spine. Yet it explained so much about who he was and how he operated. She thought about the scene with his father. "What about children?"

He shrugged. "It is possible, even encouraged, for an Argonaut to have young outside marriage. After all, 'go forth and multiply' was, and still is, the slogan of the gods, and screw anything that gets in their way. That mentality has been passed down to us tenfold. But that's all it is. Sex for fun and procreation…if the time is right for the *gynaíka*. An unbound Argonaut will never be emotionally involved with his younglings. He has no real ties to them."

The type of man he described seemed so different from the one she was getting to know. She'd glimpsed tender moments from him, even back at her house before she'd known what he was. Surely an Argonaut who'd called her "beloved" right from the beginning couldn't be as callous as all this.

And then a thought occurred. One that tightened her stomach and sent a wave of unease rolling through her. "Do you have children?"

"No."

"But you said—"

"My father was one of the lucky ones, *meli*. An Argonaut who found his other half. I grew up in a loving household, unlike my kinsmen. When, *if*, I have younglings, it will be with the *gynaíka* who is my soul mate, no one else."

She breathed out a sigh of relief, though why his answer pleased her, she couldn't say. For reasons she didn't want to examine, she couldn't bear the thought of him with someone else. At least not right now, when she was seated precariously on his lap and his hands were running up and down her back in that languid way that made her want to take a bite out of him.

And that's when she remembered what he'd said on the hike up here.

Thankful he couldn't see her blush, she said, "So, um, about that. You said there was one way you could tell if someone was your soul mate. I suspect that means you've had plenty of practice in the whole soul-mate-searching thing."

He stirred again beneath her, and oh, yeah. This time there was no mistaking his arousal pressing against her hip. Her skin tingled at the contact, and she remembered the erotic way he'd touched her that night at her house. If she turned ever so slightly and slung her leg over his hip, she could be sitting on top of all that hard steel, exactly where she suddenly needed it.

"I've never had any reason to wonder," he said in a low voice. "Until now."

Casey's heart kicked up, and in the silence she knew he had to hear it too. "Why not?" she asked, even though she knew this was a dangerous road to travel.

"Because I hadn't met you. And I didn't dare think to look in the human world for my other half."

Oh, boy. Had he just said what she thought he'd said? Okay, ignoring the part about her maybe being his—*gulp*—soul mate, was it possible he'd never been with a human?

Her blood went hot at the thought. Casey wasn't stupid. The man was more than two hundred years old and radiated raw sexual heat that would undoubtedly make even the strongest woman throw herself at his feet and rip off all her clothes at just the crook of his finger. And judging from Casey's spotty memory, she'd done just that. Which meant he was well experienced in the sex-for-fun thing he'd mentioned earlier. But the idea he'd had all that practice with only women of his kind and not humans? Oh, yeah. That electrified her. Jacked her up. Left her burning hot and wild.

Because it meant this was as new to him as it was to her.

A slow ache pulsed deep in her core, slid lower until she had to press her thighs together to keep from moaning.

What would he be like as a lover? Hard and hot and demanding, she was sure. Would she be strong enough to take it? Would she even care after he had his way with her?

Sultry images lit off in her brain. His mouth on hers, his skin pressed up against hers. His body bending hers over the couch, as he'd done once before, to drive deep inside her.

The hand he'd been using to stroke her back slid down her arm to rest on her thigh. A shiver rushed over her skin, and all she could think about was how good it would feel to have his hands on her bare flesh again.

"I can hear your heart," he whispered in the silence between them.

Oh, yeah, ya think? Casey bit her lip as his fingers traced a lazy pattern across her thigh.

"Do you feel all right?"

No, she didn't feel all right at all. She was exhausted and weak. Compounding her illness was the fact she hadn't eaten in nearly two days. She felt as if she could sleep for a month and still never catch up, but at the moment none of that mattered. Because all her energy was focused on what he was doing to her body with just the barest touch from his talented fingers.

"Acacia?"

His warm breath fanned over her face, telling her he was closer than she realized. One slight move and she could claim that rugged mouth as her own. His fingers inched higher on her thigh until they brushed the juncture of her hip. She sucked in a breath and waited.

"Are you afraid of me?" he asked.

One millimeter. All she had to do was lean forward a fraction of an inch and she could kiss him.

"What's it saying?" she whispered.

"What's what saying?"

"My heart."

He let out a long breath that washed over her cheek as his fingers danced up her rib cage. And then his hand hovered over the left side of her chest, right over her heart. "Hopefully the same thing mine is saying."

She swallowed. Hard. And knew there was no turning back. "Do you? Have a heart, that is, Theron?"

"I didn't think so," he said in that husky voice. "But I'm not so sure anymore." He hesitated, barely brushing her mouth, and moved his hand to graze her arm. "Kiss me, *meli*. Kiss me like you did—"

She didn't let him finish. She pressed her mouth to his until she was lightheaded. In reflex, her hands slid up his chest, around his neck to brush his silky hair back from his face. His muscles tensed and his arms twined around her as he pulled her tight against him.

A groan tore out of him. He changed the angle of the kiss, ran his tongue along the seam of her lips and urged her to let him in. She wondered, momentarily, if she was making a monumental mistake. Then moaned as he shifted her into better contact with his hips and finally acquiesced, opening to him on instinct and taking him deep. In a rush she pushed aside the thousand reasons this was wrong and focused on how good it felt now. How good *he* felt here.

Not just in her skin and in her body. But in her soul. That connection to him she'd felt from the very beginning erupted again as she tipped her head and ran her tongue along his. The growl of satisfaction resonating from his chest only fueled her need, and she slid her fingers around to cup his face while she kissed him deeper and reveled in the way his body hardened beneath her and his lust grew exponentially with hers.

"Meli," he whispered against her mouth. "I dreamed of touching you like this again."

He did? Oh, God. She was quickly losing control and didn't even care. His mouth nipped its way to her ear, where his hot and wanton breath against her neck made her whole body quiver and her sex clench. Hands still on the sides of his face, she closed her eyes and tipped her head, giving him as much access to her throat as he wanted, loving every lick and suck and kiss he pressed against her.

Time was forgotten. The circumstances that had brought them here became trivial. All she could focus on was shedding the clothing separating their bodies and sliding across his naked flesh until he filled her with his heat.

His fingers ran down to the edge of her shirt while he kissed her neck, up and under until he skimmed the bare skin of her abdomen and her stomach tensed. She turned her head, bringing his mouth back to hers, and groaned long and deep when his fingers brushed her silk-covered nipples.

She shifted in his lap, slipping her leg over his until she was straddling him. One of his hands continued to tease her breasts while the other slid to her hips and pulled her down so she was sitting on his erection and he was rubbing right where she wanted him most.

"Meli." His voice turned frantic, his mouth possessive against hers. Before she felt his hands move, he had her jeans unsnapped and his fingers were sliding inside and down through her moist curls. "I need to feel you come."

She wrapped her arms tight around his neck, moaned at his erotic words. Closing her eyes, she lifted just enough to grant him access. His finger slid lower while his mouth returned to her neck, licking and sucking, and then everything went white-hot. She shuddered violently at the first touch. Just as his fingers slid into her folds and electricity rippled through her center to every cell in her body.

He chuckled against the column of her neck, slowed his strokes but continued to tease and torment with the sweetest touch. "Gods, how you please me."

Her chest rose and fell as she drew in ragged breaths. She should have been embarrassed. She'd never climaxed like that, so fast and with such little stimulation. But this man—Argonaut—whatever, had the strangest control over her.

"Don't sound so proud of yourself."

He laughed again, and the husky sound warmed her from the inside out. As did the curve of his lips as he kissed her throat and ear and moved around to take her mouth again.

His hand stayed in her pants, but he eased it around to her backside, pulling her close until his arousal was pushing against her jeans. He deepened the kiss, and in the silence between them, she heard his strong and steady heart pounding in time with hers.

Yes, he had one. If he'd been interest only in getting what he wanted, he wouldn't have bothered to pleasure her so thoroughly. Even now, after she'd had her release, when she was limp and sated, he could easily flip her to her back and drive into her without even a protest from her lips, and he knew it. But he didn't. Instead he continued to kiss her slow and gentle, like he wanted to draw out the moment. Like she mattered to him.

She reached for the button on his pants, knowing then she was going to take him in, as deep as he wanted. Not because she needed to know if he was her soul mate, but simply because she wanted him. Because she had always wanted him.

"Yes, *meli*," he purred. "Touch me. I want to feel your hands on me. However you want."

Her pulse quickened. Her throat grew thick with desire. She was just about to dive beneath his waistband and take matters into her own hands when she heard a small voice behind her ask, "Casey? Where are you?"

Casey froze. Then common sense slammed into her, and like a guilty teenager, she scrambled off Theron's lap and fixed her clothes. Her face heated at what she'd been about to do and how easily she'd forgotten they weren't alone. Thank heavens for the darkness.

Flushed, Casey pushed to her feet and wobbled, all the blood rushing from her head with the sudden movement. Theron grabbed her at the arms from behind and steadied her. The man moved like a silent shadow. She hadn't even heard him rise.

"Casey?" Marissa asked again, this time in a frightened voice.

"I'm here, honey." Reaching out a hand, Casey crossed the room toward Marissa's voice and finally found the child. She drew the girl into her body in a hug. "It's all right. Everything's fine."

Marissa pushed Minnie against Casey's torso. "Look! Minnie found us."

Casey dropped to a crouch in front of the girl. "I know. Theron brought her."

"Theron's here?"

From across the room, the flashlight flicked on. The bright light burned Casey's retinas for a minute, but when her vision adjusted, she looked over to see Theron standing near the far wall, looking every bit the dark and sexy hero she'd very nearly boned the hell out of only moments before.

She blushed again and quickly looked back at Marissa. The girl had a sappy smile on her face as she glanced between the two of them. The child couldn't possibly know what they'd been up to only moments before, could she?

"I told you he'd come back for you," Marissa said, nudging Casey with her shoulder. "The old lady with the string told me."

Casey's brows drew together. "The one you saw before?"

Marissa nodded.

Was the child talking about Lachesis? The Fate who drew out the life thread? Assuming Casey bought into all this freaky Greek myth stuff, if Marissa could really see into the future, maybe she knew the answer to Theron's burning question. Maybe she could tell them right now if they were really destined to be together...

Casey took Marissa's hand in hers. "Marissa. Honey. What else did the lady with the string tell you?"

Marissa turned clouded gray eyes on Casey. "About you?"

Casey shook her head. "No. About us. Me and Theron."

Marissa's stare bore into Casey, and just when Casey was about to wave her hand in front of the child's face to break the trance she seemed to have slipped into, Marissa's pupils expanded until there was nearly no iris left and the only thing was a gaping black hole in a sea of white. "She said you're going to see Tartarus. And Theron is the reason you're going."

CHAPTER TWENTY

Isadora jumped at the sharp rap against her window.

It was nearly midnight. Her latest sentry, Gryphon, was keeping guard and talking smack with anyone who ventured by. The last time Isadora had checked, he'd been flirting up a storm with the kitchen help—a young girl no more than thirty—who'd brought up Isadora's dinner.

Isadora had heard laughing beyond her suite. And of course she'd peeked. She thought back to the way the giant blond Argonaut had twirled the *gynaíka*'s red hair around his finger and looked down into her eyes with that mischievous glint. And the way the girl had seemed mesmerized by him even before he'd opened his gorgeous mouth to whisper in her ear.

There was something disgustingly wrong with her world. The strongest and most virile males were the Argonauts. They also happened to be the most attractive and the most dangerous—on more than one front. Oh, she'd heard rumors about their sexual appetites and the way *gynaíkes* supposedly threw themselves at their feet, but she'd never had the chance to view any of it in action firsthand.

Now? Good gods. The sexual heat the two had been throwing off could be felt all the way inside Isadora's room—even with the door closed.

Was that how Theron reacted to other *gynaíkes*? Is that what she could expect once they were married? Him flirting and making plans with other females? She knew there was no chance she could ever satisfy the guardian. In fact, what if he was off with another *gynaíka* right now?

Surprisingly, the thought didn't upset Isadora. If anything, it gave her hope. Because if there was someone else out there for him, perhaps there was still a chance he wouldn't want to marry her after all.

Frowning, she glanced at the door. And thought back to the way Gryphon had touched that girl outside. She'd seen that lust-filled look on a man's face before. When she'd been in that human strip club looking for her sister.

Her skin tingled as she thought back to the patrons of the seedy establishment. What kind of man went there? There'd been plenty of roughnecks, a few higher-class individuals, and a whole lot of young men—college kids?—who'd obviously been out for a good time. But the one man her brain kept skipping back to, and the one that had shocked her more than any other, was the scarred blond behemoth Acacia had talked with briefly that night.

Who was he? How did they know each other? And why had he been staring at Acacia so intently?

The tapping at her window again brought her head around. She stared toward the dark glass, didn't see anything, then nearly came out of her skin when something hard hit the pane.

Rising slowly from her chair, she rubbed her hands down her thighs and stepped toward the darkness. Her reflection peered back at her, thin and pale. She ignored the image and looked beyond. To the twinkling lights from the city below shimmering in the distance. Narrowing her eyes, she saw nothing out of the ordinary.

"Red's a good color on you, Isa."

Isadora whipped around so fast, she nearly lost her balance.

From the middle of the room, Orpheus laughed. "Don't tell me you weren't expecting me."

Isadora pressed a hand against her stomach. "You startled me, that's all. You know I hate it when you poof in like that."

Orpheus shrugged, his light brown hair falling into his eyes in the process. "Some *ándres* can lift tall buildings. I simply poof through them. There are worse powers to have."

Yeah, she could think of something worse. Like not having any powers at all anymore.

She pushed that lovely thought aside as her gaze swept over Orpheus. He was built like the Argonauts, so tall she had to crane her neck to look up at him. Broad shoulders, narrow hips, roped muscles. As he hailed from Perseus's line, he could have served with the guardians, had he not been passed over in favor of his younger and stronger brother, Gryphon.

And wasn't it just convenient Gryphon was standing outside her room right now? Good thing Orpheus had poofed in here after all. The last thing Isadora needed was a hand-to-hand in the middle of her sitting room.

His sandy brown hair was longer in the front to fall over his eyes, shorter in the back; he wore a black T-shirt, low-slung black jeans, clunker military boots and a long black leather trench coat. She, like every other Argolean—maybe *more* than other Argoleans—was fascinated with human styles and peeked through the portal just to see what they were doing and wearing. But unlike other Argoleans, Orpheus made a habit of bouncing back and forth from world to world unnoticed to satisfy his deviant pleasures, and he didn't care what anyone thought of him. That was obvious in his speech and dress. And in the way he carried himself as if ready to pounce on anyone who looked at him sideways. If he wasn't careful, he was going to wind up dead from it.

Orpheus tipped his head to the side. "You don't look so well, Isa. Don't tell me you're pining for your Argonaut. Word on the street is he ditched you."

Isadora glared. "Not that it's any of your business, but Theron's taking care of Argonaut business before our...binding ceremony."

A ghost of a smile curled Orpheus's mouth, and Isadora cursed herself for the stammer that proved just how freaked-out she was by the whole marriage thing. Showing weakness in front of Orpheus was a bad idea.

"Sounds exciting. Both the business at this important time and the binding ceremony he's not bothering to prep for. You'll forgive me if I don't attend. I figure if the groom can't make it a priority and all that, why should I?" He flopped onto a plush white sitting chair across the room while Isadora clenched her jaw. "I mean, let's get real, Isa. If the big, bad stud were here now taking care of *family* business, I wouldn't be, would I?"

"You are an ass."

Orpheus's smile widened. He kicked his feet out to rest them on the low glass coffee table. "Aw, now Isa. You hurt my feelings. You really do. Here I am, giving up my precious sleep to help you—again—and what do you do? You hurl insults at me." He tsked and shook his head. "Breaks my heart. It really does."

Orpheus wasn't here simply because he was worried she would spill the beans on his secret, but because he knew she was desperate enough to call him. And that put him in the driver's seat. Refusing to show him an ounce of weakness, she lifted her chin. "What's it going to cost me?"

"Depends." He arched one wicked brow. "What exactly are you asking for?"

She thought for a minute. Then said, "Persephone."

His rolling laughter was like fingernails scraping down a chalkboard. "Wait, let me check." He held up a finger, glanced around as if he were listening for something, then shook his head. "Yeah. No. She won't give you five minutes."

"But she would for you," she said quickly, ignoring his sarcasm. "If you asked her."

His expression said that wasn't a guarantee. "Even if I wanted to, her SOB of a husband won't allow it."

"He doesn't have to know."

Orpheus's eyes narrowed. "And how do you plan to keep Hades from knowing? Did your Argonaut teach you that Jedi mind-trick thing?"

She ignored the comment, because she wasn't exactly sure what it meant. She wouldn't need mind tricks if she had Orpheus's cloak of invisibility. He used it to sneak into the beds of the human women he ravaged, and he'd let her borrow it before to cross through the portal unchecked when she'd gone looking for Acacia. The cloak was so strong, it worked on both humans and gods alike.

"Oh, no," Orpheus said, reading her expression. "Not on your life."

"I may not have much of a life left. And you're the only one who can help me, Orpheus."

His eyes flashed green in that daemon way of his, then returned to their normal shade of gray. For a moment, fear raced through her, but she beat it back. She was the only one who knew of his true lineage—she and his father, a past Argonaut who was now, conveniently, dead. Not even Gryphon knew his brother was half daemon. The only reason Isadora had discovered the truth was because she'd secretly followed him into the woods one night, where he often trekked alone for reasons she didn't understand, in the hopes of convincing him to help her, and had seen what he could turn into.

She inwardly shuddered at the thought. She could have slinked away. Could have returned to Tiyrns and turned him in. But a vision had stopped her. It had been the last one of the future she'd had before her powers had dried up. And in it, Orpheus—in his daemon form—had saved her.

He looked toward the dark windows. "I don't owe you shit."

She knew he was lying. He knew she held his fate in her hands. One word from her and he'd be executed. If Argoleans discriminated against humans, it was nothing compared to what they'd do to a daemon living among them.

Silence stretched between them. She half-expected Orpheus to poof his way right out of her suite. And then he said, "Tell me why."

"It's personal."

"Tough shit. If you're asking me to go out on a limb to get you Persephone, then you better cut the personal crap."

Isadora bit her lip in indecision. In the end, she knew she didn't have a choice.

Before she lost her courage, she reached for the hem of her skirt and slowly lifted so he could see the marking high on the inside of her right thigh. The winged omega symbol. The one she'd never understood until recently.

Orpheus's eyes grew wide and he swore in his native tongue.

Yup. He obviously knew what the mark meant. But then, being half daemon, of course he would.

She dropped her skirt back into place. His smug expression had been replaced by a "holy *skata*" one she knew she would never forget. "I need to see Persephone because she's the only one who can influence Hades to alter the pact."

His shocked gray eyes slowly lifted from where he was still eyeing her skirt up to her face. If there was one other person in all of Argolea who didn't want to see the prophecy come true, it was Orpheus. "And what if he won't?"

"Then you and I are both likely dead." She narrowed her eyes. "Now tell me, are you going to help me or not?"

They left at dawn, when the first light of morning was spilling over the horizon. Theron let Acacia lead the way, while he took up the rear to keep an eye out for any wayward daemons lying in wait.

So far so good. He knew none of the three from the day before had been able to send a signal back to Atalanta about their location. At some point they'd be missed, but hopefully by the time anyone in Tartarus noticed they were gone, Theron would have Marissa and Acacia far from this valley and out of harm's way.

Gods, but he couldn't get the little girl's words out of his head. Each time he looked at Acacia he saw the surprise in her eyes at Marissa's premonition. He understood Acacia didn't believe it. He knew otherwise.

A heavy weight pressed down on his chest, making it hard to breathe. Though he knew what was expected of him, had even accepted what he *would* do for his race, the thought of Acacia's fate had never once been a question in his mind. The Elysian fields, yes. Perhaps even the Isles of the Blessed—the afterlife where the blessed heroes dwelled—because of her connection to the royal family. But not once had he considered the fact she might be condemned to Tartarus.

And why hadn't he? It made perfect sense that a pact made by Hades would not end well for the loser.

"I think we're getting close," Acacia said from up ahead.

Shaken from his thoughts, he looked up to see the soft sway of her hips as she moved. They'd made good time, even with Marissa in tow, but Acacia's pace had slowed the last mile or two. He knew she was weak and growing weaker by the minute. Just as he knew there was nothing he could do to help her.

A lump formed in his throat at the thought, that weight in his chest multiplying. Marissa sat perched on his shoulders, her hands and cheek pressed to the top of his head, where she'd been sleeping for the past hour. Working to keep the child balanced was the one thing that had distracted him from thinking too much about Acacia. And about what he was doing to her himself.

He never should have touched her. In her house, in her room at the colony, last night in that dark and sultry cave. Just the thought of the way her body felt, so soft and moist and giving, jacked him up and made him think about what it would be like to sink inside her and forget about the rest of the world. Never before had he met a *gynaika*—or a woman—who'd made him forget his duties.

Why did it have to be her?

"Do you hear that?" Acacia stopped in his path. Theron nearly ran into her before realizing she was intently listening to something in the distance. She reached a hand behind her to stop him. Just the slight brush of her fingers against his chest sent electricity zinging along his nerve endings.

He forced his mind away from what those fingers could do and drew in a long breath. He smelled fresh wood and fire, and the unmistakable scent of burning flesh.

Alarm bells rang in his head even as Acacia turned questioning eyes his way, and he realized she smelled it too. "What is that?"

He had a feeling he knew. And *skata*, he didn't want to tell her.

Worry rushed over her features as she read his expression. Then she turned and rushed ahead down the path.

"Acacia!"

From above, Marissa was jolted awake. She sat up taller on his shoulders. "What's happening?"

"Nothing, child. We're almost there." Theron gritted his teeth as he ran after Acacia and tried not to lose Marissa.

They reached a clearing, and the trees opened to an area void of shrubs and brush. A circle had been outlined in rocks, and at the center sat a large, blackened stone, four feet high and as long as a man, flat on top as if it had been chiseled to form a table. Around the base, piles of wood fueled flames that leapt and licked at the stone tablet and the body that lay on top, burning in the dawn.

Nick stood with his back to them, something bunched in the hand at his side. On the far side of the table, a small group of people huddled together, weeping as they watched the body burn.

Mourners. The burning of the flesh was said to release the soul to the afterlife, but it only worked if the heart remained in the body.

Let there be a heart.

"Oh, my God," Acacia whispered at his side.

Theron eased Marissa to the ground, and a woman came racing their way. He recognized her from the day they'd arrived in the colony.

"Marissa!" the woman screamed.

The girl was swept up into her mother's arms. The woman muttered incoherent words of comfort as tears streaked down her face and she clung fiercely to the small child. She mouthed a thank-you to Acacia and Theron before turning back to the group of mourners.

Nick turned slowly to look their way, and Theron saw what the man held. A jacket. Bright red. Leather, with shiny silver grommets running up and down the sleeves.

Acacia saw it, too. Her hand went to her mouth as the blood rushed from her cheeks. "Dana. Oh, God, Dana. No."

She swayed on her feet. Theron caught her before she went down. And cursed himself and those bloody daemons. He glanced up to Nick for help, not understanding Acacia's link to the woman, but knowing instinctively that they'd been friends.

Nick shook his head, and though there was murder in his eyes at what had been done, there was also heartfelt regret. He turned back to the fire.

"Meli," Theron said gently, putting his body between her and the fire. "Don't look."

"No." She gripped his forearms. Tears streamed down her face. The anguish he saw in her eyes nearly broke him. "It can't be Dana. It just can't. She was talking about leaving town. She was at the store. With me. Just before you showed up. Just before those things…" She closed her eyes tight and curled her hands into fists against his shirt. "You don't think they found her"—her eyes popped open—"because of me, do you? Theron. You don't think—?"

He gathered her close against his chest, cutting off her question. She struggled, but he held her tight. How could he tell her that was exactly what had happened? His sense of smell was strong, and even amidst the flames, he hadn't detected the scent of her heart. Which meant the daemons had cut it out of the Misos in payment to Hades before they'd killed her, as was their pattern. No way he could tell Acacia any of that. Or where he suspected her friend's soul was right now.

Voice thick with emotions he'd never felt before, all because of the woman in his arms, he said, "Come on. There's nothing we can do here."

Her anguish was palpable, but she turned and walked with him toward the trees. "I don't understand this world you live in," she mumbled as she swiped at her eyes.

No. Of course, she wouldn't. Sometimes he didn't either. He drew her closer to his side.

"I'm so tired, Theron," she whispered.

He lifted her into his arms. When she didn't protest, he knew she was more fatigued than she was letting on.

His heart pinched. She was fading quickly. And the events of the last two days weren't helping.

They made it ten yards into the trees when he sensed the air change. Acacia sensed it too, because she stiffened in his arms. "I have a bad feeling," she whispered against his neck.

So did he. He set her slowly to her feet.

The first scream erupted at their backs before either of them turned.

CHAPTER TWENTY-ONE

One thing Isadora could say about Orpheus. The *ándras* knew things no one else did. Like where the gods hung out and how to breach their inner sanctum.

"I can't go in with you," Orpheus said as he pulled the hood of his black cape over his head to hide his face. "The cloak only works for one, and no way in hell I'm getting trapped on Olympus. Zeus has called one of his blitheringly boring summit meetings, so the gods will all be congregated in his temple, no doubt falling over themselves in an attempt to impress the pompous POS. You know the difference between a brownnoser and a shithead, right, Isa?"

Isadora frowned.

"Depth perception." Orpheus chuckled at his own joke.

"What about Persephone?" Isadora asked, trying to refocus him.

His cocky grin faded. "She'll be where I told you."

"How can you know for certain? Maybe she—"

"Trust me. She'll be there. Any time she can get away from her mother, she heads for the trees. There's more to destroy there."

Trusting Orpheus went against everything in Isadora's gut. But she didn't have another choice. She was out of options, and if this didn't work...

She ignored the sickness brewing in her belly and lifted her chin. "Where will you be?"

"Hiding out here, like the lower life-form I am." He glared at her from beneath the hood. "You screw this up, Isa, and we're both fucked."

She nodded once. "I won't."

On one more deep breath, which didn't do a thing for her tummy, she pulled the hood over her head and turned for the gates that granted access to Mount Olympus. For the love of all things holy, she was about to walk on hallowed ground.

Okay, correction. For her sake, she sure hoped good ol' Zeus didn't catch wind she was here. The god was not known for understanding, and his temper was worse than all seven of the Argonauts put together, on a bad day.

She held her breath as she walked cautiously up to the gates. When neither sentry looked in her direction, she realized they couldn't see her. Orpheus's invisibility cloak was working. Confidence growing, she slipped past the guards without even a glance and paused at the base of the winding road toward the temples.

Please let Orpheus be telling the truth...

She turned left instead of heading up the road and followed a low stone fence past wheat fields and olive orchards, until she came to the forest. Large trees she didn't know how to name towered above, blocking out the sunlight. Low brush and trailing vines littered the ground.

She walked a quarter mile in the dim light before she noticed the shrubs and plants around her looked sickly and wilted. As she delved deeper into the forest, the ground became black, looked almost burned, and what little plant life was left was withered and dry.

Humming from ahead brought her feet to a halt, and she peered through the blackened tree trunks toward a small pond. Around the edge, the grass was brown and brittle. Even the tree branches protruding over the once-green oasis were drooped and void of leaves. A great sadness radiated from the space. And in the center of the pond, hovering inches above the surface, lay Persephone, floating on her back. But the only parts of her body touching the water were her fingers as they splayed over the surface of the pond.

Even reclined and in a state of miserable relaxation, she looked like a regal queen. The Queen of the Underworld. The queen of death and destruction. Which was exactly what she was.

Isadora's nerves kicked up. She glanced back the way she'd come as worry and self-doubt raced down her spine. She had the goddess alone. Just like she'd wanted. But suddenly her tongue was thick and her throat was bone-dry.

Persephone's hair was dark, her body lithe and graceful. She looked like a siren, but a thousand times stronger and a million time more dangerous. And she was way more intimidating than Isadora had expected.

"I wondered how long it would take you to get here."

Isadora froze. Glanced around again. The goddess couldn't possibly be speaking to her, could she?

"Of course I'm talking to you," Persephone said, turning her head and pinning Isadora with deep green eyes the color of an Irish field. "Do you think I don't know what you and your half-daemon friend are up to? You were only permitted to pass the gates of Olympus because I figure anyone as desperate as you deserves to be heard. And because your anxiety amuses me." She heaved out a long sigh. "I do so get bored here."

Isadora opened her mouth to speak, but nothing came out.

"Not so desperate now, I see." Persephone looked back up to the sky. "And here I thought this was going to be interesting. Apparently you lack the panache of your father."

"M-My father?" *Oh, good one, Isa. Way to get right to the point.*

"It's been twenty-seven years since King Leonidas stood where you stand now. Asking very nearly the same thing."

Suddenly, getting to the point didn't seem so important after all. "Wait. My father came to you?"

Persephone's irritated eyes darted to Isadora. "Did I not just say that? Keep up, girl."

As far as Isadora knew, her father hated the interventions of the gods. In fact, he'd do just about anything to keep them from meddling in Argolean affairs. "Why did my father come here?"

Persephone huffed and lifted a hand to let water drip off her long, elegant fingers. "To ask me to use my influence on Hades. Isn't that why you're here?"

Wow. News flash.

"Yes," Isadora said, stunned. "But I still don't understand why my father would intervene."

Persephone rolled her eyes and recited in a dull monotone: "There shall be two in every era, born of god and earth and men. One of strength and one of courage, two separate halves to bring the end. And they shall be known by the markings they bear, united in the twenty-seventh year. Only joined will the strong survive, to dissolve the pact and bring the end to life."

A ghostly smile curled Persephone's lips. "Morbid, isn't it? But that's my husband for you. Although that wasn't the original text. Originally it said, '...united in the coming year.' King Leonidas came here to ask me to barter for the addition of those twenty-seven years."

At what Isadora knew was her perplexed expression, Persephone huffed and added, "In the past, Atalanta's daemons were always able to locate the human half of that equation, thereby keeping the prophecy from coming true."

Isadora's stomach rolled. "He bartered to keep her alive just so she could die later?"

"All for the greater good." Persephone's brow wrinkled. "Don't tell me you're a bleeding heart for humans. They're so...lower class."

"She's not just a human. She's...my sister."

"That's just biology."

At that moment, Isadora knew this goddess wasn't going to help her. She forgot about strategy and spoke from her heart. "No, I don't believe in sacrificing one for the good of many. Unlike you and the other gods up here in never-never land, I don't view them as chess pieces to be placed at my whim. My father is a coward and a liar, and my coming here was very obviously a mistake." She turned on her heel.

"Very good, Princess." The laughter in Persephone's words stopped Isadora's feet. "You may just make an adequate queen, after all."

Isadora glared over her shoulder at the goddess, who was now standing upright but still hovering over the water. "I'm so glad you approve." *Not.*

She was just about to leave again when Persephone suddenly appeared in her path, looking—now—very much the queen she was. "I said, 'may.' Not 'will.' A lot depends on what you do next." She tipped her head. "I believe I will grant you audience with Hades. I'll even take you there."

Persephone's eyes sparkled at the excuse to see her husband again. Around them, the pond and forest burst to life, the colors and fragrances overwhelming the senses. And Isadora caught her breath at what was being offered to her for reasons she didn't quite understand. "But of course, nothing is free, and we haven't discussed the issue of payment yet."

"I don't have anything—"

"I want your gift of foresight."

"But I—"

"Don't have it? Not right now you don't, but it will return. And when it does, I want it. For one month."

Isadora's eyebrows drew together. "But you're a goddess. Certainly you don't need something as simple as my power."

Persephone shrugged in a nonchalant way, but Isadora could tell this meant a great deal to her. "Curse of the gods. Supreme cosmic power but no way to look into the future. None of the gods can. Free will and all that crap. But to be able to see ahead, whatever I choose?" Her eyes shone with a devious light. "That would elevate me to the plane of Zeus."

A chill slid down Isadora's spine. "But my powers don't work that way. I can't choose which events I see. And though I have glimpses of the future, I don't know when the events will happen."

Persephone's eyes flared to a glowing jade, and malicious intent slid across her perfect features. "Don't bother yourself with that, Princess. Your powers in my hands will be quite different. I guarantee it."

Dread welled in Isadora's stomach. Would it be wise to grant the Queen of the Underworld such power? Just what did the goddess plan to do with it anyway?

"Choose now. Your sister's life for one month. I grow bored with this conversation."

One month. Nothing bad could happen in one month, could it? Isadora hoped not, but in the end what the gods did was of little concern to her. Her world was far removed. And her sister's life and the lives of many Argoleans hung in the balance.

She lifted her chin and pushed the fear at what she was about to do out of her head. "Take me to Hades."

"No sweeter words were ever spoken." A wicked smile slid across Persephone's face as she held out her hand. "As you wish, my dying little queen-to-be."

"Do you still have the weapon I gave you?"

Casey's adrenaline spiked. She watched a horde of daemons rush out of the trees on the far side of the clearing and charge the circle of mourners.

"Acacia!" Theron pulled his dagger with the thick blade from his back and glanced up at the canopy.

Fear clogged Casey's throat as screams and fighting erupted in the clearing, but somehow she had the presence of mind to nod. She made sure the blade was still strapped to her calf where she'd put it this morning.

"Can you climb?"

"Climb? What—?"

He looked up again. "I'll boost you up. Get as high in the trees as you can. Anything comes up after you, scream. Loud."

"Is that supposed to be funny?" He was developing a sense of humor *now*?

He picked her up as if she weighed nothing and forced her to grab the first branch in the old-growth Douglas fir. "As high as you can, Acacia. Only use the weapon if you have to, and scream as loud as you can. I'll be right here."

He was leaving her?

"Wait." Frantic, she grasped his arm even as he pushed her higher into the tree, and she had no choice but to grab on or fall. "Theron—"

He clasped her hand and locked his eyes with hers until it felt as if he was seeing the darkest place of her soul. Her breath caught at the intensity of his gaze. "I won't let anything happen to you, *meli*. Marissa was wrong. I will never let anything happen to you. Tell me you believe me."

She nodded slowly and whispered, "I believe you."

His eyes searched hers one last second before he nodded upward. "Go. Now."

Casey hesitated only a moment to watch Theron charge into the battle happening in the clearing. He was all hulking muscle and deadly intent, joining Nick, who, along with a few other men from the colony, was beating back the dozen or so daemons who'd converged on what she could tell was a funeral.

God, Dana.

Weapons clashed with fangs and claws. Shouts and cries mixed with snarled grunts as fists met bone. When Theron was tossed to his back and a daemon charged for him, Casey slammed her eyes shut and shifted to look away.

Heart in her throat, she reached up and grabbed the next branch. Her hands shook as she climbed, the knife Theron had given her a solid weight pressed against her leg.

Please God, don't let it slip and fall out.

She wasn't fond of heights and she felt like a fool hiding out in this tree when people were possibly dying below, but if those monsters were here for her, she wasn't stupid enough to hang out in the open.

Her hands burned as bark scraped her palms raw. She groaned at the ache in her arms as she climbed higher and told herself if she came through this alive—and Dr. Jill found a cure for whatever was wrong with her—she was definitely starting that workout program she'd been putting off for far too long. The sounds of the battle drifted up to her, but she blocked them out, tried not to listen for Theron's voice. One thing, however, got through. A feral growling coming from the base of the tree.

She froze. Hoped she blended into the limbs. And prayed she was imagining things.

The growling grew louder. And then the entire tree began to shake.

Casey shrieked. Her fingers closed around a branch just as she lost her footing.

"There's nowhere for you to go, half-breed," the daemon below snarled. "Come down."

Casey flailed out with her feet and finally found a thin branch that bent slightly under her weight. She pushed herself higher as her adrenaline spiked. A few more feet to that thicker branch above and she could let go with one hand and grab the knife.

"Come down!" the beast thundered.

"Fuck you!"

With a ferocious roar the daemon grabbed the trunk of the tree and shook violently. Casey screeched as the branch she'd been standing on snapped. Bark abraded her palms. Her fingernails dug into wood, sending slivers deep into her skin as she hung on with all her strength. Her body was thrown right and left as the tree bowed under the great force jerking it back and forth.

And then the unthinkable happened. The knife slipped out of its holster. Frantic, she tried to catch it with her shoe, but it was too late. Her only weapon fell free just as her hands slipped a fraction of an inch on the branch above.

The daemon saw her falter. And the SOB actually laughed.

Oh, shit.

Sweat broke out on her forehead. She was going to fall. She was sixty feet up, with no weapon and no one to save her. If, that is, she survived the drop.

Oh, shit, oh, shit, oh, shit.

"Theron!"

The branch she was holding snapped like a twig. And then all she felt was air.

Hades wasn't alone. He'd know that damn flower scent anywhere.

His head jerked up, and he leapt off his throne so fast he nearly tripped down the five marble stone steps. He made it as far as the archway before the double wood doors were thrown open and Persephone flung herself into his arms.

"My sweet," he crooned, gathering her close and kissing her hard. Her hands flew to his face, her mouth was possessive against his, warming the coldest space inside him. "Missed you...so."

She groaned against him, frantic as her hands ran under his shirt and across his skin. "Oh, god."

He chuckled and turned her around, pushing her back toward his throne and the solid stone table just to the left he knew she liked so very much. "I am. All yours. Now tell me how you got away from the wicked bitch of the west."

She wrapped her arms around his neck, pulled back and chuckled herself while he kissed her throat. "Don't talk about my mother like that. You know I don't like it when you take that tone."

Since she sounded anything but upset, he licked the column of her neck, slid his hands around to her ass and lifted her so he could get her to the table as fast as possible.

"Hades, wait. We have business first."

"Business?" And that's when he noticed the slight creature standing in the corner of the room, just inside the door. He dropped his queen to her feet and whirled back around. "She's human."

"Argolean," Persephone said, placing one of her delicate hands on his chest. "Future Queen of Argolea, actually."

Oh, now this was interesting.

He looked down at the slight *gynaíka* with her big brown eyes and nearly white hair. He could tell she was sick, but she held an air of authority that intrigued him. One he doubted she was even aware of. "Come in," he barked.

She hesitated, then cautiously stepped forward.

In the light she wasn't simply beautiful, she was magnificent, and he knew interest flared in his eyes before he could stop it. Persephone saw it, too. She punched him hard in the stomach and glared at him. "Not her. And not when I'm standing here, you jackass, or I'll make you both sorry."

Hades coughed and rubbed a hand over his abdomen, then laughed when he saw the *gynaíka*'s frightened eyes dart between him and his queen. "She's too small. I'm pretty sure I'd split her in two. Besides, I gave up virgins last year." He looked back at his wife. "Really, Persephone, if you were going to bring me a treat—"

Persephone socked him again, and he doubled over, laughing twice as hard. She was the only creature in the world allowed to raise a hand to him, and he loved every moment of it.

Persephone's eyes flashed. "Pull your head out of your pants for ten seconds. She's here about the pact."

That got his attention. "My pact?"

"Is there any other?"

A wicked smile slid across his mouth. "Oh, now this *is* interesting. What is it you want, little queen?"

The *gynaíka* took two steps closer, then stopped. Fear flashed in her eyes, but she lifted her chin, looking every bit the regal queen she could become. "I—I ask that your pact be broken. Or at the very least, postponed."

He lifted one eyebrow as he drew his queen to his side, amused at the Argolean's audacity. "And why should I do that?"

"Because..." The *gynaíka* swallowed. "Because I'm one half of the prophecy."

Well, duh. He'd already figured that out, but he was intrigued enough to hear the rest of what she had to say. "And the other half?"

"My sister."

"And let me guess," he said, slowly running his hand up and down Persephone's spine. "You've come to ask me to spare the human's life."

"She's not just a human. She's a Misos."

"Even better." Hades scoffed. "Useless. I don't know why your kind can't keep their pants zipped." Persephone punched him in the arm. His head swiveled her direction. "Do that again once more, wife, and I'll make you pay."

Desire lit her eyes. "Promise?"

He growled low in his throat and leaned in to take her mouth again.

The Argolean's coughing brought his head up in irritation. He pinned the exasperating creature with a look. "Why in all that is evil in my realm are you still here?"

"Hades," Persephone warned.

He sighed, knowing he wasn't getting inside his queen until he appeased her and dealt with this situation first. "Very well. You do realize the ramifications of this, correct?"

The *gynaíka* nodded.

"And you realize that by interfering, you set events into motion that cannot be undone?"

The *gynaíka* hesitated, looked between them and nodded again.

Hades shrugged. "Fine. Your human's life is spared." The *gynaíka* breathed out a sigh of relief. "But not without a price."

"But Persephone said—"

He nuzzled his queen's jaw. "Whatever bargain you struck with my conniving wife is between the two of you. I still require payment. One soul. Yours or hers. I don't care which."

"Now?"

"Now could be interesting," he said, smiling down at his wife, "but the time isn't of my choosing."

The *gynaíka* looked as if she would be ill. Which pleased him. It very much pleased him.

"Well?" he asked. "What do you say?"

She glanced at her hands, seemed to struggle with some internal debate, then closed her eyes. "Mine," she whispered.

His laughter bubbled up from the depths of his soul as his eyes ran up and down her slight and very feminine body. Oh, what he would enjoy doing to her, with Persephone's approval or not.

"Make yourself comfortable, little queen." His hand slid down to Persephone's ass. "The show's about to begin."

The *gynaíka's* eyes snapped open, and shock registered in her fine features, igniting a whole new set of bargains in his head. Ones that involved not only him, but his wife as well. "I'm not going home?"

"Not yet." Hades's smile widened. Catching on, Persephone's did, too. "Not yet. Not until we're both done with you."

CHAPTER TWENTY-TWO

She smelled lavender. And leather. And something she thought had to be thyme.

Which was strange, because thyme wasn't a scent she could normally stomach. Today it smelled like heaven.

Casey drew a deep breath and tried to roll over. A stabbing pain in her side kept her from getting too far, and she pried her eyes open, wondering just what the heck was going on.

The first thing she noticed was the fire roaring in the massive marble fireplace across the room. A quick glance down and she realized she was in a bed with crisp white sheets and a fluffy comforter. She was clean, her toes were toasty, her pillow was soft, but this wasn't a room she'd ever been in before.

She tried to sit up as her brain slowly came back on line. The last thing she remembered was being in that tree, the daemon shaking it vigorously, her fingers slipping and…

She turned her head and saw Theron asleep in an armchair next to her bed.

His hair was damp, as if he'd recently showered, and he was dressed in faded jeans and a tight black T-shirt. His perfect feet were bare, propped up on the side of the mattress, his head tipped to the side, his eyes closed as he caught a few z's. He looked like an angel fast asleep, and try as she might to squelch it, Casey's heart did a little flip at the sight of him.

On closer examination she saw the bruises and nicks on his arms and face and remembered back to the way he'd fought in the clearing. Then realized this was no angel. He was a warrior. And somehow, he'd rescued her again.

Damn hero complex.

She wiggled his toe. "Wake up, sleeping beauty."

He jerked awake and dropped his foot to the floor. Eyes sleepy and sexy and a little dazed, he stared at her. Then moved so fast, she couldn't track him. One minute he was on that chair, blinking as though he didn't know who she was, and the next he was with her in the big bed, pulling her into his arms and holding her close.

Okay, not a bad way to wake up, all things considered. Casey's heart kicked up as he ran his hands up and down her spine and spoke soft words in her ear in a language she didn't understand.

Oh, man. She'd always been a sucker for the foreign-language thing.

"Either I was asleep a lot longer than I thought or you're just happy to see me," she teased.

He didn't laugh at her joke, but his big body relaxed against her. "You've been asleep for nearly eight hours, *meli*. I was worried."

Eight hours didn't sound so bad. Considering she'd knocked herself out during the middle of a war, though...

"Where are we?" she asked against him.

"My home."

His? Really?

"You're completely safe here. The daemons can't get into Argolea."

They couldn't? She wanted to ask why, but was distracted by the realization that...she was in Argolea.

Wow. That was just...wild.

"How did I get here? I thought Nick said I had to willingly cross the portal. I don't remember doing that."

He ran a hand down her hair, smoothing the stray locks back from her face. "You were a little out of it from the fall. Nick helped me bring you here. Yes, you agreed to cross, but you were going in and out of consciousness at the time. It doesn't surprise me that you don't remember."

"Nick's here?"

He shook his head. "He went right back."

Back. To that battle. To the daemons attacking his people. *Her* people.

She grasped his forearm. "Marissa—"

"She's fine. Nick and the others beat them back. They've been doing this for a long time, *meli*."

Was that sadness in his voice or had she just imagined it?

And then she thought of Dana.

She dropped her head against his chest as a wave of grief rolled through her. "Where did he find Dana?"

His hand traced a lazy circle on her back. "I don't know."

But he did. She could hear it in his voice. Feel it in the tingle at the base of her spine, near her birthmark. Just as she sensed he wasn't about to tell her the details. Because it had something to do with her. "I didn't even know she was one of them. Us. Me. I should have. I always sensed she was different. She..." Casey closed her eyes tight. "We led them to the colony."

"No. What happened wasn't your fault. What happened to your friend wasn't your fault. It was just...circumstances. Sometimes bad things happen for no reason."

She knew that. Her whole life was filled with those rotten circumstances. But it didn't make reality any easier to accept. And she missed Dana with a ferocious ache she wasn't sure would ever ease.

When she finally let go long minutes later and looked up, the scratches and bruises on his face again reminded her of what he'd done. She ran her fingers over his cheek. "You look like you've been wrestling with a mountain lion."

His sad smile nearly melted her heart. "I'm fine, *meli*. You were the one..." He closed his mouth, seemed to gather himself. "When I heard you scream... I shouldn't have left you alone."

Casey's heart thumped against her ribs at the emotion she heard in his voice. She closed her hand over his. When their fingers intertwined, she had a flash of the battle. Of his fighting daemon after daemon, saving the lives of the Misos, hearing her scream and rushing for the tree just in time to catch her before she hit the ground. She saw her body slam into his and the way they rolled, the way he took the brunt of the force and shielded her from harm. Then was on his feet again in a flash, clashing with the daemon at the bottom—the one waiting to kill her.

My hero.

The words revolved around in her head as she stared at him. And in that instant she knew. Whether she really was his or not didn't matter. She'd fallen for this very unlikely hero who'd slipped into her life and turned her entire world upside down. Two days ago she'd been so angry with him, she could barely see straight. But now...

"What?" he asked.

"Nothing. I just..."

Now she loved him.

Her chest grew tight at that thought. Holy cow, was it possible? Could she...love someone? Especially him? He was an Argonaut. One of his race's guardians. She still wasn't entirely sure why he'd brought her here. And he despised humans.

"Are you all right, *meli*?"

No, she wasn't *all right*. She was on the edge of freaking out. She shook her head to try to clear the fuzz and looked down at their joined hands. Then remembered the vision she'd had of him and his father in those woods. "What did he say?"

"Who?"

"Your father. Before he died, he said, '*To peprōmenon phugein adunaton, gios mou.*' What does that mean?"

Something unsettling crossed his face. But he didn't look away. "He said, 'It is impossible to escape from what is destined, my son.'"

She looked back down at their hands. *What is destined.*

Was coming here destined? Was meeting him part of her destiny? She didn't buy into all that crap about soul mates and finding the one person you were fated to be with for life, but at the same time she couldn't ignore that there was something pushing her toward Theron and had been from the very beginning. Something that seemed...almost out of her control.

Was that love?

His fingers wrapped completely around her hand, engulfing hers in his. He stroked his thumb gently over her skin. "It's an ancient Greek saying. A reminder that each of us is born with a purpose."

Purpose. That made sense. "And what's your purpose, Theron?"

His thumb stopped moving, and when he looked down at her, it was as if she could see forever in his dark eyes. "For as long as I've been alive, it's been about doing what I was trained to do for my people. But now...I'm not so sure anymore."

Her heart skipped a beat. And another. And another.

And right then she knew.

She did love him. Which was scary and electrifying all at the same time because she'd never been in love before. Somehow over the past few days, she'd fallen for this big, bad guardian in a way she knew she'd never totally recover from. And the fact he was still struggling with figuring it all out himself was sort of endearing.

And completely empowering.

She needed to do something about it before she lost her nerve.

Ignoring the ache in her side from hitting the hard earth, she leaned in to kiss him. He sucked in a breath as she closed the distance between their mouths, held it while her lips brushed his, then went lax beneath her touch.

A smile pulled at her lips. How fascinating that she could turn such a virile warrior to jelly just by kissing him. And how enthralling that he reacted this way to *her*.

No one else ever had. Oh, she'd had a handful of lovers—in college, later when she'd been traveling—but none had ever fired her up like Theron did. None had *ever* seemed unable to get enough of her like Theron did.

He tipped his head and opened his mouth to her, drawing her deep into a kiss he took charge of. His hand slid into her hair as he dragged her closer until she was against his chest and very nearly on top of his lap as she'd been in that cave.

Oh, yeah, she could get used to this. The way he took what he wanted, but was gentle and giving in the process. Almost as if her pleasure meant more to him than his own. Why hadn't she given in to this earlier?

"Meli," he whispered, shifting his big legs and pushing her back on the bed. "What you do to me. Ah, gods."

Her whole body quivered at the desire in his voice. She reached for him and pulled him down on top of her. He was still gentle, settling his weight on his elbows, easing down into the cradle of her body until his erection prodded between her legs. But instead of stripping her bare and driving deep, as she expected him to, he brushed her hair back from her face with both hands and gazed at her so long, that tingling near her birthmark kicked up all over again.

Something was definitely wrong here.

"You are so beautiful," he whispered, running his thumb softly along her temple. "So beautiful and so fragile. Like the most exquisite crystal in my hands."

Okay, that was sweet but...there was more he wasn't saying. She could see it in his eyes. Like he knew something she didn't. She searched for answers in his face as his words whirled in her head. Beautiful. Fragile. Breakable.

Those weren't words she'd ever use to describe herself. Unless she was sick.

And suddenly it all made sense.

What if the whole mystery illness Dr. Jill had found wasn't such a mystery after all? What if it had to do with her Argolean half? And what if that's what was making her sick? It explained why her long-lost father was looking for her. Explained Theron's sudden search for her and the need to bring her here before her time was up.

Holy...*hell*. Was her time nearly up?

She searched his face, hoping for some sign she was wrong, but she didn't see it. All she saw was...pity. A lump formed in her throat. "How long do I have?"

If her question surprised him, he didn't show it, and that fact just cemented her suspicions. "I don't know," he said softly.

Wow. Now there was a mood buster. She was too stunned to feel anything other than disbelief as she ran her fingers through his dark hair. The strands were like silk against her skin. Soft and real and solid.

"I'm going to do whatever I can to help you, Acacia." His resolute voice drew her attention back to him. "Nothing's changed. I'll still protect you."

His eyes were hard and intense, and she saw then he was a man who always got his way. He didn't know how to fail.

"But you can't, can you?" she said. "Because what's happening to me isn't something that can be fixed."

His eyes slid to her hair, where he played with a stray lock without answering. But it wasn't only pity she saw on his face anymore, it was secrets. And sadness.

"Don't hold out on me, Theron. If you know what's wrong with me, I want to know too."

He sighed, as if he didn't want to answer but knew he was stuck. "I don't know. Not completely."

"Best guess, then."

He hesitated so long she was sure he wasn't going to answer, and then he said, "If I had to guess, I'd say your body isn't strong enough to handle all the changes you're going through right now."

The changes. Meaning her Argolean side coming out of nowhere. Which explained why she was suddenly having glimpses into the past. "Is it normal for people in your race to come into their powers? To go through a change of sorts?"

He looked back to her eyes and shook his head, and she didn't miss the shot of gut-wrenching sorrow there. "No. But it could be different for a Misos. Nick would know. We could ask him."

We. The one word both electrified and scared her all at the same time. Because she wanted to read so much more into it than what he implied.

Which was dumb, considering she was growing weaker by the day. Nick couldn't help her. If he could, he would have already. And that meant this was a losing battle. And Theron knew it. Her chest tightened with the reality she was suddenly facing until all she wanted to do was forget.

Threading her fingers in his hair, she pulled his mouth back to hers. "Just kiss me, Theron."

He hesitated, and she sensed the war inside him between what he wanted and what he deemed right. But when her fingers touched his cheek, his restraint broke. Suddenly he was kissing her deeply, pushing his hips into hers, driving her deeper into the mattress, filling not only her mouth but her heart and soul as well.

"Yes, yes, yes," she mouthed against him. This was exactly what she wanted. What she'd wanted from the first moment she'd met him but was too afraid to ask for. Now? Now there was no reason to hold back. She ran her hands up his spine and groaned when he shifted his weight, pressing into the one spot she needed him to touch most.

His tongue slid over and around hers, stroking until she felt her entire body come alive. He nipped at her bottom lip and she felt a lick of pain, then sucked the spot until she melted. Just when she was sure she couldn't stand a second more teasing with his mouth, his lips blazed a trail across her jaw to her ear, while his hand found the edge of her shirt and slid along her abdomen, sending sparks down the column of her neck and the length of her torso. "You're a gift, Acacia," he said against her neck, kissing, licking, lavishing her with his touch. "One I never expected."

She was already on fire and he'd barely even kissed her. She pulled his mouth back to hers. "No, you are."

He obviously liked that, because he slanted his mouth over hers again and kissed her deep, and when his hand found her breast again, they both moaned in unison.

For this moment at least, she wasn't exhausted and weak. She was powerful. She loved what he was doing to her mouth with his own, to her breasts with his fingers, but she wanted more. She wanted as much as he could give, for as long as he could give it. And she wanted to give him all of it back tenfold.

"Theron," she mumbled against his lips. "I want you. Now. Here. No more waiting."

He eased back just enough to look down at her. "I don't want to hurt you."

She ran her finger along the exposed vee of his chest. "Based on personal observation, I have a good idea what I'm up against." She lifted her hips to his and watched desire flash in his midnight eyes. "And I'm pretty sure I can handle you." She slid her fingers down his chest to the waistband of his jeans. "I know I want to."

He groaned and pushed that impressive erection against her softest spot until she shivered. "You tease me, *meli*."

She smiled as she fumbled with the button on his jeans. "No, guardian, I promise."

A slow grin spread across his face just before he kissed her. He found the front latch on her bra and released it, finally touching her, skin on skin, just the way she wanted, until her nipples pebbled into stiff points. Cool air washed over her when he pulled her shirt up and lowered his mouth to her breast. And when his tongue found her nipple, electricity raced through every cell in her body.

She arched her back. Offered him more. Moaned in desperation when he released her breast and lifted his head.

"Don't stop. Theron—"

"Shh."

Her eyes flew open. She looked up and saw he was intently listening to something.

The heavy footfalls outside registered for both of them at the same time. He climbed off her quickly and reached the door in three long strides. "Stay here. I'll be right back."

Theron exited the bedroom and closed the door firmly behind him. Dazed, Casey readjusted in the pillows, pulled her shirt down and fixed the sheets. Then listened closely. She heard Theron's deep voice, followed by two other male voices she didn't recognize. She couldn't make out any of their conversation.

He'd said the daemons couldn't get into Argolea. And that Nick had gone back to the colony. Whom then was he talking to?

The footsteps receded until all she heard was silence. She waited for Theron to come back into the room, but he didn't.

Curiosity finally got the best of her. She climbed out of bed, fixed her clothes and headed for the door.

The bedroom opened to a long hallway. Skylights in the vaulted ceiling filtered in sunlight and cast shadows along the floor. Dark wood ran beneath her bare feet as she headed toward what she hoped was the main part of the house. As she drew closer, she heard voices again—Theron's mixed with the other two.

The scent of thyme was stronger here. She drew a deep breath as she reached the end of the hall and stepped into a massive living room done all in masculine greens and burgundy. The ceiling was at least twenty feet high, made of thick pine beams and rustic materials. Another fireplace built entirely of river rock graced one whole wall. Next to it, a sea of windows looked out into a wonderland of woods made up of wild olive, myrtle and strawberry trees.

She gasped at the beauty, and stopped dead in her tracks. In her peripheral vision she saw movement, and swiveled her head in time to see the two men standing with Theron near the windows gape at her as if she were a three-headed beast.

"Holy Hera," the blond one said. "She's human."

"Acacia." Theron immediately crossed the floor to her. "What are you doing out of bed? You shouldn't be up and around."

"I…" She glanced around him at the other two, clearly as shocked by her as she was by them, and didn't know what to say.

Both were nearly as big as Theron, with the same strange markings on the backs of their hands. The blond was David Beckham handsome, with a youthful face and a wicked glint in his silver eyes. His short hair was unkempt, and the thin mustache and goatee was damn sexier than she would have expected.

The other was dark and mysterious, with eyes she sensed saw way more than he let on. A thin scar ran over his upper lip, and his golden skin glowed in the light coming through the windows.

But it wasn't their good looks that gave her pause. It was the power she sensed from both of them. As if it radiated off their bodies and swirled in the air around her. She knew immediately these were Theron's guardian kin. Two Argonauts. Up close and in the flesh. Theron's comment about women throwing themselves at their feet? Yeah. She got that now.

The blond marched toward her. Theron immediately put his body between her and the guardian and spoke in a language she didn't understand. His words sounded oddly Greek, but were different at the same time.

The blond guardian stopped mere feet away. Stared at her around Theron's shoulder with cautious eyes while Theron continued to speak in a harsh tone she hoped was a warning not to harm her. The other guardian stayed rooted in place across the room, still shocked and staring, but even still, Casey swallowed back a lick of fear. If one of them wanted to squash her like a bug, he could in an instant.

When Theron stopped speaking, the blond guardian's eyes flicked from her face to Theron's and back again. And then he did something she never would have expected. He dropped to one knee in front of her and lowered his head.

Casey's eyes grew wide, but before she could ask what was happening, Theron wrapped a hand around the guardian's arm and pulled him to his feet. "Enough, Zander."

Zander stood to his full height but bowed his head one more time her way. "Many apologies. I didn't realize who she was."

Theron slanted an uncomfortable look her way before turning back to his guardians. He said something again in that native tongue Casey was coming to despise, and then the dark guardian finally spoke up.

"Leonidas wants to see you."

Her father?

Theron's eyes narrowed. "How did he know I was here?"

"He didn't," Zander said. "Cerek and I came to see if you were back. We were going to cross over and look for you if you weren't, but I guess we won't need to now." He nodded Casey's way. "You're taking her, I assume."

Theron quickly said something again in that native language, and both guardians looked bewildered. Casey didn't have a clue what was going on, but she sensed when something wasn't right, and big red warning flags were raised in her head.

Just what was Theron hiding from them? From her?

"Theron," the one named Cerek said in a placating tone. "It's not wise to—"

"Enough," Theron barked. Casey jumped at the sound of his hard voice. "It's not open for discussion." He glanced at the blond guardian. "Zander will go with me. Cerek, you'll stay here."

Casey's gaze shot to the dark guardian, who looked as enthused by that order as she was.

Casey touched Theron's arm. "Theron. I—"

He turned her way, and she saw then the man he'd been when he came into her store that day. Hard. Unfeeling. Full of purpose that had nothing to do with her. She hadn't realized just how much he'd softened toward her until this moment.

As if he knew what she was seeing, he gently took her hand and turned her toward the hall. "Come, *meli*. You need to rest."

She let herself be pushed along, partly because she didn't have the energy to argue and partly because she was still trying to make sense of the strange encounter. But behind her she heard Cerek say, "*Skata*. Did you hear what he just called her?"

That tingling ignited across her back again as Theron led her to the bedroom and tucked her into the massive bed.

"I won't be long," he said. His eyes were once again soft and gentle, but there was an edge to them that hadn't been there before.

"I could go with you if you want—"

"No," he snapped.

She recoiled, and he quickly sat on the side of the bed and took her hand. Turning it palm up, he rubbed his thumb over her skin. "No," he said softer. "It's Argonaut business. You'll be better off here. And besides, I want you to get some rest."

"You said the daemons couldn't cross into Argolea."

"They can't. The portal's safely guarded."

"Then why did you tell Cerek to stay?"

His thumb rubbed a soft trail over the inside of her wrist. "Because I feel better knowing he's here, that's all. You have nothing to worry about, *meli*."

Yeah. Like she was buying that one. She was just about to ask him what was really going on when she looked down at where he touched her. "You're not doing that mind-control thing on me again, are you?"

He chuckled. "I was trying. Is it working?"

"No."

He smiled then as he looked up. That same sexy grin that had nearly melted her before. At her house. In that cave. Here, right now. "I never was very good at it."

His smile faded as he let go of her hand and stood. "I'll be back soon. If you need anything, ask Cerek. He won't harm you."

She found his last comment oddly unnerving, but before she could ask what that meant, he was leaning down. She lifted her face for his kiss, only to be disappointed when he pressed his lips to her forehead. Then he was gone.

With a frown, Casey eased down into the pillows. She could smell Theron here, as strong as if he were lying beside her. The scent of thyme wasn't as prominent in the bedroom, but it was still definitely somewhere in the house.

She closed her eyes and tried to figure out what was going on. Why wasn't he being honest with her?

Her mind spun with possibilities, but before she could spend anymore time wondering, sleep claimed her.

CHAPTER TWENTY-THREE

"Imbeciles!"

Atalanta roared out her frustration as she slammed her hands down on the altar of her temple. The solid stone split in two with an earth-shattering crack and fell together at her feet.

Two steps down, in front of the now-demolished altar, Deimus dropped his head in supplication. Behind him, and several feet away, three other daemons did likewise.

They were morons. All of them. And they were fucking up her plans.

She rounded the mess, her bloodred skirt flying behind her. "She lives and the half-breeds survive. You are useless, Deimus!"

He didn't lift his head or try to defend himself, even as she reached for the sword at his hip, unsheathed the blade and plunged it deep into his chest in one mighty thrust.

Slowly, his head came up, and his green eyes widened until the whites were all she saw. The shock that ran over his face only fueled the venom in her veins as she twisted the sword, exacting as much pain as possible.

He gasped. Fell to his knees at her feet. Blood pumping, she braced one foot against his chest and yanked the blade out, then thrust her arm out to the side so the blade sliced through the air and severed his head. It rolled down the stone steps with a sickening thunk. Gritting her teeth, she pushed with the sole of her foot until his body followed suit and came to rest near the head at the base of the temple steps.

The other three daemons looked down in horror.

"Thanatos," she barked. "Come forward."

The daemon in the middle cautiously looked up, and though he hesitated a brief moment, he obeyed, coming to rest where Deimus had once stood.

She liked that he didn't quiver, though he had to be pulsing with fear. "Pledge your allegiance, here and now."

He dropped to one knee and bowed his head. "I vow to serve the goddess until death."

Oddly calmed by his vow, she lifted her shoulders, straightened her spine. "Who is your master?"

"You are, my queen."

"What is your quest?"

"To destroy Argolea and all that it represents."

Atalanta drew a steadying breath. Because of Deimus's ineptitude, she'd lost the half-breed. That didn't mean it was over, though. She knew of Hera's curse. She'd just have to believe the Argonaut wouldn't go through with the joining of the Chosen. And she still had other means of vengeance.

She pulled Thanatos's sword from its sheath and placed the flat end of the blade against the top of his head. "You, Thanatos, daemon of death, are hereby knighted the commander of my army." Electricity flowed from her hand, down the blade and into Thanatos as the extra strength granted to that of her archdaemon seeped into his body. "Do not disappoint me. My patience grows dangerously thin."

She lifted the sword and held it out to him. "Now rise. And go forth to kill. I want blood."

"Yes, my queen." Thanatos bowed, turned and stepped over Deimus without a look.

Alone, Atalanta drew one deep breath, then glanced to the blackened column on the right side of her temple. "Come closer, Maximus."

Silence met her ears. But she sensed his breathing. And his fear. And it fed her. As it always did.

Slowly, two feet shuffled from behind the massive column, and the child stepped out of the shadows, eyes wide as saucers, face drawn in terror.

His striking resemblance to his father always stopped her. The blond hair, the chiseled features. The power. At ten he was big for his age, already hinting at the warrior he would one day become. Her warrior. Trained, molded, nurtured *by her*. "Closer."

He stepped toward her, careful, she noticed, never to look at Deimus's mutilated remains but to keep his eyes on her. When he inched close enough, she grasped his hand, her fingers sliding over and around the markings that started on his forearms and ran down to entwine his fingers. She jerked him down the stone steps until he was standing over Deimus's body, his back pressed up tight against her stomach, her hands cemented on his shoulders to hold him in place.

She felt him tremble and smiled as she leaned down to whisper in his ear. "Look closely, *yios*, and tell me what you see."

"I—I see…in-ineptitude."

Already, he'd learned so much, but there would always be more. "Ineptitude, *what?*"

"Ineptitude"—he swallowed, hard—"*Matéras.*"

Mother. Her smile widened. "And what is your *matéras*, above all else, Maximus?"

He hesitated. She felt it. Knew the internal war between good and evil that lived inside him was raging hot and fierce. The internal war she would beat out of him until he turned to her fully and without conscience. "M…merciful."

Her smile faded as she slid her arms down his chest and around to pull him tighter against her. The breath left him on a gasp, and still she tightened like a boa constrictor, knowing…*showing* that she held the ultimate power over him and always would. "Yes, *yios*. Your *matéras* is merciful," she growled in his ear. "So merciful, I am the only one who can save you. You know that to be true. And you would be wise to remember it. *Always.*"

She held him long enough to know she'd made her point, until it was all he could do not to scream for a breath. His muscles tightened against her, but he knew better than to fight. Knew if he did, he would wind up in much, much worse shape than he was in now.

When she released him, he drew in a gulp of air and fell forward to land on his hands and knees on Deimus's decapitated body. Blood stained his skin and clothing as he pushed up quickly, stumbled and tripped over the monster. But when he turned, breathing deeply, and his brilliant silver eyes finally lifted to hers, there was no longer fear smoldering in their depths, but determination.

Determination and a hatred forged by her hand.

Pride rushed through her. Oh, yes. It was beyond time he assumed his rightful place at her side and learned the full extent of her power. Especially now, when he may just be the key to her plan after all.

"Tomorrow you join Phobus in the training circle."

Not a flicker of emotion ran over his features at the news that in a few short hours he would be fighting daemons like the mutilated one at his feet to the death. No fear, no horror, no disgust or railing that he was still a child. There was simply...nothing. Her pride swelled. Already he lacked the humanity bred into the Argonauts that would eventually be their downfall. His training would finish the job to turn him fully her way.

"Leave me now."

He did. Without a single word. Shoulders held high, head up, back straight with a confidence born of the guardian class. Her eyes followed him as far as the outer wall around her temple before she turned her back and climbed the steps of her altar. And as she did, her gaze swept once again over the River Styx that so often was her only source of pleasure these days.

"He is a beast of burden, Meleager," she said on a sigh. "But one day soon, he will be the son we should have had."

Silence. Not that she expected Meleager to answer her. He never did.

She ran her hands over her cold arms. Shivered. Thought of all the day had brought.

It wasn't over yet. She was the greatest hero to ever walk the earth. Her father had known that. Meleager had known it and died because of it. The rest would know it as well.

"Soon," she muttered, staring at the water. "Soon I'll have my revenge."

Zander knew a dead end when he saw one. Hell, he was a living dead end, wasn't he? And hadn't he told Theron a thousand times the same damn thing Theron had just told him—that he was fine, and to leave his ass alone?

Yeah, he had. But this wasn't about Zander. It wasn't even about Theron, not really. It was about the Argonauts. And the Chosen Ones. And the future of every person in their race.

"What's Phineus doing outside Isadora's room?" Theron asked, glancing toward Isadora's suite as they passed, trying—unsuccessfully—to change the subject. Again.

"The king ordered she be guarded," Zander said, judging Theron's reaction as they moved toward the king's suite. Theron hadn't said much since they'd left his house. And his silence and the memory of the way he'd called the Chosen One *meli* kept swirling in Zander's head.

He seriously hoped this wasn't what he thought this was. Theron was all business all the time. He wasn't prone to human emotions. And he'd never fall for a female he shouldn't fall for. Not like Zander.

When his kinsman only harrumphed and focused on the stairs ahead as they climbed toward the fourth floor, every step visibly tightening his shoulders and making his jaw tick like a time bomb about to go off, Zander knew his suspicions were correct. He cursed under his breath.

The leader of the Argonauts *had* fallen for the female. For the Chosen One to boot. Of all the stupid, meaningless moves... Hadn't he learned a thing from Zander's mistakes?

Zander's frustration grew as their boots clunked across the marble landing outside the king's chambers. But it ground to a halt when Theron opened the outer door and Callia stepped from the king's bedroom suite. Just that fast, Zander's chest ignited as if he'd taken a searing blade into the depths of his flesh.

This was why he hated coming to the fucking castle.

A servant jumped from where she'd been sitting behind a desk and bowed. "The king is expecting you, guardians."

Callia's gaze darted up, skipped over Theron to Zander, then quickly darted away as if she couldn't bear to look at him. And why the hell that pissed Zander off was as foreign as the rush of pain he thought he'd let go of long ago.

He was immortal, dammit. A fierce fighter who wasn't afraid of anything. And yet five minutes in this castle and he wanted to run away screaming like a little *gynaíka*.

His mood slid to black. Oh, lucky him. He had all of eternity to get over this one.

At Zander's side, Theron's eyebrows drew together and he glanced between them, obviously sensing...something. But like

Theron earlier, Zander did not want to get into it. No way, no how. He shook his head and muttered, "Don't ask."

Theron didn't. He glanced back at Callia instead. "How is he?"

Callia's gaze snapped Theron's way, and she lifted her chin. "He's resting. Not too long. I don't want him anymore agitated than he already is."

Theron nodded once. "We won't be long."

Callia cast a quick look Zander's direction, then headed down the long stone corridor without another word, just as she always did when their paths crossed, her shoes clicking softly in her wake.

That anger hovered on the edge, pushed at Zander from all sides and tempted him to take the bait. He didn't want to give in to it, but when Theron made a move to open the king's door, Zander saw himself and every one of his wrong turns. He moved without thinking and stopped Theron with a hand on his arm. "Hold up. Before you go in there." *This isn't your problem.* "What in Hades is going on with the half-breed?"

Theron's jaw clenched. "Nothing."

"Nothing?" Zander dropped his arm but he didn't back down from Theron's defensive posture. So much for it not being his problem. Deep inside he'd be damned if he let one of his kin go through even an ounce of what he had. "It didn't look like nothing from where Cerek and I were standing."

Theron's jaw twitched again. "It's none of your business. It's between me and the king. Let it go, Argonaut."

"Not my business?" Zander stepped between Theron and the king's door before the leader of the Argonauts could dismiss him. The flash in Theron's eyes warned him he wasn't in the mood to be toyed with. Well, fuck it. Zander wasn't in a mood to dick around either. Not after the last few minutes. "The hell it's not. Theron, this concerns all of us. And our futures."

Theron pursed his lips and took a step back. At his silence, Zander pressed on. "What the hell are you doing, man? She's a half-breed."

"I know."

"And the Chosen."

Theron dropped his head and rubbed a hand over his brow. "I know."

Pity crept into Zander's chest. Pity for his kinsman, who was obviously totally conflicted right now. But Theron needed to know his superhuman strength wasn't going to save him this time. He was about to hit rock bottom. Over a female. And Zander knew all too well just how bad that fucking hurt. "You gotta let her go, Theron. This isn't going to end well and you know it. You're just prolonging the inevitable and making it worse."

Theron's head snapped up, and fire rekindled in his eyes. "Who am I making it worse for, Guardian? For the king? He's dying. In a few weeks he won't give a shit about any of us. For Isadora? No one even knows what's going to happen to her. For our race?" He scoffed. "Most in our kingdom don't even understand what the hell we do for them. The Council's made sure of that. Why should I give a rip about them?"

Theron's uncharacteristic reactions set off warning bells in Zander's head. "Because it's your duty."

"My duty's changed."

"Theron—"

"No," Theron reached for the door. "I'm sick of sitting back while he plays god. You don't have a clue what he's done, Zander. Not a fucking clue."

Theron pushed by Zander and thrust the king's door open. Immediately the scent of healing herbs and the odor of sickness permeated the air. Reluctantly, Zander followed, though what he wanted to do more was pound some sense into Theron before the guardian made the biggest mistake of his life.

The heavy velvet curtains were pulled closed, emitting only a line of light around the edges of the fabric that did nothing to lighten the room. Sheets rustled on the bed. "Who's there?" a weak voice asked.

It took Zander moments to find any familiar features in the frail *ándras* propped up in a mountain of pillows. The king's cheeks were hollow, his eyes sunken. The skin seemed to hang off his bones and his hair was now snow-white. He looked as if he'd aged fifty years in the last few days alone.

"Speak up," the king barked. "Who's there? I may not be able to see anymore, but I know I'm not alone."

"You sent for me," Theron said in a dry voice. "I came."

The king's face softened. "Theron. There you are, my boy. I was beginning to worry."

Theron's jaw tightened.

"Tell me," the king said with excitement brewing in his voice. "Did you find her?"

Theron glanced at Zander, and in his eyes Zander didn't miss the warning: *Don't fucking say a word.*

Shit. Zander stiffened, knowing a train wreck when he saw one. This was about to go from bad to worse, and there was virtually nothing he could do to stop it.

"I found her," Theron said simply, refocusing on the king.

The king breathed out a long sigh of relief. "Thank Hera. You brought her with you? Where is she? We need to unite her with Isadora. My daughter isn't well."

"They're *both* your daughters," Theron snapped.

The king went still. Zander took a step farther into the room, adrenaline pumping.

The look Theron sent Zander could have boiled blood, but Zander ignored it. Right now he just wanted to make sure Theron didn't pummel the king. And holy shit, wasn't that ironic? *He* was the Argonaut who normally had to be talked down from a rage, not the other way around.

Theron transferred his glare to the king. "Aren't you curious about her at all?"

The king stayed silent and unmoving. And his total lack of emotion ignited a fury in Theron that Zander had never seen before.

The Argonaut's coal black eyes grew so wide they seemed to consume his face. His hands clenched into fists at his sides and every muscle in his body bunched for battle. "Well, let me tell you. Her hair is dark, her eyes are violet, just like yours. She's tall and slim. Athletic. The opposite of Isadora. Built more like you. She runs her own business. Has traveled all over the world. She's kind and gentle and smart enough to put me in my place. And there's not much that scares her. When she was surrounded by daemons she kept her cool. Even had the strength to save my ass. More than once."

"Enough," the king said.

"She cares little about herself. Would give the shirt on her back to someone in need if she could. And she's full of more humor and goodness and life than you or I will ever know."

"That's enough," the king said between clenched teeth.

Shit. *Shit.* Had Zander thought Theron had fallen for the half-breed? The Argonaut hadn't fallen. He'd dived in headfirst. Without—obviously—fucking thinking.

"Theron," Zander cut in, trying to defuse the situation, even though he knew he was the last person in the universe who should. Cerek was the peacemaker, not him. "That's it."

Theron shot Zander a blistering look. "Fuck you, Zander."

The rage Zander struggled against every day bubbled up to explosive levels. Curling his fingers into his palms, he breathed deep and reminded himself Theron was his kin. And that he was hurting. Zander could identify with that, even if all it did was remind him what an idiotic fool he'd been once.

"I said, enough," the king repeated firmly.

"Yeah, you know what?" Theron mocked, swinging his gaze back to the king. "I don't think so." He took a step closer to the foot of the bed. "Do you have any idea how she reacted when she found out she was half Argolean? She pitched in and helped the Misos—a race she knew nothing about. A race you told me didn't exist. An offshoot of ours that's been on the front lines battling the daemons, while we sat back and did nothing. *Nothing!* Do you know how many there are out there? How many have died? Been maimed? What they've gone through because of you?"

The king didn't answer, and Zander found himself staring at his kinsman, unable to believe that what he was hearing was true.

"Hundreds," Theron said, eyes blazing. "In that colony alone. *Thousands* the world over."

"Holy Hades," Zander whispered.

"That is enough!" the king screamed.

The king was visibly shaken, and sweating from his old and wrinkled brow, but Theron didn't back down. "If she knew why I brought her here, she'd probably sacrifice herself for you and your noble cause. Because that's the selfless kind of person she is. But I won't let her."

For the first time, the king's eyes lifted, and he squinted hard to see. "What did you say?"

"I said I won't bring her within a mile of Isadora," Theron said calmly. "Consider your prophecy null and void."

Zander sucked in a breath.

The king's face went ashen. "You do not know what you are saying. Isadora will die."

Theron tipped his head. "And why does that concern you, *Leo*? Is it because you lose an heir to the throne in the deal or because she's your daughter? Because as long as I've known you, you've cared for Isadora about as much as you care for the Misos. And we all know how much anyone outside these sacred walls matters to you."

The king's white face went beet red, and he struggled forward in bed. "You do not know of what you speak!"

"I speak the truth!"

In the silence that followed, Zander wasn't sure what to do. Theron's rage was so close to the surface, he was vibrating. And Zander didn't put it past the Argonaut to cross the floor and hurl the old man against the wall. He understood that rage and need to annihilate. Hell, he lived with it daily. And he felt it now. From his friend. From himself. From the flickering image still lingering in his head of Callia brushing him off outside this very door and the unwanted emotions that action stirred inside.

"I've seen them," Theron said, shaking his head. "I've seen what they've been through. And yet you did nothing. *We* did *nothing*! And now you want to set Atalanta free from Tartarus so you can truly start your precious war? Unleash the daemons? I won't let you do that. I won't let you kill one more person to make your twisted prophecy come true. Not even for Isadora. You can call on all the gods on Olympus to come to your aid, but know this now. I'll never let you get near Acacia. I'll die first."

The king gasped. Theron turned for the door.

"Your father understood," the king called at his back. "He had more honor in his right hand than you've got in your entire body."

Theron's fist hit the wall near the door so hard, it created a crater the size of a window. He pulled his arm from the rubble and glanced over his shoulder toward the king. "My father's dead, you son of a bitch. And you can join him, for all I care."

Theron stormed out of the room, leaving a seething tension in his wake. One that washed over Zander like a wave, pushing and pulling him in the current left behind. The bond he had with his forefather Achilles, with Theron, urged him to follow and say "Fuck you" to the world. But that part of him that struggled with what was right and what was expected of him rooted his feet in place.

"Argonaut," the king rasped. "Are you still here?"

Yeah, he was still here. Just like always. Spending eternity fighting the same damn things he'd been fighting the last eight hundred years of his neverending life. "I'm here."

"You've just been appointed leader of the Argonauts. Gather the rest of the guardians. I want that Chosen brought to Isadora now. And if Theron stands in your way, you have my permission to use whatever force necessary to remove him."

Holy...fuck. Zander's brow lifted in utter shock. That was not what he wanted. Not by a long shot. He was a fighter. Not a leader. Not ever.

"I think—"

"Go. Now," the king snapped. "If you can't follow orders, I'll find someone else who can."

He was being dismissed? Like that? Not likely. It didn't matter that the order came from the king. At that moment, Zander had a memory flash. Of another *ándras*. Dismissing him in much the same way. As if he were nothing.

That time it had been because of a female, too.

That rage pushed up against the barrier of his control. And Zander narrowed his eyes. "Theron's stronger than all the Argonauts put together. And if what he just said is true, he's got every reason to stand against you, Your Highness."

At the king's gasp, he turned for the door. "I won't be your patsy. Not yours. Not anyone's. Get yourself another guardian."

Casey threw back the covers on a long sigh and climbed out of Theron's big bed. She couldn't sleep. Her body was exhausted, but her mind was racing. The catnap she'd taken had only made her insomnia worse.

And that blasted tingling on her lower back just wouldn't go away.

After a hot shower that did nothing to relax her, she dug through Theron's dresser and found a white T-shirt that hit at her knees. The thing was huge, but she smiled as she pulled it over her head. It smelled like him and was soft against her skin, and that, at least, was comforting.

Barefoot, she headed down the long hallway, intent on investigating a little, if she was going to be stuck in his house alone.

At the entry to the massive living room she paused, and when she didn't see Cerek, she crept into the room and looked around.

The scent of thyme was strong here, and one look told her it was coming from an incense burner across the room. She moved closer to look. Yep, that's what it was. Weird.

She turned away, studied the decor. It pleased her beyond belief that there were no feminine touches. The colors, furnishings, even art on the walls were all very masculine with sleek lines and bold patterns. No girlfriend had decorated this place for him. He'd done it himself.

She ran her hand over the top of a sofa table as she passed and remembered what he'd said to her in the woods. *In my world, an* ándras *can tell if a* gynaíka *is his soul mate by sharing a bed.* She chuckled at the ludicrous thought. Then sobered as her cheeks heated and warmth slid down her abdomen.

It didn't make sense. As sick as she knew she was, she shouldn't be contemplating sex with a guardian as strong as Theron. But she was. In fact, she'd shored up her courage and decided that was exactly what she wanted. She couldn't stop thinking about the way he'd kissed her before Zander and Cerek had arrived. About the way he'd touched her. About what would have happened had they not been interrupted.

In serious need of a distraction, Casey headed for the kitchen and told herself she'd find something to eat. Theron was right. She needed to keep up her strength for whatever was ahead. And especially for the night she wanted to have with him when he returned. She'd worry about everything else later.

She pulled the giant refrigerator open and peered inside. Sandwich fixings, what looked like leftover pasta, some kind of meat she didn't even want to look at, bottled water, beer and juice. No soda. A smile played across her mouth as she reached for the container of juice and remembered the meal she and Theron had shared back at her house. For the most part, things in this world seemed pretty normal to her. Everything except the no-soda thing.

She was just pouring herself a glass when she heard muffled voices outside the kitchen window. Cerek was on the porch talking to someone just out of her view. Her adrenaline pulsed as she tried to peer around Cerek's massive body. Who else would come out here?

A moment later she got her answer when the kitchen door swung open and Theron stomped into the house.

Her heart kicked up as she lowered her toes and smiled at him. "Hi, honey. How was your day?"

One look from his sullen eyes and her smile faded. *Okay, not such a good day after all.*

He crossed to the refrigerator and closed the door she'd left open with a snap. "What are you doing out of bed? I told you to lie down."

"I didn't realize it was an order."

"It wasn't. It was a suggestion. A very strong one. Now go back to bed."

Casey stared at him. That tingling came back stronger than ever. He was in a mood for some reason. She could either fight with him or try to soothe him. The latter sounded a thousand times better.

"Stop worrying, Theron. I'm fine." She tried a smile. "I missed you."

His eyes softened, just a touch, so she pushed up that courage again and crossed to him. She lifted his hand with the intention of kissing it, but the swollen red cuts across his knuckles stopped her. "What happened?"

"Nothing." He quickly drew back and walked to the sink, where he turned on the water and washed his hands, cringing slightly as the soap touched his open wounds.

"That's not nothing."

"Let it go, Acacia," he said, not bothering to look at her. "It's none of your business."

None of her business? Whoa. Wait. She loved him and wanted to help ease whatever was wrong, and it was none of her business? He'd gone to see her father and come back not only in a surly mood but with cuts across his skin, and *that* was none of her business?

"You're a rotten liar, Theron."

"Argonauts can't lie. It's a curse."

Her eyes narrowed. "Then they omit extremely well. You're the king of omissions."

He ignored that barb and instead grabbed a towel from the drawer. "I have some things I need to do. You really should lie down and get some sleep."

That was it. Breaking point.

"Argh!" She crossed the kitchen, grasped his arm and pulled as hard as she could until he faced her, then shoved him in the chest until his back hit the counter. "Your little secrets are really starting to piss me off. And I swear to God, if you tell me to go lie down one more time I'm going to slit my wrists! Or yours."

His eyes widened at what she knew had to be her crazed features, but she didn't care. She'd had enough.

"Acacia."

She mimicked his confused expression and punched him hard in the shoulder. "Theron!" Pain zinged up her arm, but she gritted her teeth and stared back at him.

Slowly, his eyebrows drew together. "Are you...teasing me again?"

Teasing him? Oh, holy hell. He might be one of the greatest guardians ever, but the man was clueless.

She glared hard. "If I were teasing you, Theron, I'd come up with a much better way to do it. Like this."

On impulse, she pulled the T-shirt over her head and dropped it to the floor until she was standing stark naked in front of him. Those befuddled yet sinfully sexy eyes of his widened until she was sure they might just pop out of his head. And considering how fired up she was right now, that wouldn't be a bad thing.

"I know I'm just a job for you, but you might want to work on your hospitality skills. They basically suck. Oh, and for the record, I'm not tired at all. But thanks for the suggestion." She turned on her heel and marched out of the room.

She might have made it all the way back to the bedroom if she hadn't been hit by a train from behind halfway down the hall. At least, that's how it felt. One second she was walking, the next she was being swept off the floor and slammed up against the wall.

Her breath left her on a gasp. She hadn't even heard him move. Somehow he caught her head so her face wasn't smashed into the plaster. And though he was gentle so she wasn't seriously hurt, the wind was knocked out of her just the same.

"You're not just a job to me," he growled in her ear as he split her legs and wedged himself tight against her backside. His hot breath fanned over her neck, sending even more tingles down her back. "And I don't tell you things, because I want to keep you safe. Not because I enjoy hiding them from you."

Her heart rate shot up into the triple digits. Too late she realized her little outburst had been childish and that she'd pissed off a two-hundred-fifty-pound Argonaut warrior with the strength of a bulldozer. "I—"

"And stripping off your shirt was a bad idea, *meli*, because now *I* know what every inch of *you* looks like." His mouth closed over her earlobe and sucked hard.

She shivered. Caught her breath. Froze when his hand streaked down her abdomen into her folds and found her wetness. Then nearly drove her to the edge.

Oh, God. This is what she'd thought it would be like with him. Fast and frantic, hard and violent. Completely and utterly bone melting.

"Theron—"

She didn't get to finish her statement because he pulled back, flipped her to face him and claimed her mouth, taking her tongue and lips and devouring them until she was his.

Air brushed over her spine, and only when she hit the mattress did she realize he'd carried her all the way back to his bedroom.

"Feet on the bed," he ordered.

Her brain was a muddled mess. She planted her heels on the mattress without question. Muffled a cry when he lowered himself to kiss her again, pushing her thighs wide in the process. His tongue snaked over hers, drew her deep and released with the erotic promise of what she knew he'd soon be doing to her body. A little voice in the back of her mind warned rough, angry, forceful sex wasn't a good idea, but as his mouth moved south to nip and suck and lick, she had a hard time listening.

His hand found her right breast, his lips, her left. He drew her deep into his mouth and sucked hard until electricity flooded her system, raced to her core, and she arched her back, seeking release. As if he could read her thoughts, his lips blazed a trail down her abdomen, lower still. Until she felt his hand on her ankles, holding her tight in place so she couldn't move as his head dipped low and his tongue made a long, possessive sweep down her cleft.

She shuddered. Had to bite her lip to keep from screaming when he did it again. Her hands clenched the comforter at her hips as his tongue licked and laved. But when he suckled her, it was too much. Stars exploded behind her eyes and the world shook.

He didn't let up. He took her to the edge again and again with that talented tongue, with those teasing lips, until she was quivering beneath him.

When he finally released her and she came back to herself, that incredible mouth of his was kissing her hip, her belly button, her ribs just beneath her breasts. Softer this time. Less frantic. Like he had a thousand years to do only this and was memorizing every second.

Nearly too limp to move, she muttered, "Wh-What was that?"

He turned his cheek against her stomach. Drew in a deep breath. "I didn't hurt you, did I?"

The change she sensed in him was so dramatic, she didn't know what to make of it. One minute he'd been out of control, crazy for her. The next, utterly still.

That tingling returned. "Theron?"

"Yeah?"

"What's wrong?"

Silence enveloped them. Then finally, he said, "Nothing. Everything's good. Just the way it should be." But he didn't sound good. If anything, he sounded...sad.

He eased up on an elbow to look down at her. "Are you sure I didn't hurt you?"

How could she tell him his secrets hurt her more than anything? "No. I liked the way you touched me. It felt good. Like you wanted me."

His eyes darkened. "I do want you."

"Then show me."

He hesitated just long enough to make her think he'd changed his mind, but then he leaned down and kissed her, and all her doubt slipped away.

She tasted herself. And him. And a lust she'd never known, as his mouth met hers. As he nibbled on her lower lip, sucked the tender flesh between his teeth, she remembered what his lips felt like on her nipples, licking, circling, drawing them deep in his mouth. Shivers of anticipation raced down her spine, and goose bumps jumped out on her skin all over again.

Her fingers found the snap on his jeans as he slanted his mouth over hers and deepened the kiss. He was hard and hot when she dipped her hand inside, and so much bigger than she remembered.

"Take these off, Theron."

"I don't need to," he said against her shoulder, pressing a kiss to her skin. His hand returned to her breast. "I get more than enough pleasure just watching you come."

That tingling kicked up a notch. And in the silence between them, she realized what was going on. "Is this about that whole soul mate thing?"

He kissed the inside of her right breast. "No. I already know the answer."

He did? She waited to hear the rest, but he only kept on kissing her. And when it was clear he wasn't going to fill her in, a little of her temper returned. Fine. He could keep all of his secrets. That wasn't what she wanted from him right now anyway.

She grasped his face and lifted so he was forced to look at her. "I want you inside me. Right now. So either lose the pants, or I'll have to remind you about that whole slitting-your-wrists thing."

He searched her face. "Are you sure? I don't—"

"Theron. Either get naked now or I'll go find Cerek to finish the job."

His eyes flashed. "Don't tease about that, *meli*. Not unless you want to see the guardian dead."

His kiss was hard and possessive, but so good. Knowing she'd won, she grasped his shirt and broke free long enough to pull it over his head. He pushed up on his hands, never leaving her mouth, and wriggled out of his jeans.

Miles of roped muscles filled her hands. When he pulled back and moved as if he were getting off the bed, she sat up and grabbed on tight. "You're not going anywhere now."

He wrapped one arm around her waist and tugged her with him as he leaned toward the nightstand. "Condoms."

"You have condoms here?"

"Of course. Our biology's the same, remember?"

Right. She should know that. Underneath, he was mortal just like her. There were so many similarities between them. So many differences as well.

She gave her head a quick shake. "You don't need them."

"Yes—"

"It's the wrong time of the month for me, Theron. And considering how fast I'm withering away, we both know I won't get pregnant." He stopped. Looked at her. In his eyes she saw he agreed, and that fact didn't upset her. Oddly enough, it reinforced her decision.

She softened her voice, on this wanting to be completely honest. "I've had three lovers in my life. None of them was special, and I was careful with each one. With you, I don't want to worry about any of that."

"Meli." His finger ran down her cheek in a move that was so tender, her heart pinched. "You honor me."

She shrugged, fighting back the feelings he stirred in her. "I just want to be with you without any barriers. Even if it's just for tonight. I know tomorrow things are going to change and you're going to take me wherever it is we're going. And from there, well, who knows? But tonight I don't want to think about it. I just want to be selfish."

"You're the most unselfish person I've ever met."

"No, I'm not." A ghost of a smile curled her mouth. "I'm difficult and headstrong and a wanderer with no focus. You just don't know me that well."

"I know everything I need to know," he whispered. "I know you're perfect."

She stared at him. And the emotions she'd been trying to hold back came raring forward. Every time she thought she had him figured out, he went and changed on her. Here she'd expected angry-warrior sex and he was switching things around, making her feel all over again, pushing her that much more over the edge in love with him.

Dammit. He really was a hero. Her very own.

"Love me, Theron," she whispered. "Just...love me. Tonight. Right now."

"Meli."

Thank the heavens above, he did just what she asked. He lowered her to the mattress, kissed her gently as he eased between her thighs. Used his fingers and lips to excite her all over again. His mouth found her ear, her throat, her breast; his fingers, her slick and ready wetness. He circled and swirled her nipple with his tongue, stroked her sleek knot with his thumb. And when he slid a finger deep inside, she groaned and lifted her hips to meet him.

He worked her over, up, close to the edge and back again, searching deep for the spot that nearly made her come out of her skin. She gasped when she felt him retreat, but then was rewarded by the tip of his cock sliding along her slit, up higher to circle her clitoris until she shuddered.

"Theron…" She lifted her head, glanced down her body to where he touched her, and went white-hot at the erotic sight before her: his strong hand gripping his massive shaft as he teased them both to new levels of sexual need, his eyes locked on the spot where their bodies were nearly joined, the veins in his neck and shoulders bulging with his restraint and his features darkening in pure lust.

All because of her.

"Theron, oh, God." She'd never been this turned on before, and it was good, so good—the tip of his cock slipping through her folds, circling her clit over and over, sliding down and back up to torment her all over again. But it wasn't enough. Not nearly enough. Frustrated when he only continued to drive them both to the edge, she arched her back, trying to draw him where she needed him most. Then groaned long and deep when he *finally* nudged her entrance and plunged inside.

"Ah, gods, *meli*. You're so tight, so wet. So…" His hips pulled back, then thrust again, this time harder. "Perfect."

She should have been tense—she'd seen how huge he was that night at her house when he'd been injured and naked, lying on her grandmother's comforter, had felt him grow in her hand when she'd stroked her fingers up and down his rigid length. And it had been a long time for her. But as she felt him press inside, one slow inch at a time, and they both groaned at the tight, slick contact, she breathed out a sigh at the rightness of the moment.

Oh, yes.

His kiss was hot. Wet. Sinful. He pushed in slowly, each move a snug glide and retreat, until finally, *finally* he was seated deep and they both paused to catch their breath.

This was what she wanted. Him. With her like this. Locked tight together, the outside world nothing but a memory.

His eyes found hers, and the tenderness she saw there cut all the way to her soul. She lifted a hand and ran it over his stubbled jaw. "Theron."

He withdrew, thrust, kept his eyes fixed on hers as his strokes grew harder, deeper, longer. His jaw clenched. A vein pulsed in his neck. Sweat dripped from his temple to splash across her breasts. She kicked her head back and moaned in sheer pleasure at his thickness plowing into her again and again. And just as she felt the peak building, he rolled to his back, pulled her on top and grasped her hips, teaching her a rhythm that nearly had her seeing double.

Her climax built, fast and urgent. And with him guiding her, she had no choice but to let go and ride the wave. It crashed over her, once, twice, three times, until she was sure she couldn't take any more. And even then it went on. Rippling through every cell in her body until all thought blew right out of her brain.

The adrenaline that had fueled her temper earlier shifted, lagged, broke. She heard him call her name, registered his length pulsing deep inside just before she collapsed onto his chest. Drawing air into her suddenly-too-small lungs, she felt his fingers digging into her hips, holding her tight to him as his body shuddered beneath her.

He was breathing hard himself and growing soft inside her. She tightened her muscles to hold him in, not ready to have him go just yet.

He groaned. "*Meli*, if you keep doing that, you won't get any sleep at all tonight."

She smiled. Released. Contracted again. His answering moan had an electrifying effect on her.

"Sleep's overrated."

He ran a hand down her back. "I think you did mention that. Briefly."

God, she loved the way he touched her. She let out a contented sigh. "If that's the way Argoleans have sex, I can see why I was your first human."

His hand slid down her spine to cup her ass before gently rolling her over. One thrust of his hips and she knew all her tightening had done its work.

He kissed her neck. Her jaw. Her lips. "Trust me when I say that wasn't normal, even for an Argonaut." He slid his tongue along the seam of her lips until she opened for him, then dipped in and took his fill. "I hope you were serious about not being tired, because where you're concerned, I can't seem to stop myself."

She held on tight as he thrust, retreated, thrust again with those gorgeous hips and that growing erection. And tried not to read too much into his words. "Ah, Theron. I love how fast you heal."

He chuckled against her neck. "Like that, do you?"

"Yes."

His smile widened. "So do I."

She gave herself up to his kiss. And ignored the tingling around her birthmark, now growing to explosive levels.

CHAPTER TWENTY-FOUR

Theron stared at the ceiling long after Acacia fell asleep.

Gods, he liked this. Way too much. Her, here in his bed. Hidden away from the world. Warm and snug and his.

His. There was a word. The irony was like a knife to the stomach.

He rolled to his side so he could watch her sleep and knew they didn't have long. The king had probably already called the rest of the Argonauts together. What he'd said in the king's chambers—with Zander as a witness—would be considered treason. He fully expected one of his kin to come charging in at any moment and drag him away.

He could hear their discussion now. Cerek the peacemaker would convince the rest not to take action until the morning. They'd come at first dawn. Play to Theron's sense of honor. If that didn't work, Gryphon would crack a joke about getting the king good, in a lame attempt to lighten the mood. Zander wouldn't care one way or the other—so long as what happened to Theron didn't affect him. And Demetrius...yeah, Demetrius would be pushing to have Theron hanged.

Too late, Theron realized he'd never told his Argonauts how much he respected them. Though they served together, fought together, none of them were close. And as he looked down at Casey, sleeping on her stomach with both arms tucked under her, her face tipped his way and one of her legs intertwined with his, he realized he'd never even thought of his Argonauts as separate individuals before. To him, they'd always been nothing more than fighters in a war they'd all been trained for. But now? Now it was as if his eyes had been opened.

He brushed a finger down Acacia's cheek, watched her back rise and fall in deep sleep. Studied the way her lashes formed spiky crescent shapes on her pale cheeks. Her courage still awed him. Last night she'd been ready to take him on. There was no other female in the universe who would dare stand up to him when he was in one of his moods, but it hadn't stopped her. She was fearless. And as selfless as he'd told the king. Everything he'd never wanted but now couldn't imagine living without.

He'd known she was his from the first taste. Long before he'd ever slid deep inside her. If he'd been more in tune with his humanity, he would have recognized it the first time he'd kissed her back in her small house. But he hadn't. Because he'd needed her to unlock that side of him he'd always repressed.

She was his curse. His soul mate. His life. And there wasn't a damn thing he could do to keep her from dying.

His finger ran down her shoulder, over her back until he found the sheet covering her gorgeous ass. He gripped the cotton and pulled it down, then eased up on an elbow and looked at her marking.

Gods, it was fading. In a matter of days, it would be gone.

His chest squeezed tight, and though he wanted nothing more than to slide back inside her and wake her from the inside out, he knew he couldn't. Shouldn't. She needed to save her strength, not use it up pleasuring him.

One glance at the window told him the moon was setting and morning would be here soon. Careful, so as not to wake her, he pulled the covers up around her shoulders and headed for the shower.

Her scent all over his body was distracting and arousing at the same time. As he lathered and rinsed under the hot spray, he told himself he was doing the right thing. The king had been correct on one count. Sometimes a great sacrifice is necessary.

He cut the water, grabbed a towel and dried his hair. After toweling off his legs, he pulled on new jeans, lifted the terry to his shoulders and froze.

Someone was outside on his porch.

Skata, he'd been wrong. They'd come for him already.

A deep male voice echoed through the closed doors. Followed by Acacia's surprised and wary one.

His heart rate jerked.

No. He was wrong. They'd come for her.

Casey sensed she wasn't alone even before she came fully awake.

She sat bolt upright and stared into the darkness. A candle flared on the low table across the room, illuminating the man seated near the fireplace.

"Don't let me interrupt your sleep," he said in a deep voice. "I do so enjoy watching the innocents."

Casey pulled the sheet to her neck in a protective move. That tingling from her birthmark intensified until it was a screaming roar up and down her spine, but she didn't open her mouth. Some hidden instinct warned her not to.

The man slowly rose, and even in the dim light from the candle she saw he was at least seven feet tall, with enough power in his right pinky to decimate her and everything in this house.

He wasn't an Argonaut. This person...being...was a god.

And oh, shit. That meant all of this was real.

He stepped toward the bed. "Yes, I am. Care to guess which one?"

She swallowed the lump growing in her throat and pulled the covers tighter to her chest. She was blindingly aware she was naked beneath the sheet. And had a horrifying thought.

What if...what if he can see through it!

His chuckle was low and menacing. "Of course I can. But don't worry. I'm not here for your sex, human. I've plenty of my own sluts to choose from. Besides, the visitor who came to Tartarus to beg for your soul was enough Argolean for me."

"Hades," she whispered.

His evil grin widened, and he bowed once. "Alive and in the flesh. I'd like to say I'm pleased to meet you, but that would be a lie. And I never lie." His eyes narrowed. "Now, ask me who my visitor was."

Her heart pounded against her ribs. She glanced around for Theron, only to confirm he wasn't anywhere near. She swallowed hard again as she looked back at Hades. "No one would go see you on my behalf."

His black-as-sin eyes glinted. "No one but your sister."

The door to the bathroom flew open. Theron, bare chested and wearing only a pair of low-slung jeans, with hair damp as if he'd just stepped out of a shower, charged.

With a flick of his wrist, Hades sent Theron shooting backward until he slammed into the wall and crumpled to the ground. Pictures and shattered glass rained down around him. Hades held his arm out, as if creating an invisible force that kept Theron from getting up.

The god's soulless black eyes refocused on Casey. "Your sister bargained with me, so that you might live."

"Acacia—"

Hades shot out another beam of energy so sharp, Theron's whole body jerked.

"Stop!" Casey leapt to her knees on the bed. Hades glanced her direction, but she knew she was no match for him. She forced the fear from her voice, for Theron's sake. "Stop. Just. Don't hurt him. I…I don't understand any of this."

"Why would anyone expect you to understand, human?" Hades looked Theron's direction with disgust. "As your Argonaut here omitted the real reason he brought you to this realm in the first place."

If the tingling at Acacia's back hadn't already been going at warp speed, it would be now. She looked toward Theron, slowly easing himself into a seated position against the wall. "What didn't he tell me?"

Hades actually smiled, and in the pit of her stomach, Casey knew he was enjoying all of this. "Should I tell her, Argonaut? Or would you like to?"

"Go back to hell," Theron snarled.

He jerked and seized as Hades blasted him again.

"Stop it!" Casey tried in vain to keep the sheet wrapped around her as she held out a hand to stop the vicious god. "Please, just…stop. You tell me the reason he brought me here."

"Don't listen to him," Theron whispered.

"To fulfill the prophecy," Hades said plainly. "Established thousands of years ago, when Atalanta sold her soul to me in exchange for immortality. You are half of that prophecy, Acacia Simopolous. The marking on your back is proof. Your half sister, Isadora, the princess and future queen of Argolea, has the same marking. Like you, she's sick and dying, but in her case, she's losing her Argolean side, whereas you are losing your humanity. Alone, you'll both die. Joined, the strongest of the two will survive to render Atalanta mortal once more and bring the beginning of the end of her war against the Argoleans."

Hades inclined his head toward Theron. "Your Argonaut was sent by your father, the king, to bring you back to meet your sister. To save her life and end yours."

Casey's eyes slowly slid to Theron, slumped against the wall, eyes closed, with his arm across his abdomen. She waited for him to deny Hades's words, to tell her they were nothing but lies, but he didn't open his mouth. He didn't even look at her.

"No," she whispered. "That...can't be true."

"The truth is never a lie. Your sister even recognized how wrong these heroes were to try to mold your destinies. It's why she came to me and bartered for your soul. And she did so against her father and her fiancé's wills."

"Fiancé?" Casey asked, having trouble following he god's words.

"Oh, darn." Hades snapped his fingers. "I guess your Argonaut forgot to tell you that as well." His obsidian eyes sparked. "The good hero Theron here is scheduled to marry Isadora as soon as the prophecy is fulfilled."

Casey's heart slammed into her ribs as she looked toward Theron. He didn't deny it. And he didn't open his eyes, even now. The guilt-ridden expression across his face confirmed Hades's claim.

Her heart shattered right there. Broke into a million pieces at her feet. The pain of betrayal in the center of her chest was as real as if she'd been stabbed with a blade.

Hades held out his hand. "Come with me and I will show you the truth, Acacia Simopolous. You will see, and you will believe."

Theron shot to his feet. "No. Acacia!"

Electricity flashed out of Hades's hand. Theron was rammed into the wall once more. He groaned and fell to the floor, this time surrounded by a pile of plaster.

"You will be safe while you are with me, human. No harm will come to you, I promise."

Tears burned the backs of Casey's eyes as she looked at the hand extended to her. Everything Theron had told her, everything she'd started to believe, was nothing more than a lie. Indecision warred within her. But one thing Hades said got through.

She had a sister. One who didn't know her but who'd gone to hell to barter for her soul. There was still one person who needed her.

"I don't have any clothes."

Hades's smile was laced with victory. "Taken care of."

Instantly, she was dressed in a white billowing blouse and matching loose-fitting pants.

Casey dropped the sheet. And lifted her hand to slide her fingers into the palm of a god.

"No! *Acacia!*" Theron screamed.

She was floating. At her side she heard Hades's voice, but when she turned her head she saw nothing but fog as thick as soup surrounding her. "It's really too bad for your crappy genetics. It's you who should be queen."

"What do you mean?" His hand wrapped firmly around hers, almost as if it were holding her together from disintegrating into a thousand microscopic pieces across time and space.

"Your sister is weak. She'll make a terrible queen, but fortunately for her, she was born Argolean and you were not."

"She had to have some courage to come to you. That's the mark of a leader, isn't it?"

He chuckled next to her. "Desperate. That's what we call her reckless actions. She's the one who should be burning thyme. Not you. Don't fool yourself into thinking otherwise, human."

Nothing he said made sense, and she was distracted by the fact she didn't have a clue where he was taking her.

"To see an army," he said. "And believe me, you will soon understand all."

"Stop reading my mind," Casey snapped. "It's rude."

His hand tightened around hers, and for a frightening moment she feared he'd let go and she really would burst apart into a thousand pieces. Right then she realized the foolishness of her short temper. But then he laughed, a low and menacing sound that seemed to come from nowhere. "Oh, you really would be the better queen. Pity the daemon who tried to mess with you. I've been watching you, you know. Wondering how this would all play out. The others in past generations, they've been so disappointing. But you…you might just do yet."

It was on her tongue to tell him to stop playing games with her when suddenly the fog lifted and they flashed onto the edge of a cliff. Casey gasped, and her arms flew out to steady herself as she teetered on the ledge. Pebbles at her feet skidded and pinged down the three-hundred-foot sheer drop to the burned valley below.

Hades pulled her back from the ledge. "Not yet. And not here. There are other plans for you." He pointed with his long finger. "Look down, Acacia. And see the army Atalanta is preparing."

Her breath left her in a rush as she saw the thousands upon thousands of daemons in the valley below. Looking closer, she realized their black skin was what was making the ground seem burnt. She took three quick steps back until she slammed into Hades's chest.

"They can't see you, human. So take a good look." She shivered as her blood ran cold. There were so many. Sparring hand-to-hand, with swords and weapons she'd never seen before. In training. For a war.

In the center stood a woman in crimson robes, with flowing black hair, doling out directions and barking orders. When one daemon was outmaneuvered by another in a duel with bare hands, the woman lifted the whip in her hand and brought it down sharply across his back until blood the color of her robes stained the ground.

Action near her stopped. But not a single daemon stepped to the rescue of the punished one. The whip came down over and over until the one lying on the ground was bathed in blood and motionless.

Casey put a hand over her mouth as she watched the beaten daemon being dragged to the side of the training area. He was left there to suffer while the rest went back to their maneuvers.

"Do you know how a daemon comes to be?" Hades asked in her ear.

Casey swallowed hard and shook her head.

"Daemons are nothing more than the soul of a human, trapped in the Fields of Asphodel."

"Purgatory," Casey whispered.

"Something like that," Hades said, sounding amused. "Atalanta loves to prey on the unfortunates, and as you can see, she's convinced many that servitude to her is a thousand times better than what they will experience with me. Some are genuinely evil and know they'll be sent for punishment. Some are just plain stupid. With her, they're reborn in the image of what she's made them. Strong fighters. Without conscience. Monsters. But there's a catch."

The smile in Hades's voice put Casey on instant alert.

"If they're killed a second time, they're mine forever. To spend eternity suffering at my hand in Tartarus, whether they were truly evil or not."

"You made her immortal."

"I did. I'm a god who's always looking for a deal. Balance in the universe. And her request? Centered on revenge? Oh, you can't get better than that."

Casey's back tingled. "What did she offer you in exchange?"

"The soul of every Argolean she kills." Casey's blood went cold. "Every half-breed as well."

Sickness swelled in Casey's stomach. "Why are you showing me this?"

"Because I want you to see. And believe." He leaned down to her ear. "What do you think she's planning to do with that army, Acacia? It's not just for looks." When she didn't answer, he moved closer, until she felt the long lines of his body against her back. Her stomach pitched. "They're going to devour the half-breeds. Decimate the Argonauts. When those warriors aren't guarding the portal anymore, Argoleans will seep into the human world and be destroyed in droves. And the daemons will spread like fire across Argolea."

"Oh, God," Casey whispered.

He chuckled in her ear, his hot and wanton breath sliding under her garments to send a shudder through her body. "Your human god can't do anything for them. I think it's time you see what it is she hates so much."

He placed his large hands on her upper arms, and they flashed through fog again until she was once more standing on a rise, but this time the view beneath her was one out of a fantasy. A lush green valley, surrounded by woods and meadows and majestic snow-capped mountains. In the center sat a sparkling city made of what seemed to be all marble, with a centralized marketplace, bustling people and a castle that looked like it had been plunked there straight out of Cinderella's fairy tale.

It was the same city she'd glimpsed from Theron's house, only closer and more real.

"Oh...my." Something warmed in the center of Casey's chest. A feeling like she'd finally come home.

"Impressive, isn't it?" Hades said at her side. "Tiyrns. The city of white. Created for a hero, wouldn't you say?" Casey could only nod. "Be a pity to see it and all of Argolea disappear."

"What do you mean?"

"Your sister, Isadora, is the only heir. By Argolean law, no one but a member of the royal family may rule the land. Your father, the king, is dying from old age. And she's as sick as you are. If she passes without producing an heir, the rule of Argolea will fall to the Council of Elders, who believe the Argonauts do nothing but instill fear. Imagine, Acacia, what will happen when your sister is gone."

Dread welled in Casey's chest, and suddenly she understood why Hades had taken her to the Underworld. "They'll be wiped out by Atalanta's army."

"Yes."

She looked back over the valley, and what was left of her heart broke.

"There's only one way to prevent that from happening," Hades said beside her.

"How?"

"Search your soul and you'll find your answer."

She did. And knew.

The only way was for her sister to live. As if she'd heard it a thousand times, the prophecy Hades had spoken of earlier ran through her mind.

And as it did, she thought of Theron and why he'd been sent to find her. All of his gruff actions suddenly made sense. Except...when she remembered the way he'd looked at her when she was beneath him only hours ago... Something didn't add up.

He'd brought her here yesterday, and still he hadn't turned her over. And when he'd come home last night he'd seemed angry, but not at her. He'd been angry with her father.

It hit her then.

He'd changed his mind. Even before they'd made love. Even knowing his actions were possibly going to destroy his world, he wasn't willing to let her die to save her sister. His fiancée.

"Answer me one thing," she said softly, staring at the castle, knowing Hades was reading her thoughts but needing to put this one question into words. "Am I his soul mate?"

"Yes."

She drew in a breath.

"Nasty gift from my brother's vindictive wife. Hera knew if Theron ever found you, he wouldn't let you fulfill your destiny."

Her destiny. Casey nearly laughed at the irony. Either way she looked at it, she was destined to die. And that truly sucked, especially when she realized she'd finally found the one place she belonged, and the one person she belonged to. But life for her had never been easy. It made sense that death wouldn't be either.

The only question left was how it would happen. On her terms or not.

She slanted a sideways look at the god beside her. "Am I to be tortured in Tartarus as well?"

His smile was actually warm, so at odds with everything else she sensed about him. "No. You'll sail to the Isles of the Blessed."

She looked back at the castle. "That doesn't sound so bad."

"It's not. It's actually quite nice."

"And if I go to her? My sister?"

"She will rule until her time is at an end."

That didn't sound so bad either.

"And what about Theron? What will happen to him?"

Hades shrugged. "The Argonaut's fate is none of my concern."

"Surely you know, though."

A bored look crossed his face. "If you go to Isadora? Nothing. Things will be for him as they were before. If you decide to go back to the half-breed colony…" He lifted one shoulder, dropped it. "He may be punished for not following orders and bringing you back."

She narrowed her eyes on him. "May be?"

His mischievous smile returned. "I'm not an oracle, Acacia."

"You're a god, though."

"Yes, but even the greatest of gods cannot tell the future. Free will and all that crap, you know."

Free will.

Casey looked out over the valley. Closed her eyes and tuned in to her senses. When not even a tingle ran over her back, she had her answer.

She opened her eyes and looked up at Hades. "Take me home."

CHAPTER TWENTY-FIVE

He felt like he'd taken forty thousand volts to the chest. Which he probably had.

Gritting his teeth, Theron scrambled to all fours and tried to push himself upright. The room spun. His head lolled on his shoulders. On a groan, he dropped down to the ground again and took several deep breaths before pushing up once more.

Stars fired off in his line of vision, but he kept going.

A roar tore out of him as he finally sat up and collapsed back against the wall. He was sweating already. Shaky. That fucking god...

Boots clomped outside on his deck seconds before he heard voices. Voices he recognized.

"In here!" he managed in a raspy voice.

The door to his bedroom flew open. Through hazy vision he saw Gryphon, Cerek and Phineus file into the room.

"Holy hell," Cerek said, coming around to help Theron to his feet. "What happened to you?"

Phineus took his other arm. "This is a sight I never thought I'd see." He sniffed. Leaned closer to look at Theron's hair. "Gods, have you been burned?"

Theron found his footing and eased free of the guardians' grips. Of all the Argonauts, Phineus would be the one to recognize singed flesh, since he had that whole fire-breathing-dragon thing down pat. "Something like that. Who's manning the portal?"

"Titus," Cerek told him.

Good. Theron had to get word to his kin not to let Acacia leave. "I need your help. She's missing."

"We know," Gryphon said from across the room. Blond hair fell across his forehead, and a day's worth of stubble covered his jaw. "Demetrius and Zander are already looking for her. The king's having a conniption. And considering what Zander said you did yesterday, you're lucky the king hasn't strung you up by your balls. This doesn't look good, man."

"How could you know that?" Theron asked. "She only left here mere minutes ago."

"Isadora was here?" Phineus asked at Theron's side.

"Isadora?" Theron glanced from Phineus to each of the other guardians in the room. "Not Isadora. Why would she—?"

And then it hit him. "Oh, *skata*. He took them both."

The dizziness returned to Theron's head. He reached a hand out to the wall to steady himself. Shrugged from Cerek's grip when the Argonaut tried to help him. Out of the corner of his eye he saw the guardians' confused expressions as they looked at each other and then back at him.

"Who took what where?" Gryphon asked.

Silence.

"The woman," Cerek finally said in a knowing voice. "The human woman he had here yesterday. Son of a bitch."

"Wait." Phineus held up a hand. "What woman?"

Theron braced his forearm against the wall. "Hades was here."

"Holy fucking A," Cerek muttered.

"Here? In the flesh?" Gryphon asked. "I thought the gods were banned from Argolea."

"Hades isn't an Olympian," Cerek said. "Only the twelve Olympian gods are banned from entering our realm. Son of a bitch."

Theron ignored them and turned a slow circle. "I have to figure out where he would have taken them. Not to the Underworld. It would have to be here—"

"Theron," Cerek warned.

"—not to the castle or the temple. Both are too busy. Somewhere private. Somewhere sacred. Somewhere... Why can't I think?" He pressed his fingers to his forehead, then without warning slammed both arms against the wall. Wood and plaster splintered into a thousand pieces to rain down on the floor as he roared out his frustration.

The room went silent. None of the guardians dared speak, because they each knew he was strong enough to rip their arms and legs off if he wanted to. And in his current mood, that wasn't entirely unlikely.

And that's when it hit him.

His head came up sharply, covered in a layer of fine white powder from the stone he'd disintegrated. *"Skata."*

"Theron, wait!" Cerek called as Theron raced for the door.

Pain forgotten, Theron paused long enough to slam his feet into a pair of boots in the hall. Not waiting for the others, he yelled, "Get Callia and bring her to the Stone Circle. Do it now!"

And then he ran.

"Where are we going?" Isadora asked Persephone through the fog.

"You'll see." The goddess squeezed Isadora's hand. "We're nearly there."

It'd been a long night. A night Isadora did not want to remember. Every time she thought about what she'd seen…

Her stomach revolted again, and she felt the bile sliding up her throat.

"Do not even think about getting sick again, little queen." Persephone's hand tightened around hers. And her sadistic laugh was the only thing that kept Isadora from losing what little dinner she'd eaten. "When this is over, you'll thank me. It's long past time you tapped into your hedonistic god side."

Isadora closed her eyes tightly. *Don't think about that. Or her. Or him. Or what they did. Don't think about anything except you and Acacia and the fact…you saved her.*

"And here we are," Persephone said.

The fog cleared, and cold air shivered over Isadora's shoulders. In front of her she saw majestic green olive trees and a purple mountain rising from the ground. She knew she was in Argolea, she just wasn't sure where. She turned. And spotted the stone table in the center of the circle.

"What is this?" Her eyes flicked over the large, flat rock surrounded by the charred remains of kindling and fuel where Argolean bodies were burned in the funeral rite that freed their souls to the Isles of the Blessed. "Why are we here?"

Persephone, a good foot taller and a thousand times more regal, smiled down at her. "Because this is where it will happen."

Isadora's chest grew cold as ice as reality hit her from all sides. "No." She shook her head. "You can't. He *promised*!"

Persephone grabbed her by the wrist before she took two steps back. The goddess was pure steel and stronger than any Argonaut. She dragged Isadora, kicking and screaming, across the hard dirt as if she were nothing more than a feather. "Yes, Princess. We can." She lifted Isadora and placed her on the stone surface, like a parent lifting a mere child. "My husband's prophecy is more important than your wants or desires."

Isadora found her arms pinned to her side. "He lied to me," she growled.

Persephone only smiled. "Not exactly. He merely… omitted."

"I'll see you rot in hell for going back on your promise." She spat in the goddess's face.

Persephone's wicked grin faded. Slowly, she released one of Isadora's arms to wipe her eye, and Isadora tensed, waiting for the punishment she knew was coming. You didn't lash out at a god and live to tell about it.

But instead of the backhand into oblivion she expected, Persephone blinked. And when her eyes resettled on Isadora, they held a note of admiration. "Very good, Princess. There may be hope for you yet. Hades will be pleased to know you have a spine underneath that pasty white skin of yours."

"Go to hell," Isadora muttered.

Persephone's grin widened. "I will. I like it there, you know. If it weren't for my mother calling me back every few months, I'd happily stay there forever." Her head came up sharply. "Ah, finally. They're here."

As Persephone eased to the side and turned to look behind her, Isadora got her first glimpse at what was coming toward them.

Hades she recognized, that sadistic son of a bitch, but it was the dark-haired woman walking at his side who held Isadora's full attention.

Acacia. Her half sister.

A strange buzzing lit off in the center of Isadora's chest, an electrical shock that vibrated every cell in her body and hummed in her ears. She recognized it because it was the same shock she'd felt in that human skin club the first night she'd seen Acacia. Only now it was growing, the humming vibrations intensifying with each step her sister took toward her.

"Stop!" Isadora yelled.

Acacia's feet paused. Her violet eyes—oh, gods, those eyes that were just like their father's—never strayed from Isadora's face. "It's okay," she said. "I've come to help you."

Panic welled in Isadora's chest, but because Persephone still had a death grip on her arm, she couldn't move. "No, it's not okay. Don't come closer. You don't know what you're doing."

"Yes, I do," Acacia said. "I know exactly what I'm doing. I'm going to save you and our people." She started walking again, and that buzz grew so loud, Isadora could barely hear. "It's what I want."

"Acacia! No!" From out of nowhere Theron charged the meadow, but before he reached the edge, Hades lifted his hand, flicked his wrist and formed a shield around the entire Stone Circle. Theron hit the invisible barrier with a crack, bounced off and fell back. But an instant later he was on his feet, pounding on the force field and screaming in a muffled voice. Behind him, others came running.

"Damn Argonauts," Hades muttered under his breath. "Always with the heroics."

Acacia stopped two feet from Isadora, and the buzzing vibrations were so intense now, Isadora couldn't move even when Persephone finally released her grip and eased out of the way. All she could do was stare.

Acacia looked once longingly at Theron, then turned to face her sister. One single tear slid down her cheek. "My name's Casey."

"Don't do this," Isadora whispered.

"I have to." She reached out and gripped both of Isadora's hands, and a popping sound lit off in Isadora's head, followed by an electrical current that rushed through her limbs. In a vortex, she and Casey were lifted off the ground and spun at light speed until a blinding radiance shone from every cell in her body. She jerked and seized, and then the world went black and the only sound was a fading buzz ringing somewhere in the darkness.

CHAPTER TWENTY-SIX

Casey came awake in a rush. The first thing she saw when she opened her eyes was sky. Crystal blue and as clear as a mountain lake.

So this is what heaven looks like.

She took a deep breath, then another. And, surprisingly, discovered she felt better. No longer tired or weak, but strong. In both body and mind.

Wow. Okay. So far, heaven's not so bad.

She turned her head to the side, and that's when things got weird. Isadora was crawling toward her across the hard ground.

No, no, no. They weren't both supposed to die. It was just supposed to be her.

"What are you doing here? You're supposed to be back there. You're—"

"It's okay, Casey." Gently, Isadora brushed dirt from her hair. "Can you move?"

"Move?" She pushed up to her elbows. "Um. No. I mean, yeah, I…" Her words trailed off as she took her first look around. And discovered she was still in the center of the Stone Circle. Hades and Persephone were standing off to the side. Beyond Hades's invisible shield, a group of superbuff men who could only be the famed Argonauts stood in stunned disbelief.

"Whoa." Casey reached a shaky hand up to her head. "That was a little trippy."

"Yeah, you can say that again," Isadora mumbled.

Dazed, Casey searched the group for Theron and had a moment of panic when she didn't see him. Then her heart lurched when she caught sight of him on his knees at the edge of the group, partially hidden behind Hades, staring in wonder, just like the rest.

Isadora pushed to her feet and whipped toward the gods. "What was that?"

"Dumb luck," Hades replied with a click of his tongue. "Looks like you were both stronger than I thought."

That got Casey's attention. Feeling at a disadvantage still plopped on the ground, she stood and brushed the dirt from her pants. "I don't understand. That means the prophecy wasn't fulfilled, right?"

"Wait for it," Hades said, holding up a finger.

Isadora and Casey exchanged puzzled glances. The Argonauts on the edge of the circle spoke in muffled voices. And then it happened.

A roar blasted up from the bowels of hell and shook the kingdom with such ferocity, it had to have registered at least 9.0 on the Richter scale.

Casey fell into Isadora, and the two sisters clung to each other as the shaking went on. When it finally ended, long seconds later, Hades's cryptic laughter filled the void left behind.

"What was that?" Casey asked, wide-eyed.

"That," Hades said with a smug grin, as he wrapped an arm around his wife's waist, "was one very pissed-off female."

"Atalanta," Isadora said.

"Yup," the god replied. "I'm sure it sucks royally to be mortal again."

Casey and Isadora looked at each other, and almost as if they could read each other's thoughts, Casey said, "I thought one of us was supposed to...you know."

"In order for the prophecy to be fulfilled, that bitch Atalanta had to make sure the perfect Argolean was never created," Persephone supplied. "One-half human strength. One-half god strength. Doesn't matter what the bloodline is, or the power, but the purity in the soul. Mortal yet immortal. One-half of each whole occurs in every generation, but because Atalanta's daemons have been scouring the world for them, they've never come together."

"Until now," Hades finished. "The prophecy never actually stated one of you would live and one would die. Only that the strongest would survive."

"Then you did lie to me," Isadora said. "You convinced me to barter my soul to make sure she was safe, even when you knew she would survive."

"*Lie* is such a strong word," Hades said. "I didn't actually know she would live. For the record though, little queen, you amused me. I was curious just how far you'd go to save a sister you'd never met."

Isadora's eyes narrowed to thin slits. "I'd say pretty fucking far, wouldn't you?"

Hades barked out a laugh and glanced at his wife. "I think she'll make a much better queen than either of us expected."

"Hm," Persephone said, looking down her nose at Isadora. "Time will tell, I suppose."

Feeling ten yards behind everyone else, Casey held up a hand. "Hold on. I still don't understand—"

Hades's eyes flashed, and Casey snapped her mouth closed. She sensed his patience was at a breaking point, and after what she'd just seen, she really didn't want to be on the receiving end of his wrath. "I really loathe that 'I don't understand' phrase of yours. Let me make it crystal clear so I can get out of this shit hole and back to my realm. Your sister still owes me her soul. There will come a day when she will be mine." He shot Isadora a wicked glance that traveled up and down her slim body.

That earned him a smack to the back of his head from Persephone. He turned to the goddess with blazing eyes. "Do that one more time, and I swear—"

His wife smiled. "Promises, promises."

His eyes flickered with an erotic light. "Guaranteed."

Persephone looked back to Casey and Isadora. "What my husband is trying to tell you is that, assuming neither of you fall off a cliff or get hit by a stupid car, you'll both live to be very old Argoleans."

Casey gasped as her knees gave out. "Five hundred years?"

Persephone shrugged. "Or so."

Thankfully, Isadora was right there to catch her.

"But Isadora—"

"Is fine," Isadora finished for her quickly. "I'll be fine. What about Atalanta?"

Persephone grinned. "Atalanta is once again mortal. She and her band of daemons were expelled from the Underworld with that little hissy fit you heard earlier."

"And that's it?" Casey asked. It couldn't be. Not totally. They'd both live, but Isadora was going to be condemned to Tartarus for all eternity? That wasn't right. It wasn't the way it was supposed to be.

Hades's dark eyes grew gravely serious. So much so, a chill slid down Casey's spine, and she knew better than to ask for anything more. "No, that's not it, human. Atalanta can't recruit any new souls to her daemon army, but she's well stocked. And with her god powers, she's possibly an even greater threat now than she was as an immortal. Especially now that she can cross the portal again. Once she's able to regroup, she'll be gunning for you and every other Argolean she can find…in this realm and the human one. And that's some entertainment I can't wait to watch."

"The Misos still aren't safe," Casey whispered, thinking of everyone back at the colony as his words sank in.

"Still as vulnerable as you now are. Cool, isn't it? Oh, and there's one more thing." A ghost of a smile played at the corner of Hades's mouth as he tipped his head and focused on Isadora. "Now that Atalanta's daemons aren't paying me the souls of their kills? And now that they aren't getting their energy and power from Tartarus? They still have to feed. Humans are fair game. And way more accessible than the Misos."

Sickness churned in Casey's stomach. She thought of those beasts and what they could do. The expression on Isadora's face mirrored her own.

Looking smug, Hades glanced at Persephone. "Well, my love, I think we've done about as much damage here as possible, wouldn't you say?"

"I would." Persephone put her hand in her husband's.

"Wait." Casey said. "Why did you do this? Why did you bring me here? Surely you don't care if the Argoleans are able to defeat Atalanta."

Hades tipped his head. "There's only one immortal ruler of the Underworld, and that's me. And the payment…," he added, glancing at Isadora again. "Well, the payment was well worth the effort on my end."

That look, the one of rank hunger and the promise of torture yet to come, sent Casey's skin prickling, and she reached out to Isadora, closing her fingers in her sister's hand tight while she kept her eyes locked on Hades.

"There is one other minor element you might want to watch out for," Persephone added smugly. "You and your sister are joined because you are the Chosen. Don't get too far away from each other for too long. Bad things will happen."

Hades looked up and around, obviously bored. "That's all the time we have for this little drama. The wife and I have some unfinished business before the wicked bitch of the west comes back to claim her."

"Hades," Persephone warned.

Hades chuckled and drew her close. "Come, daughter of the bitch."

Persephone smiled over her shoulder as Hades pulled her in for a kiss. "Don't forget our deal, little queen. One month." And with that, both she and Hades disappeared.

"One month for what?" Casey asked, looking toward Isadora when they were alone.

Isadora's face was pale, and she didn't meet Casey's eyes. "Nothing. Look, Hades's force field is gone."

Casey glanced up. The Argonauts and one strikingly gorgeous woman were slowly stepping into the circle and walking toward them. All of the guardians were brawny and built, and each one was even more gorgeous than the next. Real-life heroes. Two weeks ago, Casey never would have believed such a man was possible, and here she stood surrounded by an entire group. The woman, she quickly learned as she introduced herself, was the king's personal doctor. Summoned, Casey suspected, to take care of Isadora in the aftermath.

Isadora introduced each to Casey, but Casey barely caught their names as she shook hands and smiled. Because she was looking for Theron in the group. And he was nowhere to be seen.

CHAPTER TWENTY-SEVEN

"Nice view, isn't it?"

Casey turned from the window outside her father's suite and dropped her arms. "Stunning."

Isadora gestured toward the Aegis Mountains in the distance. "Better view from up there if you ever feel like a hike."

"I know. Hades showed me."

Isadora's smile faded at the mere mention of the god's name. Today the soon-to-be queen wore a long peach gown with a straight bodice and elbow-length ballet sleeves. Her blonde hair spilled down her back in waves, and she looked regal and grand and very much the princess she was, though Casey wasn't clear why her sister had to dress the part even in private.

But there was something very sad about her. For a while, Casey had convinced herself it was Hades's contract on her soul weighing heavily on Isadora's shoulders. But the more she got to know her sister, the more Casey was convinced there was something more going on. The troubled look in her sister's eyes had something to do with what had happened when Isadora had been in Tartarus. Casey had asked, of course. But Isadora had never uttered a single word about what had gone on there. And from the looks of it, she never would.

Casey heaved out a sigh. And told herself, *In time.* She was still learning a lot—and there was always more to learn—about Argolean customs and royal workings and just what place she had here. More often than not she was overwhelmed and a little homesick, but one thing they'd quickly learned was just how tightly she and Isadora were bound. If one got too far away for too long, the same symptoms they'd each experienced before came back.

They'd yet to push the boundaries, and each was curious to see how far and how long they could be separated, but they had time for all that. Like five hundred years' time.

And five hundred years was plenty of time to figure out what had happened to Isadora, and how they were going to break Hades's bloody contract.

She looked back out the cathedral windows over the parapet to the city below and watched as a woman—a *gynaika*—stepped out of a shop door, stopped on the sidewalk, then disappeared into thin air.

Okay, now *that* was something else Casey was having trouble getting used to. Here in Argolea, cars and other forms of transportation weren't needed, because the people all had the ability to poof from place to place like *Star Trek* characters being beamed around. Isadora had explained it was a gift from the gods, a benefit of living here as opposed to on Earth, but that there were still limitations. You had to be outside to flash, and walls and structures created barriers that were impenetrable, but it sure made moving from one end of the city to the other quick and easy. And really, it was pretty cool. Casey, of course, had inquired if this was an ability she'd soon develop and was told it was possible, due to her lineage, but so far, no go.

Just another disappointment in a long line of disappointments throughout her life. Her very *long* life.

"How was he today?" Isadora asked, clasping her hands behind her back and pulling Casey from her melancholy thoughts.

"He's fine," Casey said, not dwelling on what she still didn't know. Since the king was dying, she was making an effort to learn as much as she could before his time was up. But it wasn't easy. Especially when the old king talked to her as if she were Isadora and drifted off to sleep in the middle of their conversations. "Sleeping now. He asked me when the wedding will be."

Isadora harrumphed because she knew the king was mixing them up all the time lately, even though they looked nothing alike. Where Isadora was petite and blonde and beautiful, Casey was tall and dark and...not. "You told him never, I hope."

"I'm not sure what to tell him." Okay, now *that* sounded like she was having a pity party, didn't it? *Snap out of it.*

"Casey," Isadora said softly. "Theron's not going to marry me. He never wanted to."

Casey's heart pinched. She hadn't seen the Argonaut in two weeks. The one who'd turned her world upside down, then vanished into thin air even before Hades and Persephone had disappeared.

She'd been trying not to read too much into that, but it was hard not to. Maybe he hadn't cared for her the way she'd thought. Maybe the connection they'd shared had been all in her head. Maybe Hades was wrong and she wasn't his soul mate after all.

Isadora shook back her long hair. "He only agreed to the marriage because my father—*our* father—thought it was the only way to keep the Council off my back. That's not an issue anymore. I'm not afraid to stand up to them. I faced down a god already. Two, actually."

Casey looked down at her hands and vowed they'd face him down again. "That's true, you did."

Isadora pressed a hand to her stomach. "Don't tell anyone, but I was quaking the entire time."

"Doesn't matter. You did it. How many Argonauts can say they did that?"

"One."

At Isadora's word, Casey's head came up. She looked back out the window.

"You know," Isadora said, "rumor has it he would have ripped Hades to pieces to protect you."

Casey frowned. "The Argonauts are a bunch of Chatty Cathys. None of them was there. They don't know what happened."

"Chatty Cathy." Humor lit Isadora's voice, but she didn't smile. Not once in the past two weeks had Casey seen her smile. "I like that one. I'm going to use it." That humor faded. "But you know what happened, don't you."

Yeah, Casey knew. It was all she thought about whenever she was alone. Because she wanted to read so much more into what Theron had done—or been willing to do for her. But if that was the case, then where was he?

"He never loved me," Isadora added quietly. "I was nothing more than another duty he was fulfilling. You…you're his soul mate."

Casey looked at her sister. "How do you know for sure?"

"Because guilt is the only thing that could keep him away. Guilt for having lied to you. For bringing you here. For thinking he could do his job and not see you as a consequence. Otherwise he'd be here right now, planning war strategy with Cerek and Zander. If there was only one word to describe Theron, it would be *loyal.* He's loyal without fault to the people he loves. And he knows he let you down."

Casey watched a bird sweep across the sky. She could think of a lot of words to describe Theron—*hot, sexy, overwhelming* and *generous.* But Isadora was right. Loyalty ruled him. After having that foundation crack, it made sense he'd be shaken now.

"What if he doesn't come back?"

Isadora pursed her lips. "I've been thinking about that. And I have an idea. If you're up for it, that is. It's a little sneaky."

"You know where he is?"

Isadora nodded. "As of yesterday, at least. Orpheus got a message from someone named Niko in the Misos colony. It seems they've got an interesting new colonist helping rebuild what was damaged in their recent daemon attack. Only he's not Misos. According to Orpheus, he's way too big and strong."

Casey's heart kicked up to the beat of a marching band. He'd gone back to the colony? To a place where everyone despised him?

Her heart filled. Of course he had. That would be his way of making amends. He'd gone to help them rebuild and start over. *Her people.* He'd gone to protect what was hers.

"The only problem is," Isadora said, "no one knows where the colony is."

Casey turned slowly toward her sister. "I do."

"I thought you might."

Theron swung the hammer with more force than necessary. The nail shot through wood and flew out the other side. Swearing at himself and the hole he'd created, he reached for another nail from the pouch in the tool belt around his waist and gently tapped it into place. Damn aluminum nails here in the human world. If it were up to him, he'd be using iron. Or fucking steel.

"You look like you need a break, hero," Nick said from across the room. He smacked a nail into place on the wall they were rebuilding and ran a forearm over his sweaty brow. "Water's in the kitchen."

"I don't want water," Theron grumbled, gently tapping another nail as if it were an egg.

"I didn't *ask* you if you wanted water," Nick said. "Gitcha ass in there anyway. You're surly as a bear and I want five minutes peace from you."

Theron shot him a droll look, narrowed his eyes in challenge and dropped the hammer into the toolbox at his feet.

Nick sent him a sour grin and went back to work.

When Theron first arrived at the colony and offered to pitch in on the reconstruction, Nick had been more than a little surprised. He'd never asked why Theron was there, and he'd never inquired about Acacia. Theron figured that meant the half-breed either already knew what had happened or he was taking pity on him.

That last thought didn't sit well with Theron, but it was the only thing that kept him from picking the half-breed up and tossing him out one of the hidden windows in the rock wall that looked down to the canyon below. "I'm not getting you one," he muttered. "You can get your own damn water."

"Hallelujah," Nick said as Theron headed out of the room. "Some twisted god up there took pity on my soul after all."

Theron flipped him the bird—a gesture he'd learned hanging around with the Misos—before he rounded the corner.

But there was no heat in the exchange, and as he walked down the hall toward the kitchen at the back of the lodge, he felt a strange sort of communion with the half-breed. He was still cautious around the man, because there was something just not right about Nick. But the scarred leader of the colony was growing on him. It took balls to stand up to a hero—especially one of Heracles's line. Nick had done it without a second thought from the very start.

A pot of soup simmered on the stove, but Theron ignored it. As he pulled open the refrigerator and looked for a chilled bottle of water, he again tried to figure out what Nick's connection was to Argolea. And just as it did whenever he thought of home, an image of Acacia lying in his bed, naked and spent from the best sex of his life, flashed through his mind.

His chest contracted as that familiar urge to go to her tightened his muscles. But he ignored it. Fought the desire from the inside out. The look on her face when Hades had told her the truth—the look of total betrayal—haunted him. Even now. Because that betrayal had been real. And there was no way he could ever forgive himself for it.

"Something smells good."

He jerked at the sound of her voice, spilling water down the front of his shirt and onto his jeans. Sure he had to be imagining things, he turned slowly and stared bug-eyed at the woman he'd convinced himself would never want to see him again.

Her smile was filled with sweetness and sinful promises. And his body responded to her just as it had from the beginning, lighting up his veins and sending all his blood due south before he could consciously stop it.

She walked to the industrial stainless-steel stove and lifted the lid on the gigantic pot. Wisps of steam rose up around her face as she drew in a whiff. His eyes ran over her sumptuous breasts, prodding the front of her fitted pink tee, down the sleek line of her hips to her beautiful backside, which filled out her jeans like perfection. And the blood in his groin pooled stronger, harder, until he was sure he'd burst.

She set the lid back on the pot with a click. "I made you soup once. I wasn't sure you liked it."

"I loved it," he said, before he thought to stop himself.

She flicked him a wicked grin. "Hmm… I'm not so sure. I think it wasn't quite ready when you had it. Needed to simmer a little longer. I was thinking of trying again. If you're still hungry. I'm better at everything the second time through."

His groin swelled at her innuendo and a little voice inside his head screamed, *Yes!* But there was one small section of his brain that hadn't turned to mush, and unfortunately for him, his conscience now ruled that part.

"What are you doing here, Acacia?"

Her smile wobbled, and though it made him more of an ass, he couldn't play the flirting card with her. Not when it would leave him bruised and more battered on the inside than he'd ever been from any battle.

"The Argonauts have been looking for you."

He tossed his empty water bottle in a recycle can and turned to reach for another. "They'll be fine without me. Zander's a better leader than he thinks."

"Demetrius is making that difficult. But then I'm sure you know how he works." She tipped her head to the side. "What's the story there, anyway? I get the feeling Demetrius doesn't like you and wouldn't be overly upset if you didn't come back, though he's the only one."

Of course Theron knew how underhanded Demetrius could be, but it wasn't his problem anymore. He wasn't the leader of the Argonauts now. There were more important things he needed to see to, like figuring out a way to protect so many in this world he'd neglected for too long. And talking about it with the woman he was never going to be able to stop loving and had no right to wasn't his idea of a party.

"No real story. Just a long-standing family feud. Zander knows how to deal with Demetrius." He brushed by her for the door. "I have work I need to get back to."

"Theron."

Her hand on his arm stopped him. And with just one touch, his resistance crumbled. He turned to look down at her and saw himself gather her into his arms and kiss her senseless until he made both of them forget just why it was he couldn't have her.

But he didn't. Because he couldn't.

"Don't walk away from me," she said. "We need to talk."

He closed his eyes because just looking at her was too painful. "Acacia—"

"No, don't do that," she said harshly, bringing his eyes open. "Don't placate me and tell me I'm being unreasonable. Because *you're* the one being unreasonable here, hiding out and ignoring your duties. My father is dying and the Council is breathing down Isadora's neck. Even with everything that happened, they still don't think she's qualified to rule. And with you gone, the Council's claiming the guardians are unstable. You can't just walk away and expect everything will be all right. It doesn't work that way."

His eyebrows drew together, and though he couldn't be certain, he had a strange feeling she wasn't here because she missed him, as he'd hoped. "Are you saying Isadora wants me to come back, knowing what happened between you and me? Are you saying *you* want me to return? Knowing"—his stomach churned—"what you now know?"

"Yes. And yes."

"Just like that?"

"Your responsibilities are bigger than what happened to any of us."

He could barely believe what he was hearing. She didn't want him back after all. "I'm not marrying her," he blurted. "I already told the king that before the scene at the Stone Circle."

"I know. So does she."

"I don't love her. I never did," he added quickly.

"That's good to know. She doesn't love you either. Not like that anyway."

He stared at her. Completely taken aback that she was showing so little emotion at his revelation. Didn't she feel any of what he did? Had he so totally damaged her that the connection they'd shared was completely gone?

Something in his heart broke wide open. "Then there's no reason for me to come back, is there?"

"Yes, there is. One reason."

He held his breath as she stepped closer. "You made a promise to protect me. Until the end. Since it looks like I've got at least four hundred and fifty years to go until I'm senile and forget that promise, I'm holding you to it. Every one of the Argonauts has told me your word is gold. So I want to know why you're so quick to go back on your promise to me, when you've upheld every other one you've ever made."

His heart bumped. Once. Twice. "Is that what I'm doing?"

She nodded. "No one blames you, Theron. You were put in an impossible position. You did the right thing."

Words lodged in his throat. "I didn't—"

She gripped his hand, and electricity crackled along his nerve endings at the connection. "Yes, you did. One for many? I would have done the same. The only mistake you made was not being honest with me. It was my choice to make. Isadora's choice. From now on we tell each other everything. No more secrets."

Hope flared in his chest even as he tamped it out. "You don't know what you're saying."

"Yes, I do. Once in a lifetime, remember? Hera's curse and all that? Did you think I missed that connection when we made love? The same one we've had since the beginning, but magnified a thousand times? Theron, *To pepromenon phugein adunaton*. Remember?"

It's impossible to escape from what is destined. Yeah, he remembered. How could he ever forget?

She stepped closer until the heat from her sexy little body made him lightheaded. "I'm your destiny and you're mine. Don't turn away from that."

He didn't want to, but he couldn't see another way around it. "Acacia, my duty is here now."

"Nick is not your soul mate."

"Nick is…" What was Nick to him? "A friend," he decided. "I gave him my word. And he needs my help more than you or anyone in Argolea."

She studied him a long beat. Then said, "Fine, then I'll stay too."

"You can't."

"Why not?"

"Because it's not safe for you. And because Isadora needs you there."

"Then I guess that makes your decision easy. Come back with me."

She wanted him. He read it in her eyes. But the reality of their situation was that he wasn't the guardian she or her sister or any of the others thought he was. And if he went back he'd be nothing but an imposter. He didn't move, even though inside, his heart was breaking. Hera was getting her way. Yeah, he'd found his soul mate, and just as she wanted, it had cost him everything else he'd ever believed in. "I…can't."

"Can't or won't?"

"Won't."

Her arms dropped to her sides. "I see."

"Acacia—"

She shook her head and avoided his arms when he reached for her. She made it as far as the door before she stopped and looked back. "You know the ironic part of this whole thing? You said Hera's curse was intended only for the Argonauts. But you never mentioned what happened to the other half of the equation when all was said and done. Free will, right?" She chuckled, but the sound held no humor. "That's a pretty crappy consolation when I'm facing four hundred plus years knowing I'll never love anyone the way I love you."

He stood there, feeling the stabbing pain in his chest as he stared at the empty doorway. Oh, gods, she loved him. Loved him even after everything he'd done and the numerous ways he'd deceived her. His heart kicked up even as he ticked through the thousand reasons they would never work.

Trivial. All of it. She's all that matters. Don't let her go.

He shouldn't. With her he'd felt alive for the first time. Sure, he'd lived for over two hundred years, but when he met Acacia, his world had finally come to life. She'd taught him about forgiveness. She'd shown him that humans were as varied and unique as the stars. She'd proved that their compassion was what made them special, and somehow, in all of that, she'd helped him let go of his anger and uncover his humanity. That piece of himself he'd shunned so long ago.

His heart pounded hard in his chest as every second with her passed through his mind. Every smile and touch, every whisper and kiss, every challenge along the way and the love she'd showered on him right from the start. Even when he hadn't deserved it.

With her he could do anything. Even lead a war he wasn't sure he knew how to win. But without her...without her there was no reason to be.

Don't let her go.

He couldn't. Wouldn't.

He dropped the water bottle and ran for the door.

"Now that's some mighty fine chicken noodle. Just can't get that on Olympus."

Theron spun around and stared at a small, elderly woman dressed in white diaphanous robes who hadn't been in the kitchen moments before, sitting at the table eating a bowl of soup. He recognized the face. Atropos, the third of the three Fates. And there was only one reason she could be here now.

Ah, gods. Not yet. Not now. Not *before* he'd had a chance to tell Acacia that he loved her.

"Bah," she muttered, lifting the spoon to her mouth. "Atropos only likes minestrone. And Clotho won't eat anything with meat in it. This"—she grinned—"this is the good stuff."

Not Atropos?

The lines around her mouth and eyes crinkled as she looked up at him. "Of course I'm not. Do I look like that old hag? And Clotho spins the thread, sonny, she doesn't stretch it. So that leaves—"

"Lachesis."

She grinned. "You get the golden ticket."

"Wh-What are you doing here?" You didn't question a Fate. To have one visit you was a sacred experience, even if it was the one come to snip the thread of your lifeline—which, thank Zeus, this one was not.

"I thought I was going to have to intervene again," Lachesis said, "considering how blockheaded you can be, but it looks like you've finally figured it all out on your own."

"Intervene? Again?"

"Come now, you didn't think that sweet little girl was making things up, did you?"

Sweet girl—Marissa. In the village.

Links fell into place. In a rush, he realized this was his one chance to find out what fate had in store for him. "The Argonauts—"

"Need a good leader," she said, ditching her smile and growing serious. "And your woman is right. That isn't Zander or Demetrius or any of the others. Only you can lead them, Theron. This war will get bloody, and many will die on both sides of the world. But if you choose not to lead them, then loss is guaranteed."

His shoulders sagged at the enormity of what she was placing on him. "How do you know I can do it?"

"Because you're of Heracles's line. You can do anything. You've found your humanity now, thanks to your woman, and that makes you an even better leader, because now you feel. Never question your ability or what destiny has called you to do. This is your *Star Wars* moment, my son. Stand up and do what you were meant to do."

His brow wrinkled. *"Star Wars?"*

She rolled her eyes. "While you're at it, try some pop culture on for size. If you want to lead your people, Theron, you need to be able to connect with them. You'll find most Argoleans as hungry for human culture as you are for that woman of yours."

She sat up straighter. "And speaking of that woman…you might want to go stop her. She's just reached the tunnel now."

He glanced to the door. "She's my curse." *And my life.* Why hadn't he realized that sooner?

"Of course she is. Why would you think otherwise?"

Why would he indeed?

A smile split his face, and he turned for the door.

"Wait," Lachesis called. "Don't you want to hear about—?"

He didn't wait. Not for anything else. Urgency overwhelmed him, and he tore out of the kitchen and ran through the lodge, skipping down the front steps and sailing across the courtyard past the waterfall and the sea of colonists suddenly turning and staring at him as if he'd lost his mind.

He hadn't. He'd finally found it. And his heart. And the courage to do what he'd been born to do. "Acacia!"

She was standing near one of the tunnel openings with Nick and Isadora, saying good-bye to Marissa. All of them looked up when he came running at them, but he didn't care. All he saw was the Misos he'd fallen in love with.

He pushed through the group, gathered her into his arms and kissed her hard and hot with everything he had in him.

When he pulled back, she looked dazed. And so damn sexy, he knew the choice he made now could never be a mistake.

Choice? Who was he kidding? There was never a choice where she was concerned. And thank Hera for that.

"What are you doing?" she asked.

"Keeping my promise." He looked up at Nick, standing behind and just to the right of her, eyeing Isadora on Acacia's other side as if the princess might just jump out and bite him. "We're going to need your help. Someone on the inside who knows what the Misos need and how best to protect them."

Nick's eyes flashed. "Who's *we*?"

"The Argonauts."

Those eyes widened. "I don't think so."

Theron glanced down at Acacia, who was smiling at him as though she'd just hit the jackpot and couldn't believe it. "He'll do it. You were right. They need me more there than they do here."

"Listen up, hero—"

But Theron didn't hear what Nick said. Acacia's arms were twining around his neck and she was pulling his mouth back to hers. "I love you," he whispered. "You're right. I'd have to be a fool to turn away from my destiny."

She was smiling when her lips met his. "My hero, the fool," she mouthed against him. "All mine. Four hundred and fifty years. How will I ever survive?"

"Don't worry. I'll protect you."

"We'll protect each other."

"Damn right."

Eternal Guardians Lexicon

ándras; pl. *ándres* – male Argolean

Argolea – realm established by Zeus for the blessed heroes and their descendants

Argonauts – Eternal guardian warriors who protect Argolea. In every generation, one from the original seven bloodlines (Heracles, Achilles, Jason, Odysseus, Perseus, Theseus, and Bellerophon) is chosen to continue the guardian tradition.

daemons – beasts who were once human, recruited from the Fields of Asphodel (Purgatory) by Atalanta to join her army.

élencho – mind-control technique Argonauts use on humans

Fields of Asphodel – Purgatory

gigia – grandmother

gynaíka; pl. *gynaíkes* – female Argolean

Isles of the Blessed – Heaven

matéras - mother

meli – term of endearment; beloved.

Misos – half-human/half-Argolean race that lives hidden among humans

ochi – no

oraios - beautiful

patéras – father

skata – swearword

Tartarus – realm of the Underworld similar to Hell

yios – son

Read on for a sneak peek at

ENTWINED

Book 2 in the Eternal Guardians Series

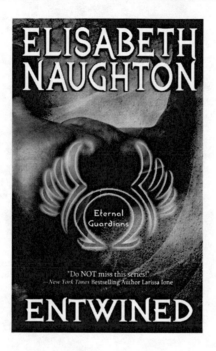

ZANDER — *The most feared of all the Eternal Guardians. It's rumored he can't be killed, and he always fights like he has nothing to lose. But as a descendant of the famed hero Achilles, he's got to have a vulnerability... somewhere.*

Forces of daemons are gathering and have broken through the barriers of the Underworld. Now more than ever the Eternal Guardians are needed to protect both their own realm and the humans'. Zander can't afford to think about what might have been with the bewitching physician he once regarded as his soul mate. But with eternity stretching before him, he also can't fathom spending his life without the one woman who makes him feel most alive. Perhaps he's found his weakness, after all.

ENTWINED

CHAPTER ONE

If he could die, this would be the perfect place to take the plunge.

Zander stood on the edge of the cliff, transfixed by the massive canyon below. A thin layer of day-old snow crunched beneath his boots as he shifted his weight on the rocks and wondered...*What if?*

The temperature was in the teens, the wind howling past his face, numbing what little he could feel of his skin. As an Argonaut, born of the guardian class descended from the greatest heroes in all of ancient Greece, he was stronger than mere humans. Stronger still than the Argoleans and the newly discovered half-breed race he now protected. Stronger, even, than his warrior kin.

No, hypothermia wouldn't kill him, dammit. Frostbite was nothing but a minor annoyance. And shit, since he was *him*, he could take a bullet to the chest and still his frickin' heart would go on beating. But this—he stared down into the abyss some six hundred yards below, which opened and darkened until all he saw was a river of deep green shrouded in a layer of thin mist—this might just do the job. A little voice in the back of his head whispered, *Just do it.*

He wasn't stupid. He spent more time with humans than any of the other guardians from his world and knew taking this leap would be nothing more than a major-ass Nike commercial gone wrong. But still...it was damn tempting. There was always the possibility he could hit that one vulnerable spot on the way down that would kill him instantly and end his immortality once and for all.

His brother in battle, Titus, stepped up next to him before he could make up his mind and peered down into the canyon below.

"Fucking nasty way to go. But you're right. It wouldn't kill you. And I'm not in the mood to pick up your broken-ass pieces and nurse you back to health today."

Zander glared at the younger Argonaut—the *way*-younger one, who, wouldn't you just know it, could take that fall and die…the lucky bastard. "Stop reading my mind. You know it drives me bat-shit crazy."

Titus smirked. Reached up to rub his hand over his mouth. In the waning light of early evening, the markings on his forearms and hands that all the Argonauts shared stood out against his light skin. It wasn't a full-out grin, but then Titus never truly smiled. "You're already bat-shit crazy, old man. And do you think I like knowing what goes on in that twisted brain of yours? 'Cause let me tell you. It's definitely not high on my thrill-ride list." He waved his big hands. "You're projecting your crap all over the place. Trust me. I'm trying not to listen."

Zander's scowl deepened, and he stepped back from the ledge, frustrated he hadn't taken the plunge before Titus started bitching, even more irritated because he knew that little free- fall wouldn't snuff him out like he wanted. He was in a foul mood and it was only getting worse the longer they went without running into any daemons.

It didn't help that he and Titus had been patrolling this particular mountain range for the last frickin' week looking for stragglers and that they'd come up empty so far. He didn't want to go back to Argolea; he didn't want to head to the colony or look for any more half-breeds hiding out in the woods. He was itching for a fight in a dark and dangerous way, which was only making him moodier than Hades. And if he didn't get one soon, bad things were going to happen. For everyone.

"Let's go," Titus said, stepping back and rubbing his hands together to ease the chill. "There's no one hanging out here, and if there was a settlement down below, we'd have spotted it. We'll head north, cut toward Mount Hood and see what we can find."

Though he didn't want to, Zander nodded. The closest half-breed colony was hidden deep in the Willamette National Forest to the south, unknown to the humans who lived around it. Consensus among the Argonauts was that there were other half-breeds, or Misos, those with both human and Argolean parentage, in hiding from the daemons who hunted them. Thanks to the colony's leader, Nick, a man who was both a half-breed himself and something else that none of the Argonauts could quite pin down, they now knew of three other colonies spread out over the globe. One was in Africa, one in the frozen wasteland of northern Russia, and another in the jungles of South America.

"Hey," Titus said with that smirk again as they started walking toward a trail that led back into the trees. "It could be worse. You could have drawn shit patrol in Siberia like Cerek and Phineus."

The mention of his two guardian brothers didn't lighten Zander's mood. "At least then I would have been away from you and your constant mind-probing."

Titus chuckled. "You need to change your outlook, Z. Immortality? It's a gift. Shit, I'd give my left arm to have that power instead of reading mi—"

Zander turned on his guardian kin so fast, Titus sucked in a breath. "It's not a gift. It's a fucking curse."

Titus glanced down at Zander's meaty hand pressed tight against his jacket. A dark warning flashed over Titus's features. He didn't like to be touched. Not anywhere. Not even by a brother. "You need to step back. Right now."

Zander's eyes met Titus's. The guardians were roughly the same size, both six and a half feet, two hundred and fifty pounds of pure muscle, but that's where the similarities ended. Titus's wavy dark hair was tied with a leather strap at the base of his neck. Ice crystals clung to his thin mustache and dark soul patch. Sure, he looked human to the average passerby, but he wasn't. And his hazel eyes sparked of knowledge and danger. The kind that were a fiery combination for anyone who crossed him.

Zander slowly dropped his hand. But he didn't back away. In a fight, he'd win, even against a hothead like Titus. He could take a beating like no other and still go on ticking. But he could be hurt. And it'd take a while to heal. As much as he wanted a good knock-down, drag-out bloodletting today, he didn't want it with Titus.

He did, however, want the brother to get it. Especially if he had to keep prowling this fucking earth for shit only knew how long with the mortal bastard. He clenched his jaw. "Watching everyone you care about die is not a blessing, Titus. I served with your father. I served with all the Argonauts' fathers. I was around when Eurandros was king and Leonidas wasn't even an itch in his pants.

And now King Leonidas is dying of old age, but not me. I'm still just as strong and healthy as ever."

The rage Zander kept buried deep inside built by the second. "You might not want to die now, Guardian, but one day you will. One day you'll be ready to go to the Elysian Fields or wherever the fuck it is the rest of you get to go when your days are done. But not me. No, I'll still be here. Doing the same damn thing I've done for the last eight hundred twenty-nine years. Watching you all die and wishing like Hades I could go with you."

He stalked off into the trees before he did something he knew he'd regret, knowing, okay, he sounded like a major pussy having one gigantic pity party. But he was sick of it. Sick of holding up his head and acting like he was all rosy and chipper at the way fate had bashed in his brain. There'd been a time—a long time—when he'd thought like Titus. When he'd actually believed the fact he hadn't yet found his vulnerability, or Achilles' heel, like his father and grandfather and every other male from his line had, was a gift. But that was before. Before he'd realized he was going to be stuck here for all eternity while everything that truly mattered was taken away from him. Before ten years ago. Before he'd figured out Hera's curse was real.

"Zander. Wait up."

He ignored Titus and kept going. Head down to block the wind. Temper and self-loathing warming his blood. Yeah, he was in the mood for a major-ass pounding. And if he didn't get away from Titus quick, he wasn't gonna care that the Argonaut was friend, not foe.

He made it thirty yards into the trees before the miserably cold temperature went bone-jarring frigid.

He came to a standstill. His head darted up. Ahead and to the right, six daemons stalked through the trees, obviously on patrol themselves. Searching for half-breeds to decimate.

A slow smile spread across his face—the first he'd felt in days. All were easily seven feet tall, with horns and fangs, catlike faces, dog-shaped ears and the bodies of men. Really big-ass, don't-mess-with-me ugly men you might meet in a dark alley on the wrong side of town after hours, looking for nothing but trouble. His smile only widened.

"Just who I was looking for. You freaks want to come out and play or stand there and look stupid like your bitch of a leader,

Atalanta? 'Cause you know, you do it so well. In fact, I see the family resemblance. You there, in front." He pointed toward the ugliest one, with something vile dripping from its fangs. "You're like, what? Her brother? No, I know." He snapped his fingers. "Her son."

The one in front, the one clearly in charge, looked at Zander and growled, "Argonaut," then sniffed the air and added, "Two." The other five daemons spread out in a U formation, surrounding Zander, then crouched, ready to strike.

And yep, that was indeed steam coming out of the leader's ears. Hot damn. This was gonna be a good one. Six against one. Maybe he could get his ass kicked once and for all. And maybe he could take a few daemons out with him in the process.

Titus jogged up behind him just as Zander reached for his parazonium—the ancient Greek dagger all Argonauts carried— from the scabbard hidden at his back. "Aw, hell. You just had to go and antagonize them, didn't you?"

"Sure as shit, I did."

Titus reached for his own dagger. "Okay, smart guy. Which ones do you want?"

"All of them."

"Zander—"

"Just stay back until I need you," he growled. "I can't die, remember? You can."

He took a step into the melee and ignored Titus's protest, but knew the Argonaut would listen and let him have the first go. If only for a few moments. Hopefully, that's all it would take to end this for good.

"Come on, motherfuckers. Show me what you've got."

With a roar, the daemons bared their fangs and charged.

This was one family squabble Callia definitely didn't want to be a part of.

"This is ridiculous. Isadora, tell him no!" Casey Simopolous turned in exasperation toward her half-sister, the future queen of Argolea.

From the far side of the extravagant bedroom suite, Callia chanced a sideways glance toward Isadora. The princess stood with her blonde head down, studying something beneath her pale pink slippers. Her hands were clenched behind her back, the gossamer pink dress all but swallowing her fragile frame. The perfect picture of submission. Not once had she flinched since her father, the dying King Leonidas, had issued his dire announcement.

This was their soon-to-be queen. This waiflike *gynaíka* who would rule over their land, command the Argonauts and lead them in this dangerous time of war. Atalanta was roaming the human realm, looking for a way to destroy the half-breeds and cross into Argolea to exact her ultimate revenge for being cast out of the Argonauts. Now more than ever it was imperative they have a leader with resolve.

But that clearly wasn't Isadora. Callia had suspected that for a while. And she couldn't help wondering if maybe Leonidas's decree was best for everyone after all.

"Isadora, you cannot let him do this to you," Casey said louder, stepping toward her sister. "This is archaic!"

"Enough!" the king rasped, attempting to sit up higher in the pillows of his gigantic four-poster bed.

Ignoring the buzzing in her head that had been going on for the last ten minutes, Callia set down her instruments and eased over to help him shift up in the bed.

The king frowned, irritated he needed any kind of help, but he didn't fight Callia. Today his mind was clear and he was making use of it while he could. "Isadora will marry by the next full moon. And that is final."

Casey's jaw twitched. "It's not right and you know it."

The king's head swiveled toward his dark-haired daughter—the one who would never be queen, simply because her mother had been human, even though Casey was the stronger and wiser choice and they all knew it—and he squinted to see clearer. Callia knew he saw nothing more than dark fuzzy shapes. "Isadora's binding to a guardian of *my* choosing will ensure the Council cannot overrule her authority. You already commandeered my first choice, Acacia. You do not have a say in whom I choose to replace him."

A heavy silence settled over the room. One Callia felt all the way to her bones. She knew all too well about domineering, controlling *patéres*. And she knew when they laid down the law, there was very little for a *gynaíka* to do but obey. Silently, she cursed their patriarchal society that gave females the opportunity to be anything they wanted so long as the male in guardianship over them approved.

Isadora still did not lift her head or look to either her father or sister. And though Callia and Isadora had never been close, a part of Callia went out to the princess. A part she didn't want to acknowledge or dredge up.

Ready to be done with the family drama, Callia gathered the rest of her things and snapped her bag closed. As personal healer to the king, she'd spent a fair share of her time here lately, making him comfortable, seeing to his maladies during his last few months, but she didn't relish it a bit. Especially not when she had a headache like this one. And every time she came to the castle there was the chance she'd run into an Argonaut. Which was a rendezvous she avoided at all costs. "I'll be back to check on you tomorrow morning."

His gnarled hand snaked out and snagged her arm before she got a step away. Even at 684 years and with his body finally giving out from old age, he was still strong. Stronger than most. "I'll need you to stay."

Anxiety pricked Callia's skin. "That's not necessary, Your Highness. And I have work at the clinic I really have to get back to."

"The new moon is but a week away. After I make the announcement to the Argonauts, I'll need you to verify my choice is in peak physical shape. I need to know he can sire an heir immediately. You'll use my office for the exam."

Callia darted a look at Isadora, who, if possible, hung her head even lower. How great it must feel to be seen as nothing but a breeding machine.

But, oh, good gods. Callia had worse things to worry about right now. The king wanted her to perform a physical exam. On the Argonaut of his choosing. Today. She could think of a thousand other tortures she'd prefer to this one. "Um. I'm sure another time would be—"

"It is not a request." He released her hand and barked, "Althea!"

His maidservant scurried into the room with a bow. "Yes, Your Majesty."

"Get me Demetrius. He's with the Executive Guard at the portal, training the newest recruits. I want him and the rest of the Argonauts assembled here within the hour."

Althea's eyes widened with the same anxiety suddenly spiking Callia's chest. "All of them, Your Majesty?"

He waved off her question with a weak flick of his wrist. "Go. Now."

"Um, Your Highness," Callia started as Althea rushed from the room. "I really think—"

"Isadora," he said, ignoring Callia's urgent protest. "Show Callia to my study and see she has everything she needs for her examination. I want you both back here when the Argonauts arrive."

Isadora didn't bother to argue. She turned silently for the door, her slippers making not even a whisper of sound across the stone floor. Callia sighed in defeat as she watched the princess leave. She had no choice but to follow.

"Acacia." The king's attention swung to his other daughter. "Find that husband of yours. Have him call back his guardians from whatever patrols they're on. I don't want to hear excuses. I want them here. All of them. Is that clear?"

Arms crossed over her chest, Casey frowned and stepped close to his bed. Dressed in a sleeveless white blouse and crisp black slacks, she didn't cower in front of the king like Isadora. And she had no qualms about putting him in his place. "Oh, I'll find Theron and tell him exactly what you're up to, don't you worry about that." She tipped her head when she reached his bedside. "This is going to backfire on you. You know that, don't you?"

The king only harrumphed and looked ahead.

"It will," Casey reiterated as she leaned down and kissed his wrinkled cheek. "Mark my words, Dad. Isadora is not going to sit back and let you run her life for her."

"Yes, she will," he mumbled. "Because she's not you."

Casey straightened, and though it was clear she was fired up over what was being done to her sister, Callia could see the compassion the half-breed had for her long-lost father. A compassion Callia wished she felt for her own father.

"You're right," Casey said. "She's not. She's stronger than I am. Stronger than all of us. And one day soon, you're going to realize that for yourself. Everyone will."

The king didn't answer. Not when Casey turned and disappeared through the door. Not when Callia grabbed her bag and followed. But as she reached the threshold, Callia was almost sure she heard the old *ándras* mumble, "I hope you're right. And for all our sakes, I hope this motivates her to finally prove me wrong."

To learn more about ENTWINED
and the rest of the Eternal Guardians Series,
visit www.ElisabethNaughton.com

About the Author

A former junior high science teacher, Elisabeth Naughton traded in her red pen and test tube set for a laptop and research books. She now writes sexy romantic adventure and paranormal novels full time from her home in western Oregon where she lives with her husband and three children. Her work has been nominated for numerous awards including the prestigious RITA® awards by Romance Writers of America, the Australian Romance Reader Awards, The Golden Leaf and the Golden Heart. When not writing, Elisabeth can be found running, hanging out at the ballpark or dreaming up new and exciting adventures.

Visit her on the web at www.ElisabethNaughton.com.

True Friendship

WHERE VIRTUE BECOMES HAPPINESS

JOHN CUDDEBACK
Foreword by Curtis Martin

EPIC

Denver, CO

| Nihil Obstat: | William C. Beckman, M.T.S. |
| | Censor Librorum |

Imprimatur:	+Most Reverend Charles J. Chaput, O.F.M. Cap.
	Archbishop of Denver
	March 11, 2003

All Scripture taken from the Catholic Edition of the Revised Standard Version
of the Bible, copyright 1965, 1966 by the Division of Christian Education
of the National Council of the Churches of Christ in the United States of
America. Used by permission. All rights reserved.

Cover and interior design by Amy Devlin and Daniel Volk.

Publisher's Cataloging-in-Publication

Cuddeback, John A. D.
True Friendship: Where Virtue Becomes Happiness / John
        Cuddeback; foreword by Curtis Martin
p. cm.
Includes bibliographical references.
ISBN: 0-9740744-0-3

1. Friendship—Religious aspects—Christianity. 2. Happiness—
Religious aspects—Christianity. I. Martin, Curtis. II. Title.

BV4647.F7 C83 2003   177'62--dc21
                                    2003110617

10 09 08 07 06 05 04 03   6 5 4 3 2 1

Acknowledgments

One of the many joys of friendship is the opportunity to thank friends for what they have done. Of course, this book on friendship could not have been produced without the help of friends. I first thank my wife, Sofia. It is within sacramental marriage that I have learned the most about friendship. To thank Sofia for the encouragement, insight, and suggestions in writing this book is only to begin to express my gratitude to her. My brother Matthew and several friends and colleagues have been my comrades in the endeavor to begin to understand, and in some way to pass on, the great wisdom of our Western Christian tradition. Among these I particularly thank Christopher Blum, Tim Gray, and Jonathan Reyes, who provided thoughtful criticism in the preparation of this text. Anand Bheemarasetti and Maria Horvath provided invaluable support in editing this text. I thank the Fellowship of Catholic University Students (FOCUS), whose commitment to this project has helped bring it to completion. Finally, I thank my students in philosophy at Christendom College: their enthusiasm, insight, and questions are always an inspiration to me.

Table of Contents

Foreword

Searching history, both secular and sacred, one is hard pressed to find examples of authentic friendship. There are certainly great people and great achievements, but what about great friendships? Yes, we see the loyalty of Jonathan, who despite the fact that he is the heir apparent to the throne of Israel, prefers faithfulness to David over personal power (1 Sam. 18-20). It is inspiring to see Elisha's fidelity to Elijah – unwilling to leave his mentor's side until the latter is carried away to heaven in a chariot of fire (2 Kings 2). But in history, betrayal seems more typical than genuine friendship; Jesus is betrayed by one of His Apostles, Brutus betrays his Caesar, even in legend Lancelot betrays King Arthur.

We should not be astonished that something so important to each of us is also so difficult to achieve. Original Sin did not just force the human family to relocate; it sent a devastating rift into our relationships – with God and with one another. Only moments after the Fall man and woman are at odds with one another, and within a generation their chil-

dren are killing one another – ever since, this world seems
to offer more heartache than consolation when it comes to
relationships. So where can we turn to find authentic friendship? Ancients, such as Plato and Aristotle, tell us about
friendship. Jesus gives us the power to live it. The proof
is right there in history. If we peel back our sometimes
overly pious perceptions of the saints we will see something amazing – they almost always come in clusters. It is
not by accident that when we think of St. Augustine, we
think of Monica and Ambrose, when we think of St. Francis we think of Clare and Bonaventure, when we think of
St. Ignatius of Loyola we think of Francis Xavier. These
Christians lived in the power of Christ and realized the joy
of the restored ability to live in friendship with God and
with one another. This ability can be yours as well, if you
will learn how to forge friendship.

Of all that we desire in life, friendship has a unique place.
Indeed, can there even be happiness without friendship?
What if you had all that the world could offer – such as
health, wealth, reputation – but no one to share it with?
Every evening you were graced with a perfect sunset, but
you could never say to a friend, "Look, isn't it beautiful?"
Friendship is the crowning gift to happiness. But, it doesn't
stop there; friendship proves itself in suffering: "A friend
loves at all times, and a brother is born for adversity." (Prov.
17:17). Even when wealth disappears, or health departs, a
friend can soften the pain. And what can compare to the
sting of being betrayed by a close friend? Friendship is
not merely part of a good life – it is at the heart of what it

means to live life to the full.

Our hearts tell us that we are made for friendship, and there is a reality that corresponds to our desire, but how do we realize it? John Cuddeback has given us a great tool: *True Friendship: Where Virtue Becomes Happiness.* Authentic friendship doesn't just happen – it is an art that must be learned, a skill that must be practiced. *True Friendship* shows us the wisdom of the ancients, what the best women and men of the past have learned about forging friendships that will endure.

But there is more. We need more than a roadmap; we need assistance in following the path. At times something within us hinders us from doing even what we know is right. If we look honestly at ourselves we find a gap between what we are and what we know we ought to be. Bridging this gap is a necessary pre-condition to finding genuine friendship. This is precisely the genius of this book; providing more than answers, it points us toward the antidote.

We find ourselves hungering for friendship, not only with a brother or sister, but in a deeper place, we hunger for friendship with God. "You have made us for yourself, and our heart is restless until it rests in you." (St. Augustine, *Confessions*). The actions of Christ anticipate the hunger in our heart. Jesus comes to us with an offer of friendship, "No longer do I call you servants... but I have called you friends." (John 15:15). His gracious initiative starts us on the path to friendship; He is the creative artist of our hearts and with His presence in our lives we begin to live the art of friendship. Where we are blind, He brings light, where

we are broken He brings healing, and where we are alone He comes to us. "I have loved you with an everlasting love." (Jer. 31:3).

It is within the friendship of Christ that we may begin to form friendships with others. St. Paul rejoices in this radical freedom to live friendship when he reminds the Christians at Thessalonica, "So, being affectionately desirous of you, we were ready to share with you not only the gospel of God but also our own selves, because you had become very dear to us." (1 Thes. 2:8). This is the freedom we have in Christ – to live life to the full. Yes, in this world we will find trials and tribulations, but we need not be alone. Friendship magnifies our joy and can bear us through life's difficulties. Can there be anything more important than learning how to become a true friend?

~Curtis Martin
FOCUS – Founder and President

Happiness and Friendship

*There is nothing so precious as a faithful friend,
and no scales can measure his excellence.*

~ Sirach 6:15

Susan could hardly believe what had just happened. She had known Mary since second grade. After all they had been through, how could it come to this? The words kept ringing in her ears: "You're just going to have to lie to your father, that's all there is to it."

On the way home from a party, Susan crossed the median and wrecked her car, or rather, her father's car. She had promised him she would never drink and drive. She had kept her word until now. Tonight, she and Mary had been drinking. Surely her father would ask her if she had been drinking. What was she to do? She had never lied to her father before, and though she was tempted, she did not want to start now. She knew that lying would be wrong, very wrong.

But Mary insisted. If Susan told her father the truth,

then Mary's father would find out too. The consequences would be serious, and so Mary would not budge. "I don't want to have to say this, but if you tell your father, our friendship is over…." All at once Susan wondered whether she and Mary really had a friendship at all.

~

Most of us assume that we know what friends are. Friends are people that we want to be with; they are those we care for, and who care for us. Indeed, at times we speak with great confidence about "true friendship" and how wonderful it is. Very few people think that they do not have friends. Even fewer think that they are not able to have friends.

Many conclude that all persons, regardless of how they live, can have true friendship. Others conclude that only the most evil people are incapable of true friendship. These conclusions are mistaken. They are a myth. And anyone who wants true friendship should come to see why. The reality is that true friendship is for those who live a certain kind of life.

Anyone can live this kind of life. If you want to have true friendship, indeed if you want to be happy, you must live this kind of life.

It should not be a great surprise that there are many of us who think that we have true friendships, while in reality we do not. Scripture points out that many live in a state of self-deception. In his first letter, the apostle John speaks

very directly: "If we say we have fellowship with him while we walk in darkness, we lie and do not live according to the truth." (1 Jn 1:6) He continues: "He who says 'I know him' but disobeys his commandments is a liar." (1 Jn 2:4) Clearly, there are many of us who think that we "have fellowship" with Jesus Christ, or that we "know him," while in reality we do not. Similarly, there are many of us who think we have true friendships, while in reality we do not.

Of course the critical question is: Why do we not have true friendships? The answer is startlingly simple. We cannot have true friendships *if we are not virtuous.* The kind of life required for friendship is a virtuous life.

Not very many people in our society would claim that they know what virtue is, or that they practice it. The lack of virtue does not seem to bother them. But friendship is another matter. Friendship, unlike virtue, is valued in our society. As mentioned, the vast majority of people think that they know what it is, and that they have it. Susan and Mary have been quite sure that they are the best of friends. But to attempt to have friendship in the absence of virtue is self-defeating. To see this point is to see one of the most profound problems of contemporary society.

The main point of this book is to unfold a bedrock truth of pre-Christian *and* Christian civilization: True friendship and virtue are *inseparable*; you cannot have one without the other. Together, they are the key to human happiness.

The Wisdom of the Ancients on Virtue and Happiness

To begin our inquiry into friendship, it will be helpful to lay

some groundwork with a brief examination of virtue and happiness. To do this, we will turn to a source to which the greatest Christian thinkers have often turned—the ancient Greeks.

In teaching philosophy at the college level, I have found that one of my great joys is introducing students to the wisdom of the ancients, particularly their understanding of what constitutes a life well-lived, or a happy life. In one of the best passages of philosophical literature, Socrates makes a defense of his way of life before the Athenian judges who are about to condemn him to death. He anticipates an offer from the jury that he can go free on the condition that he no longer practice philosophy. Socrates proceeds to explain:

> *Gentlemen of the jury, I am grateful and I am your friend, but I will obey the god rather than you, and as long as I draw breath and am able, I shall not cease to practice philosophy, to exhort you and in my usual way to point out to any one of you whom I happen to meet: "Good Sir, you are an Athenian, a citizen of the greatest city with the greatest reputation for both wisdom and power; are you not ashamed of your eagerness to possess as much wealth, reputation and honors as possible, while you do not care for nor give thought to wisdom or truth, or the best possible state of your soul?" Then, if one of you disputes this and says he does care, I shall not let him go at once or leave him, but I shall question him, examine him and test him, and if I do not think he has attained the goodness that he says*

*he has, I shall reproach him because he attaches little
importance to the most important things and greater
importance to inferior things.* (Apology 29d-30a)

I take this last thought as representative of a pivotal insight in Socrates' thought, an insight shared by Plato and Aristotle. The key questions about a human person's way of life are: Does the person understand what is truly most important, and does the person live in a way that reflects this understanding? To live as though what is most important is really most important is to live an ordered life, a good life, a happy life. To live as though inferior things are most important is to live a disordered life, a bad life, an unhappy life. The great Greek philosophers had a profound appreciation for the nobility of a human life well lived and the tragedy of a life not well lived.

But what in fact are the higher or most important things in life? In his response to the jury, Socrates indicates that they include wisdom, truth, and "the best possible state of your soul." According to Socrates, humans have a soul, which is higher and nobler than the body. This insight is pivotal. If the body is what is highest in a person, then what is the point of life—to be well-fit, or to be healthy and wealthy? Something deep inside the human person cries out that there is much more. This leads to the further insight that simply flourishing bodily cannot constitute "living well" for a human (although it does for a bird or horse), since there are higher human goods—those of the soul. This is where the notion of "virtue" comes in.

TRUE FRIENDSHIP: Where Virtue Becomes Happiness

The Greek word for virtue means "excellence." The philosophers insist that virtues, which are excellences of the soul, are the highest human goods. Therefore, to live a good human life, or a happy human life, is to live a life of virtue. All humans live; but only some really live well—those who live the life of virtue. Thus, in Socrates' immortal words: "The most important thing is not life, but the good life." (Crito 48b) In other words, human life is not just about being "alive" in body; it is about living well. And living well for humans means first and foremost to have excellence in the soul, or to live virtuously.

Socrates was absorbed with the dismaying fact that very few people actually live a good life, are actually happy. There is a paradox here. On the one hand, there are few who explicitly believe that true human happiness consists in the fulfillment of bodily desires. Most people will grant that there are "goods of the soul" that are more important. Indeed, who would want at one's funeral to be praised for being fit or wealthy? Surely we want to be remembered for some higher qualities. And who has not experienced the deep emptiness at the end of a day lived as though bodily pleasures were what brings happiness? On the other hand, very few people truly live as though what is most important is really most important. It seems that Socrates' reproach to the Athenians applies to many of us who say that we *know* what is most important: "Are you not ashamed of your eagerness to possess as much wealth, reputation and honors as possible, while you do not care for nor give thought to wisdom or truth, or the best possible state of your soul?"

Socrates was very concerned about this matter. We should be too. As he says later in his trial: "It is not difficult to avoid death, gentlemen of the jury, it is much more difficult to avoid wickedness, for it runs faster than death." (*Apology*, 39b)

Living a virtuous life requires much more than just *knowing* what is most important. Virtues are all about *living out* the truth that you know. Aristotle, who was a student of Plato, who was in turn a student of Socrates, is the philosopher who gives us the most developed understanding of the virtuous life. In his masterpiece of morals, the *Nicomachean Ethics*, Aristotle explains that living a virtuous life is precisely what constitutes living a *good* human life, which is to say, human flourishing or happiness. The heart of his explanation is this: There are two fundamental truths about every natural thing ("natural" here simply refers to things not crafted by man). The first is that it has a given structure, called its "nature." An apple tree, for instance, has a nature; this is the structure shared by all apple trees, which allows us to recognize an apple tree as an apple tree. The second truth is that each thing has a goal or state of flourishing, called its "end." The end of the apple tree is to grow in good health to full stature and then produce well-formed apples. It is obvious that in all that an apple tree "does," this is its goal or end, this is what it is "trying" to do. Anyone who knows apple trees can discern well enough the nature and the end. Now, it is particularly in knowing the end or goal that one can judge between a *good* and a *bad* apple tree. A good apple tree is one that either has achieved, or

7

is achieving, the goal of all apple trees. A bad apple tree is one that is not. Further, those things that are conducive to or lead to an apple tree's health and production of fruit are said to be "good" for apple trees. Similarly, what injures the tree's health and production of fruit is said to be "bad" for apple trees.

It is worth noting that sometimes the goodness or badness of something for the tree is not always immediately apparent. In other words, what *appears* at first as bad, might in reality be good, or vice versa. For example, the pruning of an apple tree, which seems at first to damage it, ultimately is very conducive to its healthy growth.

Now while human nature is much more complex and noble than the nature of a tree, the same basic truths apply. *There is a natural goal or flourishing for human beings, and persons and their actions can be judged as good or bad in terms of this end.* What is the end of human persons? Aristotle answers that it is a life of complete virtue.

This point must be appreciated. Aristotle is not only saying that if one is to live well, virtue is necessary. He is saying that to live the whole range of virtues *is* to live well. And thus, since to live virtuously is the goal or end of human life, all other things in human life are ultimately judged as good or bad by their relation to virtue. What is conducive to virtue is good for a person, what hinders virtue is bad for a person. Thus, since ethics is all about living a good or happy human life, and a good or happy human life is a life of virtue, the bulk of Aristotle's *Nicomachean Ethics* is about virtues: What are the different kinds, how do we

develop them, etc.

But first we must step back and ask just what is a virtue? It is a *habit*, or a firm disposition to act in a certain kind of way. Experience shows that performing actions of a certain kind gives a person a sort of disposition or tendency to perform that kind of action again. This is why we "practice" various actions—such as playing the piano, or doing math problems—knowing that performing the actions, especially over and over again, makes it progressively easier to do them. We also know how important it is to practice correctly, for the way that we do the actions now is the way that we will tend to keep doing them. Aristotle would put it this way: Performing good actions, such as giving help to those in need, develops a habit of doing those good actions, while performing bad actions, such as stealing or lying, develops a habit of doing those bad actions.

The simplest definition of virtue then is that it is a *good* habit. Let us note what the *Catechism of the Catholic Church* says about the virtues known as cardinal virtues. These definitions are fundamentally the same as Aristotle's. Justice is "the moral virtue that consists in the constant firm will to give their due to God and neighbor." (*CCC* 1807) For an example of justice we can think of the employer who always pays his employees a living wage, even when he could get away with giving less. Fortitude, or courage, is "the moral virtue that ensures firmness in difficulties and constancy in the pursuit of the good." (*CCC* 1808) An example is a young mother whose husband has left her, who perseveres in fidelity to her marriage (assuming that it was

a valid marriage) and to the proper raising of her children. And temperance is "the moral virtue that moderates the attraction of pleasures and provides balance in the use of created goods." (*CCC* 1809) An example is the young person who disciplines the sexual desire and is committed to waiting for marriage. Note how in each instance the virtue is a firm disposition, or a kind of inclination in the soul. This is what is captured by the term "habit." Therefore, having a virtue, a good habit, means being firmly disposed to perform good actions, and to perform them with ease, and even joy. On the other hand, having a vice, or a bad habit, means being disposed to perform bad actions.

Having virtues or vices basically defines a person's moral character. To see this we must appreciate that most of our actions spring from our habits. Throughout the day a person acts and reacts primarily through established habits of acting and reacting. Consider yourself in the following situation. A five-dollar bill drops from the pocket of a person walking in front of you on a crowded street. After you pick it up, what will you do? The answer is: You will most likely do what you have done in other similar situations before. It would be very unusual, for instance, if a person who habitually returns property to its rightful owner (this is a part of justice), decides at that moment: "Today, I'm going to keep this for myself!" Similarly, a habitual thief (a form of injustice) will almost surely keep the five-dollar bill, considering today his lucky day. How does a person respond in a situation of danger or a situation of personal provocation? Does that person respond with courage and good temper,

or with cowardice and unbridled anger? The response will tend to be from habit: virtue or vice.

The "virtuous" persons are those who, through a desire to do what is good and right, have disciplined themselves and consistently directed their appetites or desires. These persons have gotten to the point where virtuous actions come very naturally, *because they are truly what they most want to do.* This is the profound beauty of virtue: Being good really becomes your own way of being. Good thoughts and actions flow from your deepest self; they flow from "who you are." This is hard for most of us to imagine because most of us are still far from being truly virtuous. Consider Mother Teresa of Calcutta. Her attitudes and actions toward the needy flowed from deep within her; they were an expression of her deepest desires, her truest self. And it showed. Those that she helped saw that she was more than a woman who just happened to help the poor. One day a dying man who was not Christian asked her, "Is Jesus like you?" She said, "No. But I try to be like Him." He responded, "Then I want to be a Christian too."

It should now be a little clearer why Aristotle insists that *to be virtuous is to be happy.* The virtuous persons are those who in everything act from a desire for what is truly good and noble. These persons have already overcome evil desires, since they now love all things according to their true worth. They always do the right things *and* enjoy doing them, since right things are what they most want to do. This is the fulfillment, the flourishing of human nature. This is the greatness for which God has made us. He wants

11

us to do the right things at all times and in all places. But more than this, he wants these actions to spring from our very core, from our own desire and love. Ultimately, he wants them to spring from love of him, and that is what it means to have the highest virtue of all—supernatural charity. Charity is a love for God, and also a love for neighbor, which should become the source and inspiration of all our actions. As a *supernatural* virtue (like faith and hope), it can only be acquired along with what Christians call sanctifying grace. Supernatural virtues are at the heart of the Christian's life. While many of the examples of virtues in this book will be of natural virtues, the ones Aristotle talks about, we will never lose sight of the fact that Christians understand a life well-lived, or a virtuous life, as including all the virtues. We will discuss charity at some length in the last chapter.

Aristotle makes a helpful distinction between two kinds of virtues. He divides them into "moral virtues" and "intellectual virtues." We can characterize moral virtues as the virtues related to how we desire and act. Intellectual virtues are virtues of the strictly intellectual or "knowing" power of man. We can characterize them as virtues of how we think or understand. The word "virtue" is often used as synonymous with moral virtue, for example justice, courage, and temperance. There are several intellectual virtues, the most important being wisdom. It is often not considered as a virtue. For instance, we might refer to a person as "virtuous *and* wise." In this usage, "virtuous" is meant as synonymous with "morally virtuous." This usage is not

a problem; there is a reason for it that we need not go into. Yet we should take note of this point, for when we consider the good human life as the "life of virtue," while we focus on moral virtue, we must not forget the intellectual virtues— particularly wisdom.

The moral virtues, again, are all about directing our desires toward what is truly good, so that what is truly good is, more and more, all that we really want. Someone might reasonably comment: "I would like to desire what is good, but I find myself desiring bad things. So I do what I can: I try to say no to my desires for bad things, and I try to force myself to do what I know is right. Isn't this enough? And besides, what more can I do?" This is very important. This person should be commended for these efforts. Yet what this person needs to see is that we are called to do more. Above and beyond doing good actions, we can and should try to *reform our desires, to change them for the better.* For example, in the realm of justice, our goal should not simply be always to give what is due to God and neighbor; it should be to do so out of a profound desire for justice, and ultimately out of love of God (again, "charity"). In the realm of almsgiving, the goal should be to give to the service of God, or to the needy, not out of a sense of duty, but out of a real desire to serve God and others. Can there be any doubt that this is how the widow whom Jesus praised in the Gospel gave her offering (see Mark 12:41-44)?

But what can a person do to re-form or change desires? As Christians we know that grace will play a major role in the reform of our wants and desires. The great St. Augus-

tine (354–430 A.D.) can be a role model for all of us. He wasted his early adult life in dissolute living. He indulged his sexual appetite, among other things. When he heard God's call, and determined to answer it, he realized that two things were required for him to change his life: unceasing prayer, and unceasing effort to change his habits. This is an excellent two-fold approach that we can imitate. We should first of all constantly pray to God to help us reform or change our desires. St. Augustine speaks of the desire that should be at the center of our hearts: the desire for God himself. He thanks God for having strengthened in him this desire:

> *Hear my prayer, O Lord; let not my soul fail under Thy discipline, nor let me fail in uttering to Thee Thy mercies: by them Thou hast drawn me out of all my most evil ways, that I should find more delight in Thee than in all the temptations I once ran after, and should love Thee more intensely, and lay hold upon Thy hand with all my heart's strength, and be delivered from every temptation unto the end. (Confessions I.15, p. 15)*

Would Our Lord Jesus ever resist the person who prays: strengthen my desire for you, *and* my desire for those other things that you want me to desire?

We must take other steps in addition to prayer to root out bad desires and to cultivate good ones. The main way to root out the bad ones is to starve them. This involves, for instance, avoiding occasions (such as certain movies, or cer-

tain parties) *and* persons, which draw us into indulging bad desires, such as desires for gossip or drunkenness, lying or sexual indulgence. The key here is to be willing to just say No. But at the same time that we are saying No to bad desires we should be saying Yes to good ones. In other words we *strive to replace bad desires with good ones.* Where there is a desire for injustice, cultivate a desire for justice. Where there is a desire for sexual misconduct, cultivate a desire for pure love and personal communion. Where there is cowardice, or an unwillingness to endure pain in pursuit of or in defense of some good, cultivate a greater love of the good to be sought or defended. The main way to cultivate good desires is to *expose ourselves to the goodness and beauty of truly good things.* Experience of what is good tends to evoke a desire for it. *Many who do not desire virtue have had little or no experience, first hand or otherwise, of the profound nobility and beauty of virtue.* Perhaps we can taste the beginnings of this in our own life. The nobility of virtue can also be experienced by turning to virtuous persons—either in person, or in writing or art. We should constantly seek to expose ourselves to virtue in all of these contexts. But the most unique and powerful experience of virtue in another person is the experience of virtue in a friend.

Now we are ready to start to think about friendship. (Note: For a fuller consideration of the nature of virtue see Romanus Cessario, O.P.. *The Moral Virtues and Theological Ethics*; Josef Pieper, *The Four Cardinal Virtues*; Tim Gray and Curtis Martin, *Boys to Men: The Transforming Power of Virtue*; and Peter Kreeft, *Back to Virtue.*)

TRUE FRIENDSHIP: Where Virtue Becomes Happiness

The Wisdom of the Ancients on Friendship

As we read Aristotle's *Nicomachean Ethics* in my Introduction to Philosophy course, my students always get a surprise as we approach the end of the ten chapters or "books." Two whole books (Eight and Nine) are devoted to examining friendship. Aristotle devotes more space to friendship than to any topic other than virtue. Knowing that he must give some explanation for spending so much time on friendship, Aristotle gets right to the heart of the matter as he opens Book Eight: "After what we have said, a discussion of friendship would naturally follow, since it is a virtue or implies virtue, and is besides most necessary with a view to living. For without friends no one would choose to live, though he had all other goods...." (Nicomachean Ethics, 1155a1-3)

Even if you had *all* other goods, you would *never* choose to live without friends. Is Aristotle simply making the obvious point that friends are good and everyone wants them? Clearly, he is saying this; but there is more. By the end of Book Nine, Aristotle has made clear that living in true friendship is equivalent to human happiness. This bears repeating: To live in true friendship is to live the good life, to be happy. But did we not just say that to be virtuous is to be happy? Yes. One of the main points of this book will be to understand how being virtuous and being a true friend are necessarily connected with each other. Indeed, they are practically the same thing.

Here someone might reasonably pose a big question. Even if this is what Aristotle thought, does he not, as a

pagan, miss certain important truths held by Christianity? This is an important question because it points to something that we should note. Divine revelation does show us truths that substantially alter the pagan worldview. But here we must keep our heads, and not throw the baby out with the bath water. St. Thomas Aquinas, a thirteenth century Dominican priest generally considered to be one of the greatest of theologians, is convinced that much of what the philosopher Aristotle teaches is simply what human reason can see about reality without the aid of God's special revelation in the Old and New Testaments. St. Thomas insists that what reason sees is never contradicted by divine revelation. God gave us reason and He intends that we use it to begin to understand ourselves and the world around us. What He reveals to us in the Old and New Testaments does not cast aside, but rather builds upon, what our reason can see on its own. This is why, in striving to understand and express complex theological issues, St. Thomas never hesitated to turn to the wisdom of the ancient philosophers.

Does divine revelation then fundamentally alter Aristotle's understanding of virtue and friendship? We will have a more sufficient answer in the final chapter of this book. For now, we can give a preliminary answer. Christians know that above the natural virtues of which Aristotle speaks there are *supernatural* virtues. They also know that the ultimate end or goal of the human person is to enjoy *friendship* with God in heaven. According to St. Thomas, the virtue of charity, which is a supernatural virtue and the perfection of the spiritual life, is defined in terms of friendship with

God. It seems then that *far from giving us cause to reject it, divine revelation gives us new impetus to try to understand Aristotle's notion of friendship.*

Christians seem to have two extra motives for examining *human* friendship (beyond the importance it has in itself), so well understood by Aristotle. First, an understanding of human friendship enhances our understanding of friendship with God. Indeed if we do not understand true human friendship, we will be hampered in understanding friendship with God. Second, and even more pressing, human friendship is the natural preparation for entering into friendship with God.

Consider the following. In his last heart-to-heart talk with the Apostles, we find the Lord Jesus saying these words:

> *This is my commandment, that you love one another as I have loved you. Greater love has no man than this, that a man lay down his life for his friends. You are my friends if you do what I command you. No longer do I call you servants, for the servant does not know what his master is doing; but I have called you friends, for all that I have heard from my Father I have made known to you.* (Jn. 15:12-15)

Christ reveals that He, the Lord of all, intends friendship with His creatures. What a stunning revelation! But if we do not have some knowledge and experience of true friendship, what will this revelation mean to us? What does a call

to friendship with Christ *mean?* It means something very specific and profound.

It helps to begin by trying to understand human friendship. It is clearly part of God's providential plan that for the most part, humans will first discover and exercise friendship with other human persons. This means that what we know of human friendship, and more importantly how we live out human friendship, is a critical preparation for the most important "relationship" in our life: friendship with God. To gain insight into friendship, in this book we will turn to what wise and virtuous persons, particularly Aristotle and St. Thomas Aquinas, have discovered from their experience of human friendship.

Yet one might ask: "Is it really necessary to *study* the nature of friendship? Friendship is so natural to human beings that we can count on it just happening through the normal course of events, without special effort." Here I answer with a firm denial. I grant that humans have a natural desire for friendship, as well as a natural "sense" of friendship. But true friendship does not simply happen. Ongoing, intentional effort is needed. True friendship is an *art*, or a habit, which must be developed through practice. While the *beginnings* of it do sometimes just "happen," or fall into place, true friendship is the result of intentional striving. Mozart had the *beginnings* of musical greatness by natural endowment and the surroundings of his upbringing. Yet his excellence in composition was the fruit of studied, persistent effort. Friendship, like great music, is a masterpiece; it happens because persons know what they want, and thus

19

develop the skills called virtues, necessary to achieve their great goal.

It becomes clear now why an explicit *study* of the nature of friendship is very helpful in building true friendships. Friendship, as a kind of masterpiece, must be developed in a specific way. The more we understand the nature of that for which we are striving, the better we are able to strive for and attain it. Would anyone consider pursuing greatness as a composer, without first studying principles of composition? And how much more important, and profound, is friendship!

While I have suggested that our call to friendship with God provides the greatest motive to examine human friendship, it is not the only motive. Bearing in mind Aristotle's point that to live out true friendship is to live the good life, we should not be surprised (although many will be) that friendship is essentially connected with all the most important things in life. In examining different aspects of friendship, this book will touch on several of these most important things.

Here is a brief overview of this book. Chapter two distinguishes the kinds of friendship and focuses on the nature of the most important kind of friendship, "virtuous friendship." Chapter three argues that friendship is a major determinant of a person's self-image, and therefore also a major determinant of who that person really is. Chapter four considers how through friendship a person forms habits—virtues or vices, and thus develops character for better or for worse. Chapter five considers how friendship is

more than a private matter between friends themselves, and how a good civil society both requires virtuous friendships among citizens, and at the same time, plays an important role in bringing about good friendships. Chapter six argues that virtuous friendships help assure that young men and women can and will engage in timely and honorable courtship, and that they will be prepared for marriage. And finally, chapter seven examines friendship with God as the root of divine and natural law, the perfection of the spiritual life, and the very end or goal of human life.

Practicing Friendship

Questions for discussion:

1. What does Socrates mean when he says "the most important thing is not life, but the good life?"

2. What are virtues, and why are they so important in life?

3. Why will it be helpful to *study* friendship?

Questions for personal reflection:

1. Sirach 6:15 says: "There is nothing so precious as a faithful friend, and no scales can measure his excellence." Do I hold friendship (not simply the person who is a friend, but friendship with this person) to be among the most precious things in my life, indeed, something whose excellence is beyond measure?

2. Do I *act* as though friendship is that precious? How can others see in my actions that I hold friendship to be that precious?

3. How often do I think about what friendship is, and how to develop it?

Friendship and the Kinds of Friendship

For there is a friend who is such at his own convenience, but will not stand by you in your day of trouble.... A faithful friend is a sturdy shelter: he that has found one has found a treasure.

~ Sirach 6:8,15

What is friendship? Before answering this question, we must consider the question itself. (It is always helpful to understand what is being asked before answering a question!) In one of the famous Platonic dialogues, Socrates asks a man named Euthyphro to answer the question: What is piety? Euthyphro, who has a reputation for wisdom in religious matters, answers the question with haste and confidence. He answers by giving an example of a pious action. Socrates explains to Euthyphro that to give an example of something, while not irrelevant, is not the same as to answer the question: What is it? "Bear in mind then," he says, "that I did not bid you tell me one or two of

the many pious actions but the form itself that makes all pious actions pious." (Euthyphro 6d) There is some "form," or as we would say "nature" or "essence" that all pious actions have in common. To point to that nature is truly to answer the question, What is piety? Now it is in a good *definition* that we express our understanding of what a thing is, or the nature of a thing. And, as Euthyphro learns in the rest of the dialogue, it is much easier to point to an example than to give a good definition.

But perhaps the ability to point to examples is all we need. Do we really need a definition? The Euthyphro dialogue contains the answer to this question. It becomes clear that an inability to give a good definition of piety casts doubt upon the ability to recognize what is or is not an example of piety. How can Euthyphro be sure that a particular action is pious if he is not quite sure *what piety is*?

What have we learned about our question: What is friendship? In asking this question we are seeking the nature of friendship, or, just what it is that makes a relationship be a friendship. If we answer this question, then we *know* we can recognize which relationships are, and which are not, friendships. This is not an easy task. Let us turn to the wise for help.

Friendship in General
As Aristotle begins his consideration of friendship in the *Nicomachean Ethics*, he takes it as a given that friendship essentially involves love or affection for some object. Of course, there are many instances of love or affection for

some object that are not instances of friendship. In which instances of affection would we say that there is a "friendship?" Aristotle points to four characteristics that distinguish a "friend" from other objects of affection. First, among objects of affection, there are only certain ones *to which* or *for which* you can have good will. To have good will for something means to wish something well. He gives the example of wine. One might have affection for wine, but one does not "wish wine well"—one would not say to it, "I hope all is going well for you." Second, among objects of affection, only certain ones can reciprocate, or return, good will. For instance, while one can "wish well" to a baby, a baby cannot reciprocate good will. Third, among objects of affection, only certain ones actually do reciprocate good will. I can have good will toward a neighbor, who is capable of returning good will but who in fact does not return it. Fourth, among situations of reciprocal good will, there is not always mutual recognition of the good will. For instance, my neighbor and I might have some kind of good will for each other, but we might not realize that the other returns it.

These points lead to a common-sense, general characterization of friendship. Aristotle concludes: "To be friends, then, they must be mutually recognized as bearing goodwill and wishing well to each other." (*Nicomachean Ethics*, 1156a3-5) Aristotle has led his reader to be able to formulate a *general definition of friendship*: It is a mutually recognized relationship of affection that occurs between human persons, human persons who have the maturity to bear

some kind of good will for one another. But just what does it mean to have good will for another? At this point, Aristotle has left this vague because there are in fact different kinds of friendships, depending on the kind of "good will" or "wishing well" that is present. This makes sense because if there are different kinds of "friendship," then the characterization of friendship itself must be general enough to include the various kinds. Aristotle next distinguishes between different kinds of friendship according to the kind of "good" that is willed in each case.

Basic Kinds of Friendships

Aristotle distinguishes three objects of affection or love: the pleasant, the useful, and the honorable good or the virtuous good. Each of these can be the "good" which is mutually willed in a friendship, and so there are three kinds of friendship that correspond to these three goods. We can call them the "pleasant friendship," the "useful friendship," and the "virtuous friendship." Let us note from the start that these are *not* mutually exclusive kinds; they are basic types. As we proceed we will see how helpful it is to distinguish these types.

In the pleasant friendship, two people find each other's company to be pleasant, or pleasurable. This friendship is basically about "having a good time" together. What each sees and values in the other is that the other is the cause of some pleasure for himself. "Pleasure" here refers to the level of what appeals to the senses. This friendship is particularly found among young people. Young people tend to

focus more on pleasure and accordingly develop relation-ships based upon it. A good example of this is two frater-nity brothers who have a friendship primarily because they party together.

In the useful friendship, each person receives some ben-efit from the presence or actions of the other, and this is the basis for the relationship. Many business relationships are useful friendships because each person provides for the needs of the other. Another example is a relationship be-tween two high-school students, where one helps the other study, in return for access to the "in" crowd.

The key divide between the kinds of friendship is be-tween the first two kinds on the one hand, and virtuous friendship on the other. The best way to introduce the "vir-tuous friendship" is to stop and consider what is shared in common by the first two kinds. The most important shared characteristic is in fact what is *not* there, what is absent. In the pleasant friendship and the useful friendship, the friends are loved neither (a) for their own sake, nor (b) because of who they are in themselves.

Let us consider (a). In the first two kinds of friendship, each person focuses on what can be derived from the re-lationship: some good received from the other person, ei-ther pleasure, or utility. The person is not really concerned about the well-being of the other. This does not contradict Aristotle's assertion that in all friendships there is some "good" willed *to the other*, because the person does want to be pleasant or useful to the other. But the person wants this ultimately because it is desirable for the other to be pleas-

ant or useful in return. The relationship is still based upon what each gets from the other.

As regards (b) where the friends are not loved because of who they are in themselves, what we find in these friendships is that each person focuses on what is "incidental" to the other, as opposed to really seeing them for who they are. The business relationship is not based on the "inner persons" of those involved, such as the baker and the farmer from whom the baker purchases grain. It is based on the reality that the farmer is useful to the baker, and vice versa. Note that the farmer's usefulness to the baker, and the baker's usefulness to the farmer, are not defining features of who they are as persons. To know that Farmer Jane is a woman who can reliably supply grain for baking is in fact to know very little about Jane. And to know that Baker Tom bakes outstanding biscuits from that grain is to know very little about Tom. A relationship based on these characteristics is not really based on the persons in themselves. Similarly in a pleasant friendship, a person's pleasantness, or the ability to bring about a "good time," is not at the heart of who the person is. It is for this reason that we say in these friendships persons are not loved because of who they are in themselves, but rather are loved because of something incidental, something that they just happen to be or do.

Does this mean that the first two kinds of friendship are bad and should be avoided? The answer is a definite No. These kinds of friendships are natural, and they have their place in everyone's life. What is very important, however, is to recognize these for what they are. Aristotle calls

them "incidental friendships." What he means is that they are not friendships in the full and most important sense. They can be called friendships because in a way they fit the general definition above, but they fall short of what full or true friendship is all about. Making this distinction is a big step toward understanding the most important kind of friendship.

Most of us have had a relationship that we thought was a "friendship" but then discovered that in some important sense it was not. What is it that we discovered? Usually it is one of the two things just mentioned regarding the pleasant or useful friendships. I have often heard someone say: He wasn't really looking out for *my* good after all; or, She just didn't appreciate me for *who I am*. This can be a devastating experience (we will consider why this can be so devastating in the next chapter). The problem here is that one or both persons thought there was a full friendship, or a "virtuous friendship," as Aristotle calls it, and it turns out that there wasn't one. Instead, there was something much more like a pleasant friendship or a useful friendship.

So what is full friendship or "virtuous friendship?"

Friendship in the Full Sense: Virtuous Friendship

Aristotle says: "Now those who wish well to their friends for their own (the other's) sake are most truly friends; for they do this by reason of their own (the other's) nature and not incidentally." (*Nicomachean Ethics*, 1156b9-10) Here is the flipside of what was said about the first two kinds of friendship. In a virtuous friendship the friends love the other a)

for their own sake, and b) because of who the persons are in themselves, that is, not because of something incidental to them. The first point is very simple, but of the utmost significance. True friends (and by "true" here we mean in the full sense, this third sense) are those who love the other in the sense of wanting what is best for them. They are able to transcend simply looking out for their own advantage. Here one's desire, extending beyond private fulfillment, is for the fulfillment, the flourishing of the friend. The second point, that the friends see the other for who they are is closely linked to the first. How can someone really desire *my* good, if that person *only* sees me as a good source of fun or as a smart study partner? I may be very funny, and very helpful in studying, but only the person who sees beyond that, and cares beyond that, to what is deep inside of me, can be my true friend.

But why does Aristotle call this "virtuous friendship?" We have seen that friendships are distinguished according to the "good" which is willed. Again, what is willed in the pleasant friendship is pleasure, in some sense "for the other" person, but ultimately so that pleasure returns to the first person. However, pleasure is not only willed or desired as something still to be achieved more and more. It is also the *basis* of the relationship because it is what got the relationship started. The friendship began when two people, such as the fraternity brothers, found themselves enjoying the same things and enjoying one another.

Now we can begin to see the profundity of Aristotle's notion of full friendship. Full friendship is that relation-

ship of mutual good will that is based upon the virtue, or true goodness, of two persons. It is *based upon* virtue because this kind of relationship can only begin when virtue or goodness is already present. It is also based on virtue inasmuch as virtue or goodness is the main thing that is willed, desired, and sought in the relationship. What does a true friend want most of all—the virtue of the friend: that it be, and increase! This fits with the insight above that a friend wants what is best for his or her friend. As discussed earlier, virtue is always what is best for a person, period.

But is it really true that a person must already be virtuous in order to have true friendship? Aristotle is insistent on this point. Of this third and most important kind of friendship, Aristotle says that it "is the friendship of men who are good, and alike in virtue." (*Nicomachean Ethics,* 1156b6) True friendship requires that a person already be, to some real extent, virtuous. We can put it like this: *To the extent that a person is virtuous, and only to that extent, can that person have a share in true friendship.* In other words, one need not be perfectly virtuous in order to have a true friendship; yet at the same time, *to the extent that one fails in virtue, one fails in the ability to have a full friendship.* Why is this so?

It is the virtuous person, and only the virtuous person, who really has the ability to desire and pursue the good of another person. To say to another person: "I want what is best for you" is one thing. To mean it is another. And to be able to help him achieve it is yet another. Anyone can say it. It takes some virtue to mean it. It takes much virtue truly to do it.

Recall our example of Susan and Mary. Mary would un-

doubtedly declare that she wants what is best for Susan. Yet, when it comes to a situation like the evening of the car wreck, Mary's inability really to want what is best for Susan comes to the fore.

Allow me to qualify these assertions through explanation. Let us first consider the virtuous person, and then the unvirtuous person. The virtuous person has become virtuous through much effort (and grace). This person habitually deliberates about (that is, rationally considers) what constitutes a *good life, and* desires and acts in accordance with what he or she has seen to be truly good. Through habitually choosing what is truly good, especially the higher goods of the soul, this person is singularly capable of recognizing true goodness in other persons, and of choosing that good over lesser goods such as pleasure and utility. It is precisely this person who is able to transcend selfish desire and truly desire and act for the good of the other. This is an amazing moment, a wonderful feat. This person, having centered a life on what is truly good, as opposed to self-gratification, is capable of an unselfish, other-centered stance. Further, this person knows from experience what is involved in pursuing the virtuous life, and through this familiarity is just the one to help another along the same way.

What about the unvirtuous? Very few persons are completely self-centered. Persons who have not grown in virtue might be able to say "I want what is best for you" *and* mean it as regards, for instance, their own family, because usually people have some real affection for their family members.

They might also mean it as regards others with whom they have grown up, or people in their "gang," etc. But a close examination reveals two major reasons why those without virtue are paralyzed as regards true friendship: a) they are normally self-centered, and b) they are basically unable to help others become happy.

Let us consider the problem of being self-centered. We noted above that the virtuous persons are those who have centered their lives, not on selfish desires, but on the higher or true human good, according to what sound reason discerns. Is this not the fundamental goal in the raising of children? Parents train children to use their reason to discern what is truly good in life, what is most important, and the ways to desire and act in accord with it. This requires effort on the part of parents *and* children. It requires effort because in order to live a good life, one must form habits (virtues) of thought, desire, and action that are often contrary to some inclinations of our fallen nature. The sure sign of an unformed teenager, or an immature adult, is a habitual inability or unwillingness to set aside selfish desires for the sake of the higher goods. It is the unvirtuous person, then, who is largely incapable of a true other-centered attitude, a true willing of the good of the other for the other's own sake, which is the heart of friendship. This becomes all the more apparent the more we realize that friendships demand a willingness to sacrifice, to give of self—something that experience makes eminently clear.

The second reason that the unvirtuous person is para-

lyzed as regards full friendship is caused by an inability to help others become truly happy. A main topic in the fourth chapter will be how friends help one another to grow in virtue, and thus in happiness. One who has not grown in virtue has either not discerned what the truly good life is, or is unwilling to pursue it. It is obvious that in either case, this person is not going to be able to help others to grow in virtue. But helping another grow in virtue is essential to friendship. It is here that the enormous tragedy of not being virtuous, or not living the truly good life, starts to become clear. Deep in our hearts, we all desire not only to be happy, but also to help others to be happy, and to be happy together with them. The unvirtuous person is frustrated on all counts. Let us be clear on this. *All of us, to the extent that we fail in virtue, are frustrated on all these counts.* This should become more and more evident as we proceed.

Let us consider another example in which the lack of virtue ruins the possibility of true friendship. A young man named James is living an unchaste lifestyle. He is a nice young man and a good college student. But for him premarital sex is a reasonable option, as long as both persons act voluntarily. James enjoys spending time with his dorm mate Patrick, and wants to have a friendship with him. But we have seen that true friendship is about persons pursuing the good life together. Now one of the main moral challenges that all young men must face is the challenge to control sexual desires. Since James is fundamentally failing in this area—or in other words, he is not willing to control

his desires (which is very different than a young man who is fundamentally in control of his desires, even though he still occasionally fails in certain ways)—he cannot truly pursue the good life with Patrick. Patrick cannot turn to him and count on him for support in his own struggles in this area. On that Saturday when Patrick needs the support of a true friend as he makes his evening plans, James is not going to be there for him.

One objection that is often raised against the claim that virtue is necessary for friendship is this: How can any of us really be friends, since we are so far from perfection in virtue? This is a critical point. We said above that to the extent that a person is virtuous, and only to that extent, can that person have a share in true friendship. Likewise, to the extent that a person fails in virtue, that person lacks the capacity for true friendship. Thus, there are degrees of capability for true friendship. Indeed, there is no upper limit: There is always room to grow in virtue and thus friendship. But there must be a bottom limit, below which there is no real capability for true friendship. I would put it this way: The minimum requirement for being capable of true friendship is that a person is dedicated to the pursuit of virtue or holiness, making it the focus of life. We would do well to bear in mind that Aristotle held that true friendships are rare, and this for one main reason: Virtuous persons are rare. But this is not a reason for despair. Rather, we press onward, with hope, in pursuit of friendship, since "He that has found one, has found a treasure," (Sir. 6:15) and "with God all things are possible." (Mt. 19:26)

A Few More Points about Virtuous Friendship

Virtuous friendship is the focus of this book, because it is this friendship that we mean when we speak of "true friendship." There is much more to say about this kind of friendship, but here, let us briefly note just a few more points about it.

Although Aristotle distinguishes between pleasant friendship, useful friendship, and virtuous friendship, he is careful to point out that virtuous friendships have *all* these qualities: pleasure, usefulness, and the virtuous good. Persons who have the virtuous or full friendship find one another most pleasant and most useful. Indeed, what or who is more pleasant or useful in the most important sense than the virtuous person? For this reason, Aristotle proceeds to assert that virtuous friendships are the most stable, long lasting, and noble of friendships.

Pleasant or useful friendships, on the other hand, tend to be short-lived. Again, unlike the friendships that are based upon who the persons are in themselves, these friendships are *based upon* pleasantness or utility. The pleasantness and utility of a person are things that easily change, and thus these relationships come and go more easily. This is particularly apparent in young people, whose friendships tend to be pleasant friendships. The person whom a nine-year old, or even a teenager, finds pleasant can change weekly. And the fraternity brothers, who only enjoy partying together, find that their relationship basically ends when the party season is over.

Aristotle expresses the unique and beautiful nature of virtuous friendship with the notion of "another self." "But the good man feels toward his friend as toward himself, since his friend is another self." (*Nicomachean Ethics*, 1170b5) Think of this. One looks upon another person as though that other were one's very self! This is the height of other-centeredness. For the friend says to the friend: It is as important to me that you are happy as that I am happy. When you flourish, when you are blessed, I rejoice with you, for it is as though it is my flourishing and blessedness. When you fail or suffer, I fail and suffer. All that you enjoy or endure, we enjoy or endure together.

The great story in Scripture of the friendship between David and Jonathan illustrates this point. Scripture records that "the soul of Jonathan was knit to the soul of David, and Jonathan loved him as his own soul." (1 Sam. 18:1)

Does this mean that friends come to have precisely the same likes and dislikes? While in some profound sense the answer is Yes (which we will return to later), we can say No: Friends retain their individual likes and dislikes as regards many things. But here is an opportunity to observe the unique unifying nature of friendship. Suppose a man loves to hike in the great outdoors. He does not expect all his true friends to love hiking too. There is, nevertheless, a sense in which any true friend of his will come to love it. He will love it *through* him, or *in* his loving it. The friend may never go hiking himself, but he loves *his friend's going hiking*, simply because as another self, he shares in his loves.

TRUE FRIENDSHIP: Where Virtue Becomes Happiness

We noted above that Aristotle warns us that virtuous friendships are rare, particularly because virtuous persons are rare. We would do well to remember yet another reason they are rare: They take time and a sustained, conscious effort.

A Final Note about the Kinds of Friendship

The most important division between the kinds of friendship is the distinction between the first two kinds, pleasant and useful friendships, and the third kind, virtuous friendship. It is critical that we understand the nature of virtuous friendship. It is the living out of *this* friendship that, for Aristotle, is equivalent to the good life.

But do not worry if you find yourself wondering: Do I really have any friends like that? We *should* wonder about that, and then do all that we can to improve our situation. We noted earlier that Aristotle's division of the kinds of friendship is not three mutually exclusive kinds. For instance, virtuous friendships usually have grown out of one of the first two kinds. This growth is slow; it takes time. Often the growth only gets so far. This is because, as we have emphasized, growth in true friendship is limited by growth in virtue. Many friendships are somewhere in between. They have elements of virtuous friendship, and one or both of the other two. But this is not the same as Aristotle's point that virtuous friendship is also most pleasant and most useful. The "mixture" we are speaking of now is a weak or limited virtuous friendship; it is one that is not fully *based in* who the person really is, and in virtue. The other

40

person is not as fully "another self" as that person can and should be.

Our goal here is to understand the fullness of friendship so that we can make an explicit effort to grow in this kind of friendship. It is for this that we naturally long. It is also this friendship that most prepares us for friendship with God, since our friendship with God should have the characteristics of virtuous friendship, raised to the highest degree.

Practicing Friendship

Questions for discussion:

1. What is the main way to distinguish between the first two kinds of friendship (pleasant and useful friendships), and the third kind, true friendship?

2. Why is it that one can only be as good a friend as one is virtuous? In other words, why is it that bad persons, or non-virtuous persons, cannot really be friends?

3. Are the first two kinds of friendship bad and to be avoided?

4. What is happening when one of the first two kinds of friendship grows into true friendship?

5. What do we mean by saying that a friend is another self? Read 1 Sam. 18:1-4 on the friendship of David and Jonathan.

Questions for personal reflection:

1. How well prepared am I for being a true friend? For instance, will my friends be inspired by my example to pursue virtue? Do I think in terms of living a good life *together with* my friends?

2.   What can I do to improve my preparedness?

3.   To what extent do I have true friendship in my life?

Exercise:
Read the following texts about the greatest Old Testament friendship—that of David and Jonathan. 1 Sam. 18:1-4; 1 Sam. 20; 1 Sam. 23:1-18; 2 Sam. 1. Look for the characteristics of true friendship.

Friendship and Self-Image

A faithful friend is an elixir of life.

~ Sirach 6:16

I will begin with an assertion that I will explain and defend in the next two chapters. Your friends profoundly affect who you are. I intend this to mean two distinct things. First, friends are a major determinant of your self-image; and your self-image, or how you see yourself, is a major part of who you are. Second, it is with friends that you form habits and develop your character. This second point will be the subject of the next chapter. In this chapter the focus is on friendship and self-image.

Let us consider first what "self-image" means, and then turn to consider the effect that others, especially friends, have on our self-image.

How Do You See Yourself?

By "self-image" I mean first of all how one "sees" oneself. While this can, of course, refer to such things as seeing

oneself as sociable or attractive, our main concern here is with a deeper level of seeing oneself. Do you see yourself as lovable? Do you see your life as worth living? Do you see yourself as belonging somewhere? Would you really be missed? Do you really have something to contribute to a community? Perhaps not every person actually poses these questions. Yet nevertheless, you know, at least in an unconscious way, that the answer to these questions is either Yes or No, and that your answer makes all the difference in the world to who you are.

Consider for a moment how important this matter is. Is not a young woman who sees her life as full of meaning, and herself as belonging to a strong community of some kind, a profoundly different person than a young woman who wonders if it would *really* make a difference to people if she disappeared? In an age in which the suicide rate has reached an unprecedented level, this matter takes on special significance. One's self-understanding or self-image is an essential aspect of who one is.

But where does one's self-image come from? How is it developed? This is a very rich and complex question for which there are no simple answers. Nevertheless, there are a few basic points that seem to be beyond dispute. First, how *other people* see and treat a person is a major determining factor in that person's self-image. We can first consider the human person as a child. It is obvious that children do not come into the world with an understanding of the world and their place in it. Children are dependent on those around them to communicate first of all by actions and lat-

er by words, a "vision" of themselves and the world. This is not to suggest that children are completely passive and play no role in the development of self-image. Certainly that is not the case. However, children are fundamentally dependent on others to "show them to themselves," to open their eyes to what it means to be a person—and to be this particular person!

As we mature this dependence on others lessens, but it does not cease. Even mature adults depend upon others to help them see themselves. For instance, to perceive clearly whether I am succeeding in my profession I must depend upon the judgment of others—not just any others, but others in my profession. I particularly depend upon others who excel in my profession. Similarly, to know whether I am living up to my calling to be a good husband, I must turn to others—first of all my wife, but also to other husbands, perhaps ones more experienced than I am. And finally, to know whether I am succeeding in living a "good life," indeed especially here, I fundamentally depend on others.

Friends and Truly Seeing Yourself

We should note that certain persons are better suited to play this role than others. When I ask myself how is my game of tennis or how good a plumber am I, I turn to the appropriate experts to help me form my self-image. But what about the most serious matters of all: Does my life have meaning? Am I living a good life? etc. Are there "experts" in these matters? Thank God there are. But who are these experts? The great Greek philosophers and Sacred

Scripture use the same word to describe them: They are the "wise." They are the ones who know the meaning of life, what true human greatness is. As Socrates says, they understand what is most important in life and live accordingly, which is to say that they live a virtuous life.

But we must go further if we are to give an adequate answer to the question: Which "others" are best suited to help us form a true self-image? What we saw in the last chapter about true friendship gives us the means to look more deeply into this question. Let us recall the two characteristics of true friendship that distinguished it from the other kinds of friendship. First, the true friend sees friends "as the persons are in themselves," which is to say that the person really understands the other. And second, the person seeks what is good for the friend, or in other words, loves the person "for the person's own sake."

Now, surely the person who can most help us see ourselves is the one who is wise *and* who sees us for who we are, as individual persons. What we are saying then is this: *A true friend is the one most apt to help us form a true self-image.* We must always bear in mind the essential connection between being a true friend and being a good person—that is, being virtuous. The true friend has the two main requirements for being the best one to help persons see themselves. Knowing the meaning of life, this person is dedicated to living out virtue *and* can see you as the individual person you are. The person can see because of having taken the time to get to know you—having broken bread together with you, as one expression says. It is probably to this person that

you have entrusted your deepest secrets, hopes, and fears. And further, this person has the secret key to insight into your person: love for you.

There is a wonderful phrase about this in Latin: *Ubi amor, ibi oculus*—Where there is love, there is the power to see (literally, "an eye"). Does anyone know you the way that one who loves you knows you? There are many reasons why love produces insight into persons. We can consider a few of them. One who loves you is willing to take the time to get to know you as you really are. One interested in friendship of utility or pleasure might make an effort to get to know you, but since the person's primary desire is to achieve an advantage, that person will not really have an "eye" for you yourself, but rather for what you can do in return. This can also be seen in the related fact that one who does not love tends not to have a "forgiving eye."

Even the most virtuous men often fall short of what they can be. To really know you, a person must be willing to look beyond your shortcomings. It is always a friend who is most forgiving. The friend sees failings precisely as a falling short of what you can do. We can put it this way: the friend is willing and able to look beyond present shortcomings, to what you *can be*. (This points to a beautiful insight into how God loves us.)

This is a precious truth, that the "lover" (that is, one who truly loves me, as a true friend does) can most truly see me for who I am. But we can take this one step further. In a very profound sense, the true friend is especially capable of *showing me* truths about myself that I am incapable of

seeing on my own, or through others that do not love me. The first such truth is that I am lovable. Let us set aside for a moment the distinction between those who are striving for virtue and those who are not. *Every human person is profoundly lovable.* This is evident in the fact that all persons are created in the image and likeness of God, and have been loved, in all their particularity, by God from all eternity. Jesus Christ is the Good Shepherd who gives His life for His sheep, each and every one of them.

Perhaps the most fundamental truth that human persons need to see about themselves is the reality of God's love for them. But how does one come to know this love? Here we begin to enter into a wonderful and mysterious aspect of divine providence. In the natural course of events, one normally discovers first that one is loved by other *human* persons. This is the natural foundation for the much greater discovery, through the assistance of supernatural grace, that one is loved by God Himself. But what is meant by "foundation" here? Are we putting a limit on the grace of God by suggesting that being loved by human persons is in some sense a prerequisite for realizing God's love for us? Let us be clear on this important point: God's grace can overcome many obstacles. Thus even a person who has never been loved by any other person *can* come to realize God's love through a miracle of God's grace. This truth, however, ought not take away from our appreciation of another truth: Human love normally plays a central role in the discovery of God's love for us. According to the design of God Himself, human persons usually discover their lov-

ableness through human love—other human persons loving them.

We can say that God has put a great "burden" upon the shoulders of humans, that they must in a very real way show one another their lovableness, or, show one another that they are loved by God. But what a precious burden this is! In God's providence human persons are the conduit, the instrument God uses to show other human persons how much *He* loves them!

We were making the point that the true friend is the one who is especially capable of showing me truths about myself that I cannot see on my own. Of course, beyond showing me that I am lovable, the friend shows me specific ways in which I am lovable, and also ways in which I am not lovable. The friend helps me to realize how and when I fall short of being the person I am called to be. For example, if Susan from our story had through a momentary weakness decided to lie to her father about the car wreck, a true friend would have responded by calling her back to her true self. "Susan, you are not the kind of person to do that!"

At this point a reasonable objection might be raised: Do I really need a true *friend* to help me see myself? Perhaps a loving family suffices for me to form a true self-image. Of course, all that has been said here should be taken as implying that the love experienced in the family is the natural and all-important starting point in the proper development of a true self-image. Experience, however, shows that family alone does not suffice. Even while still a child, and more and more so as one grows older, the human person looks

beyond the family to develop relationships.

Consider a girl who complains: "I don't have any friends." Her mother responds: "Well sure you do, you have Daddy and me and your brother and sister." The girl retorts: "You all don't count; you have to like me, you're my family!"

It does no dishonor to the beauty and importance of family relationships to recognize that the girl has a point. It is very important that this girl appreciate the true love that her family has for her, but it is also important that she begin to experience true friendship outside the family. True friendship that comes from a peer outside the family provides a special completion or furthering of the love experienced inside the family. It has a special quality of "gratuity"—having been completely freely given, and a quality of "objectivity" that love from inside the family does not necessarily have.

This point is seen perhaps most clearly in one unique instance of true friendship: the true friendship that should develop between spouses. It is often the great joy of a happily married person to say, "Only now am I most fully discovering who I am, through the love of my spouse."

In summary, through true human friendship we naturally come to see who we are, and who we are called to be. We come to have a sense of self as one who is lovable and worthy of the attention and affirmation of others. This should be appreciated if we are to appreciate the place of friendship in human life, and if we are to appreciate the importance of having true friends. One of the main causes of the tragedy of a person's not having a true self-image is

the lack of true friends.

Our treatment of friendship and self-image will not be complete unless we note that bad friends can actually create a bad self-image. We should first say a word about what a "bad friend" is. As noted earlier, it is not bad to have what Aristotle called friendships of pleasure or utility, as long as they are recognized for what they are. In other words, persons should realize that it is not with *these people* that they really share their lives. There is a problem, however, when persons want to share their lives together, but do not pursue the good life together. Or another way of putting this, is that a "bad friend" is one with whom you share your life, but who draws you away from the truly good life, from virtue.

We will consider the influence of bad friends more in the next chapter, but here let us simply note their negative effect on self-image. It is the true friend who can see you for who you are, and love you for your own sake. The bad friend cannot and does not do this. This person, then, is in no position to help you see yourself. Indeed, a bad friend often causes a person to have a skewed vision of self, as well as of the meaning of life itself. How does this happen? The bad friend does not pursue true goodness. As a result, this person tends to approve and encourage things in you that ought to be disapproved and discouraged, and disapprove things in you that ought to be approved. Think of the fraternity brother who praises his buddy for his ability to out-drink the other guys. "You're amazing, you're the best." Again, it is natural that we see ourselves through the

eyes of our friends. In the case of the bad friend, we simply will not be seeing ourselves in the right light.

Love for Those Who Do Not Pursue Virtue

I said above that when we consider the lovableness of *all* persons, we can set aside the distinction between those who are striving to live a good life and those who are not. Let us close this chapter with a little more consideration of this point. It would be fitting, although sadly it is often not the case, that all persons have loving families, as well as friends outside the family. Love from family and friends would take the form of appreciating the persons in their particularity, and wanting what is best for them. These two aspects are included in any true love for a person: an appreciation or affirmation *and* a wanting what is best. Thus, to say "I love you" is to say, "I affirm you as good, and I want more good for you."

Again, all persons—even those who can be called evil persons—are worthy of love. God loves each and every one of us. In other words, He says to us: I affirm your goodness (which I have given you!), and I want you to grow in goodness. But *true love* (whether in God or in us) *does not affirm or approve of evil.*

What happens when one loves a person who pursues an evil path in life? One should have this disposition toward the other (but does not necessarily put it in words): "I affirm you as the particular person, the particular creature of God that you are, and I want what is best for you. But since you are not pursuing what is best for yourself, I cannot approve

of how you are living. I want nothing more than for you to discover who you really are, and what you are called to be. I want you to pursue the good life of virtue." Of course, this person will do everything possible to aid the other in changing for the better. Prayer is always the first, and at times the only, recourse. "Lord, help us, and all those we love, to live the life that you call us to live."

We saw in the last chapter that true friendship requires that both friends pursue the virtuous life. Indeed, friendship is all about pursuing the good life *together*. In the preceding reflection, we see this same point yet again. If the unvirtuous person who is truly loved by another person does not start to turn his or her life around, then the person is in effect rejecting the offer of friendship from the first person. To the loving call to "be all that you are called to be," this person responds: "I want to live my life my own way." This leaves the person in a lonely and tragic isolation. Two persons pursuing virtue, on the other hand, can be united in their pursuit, and can continually call one another to new heights. This is the subject of the next chapter.

Practicing Friendship

Questions for discussion:

1. Is self-image an important part of who a person is? Why?

2. Where does self-image come from?

3. What is the role (or should be the role) of friends in the development of self-image?

Questions for personal reflection:

1. Is my self-image true to my self? How am I too critical of my self? How am I not critical enough of my self?

2. How do I receive affirmation from family and friends? Do I take it for granted, or do I receive it with gratitude?

3. How do I express affirmation for my loved ones? Do I assist them in true character assessment? How, or how not?

Friendship and Virtue: Moral and Intellectual

Whoever fears the Lord directs his friendship aright, for as he is, so is his neighbor.

~ Sirach 6:17

The thesis of this chapter is that it is with "friends" that persons form habits and develops their character, for better or for worse. I put the word "friends" here in quotation marks because I am using the word very broadly. Here I mean anyone with whom persons share their lives. Almost everyone has "friends" in this sense. These are the people that a person turns to in times of rejoicing and in times of trial (how these people will respond at these times will vary). It is with these people, with these "friends," that a person develops habits, either good ones, called virtues, or bad ones, called vices. What kinds of habits are formed depends, of course, on several things, but most especially

on the moral character of the persons involved. For it is a fundamental truth about human nature that people want to live and act "together with" their friends, and that they will tend to act as their friends act. It should be clear that the choice of friends is just about the most important decision a person makes. A person who has what we have been calling true friends will tend to form good habits, or virtues. A person who does not have good friends but rather, in place of good friends, associates with people not pursuing virtue, will tend to form vices. The importance of this truth must not be underestimated.

What Do Friends Do?

Before turning to a more specific consideration of how true friends grow in virtue, let us turn again to Aristotle for an insight that will help us understand a little more about true friendship. In his treatment of friendship, Aristotle asks a very simple question: Just what do friends do together? In other words, given that friendship must surely be expressed in actions, what kind of actions most constitute the living out of friendship? Aristotle answers with two kinds of action: Friends "do good for one another," and they "live together." (*Nicomachean Ethics*, 1157b7)

The first of these comes as no surprise. Since a true friend wants what is best for the other, for the other's own sake, it makes sense that the true friend will work toward helping the other in whatever way possible. This is to do good for one another. The second kind of action mentioned by Aristotle might sound a little strange. Do friends always

"live together?" If we understand "live together" properly, the answer is Yes. This is the point we made above when we said that persons naturally want to live and act together with their friends. This is not a matter of *where* one lives; it is a matter of *how* one lives. Friends want to do the same kinds of things, and they want to do them together; they want particularly to share the most important things in their lives. Aristotle is insistent on this point. In fact, he emphasizes this even more than doing good for one another. He says: "For there is nothing so characteristic of friends as living together, since ... even those who are supremely happy desire to spend their days together." (*Nicomachean Ethics*, 1157b19-21) We can say that friends want to live the same life together. To live the "same life" does not simply mean to live the same kind of life, it means to live literally the same life, to act together. As an analogy, this is not just about both being surgeons, it is about performing the same surgery. I want my friend to live a good life, the same kind of life that I want for myself. But more than this I want to be good *together with* my friend; I want to spend our days together; I want our lives to coincide in a very real way.

An excellent example, indeed perhaps the best example there is, of an action in which friends want to share, and in which their lives can be said to "coincide," is the action of conversation. We will consider the nature and importance of conversation later in this chapter. Here we might simply notice how conversation, when done well, can be an action which is so clearly not just "mine" but "ours."

We have seen then that there are two main ways of char-

acterizing what friends "do together:" They do good for one another, and they live together, in the sense of sharing their lives together. If we look closely, we will see that at the root of both of these things is a truth we keep coming back to: True friends must be mutually committed to pursuing the virtuous life. If two persons are really to be united in doing good for one another, they must share a vision of what life is all about. If they have different notions of what constitutes a life well-lived, then they will have different notions of what it means to do good for one another. True friends understand that the most important thing that they can do for one another is to help each other walk down the path of virtue. And, of course, as regards sharing their lives together, it can only really be a sharing of lives if they share a common vision of what they want to make of themselves in life.

We turn our attention now to how friends grow in virtue together, first as regards moral virtue, and then as regards intellectual virtue.

Moral Virtues and Friendship
The seeds of virtue should be planted early in life, in the bosom of a strong family life. Parents exercise the most formative influence in the early stages of character development. Yet, as noted last chapter, as children grow they begin to turn more and more to people outside of the family. Note: This is not to suggest that one cannot develop true friendships within one's own family, too! When a child develops such a friendship with a sibling, we can say that

the relationship has gone beyond simply being siblings—as when for instance a person says, "My brother is also my best friend." A main concern for parents is whether their children are developing relationships with others who are committed to virtue. As I asserted at the beginning of this chapter, persons tend to become/act like those who are their "friends" in the broad sense. Let us take a little time to examine this point.

The term "peer pressure" usually signifies a negative influence that friends and associates can have on a person, usually a young person. Often parents rightly bolster their teenagers against the influence of bad peers by encouraging them to stand strong in their own convictions. "Be your own person and do not worry about the others" can be very fitting advice. Yet it is important to notice that the pressure or influence exerted by peers need not be negative. And the fact of being influenced by peers is not in itself something negative. It is very natural that persons be influenced by those around them, whether the person is young or old. In the case of the young, however, there is more at stake because young persons are still maturing—which means that they are still "becoming themselves." As persons grope toward maturity they turn to others for help and companionship. Thus, it is of particular importance that the young have friends of good moral character.

Let us consider the following two imaginary scenarios to illustrate how true friendship helps to develop moral virtue. There are two young men, Francis and Thomas. Francis and Thomas are both convinced that goods of the soul are

the most important human goods, and that always doing the "right thing" is more important than riches, comfort, or the respect of others. They are just like any other person in their desire for companionship, and each wants to live his life "together with" others. Put more simply, each wants to have friends (in the broad sense). Now Francis does know someone that fits our description of a true friend: That person shares Francis's desire for virtue, and he knows and cares for Francis as a person. Thomas, on the other hand, does not have such a companion, but rather spends his days with others who do not share his desire for virtue. (How each came to this point is irrelevant; the point of the examples is simply to illustrate how helpful a true friendship is.)

Francis has a monumental advantage in the pursuit of virtue. First of all, in pursuing those things that are most important to him, he has peer companionship. The road to human greatness, to virtue, is a difficult and uphill grade. When the way to follow is not clear, his friend is there to help him discern the right path. When the way is clear, but will require much sacrifice, his friend is there to encourage him and even shoulder the load with him. When it is tempting simply to turn back, to give up, his friend is there to say: "You can do it; we can do it."

We can be more specific. When Francis's complaining about his neighbor starts to be uncharitable, his friend suggests assuming a different attitude. When conversation among the guys turns to inappropriate discussion of women, Francis and his friend support one another in an effort to change the topic. When Francis is suffering from the

tragic death of a family member, his friend not only grieves with him, but also helps him put the matter in the perspective of divine providence. This list can go on and on.

We need not go into great detail in considering Thomas's life. There are two main things to notice. First of all, if Thomas were in any of the above situations, it is very likely that he would not receive the kind of assistance that Francis did. In fact, he may well have to face negative pressure. When, like Francis, in a moment of weakness Thomas acts uncharitably, he may be joined and encouraged by his comrades. The difference is dramatic.

Growth in moral virtue is a project of monumental proportions. "Disciplining and reforming desires" sounds so simple. But how many really succeed? The words of Our Lord come to mind here: Narrow the way and few there are who find it. What we are suggesting here is that friendship is one of the most critical natural helps to walking the straight and narrow path.

Friendship, the Intellectual Virtues, and Good Conversation
Wisdom was mentioned above as the most important example of an intellectual virtue. We should make a distinction between two different virtues, each of which can be called a wisdom.

There is what Aristotle calls "speculative wisdom." This wisdom is a habit of insight into the highest truths of reality: truths about God, the universe, human nature, the meaning of life, etc. This kind of wisdom, which from now on we will simply call "wisdom," is all about the kind of

truths that one *contemplates*. Contemplation is a very special action in which a person fixes the mind's eye on something wonderful. Examples of contemplation are the monk who is absorbed in considering the infinite mercy of God, or the farmer who stops his work to consider how the beauty of nature reflects the glory of God.

The other kind of wisdom Aristotle calls "practical wisdom," and it is listed among the cardinal virtues as "prudence." The *Catechism of the Catholic Church* defines prudence as "the virtue that disposes practical reason to discern our true good in every circumstance and to choose the right means of achieving it." (*CCC* 1806) In other words, prudence is the habit of discerning what is the right way to act. It is the habit of being able to see just what virtue requires of us in all the circumstances of life.

All intellectual virtues are habits of knowing, or having insight. Wisdom is the virtue of insight into the highest realities, while prudence is the virtue of insight into how one should act.

Intellectual virtues, just as moral virtues, are not easy to form, and they require time and effort. Most everything said above regarding how friends support one another in forming moral virtues could be repeated about the intellectual virtues. It is not necessary to repeat those points. I simply want to focus our attention on a point that Aristotle considers to be of central importance in friendship: the role of good conversation. Good conversation is in fact crucial for the formation of both moral and intellectual virtue, but it has a more immediate relevance to intellectual virtue.

Conversation is, or should be, about the communication of truth, which is nothing else than a sharing of *insight*. Friends help one another grow in insight and grow in the habits of pursuing greater insight.

It has been said that our culture has lost the art of good conversation. There is of course no single cause at which to point a finger. Contemporary cultural habits, such as how we spend our free time and entertain ourselves, do not foster conversation. For instance, families and friends gather around the television (if they even gather there) as opposed to around a fire, and this removes a natural context for conversation. Many other high-tech forms of entertainment, such as the myriad "games" now played on computers, tend to isolate people. The general fast pace of society and the often engrossing attention given to practical endeavors, such as excelling in the marketplace, also remove the opportunities for conversation which were more abundant in a slower paced society.

The influence of the above trends—and many other "external" factors—should not be underestimated. At the same time, there are even more serious "internal" factors, or in other words, factors that pertain directly to one's character. Good conversation demands, and this should come as no surprise, a certain amount of moral virtue. The conversation we are calling "good conversation" is an activity in which two or more persons come together to pursue truth. This communal pursuit of truth requires, among other virtues, humility, patience, and perseverance. Consider how difficult it is to have good conversations with

those who are concerned more with image—how others view them, than with attaining the truth. And how can there be a good conversation with a person who, when the matter becomes difficult says, "Oh well, I guess it doesn't really matter anyway"?

But there is more. In addition to the virtues that enable people to engage in a communal pursuit of truth, there must also be some familiarity with the important matters to be discussed! This is of great significance. We need to feed our minds and often consider in our own minds the important matters of our faith and life. There should be an "interior conversation" within ourselves that extends to our conversations with others. Consider the words of Moses regarding the greatest commandment:

> *Hear, O Israel: The Lord our God is one Lord; and you shall love the Lord your God with all your heart, and with all your soul, and with all your might. And these words which I command you this day shall be upon your heart; and you shall teach them diligently to your children, and shall talk of them when you sit in your house, and when you walk by the way, and when you lie down, and when you rise.* (Deut. 6:4–7)

And the Psalmist says, "Blessed is the man... his delight is in the law of the Lord, and on his law he meditates day and night." (Ps. 1:1-2) Those who ponder the law of the Lord day and night, and carry it upon their hearts, are the persons who will want to discuss that law with friends. Indeed,

they and their friends will have much to discuss! But how many of us find ourselves not having much (of real significance) to discuss? Our conversations, even with our friends, most often revert to the weather, the economy, sports, or the latest tragedy reported in shocking detail in the news.

Given that there has been a decline in the art of conversation, what can be done about it? This is almost as difficult as asking what can be done about a decline in virtue. But let us take this opportunity to clarify a major theme of this book. Friendship is intimately linked with the highest human goods—particularly moral and intellectual virtue. They, friendship and virtue, must ultimately be restored *together*. In other words, the more that we develop virtue, the more we can exercise true friendship. And the more that we exercise true friendship, the more we will grow in virtue, especially since true friends want nothing more than to grow in virtue together.

As regards good conversation, then, friendship is a critical aid. True friends want good conversations and will help one another and draw one another into good conversations. Friends will benefit from the insights of one another, as they constantly share the fruits of their personal meditation and contemplation. And in fact, some truths will be discovered in conversation, which each friend never would have discovered separately. There is something irreplaceable about two minds working together, in a context of mutual affection and trust, to uncover the deepest truths.

Having said that friendship enables good conversation, we can look at the inverse and note that good conversation

is very important for the growth of friendship. To the extent that we, either as individuals or as a community, work to bring about good conversation, we will be simultaneously enhancing the possibility for true friendships. Avoiding the negative "external" factors mentioned above, such as constant noise and distraction, is a critical first step. Beyond this, we can more and more accustom ourselves to the hard work of study (taken in a broad sense as something that everyone, not just students, can do) and meditation and prayer, which feed our minds and inflame our hearts. What is prayer itself if not a good conversation with our Lord? We will return to this point in the final chapter. Now we turn to some reflections on friendship and its relation to the larger community.

Practicing Friendship

Questions for discussion:
1. Is friendship something I have or something I do? Explain.

2. Why is friendship such a good context, even a necessary context, for the formation of moral virtues? (Make sure you remember what a moral virtue is.)

3. Read 1 Sam. 23:1-18. What might it mean that Jonathan "strengthened his (David's) hand in God?"

4. What is good conversation?

5. What are the necessary conditions for good conversation to occur?

Questions for personal reflection:
1. Do the people I call friends help me grow in virtue?

2. Do I help the people I call friends to grow in virtue? How might I do this better?

3. How often do I have good conversations? If seldom, why?

Friendship and Society

When it goes well with the righteous, the city rejoices... By the blessing of the upright a city is exalted...

~ Proverbs 11:10-11

There is 'an interdependence between personal development and the improvement of society.'

~ CCC 2344

Having achieved some understanding of the nature of friendship and its role in the development of human character, we broaden our scope in this chapter to consider the connection between friendship and society. It might seem that this is an unimportant side-point about friendship. Aristotle and St. Thomas Aquinas think otherwise. To understand the true significance of friendship in human life, and indeed to understand human life itself, we need to consider the social nature of the human person. Aristotle and St. Thomas hold that just as surely as it is natural for a person to belong to a family, it is natural for a person to belong to a civil society. (The beginning of St. Thomas's political treatise *On Kingship* is very clear on this point.)

Let us consider first what civil society is, and then we will be in a position to consider two things: Why a good civil society needs friendship, and why friendship needs a good civil society.

What Is Civil Society

The term "civil" is added to "society" to distinguish this society from other communities or groups that can also be called societies, such as the church, family, or a club, or other organization. The civil society, which from now on we will simply call "society," is the society which the Greeks called the polis or city, and which today is commonly called the nation or state. This society is very different from any other kind of society because of its "self-sufficiency." In other words, only a society as large and complex as the civil society is able to provide for all human needs, and thus only this society is what is called a "complete society." A family or a village can provide for many human needs and will normally suffice to keep people alive. But only a complete society, or civil society, which is of course much larger than a village, can provide for the fuller range of human needs.

A couple of examples here should make this clearer. It is only in a civil society that there can be a well-developed system of law. The rules of a household, important as they are, do not approach being a full system of law; indeed, they are most effective *within* a society with a good system of law. It is also only in the context of a civil society that artistic and cultural expressions can be highly developed. It is for these and many other reasons that Aristotle says

74

that a family or village by itself might be able to provide for "life," but a civil society is required for the sake of a "good life." The good life in this context means human life with the various higher aspects that are only achieved through the communal effort of society. The great philosophers have a critical insight here: Human flourishing is so great and noble that it requires persons working together in a serious and complex fashion. Human civilization, though we tend to take it for granted, is no minor achievement! And true human civilization is all about enabling the highest refinement and perfection of human nature.

Hearing the above, one might reasonably ask the following question: If people are going to work together for the greater perfection of human nature, do they not need to share a common vision of human greatness? The answer must be an affirmative one. In other words, if a society is to succeed in cultivating human nature well, then there needs to be at least a fundamental agreement regarding what constitutes human greatness (that is, virtue). Most of the prevalent theories of civil society today simply emphasize the need for society to safeguard the freedom of individuals. While this freedom is of the utmost importance, Aristotle and St. Thomas would be quick to point out that civil society should be concerned with freedom but also *much more*. The best civil society is one whose laws and structures are designed not only to protect life and freedom but also to provide a context for the growth of its members in virtue.

To examine more specifically what this means and how it might be carried out would take us beyond the scope of our

book. But in order to appreciate the relationship between society and friendship, it is important that we keep in mind that Aristotle and St. Thomas held that a civil society ought to be judged in terms of how well it promotes the virtue of its citizens.

Society Needs Friendship

Aristotle writes that: "States it seems, are maintained by friendship; and legislators are more zealous about it than about justice." (*Nicomachean Ethics*, 1155a23) He proceeds to give a reason for this assertion. Of the utmost importance in a state is "unanimity" and "concord;" and friendship, more than anything else, brings about unanimity and concord. This, it seems to me, is a brilliant point. We have seen how, in friendship, persons are united in their love of one another and in their love of virtue. Friends share a vision of the good life and strive together to achieve it. Friendships thus provide "mini-communities" within the larger community; they are a basic unit, as it were, of striving for perfection. In this way the mini-community of friendship is very similar to the most basic, natural unit of society, the family.

Strong families that foster faith and good morals provide the necessary foundation for a good civil society. Where then does friendship fit in? First of all, friendship *within* the family is an important aspect of the strength of the family itself. And further, friendship *between* families, obviously most of all between parents, is what particularly strengthens those families and enables them to be more substantial units or cells of striving for greatness. Several

families united by the bonds of friendship constitute, in fact, the healthy proximate environment in which persons live out most of their lives. It is among family and friends that we spend most of our time, and it is among them that we form our habits, be they good or bad.

An example will help illustrate the centrality of this community of family and friends in our lives. Consider a young man who goes off to serve his country by military service. He sees himself, and rightly so, as serving his country—the civil society in which he lives. But probably foremost in his mind as he goes to serve are his family and friends. In a very real way, when he is fighting to defend his country, he is fighting to preserve their way of life. He realizes that the common good of the civil society is the great good for which he is willing to sacrifice his life. Yet at the same time, it is only natural that he focuses his attention on that mini-community of persons among whom he has been formed and lived most of his life. The point here is that a person has a place *in* the civil society *through* having a place among family and friends. Consider how absurd it would be for a person to say: My only community, my only place of belonging, is the national community, for example, the United States of America.

We can conclude that the character of the "mini-communities" of family and friends determines the character of the national community, the civil society. Aristotle says that legislators are most concerned about fostering true friendship among citizens. How much sense this makes! To the extent that there is true friendship among citizens, society

will be formed by persons, or groups of persons, united with one another in the pursuit of virtue.

Friendship Needs Society

What do we mean when we say that friendship needs society? We said before that the possibility of a good civil society is directly dependent on the existence of true friendships among citizens—the stronger and more widespread the friendships, the better the civil society. Here we make the opposite point that true friendships are, to some extent, dependent on the existence of a good society. This dependence is different from, and not as absolute as, the opposite dependence. An example will help illustrate this point.

Let us compare the relation between friendship and civil society to the relation between a soccer player and a soccer team. A soccer team will never be excellent if it is not composed of excellent (though not necessarily superstar) players. Similarly, a civil society will never be a truly good one if it is not composed of persons among whom there are true friendships. This much is clear.

The other "direction" seems a little less clear. Can there be an excellent soccer player without an excellent team? Clearly there can be such a situation, but we must look a little deeper. Perhaps right now an excellent player is stuck on a bad team. But how did that player become excellent? Soccer players will attest to the fact that a person cannot really *become* a good player without having played with good players on a good team. The famous Pelé did not become

the player he was by kicking around a ball in his back yard, nor even by playing with just one or two of his buddies. By its nature, soccer is a communal activity, and thus training in it must be done among a good "community" of players.

This points to a fundamental truth about friendship and civil society. A good civil society provides the natural context within which good friendships can grow. Now I do not assert that it is impossible to form true friendships in a bad civil society. I do, however, assert two things. First, a good civil society provides significant help in forming true friendships. And second, to the extent that a civil society is not what it should be, persons are hampered in their efforts, or have more to overcome, in forming true friendships.

We need not go into these points at great length. It is important, however, perhaps especially today, to have some appreciation of the difficulties associated with living in a society that falls short of being what it should be. (The causes of the decay of civil society are beyond our scope.)

One of the most serious ways in which the flaws of a civil society are manifested is in its laws. It is hard to estimate the negative effect of bad laws on a society. Consider an example in the area of protecting human life. The negative effects of laws that permit abortion, for instance, are multiple. The first casualties are, of course, the unborn persons whose lives are forfeited. But not only does the law allow those particular lives to be lost, it also allows persons to form the evil habit of taking innocent life, a habit which can lead to the destruction of even more life and to the destruction of the moral character of the persons in question.

And further, beyond allowing or forbidding actions, law also speaks to the community. Since it speaks of the judgment of the community regarding right and wrong in action, it has a formative effect on the judgment of citizens regarding right and wrong. For centuries philosophers have referred to the "teaching aspect" of law. A society with bad laws, then, tends to form its citizens, and particularly its youth, with a corrupted judgment about right and wrong.

Besides in its laws, the flaws (or strengths) of a society are manifested in customs and cultural expressions. By "customs" we mean social habits of living that are passed down in a society from generation to generation. How the elderly are treated in a society, for instance, is not so much a matter of law as a matter of custom. How young men and young women interact, and the basic structures of dating or courtship, are also a matter of custom in a society. But custom has a very similar effect to law: It has a formative influence on the personal habits and judgments of citizens. In a society in which there are, for instance, bad customs of how young men and women date, it is very difficult for youth, even those from good families, to swim against the current in this area. (More thoughts on this in the next chapter.)

It is hard to comprehend the full extent of the influence that laws and customs of society have on the lives of citizens. Living in an age where many societies reject basic principles of natural law and treat religious faith as something which must be kept completely out of the "public square," many of us have simply become accustomed to

"having to be different" from the society around us. But this is easier said than done. The fact is that a decadent civil society places unique obstacles to the project of seeking virtue and thus, also, the project of forming true friendships. These obstacles can be overcome, particularly through the help of supernatural grace. But obstacles they remain, and we must reckon with them constantly. It is small groups of families, united by bonds of friendship, which are in the best position to reckon with these obstacles.

~

We could call friendship an art, acknowledging that it is something beautiful and noble, *and* that it must be cultivated—it does not simply happen by itself. Recall what we said about the composer Mozart: his excellence was cultivated and developed through persistent, ordered effort. We could further call friendship the art *of happiness*, recognizing that it is not just one art among others. It has a unique position in its connection to virtue and holiness, to human fulfillment and happiness. To see this point is to see something essential about human persons (indeed about any *persons*)—their happiness is constituted by a union, or communion, of persons.

What we have considered in this chapter has brought out another critical point. Certain arts, particularly the more noble ones, can only be achieved through communal effort. It goes without saying that friendship requires a kind of communal effort. But we have seen here that friendship in-

volves more than just the friends themselves. Let us think again of Mozart. His excellence in the art of music came about because of his persistent effort in the context of his musical friends. But they were not working in a vacuum. Rather, they were the inheritors of a rich and noble tradition of music, passed down in a broad community, that provided the necessary foundations for their work. Similarly, the art of friendship is something that needs to be "passed down" in certain ways (as for instance, we are turning here to Aristotle and St. Thomas for an understanding of it), and practiced by a larger community.

Our image of the soccer team can help us glean one final insight. We have noted the difficulty of becoming a good soccer player if one is not on a good team. But there is more to see here. What is soccer ultimately about anyway? Is it about there being excellent players, or there being excellent teams? Is it not the case that the very fulfillment of being an excellent player is to be an excellent player playing on an excellent team? Yes. What does this mean for friendship and society? Aristotle and St. Thomas say that friendship finds its natural place and its fulfillment in a flourishing broader community. In other words, friends can most of all be what they want to be, and what they are called to be, exactly when they are members of a broader flourishing community. The Greeks had a wonderful insight. The height of human greatness is the greatness of a community, a community whose backbone is friendship.

It is important to note here that as a Christian, St. Thomas sees something that Aristotle could not see, namely, that

there is a *supernatural* community that is even higher than the civil society: the Church. All that we have said about the civil society, the highest natural community, can and should be applied to the supernatural society. The Church needs good friendships, and friendships need the Church and find their fulfillment in her. Especially in an age of decadent civil society, it is a great joy and consolation to recall that we are first of all members of a supernatural community, a community against which the gates of hell shall not prevail.

Practicing Friendship

Questions for discussion:

1. Why is it inhuman to "live alone?"

2. Why are friendships so important for the broader community or civil society?

3. Why is society important for friendships?

4. What extra challenges are there for people developing friendship in a decadent society? How might these challenges be met?

Questions for personal reflection:

1. Do I recognize the extent of my dependence on others: friends, family, society?

2. How do I act so as to build up the communities to which I belong?

3. Am I aware of the dangers of living in a society that does not value what I value? How do I respond to these dangers?

Dating, Marriage, and Friendship

. . . but for the man there was not found a helper fit for him. So the Lord God caused a deep sleep to fall upon the man, and while he slept took one of his ribs and closed up its place with flesh; and the rib which the Lord God had taken from the man he made into a woman. . . .

~ Genesis 2:20-22

The *Catechism of the Catholic Church*, in a section emphasizing the importance of proper preparation for marriage, states the following:

It is imperative to give suitable and timely instruction to young people, above all in the heart of their own families, about the dignity of married love, its role and exercise, so that, having learned the value of chastity, they will be able at a suitable age to engage in honorable courtship and enter upon a marriage of their own. (CCC 1632, quoting *Gaudium et Spes* 49'3)

In one rich sentence the Catechism paints an excellent portrait of "courtship," which we will call dating. First, it reveals the heart of the traditional understanding of dating: the essential connection between dating and marriage. In other words, dating is all about preparation for holy matrimony. Further, the Catechism refers to two critical aspects of proper dating which actually stem from its essential relation to marriage: that it be honorable, and that it be done at a suitable age. In this chapter we will consider these points in an effort to come to a better understanding of dating. The main thesis of this chapter is that true friendships help assure that young men and women can engage in *honorable* dating, at the *proper time*, and that they will be prepared for the friendship of marriage.

Dating: What Is It?
We should first be conscious of different ways that the word "dating" is used. Taking someone on a "date" can simply mean going out for coffee or to a movie. Thus we can speak of "dating" and mean just this phenomenon of men and women going out together, either as a single couple or in larger groups. This sense of dating is not the main way that the word is used today. The more prominent sense of "dating" names the situation in which a man and a woman, desiring to be with one another precisely as man and woman, develop a relationship with one another, a relationship which is more or less exclusive. (This dating might also be called "going steady," although we would call it dating regardless of whether there is an explicit understanding to

go steady.) This relationship can be based on any one of the three kinds of friendship we have discussed (of pleasure, of utility, or true friendship); often it is a mixture. We will discuss this shortly.

Now while most everyone can agree to a general description of dating, there are diverse understandings of *what the purpose or goal of this relationship is*. I stated above that the key point in the quotation from the Catechism was an assertion that dating is fundamentally about *preparing for marriage*. This point has monumental importance for us for two main reasons: a) it tells us what dating should really be, and b) the vast majority of our society does not accept this point. Today dating is usually seen as something that people do simply because it is fun or fulfilling or recreational. And when it is seen as a way to find a marriage partner, it is still often not seen as a preparation for a covenant commitment. The contemporary incomprehension of the true purpose and meaning of dating is particularly evident in *how* people date and in *when* people date. On the other hand, as noted above, understanding dating as a preparation for marriage means knowing how to date ("honorably") and when to date ("at a suitable age"). We will consider each of these after looking first at the goal of dating: marriage.

Marriage: A Unique Instance of Friendship

One of the most striking aspects of marriage is that it should be a unique instance of true friendship. The Catechism says the following about marriage: "The matrimonial covenant, by which a man and a woman establish be-

tween themselves a partnership of the whole of life, is by its nature ordered toward the good of the spouses and the procreation and education of offspring." (*CCC* 1601, quoting the *Code of Canon Law*, 1055) A document of Vatican II has this to say:

> *Thus the man and woman, who "are no longer two but one" (Mt. 19:6), help and serve each other by their marriage partnership; they become conscious of their unity and experience it more deeply from day to day. The intimate union of marriage, as a mutual giving of two persons, and the good of the children demand total fidelity from the spouses and require an unbreakable unity between them.* (*Gaudium et Spes* 48 ' 3)

We have characterized true friendship as a relationship between two persons who, wanting what is best for one another and working for each others' good, share their lives together. The above quotations emphasize these very points about marriage.

We do not have time here to consider the wonderfully complex subject of marriage at any length. There is one point, however, that we will insist upon here: *Spousal life lived to its fullness implies living a true friendship.* Marriage is a union of persons who should help perfect one another and be fruitful. True friendship especially unites persons, perfects persons, and allows persons to be fruitful. Now spouses *can* be united through a mutual commitment of faithfulness, without being friends in the fullest sense. Spouses *can*

help perfect one another, without being friends in the fullest sense. And they *can* be fruitful, without being friends in the fullest sense. Indeed, even if they are not friends, they are still bound by honor, and a moral obligation to pursue union, mutual helpfulness, and fruitfulness.

But how much more united, mutually helpful, and fruitful are the spouses who have pursued the noble good of growing in friendship! How much more *happy* are those spouses who strive with each other, more than with any other human person, to grow in love, to grow in virtue, to grow in wisdom. Realizing that they are called by God to work out their salvation *together*, they live a kind of shared-life that is beyond the sharing possible for any other friendship in this life. The blessing of children is a kind of incarnation (literally: a putting into the flesh) of *their* love for each other. Their ability to raise and educate these children well is directly proportional to their success in growing together in virtue and wisdom. We might consider it this way: True love between spouses expresses itself first in their love for one another, which leads them to help one another grow in virtue. This love, blessed by God, also bears fruit in the gift of children. This same love, which first bore fruit in mutual growth in virtue, then continues to bear fruit in the proper raising and educating of children.

It is this understanding of marriage that should form our understanding of dating. If dating is a preparation for marriage, then it must be conducted in such a way and at such a time as best to lead into marriage. Let us turn then to how to date.

How to Date

Just what it means to prepare for the vocation of marriage is more complex than it seems. The most basic aspect is that dating is the means by which we discern whom we are called to marry. It is, for obvious reasons, of the utmost importance that a person carefully discern with whom to share one's very self and work out one's salvation. Yet dating is not simply about "finding the right person"—be that ever so important. It is also about *preparing oneself* to be married. Preparation in this sense means honing those good habits that are critical to all true friendships, such as self-sacrifice and patience. Further, it means growing in insight into the unique characteristics of a specifically nuptial relationship, such as exclusivity and total commitment. Dating, then, is much more than having fun, and it is more than seeking personal fulfillment. It is a very serious and beautiful enterprise, in which two people develop as individuals and prepare themselves for an irrevocable commitment.

As regards *how to date*, I have three suggestions. They can be encapsulated as follows: a) you will only have as much between you, as you have above you, b) you show charity, through your chastity, and c) you date "within" a community.

Clearly a main focus in a dating relationship is to get to know the other person, and for the other person to get to know you. But how is this done? It is not done by hours of gazing into one another's eyes. Gazing into another's eyes is really meaningful when you already know that person. You get to know one another best by standing next to one

another and looking outward, indeed especially upward, together. You start to share your *life* with the other person.

You start to enact life together by doing those things and discussing those things that are the most important things in your life. Meaningful conversations which, as we have seen, are essential in a true friendship, are also essential in the dating relationship. Who are you? At the end of the day, what gives meaning to your life? As a Christian who is mature enough to be discerning a specific vocation in life, the root answer is: my faith, my relationship with Jesus Christ. But there is also more to you: What else do you do, and enjoy, value, and desire? These things should be done together and shared together. In this way, you are in a good position to discern whether the two of you are called to be spouses. Our Lord said: Where your treasure is, there will your heart be also. (Luke 12:34)

If you slowly show one another what you treasure, you will be showing one another your hearts. There is nothing that unites two people like a shared commitment to something great. A shared commitment to losing weight gives you a simple common goal; a shared commitment, however, to growing in maturity and holiness gives you a solid basis for the nuptial bond.

You show charity through your chastity. The point here is simple. One of the greatest challenges dating couples face is the challenge to be chaste. What we mean here by "chaste" implies a refraining from, as the Catechism calls them, "the expressions of affection that belong to married love."(*CCC* 250) Here is perhaps the main way that those

dating have the opportunity to demonstrate their unselfish love for one another. It goes without saying that the lack of willingness to control one's desires in this area is a sign that the relationship will not last, since it lacks a real commitment to the well-being of one another. Marriage is essentially a total self-donation in unselfish love. Unchastity, as a form of selfishness, attacks the dating and marriage relationship at its very root. Chastity, on the other hand, is an expression of true love. It is a gift that those who are dating give to one another and which endures into and throughout marriage.

The best thing to do is to meet the challenge head-on. As a dating relationship progresses, couples should talk to one another about the importance of chastity. Physical intimacy should be seen as a natural sign of an *established commitment.* In this light it is easy to see that premarital sex is always wrong. Even if I am "certain" that I am going to marry someone, if we have not yet made the marriage vow itself, then we do not have a real, permanent commitment. The focus of the time of dating (and engagement, too) should be on developing a personal relationship in preparation for a permanent commitment, not on acting as though the commitment has already been made.

Consider this: Why are so many young men and women seriously scarred when a dating relationship is broken off? One main reason is that premature physical expressions of affection have fostered a false sense of intimacy. One of the many benefits of chastity is the safeguarding of men and women from this scarring. In the event of a break-up, the

couple that has been chaste is much more likely to separate in friendship, having experienced the joy of a relationship based in mutual goodwill and respect. Indeed, it is worth bearing in mind that very few people look back on a time of dating and think: "Gosh, I wish we had started kissing earlier." There are many who look back with regrets of another kind.

It is not within our scope to give universal guidelines for the expression of affection—although I do want to emphasize how important it is that individuals and couples look into this matter. (See, for instance, the section of the Catechism entitled "The Vocation of Chastity," *CCC* 2348.) In a culture in which the norm is to ignore these critical principles, honorable dating requires heroic effort and vigilance, and the help of friends. On this note, we turn to our third suggestion: You date within a community.

"Community" here should be taken to include the small community of one's truest friends, the community of family, and the broader community beyond the family. What do we mean by dating "within" these communities? The focus here is not on literally where dating goes on, in the sense of physical place—although that is a part of it. The question here is more the spirit and attitude of dating. For instance, do a couple that are dating see themselves as "on their own" in their dating? Is dating seen as something that is done in a vacuum and as something that is simply the couple's own business? Traditionally dating was seen as something that goes on in the heart of the family. A young man would "come courting" and pursue a relationship with a young

lady primarily within the confines of her own home. While that system might not have been perfect, it did have the community aspect that we are now emphasizing.

The two keys to dating within a community are *support* and *accountability*. Dating obviously involves special challenges that friendship between men and friendship between women does not. The support of family and friends, in the form of encouragement, advice, etc., is a critical aid in meeting these challenges. Further, it is very beneficial for the couple to feel accountable to family and friends. This does not mean that family and friends interrogate the young man and woman after each time that they have seen each other. Rather, the point is that the young man and woman should know that there are loved ones who want the best for them, and expect the best from them. This accountability does not call for an over-bearing, chaperoning presence. It does, however, call for the family and friends of the couple to seek to "hold them to" certain standards. This accountability means that the young man and woman realize that they are not isolated individuals but are the object of a concerned love. And further, it is family and friends who are in the best position to provide an objective, outside view of a relationship. Advice from these persons who really know the persons dating is often indispensable to a couple. How many pitfalls can be avoided by dating "within" a community!

As already stated, dating within a community is primarily a matter of spirit and attitude, as opposed to where a couple spends their time. One example of how this can be

lived out is in the habits that a young woman has of discussing with certain family members or close friends the various aspects of dating in general, as well as specific challenges that she and her boyfriend are facing. Another example is in the effort that she makes to invite her boyfriend "into" her relationships with friends and family. This points toward the fact that habits of *where* a couple spends time are in fact also very important. I will be blunt here: Most dating couples spend too much time alone. Of course time alone is very important in a dating relationship. It is a good thing. But too much of a good thing can be a bad thing. Unfortunately, couples that spend too much time alone tend to have an attitude of separation or isolation from friends and community.

Here is a practical suggestion. Couples can resist the temptation to look upon time alone as the only "real time" that they spend together. They can cultivate habits of group interaction—interaction with friends, family, and larger communities (such as a parish). These groups are the natural context for discussing, praying, working, reading, recreating, etc. In this way, time alone might actually take on a more special character. It is seen as a special gift, a foretaste of the married state.

When to Date

As regards the right time for dating, the traditional wisdom is: If you are not fundamentally ready for marriage, then you are not ready to date. A full treatment of what being "ready for marriage" means is beyond our scope. It can

suffice to say that it includes both readiness in a material way and readiness in a spiritual way, or personal maturity. I suggest that for many, though not all, this means not dating before the final year or so of college. It is not surprising that in our society young people are dating earlier and earlier. If dating is simply about fun and personal fulfillment, then why not date early? Yet if dating is a serious preparation for the vocation of marriage, then we have a very good reason to make the sacrifice of postponing dating.

But what is one to do in the meantime? Should one languish in isolation from the opposite sex before one is ready to be married? No. There is much to do and experience, that should be done and experienced *prior* to dating and marriage. Indeed, these things are essential preparations for dating and marriage. Here I offer two suggestions. First, it is essential that young men and women first develop healthy friendships within the same sex. In these friendships, young people can grow in maturity and develop the basic habits of personal relationships, without the challenge or distraction of the "romantic" element. Second, young men and women should develop habits of interaction with the opposite sex, yet primarily in the context of wholesome group activities, and in non-exclusive, non-romantic relationships.

Perhaps we should look a little more deeply into these two suggestions. One of the things that we have seen about friendship is that it does not just "happen" without much effort; it is like great art in this way. Friends-to-be must develop habits, for instance, of discerning the inner thoughts,

desires, and needs of the other person, and often this is not easy. Now, we do not need a psychologist to tell us that this is particularly challenging in the case of a man and a woman—be it an explicitly romantic relationship or not (since, of course, a non-romantic relationship between a man and a woman could turn into a romantic one). Given the extra challenges in other-sex relationships, it seems clear that a person can best develop the habits of friendship in the context which, particularly for young people, is naturally more welcoming and comfortable. It is not without reason that younger boys and girls tend to herd together among themselves. This is very natural. It is a sign of grave corruption that boys and girls today are being conditioned to become romantic and "sexually aware" earlier and earlier.

I am certainly not suggesting that boys and girls should not have contact with one another. In fact, they should develop non-romantic, non-exclusive relationships. Boys and girls both go through a stage when they prefer to be among their own sex. When they start to come out of this stage, normally as they enter into the teen years, they have reached a very important moment in their lives. It is at this time that cultures traditionally were very attentive to guide the youth, to watch-over and direct their desires and activities. Teenagers must begin to learn to interact with one another as honorable young men and women. For this end, young people benefit most from wholesome *group* activities. They need help in this area from mature, virtuous men and women, including their parents and older peers, who can

act as role models and guides. This is where the family is so important. One of the great tragedies of contemporary culture is the way that teenagers and young adults leave their families behind in order to interact, alone and isolated, with their peers. The family itself, extended to include *its* relatives and friends, naturally provides the best context for young adults to interact with members of the opposite sex, and thus grow in maturity.

But again, in the teenage years, and sometimes a few years beyond, the main focus should be on developing friendships within the same sex. Developing these relationships is itself a major factor in the process of maturation and thus in becoming ready for dating and marriage. As noted in chapter two, central to human maturity is the ability to look beyond one's own needs and to consider what is simply good or best in itself. In other words, the heart of maturation involves growing in virtue. The experience of true friendship is critical for maturation and therefore is critical to being prepared for marriage, or even prepared for the *final preparation* for marriage—dating.

Please allow me to emphasize this: The conviction that young people should wait until they are truly ready for dating is rooted primarily in the dignity and beauty of dating as a preparation for marriage. This is not to be confused with a common contemporary attitude that says: Postpone marriage so you can live your own life to the fullest first. This bad attitude does not put off the "fun" of dating, but rather puts off the commitment of marriage. My position

is also not to be confused with an overly scrupulous attitude of assuming the worst about self, and thus persistently assuming that one is not ready for marriage. I do not suggest *indefinitely* postponing dating and marriage. I do suggest growing in maturity, virtue, and friendship *first*. To do this in our society is to swim against the tide.

Practicing Friendship

Questions for discussion:
1. What does a true understanding of dating mean for *how* I should date?

2. How does a true understanding of dating affect *when* I should date?

3. Just how different is the contemporary practice of dating from a true understanding of dating?

Questions for personal reflection:
1. Am I willing to be radically different from society in the area of dating? How might I do this?

2. What will help me act according to a true understanding of dating?

3. Can I explain and defend these points to those around me?

Charity:
Friendship with
God and Neighbor

. . . but I have called you friends . . .

~ John 15:15

I suggested in the first chapter that as Christians we have two special motives for examining human friendship. The first is that an understanding of human friendship enhances our understanding of friendship with God. The second is that human friendship is a natural preparation for entering into friendship with God. Now that we have spent some time examining human friendship, we are more ready to turn to the very perfection of the Christian life: supernatural charity, or friendship with God. After examining friendship with God, we will conclude by considering how this friendship ultimately transforms human friendship.

Charity as Friendship with God

We have emphasized that the main way of characterizing

what friends do together (and really, friendship itself is all about what friends do together) is that they share their lives, or that they act together, particularly in such human actions as conversation. For Aristotle, this very point raised a serious problem when it came to a question of great significance: Can a human person have a friendship with a divine person? Aristotle gives an answer which is as crushing as it is insightful: No, human persons and God cannot be friends—because they are too different, their lives are too far apart. Now from the viewpoint of natural reason, that is, reason unaided by divine revelation, this answer makes complete sense. Indeed it is the correct answer for the human predicament *without grace.*

But something extraordinary happened, almost four hundred years after Aristotle's striking analysis of friendship. I like to think that the words of Aristotle were echoing in the ears of the God-man when He was having His last heart-to-heart conversation, in this life, with His apostles. He says to them:

> *These things have I spoken to you, that my joy may be in you, and that your joy may be full. This is my commandment, that you love one another as I have loved you. Greater love has no man than this, that a man lay down his life for his friends. [And now the line that would stop the heart of Aristotle.] You are my friends if you do what I command you. No longer do I call you servants, for the servant does not know what his master is doing; but I have called you friends, for all*

*that I have heard from my Father I have made known
to you.* (Jn 15:11-15)

How dramatically have the actions of the God-man Jesus
Christ changed the human condition! Now, and only now,
can a human person really be a friend of God. Now a human person and God can be friends because He, first of all
unilaterally, has shared His Life with us. How wonderfully
He expresses this very point when He says that now He
calls us friends "for all that I have heard from my Father I
have made known to you!" We might say that He has invited
us into the divine conversation itself. From the limited perspective of natural reason, from the noble Aristotle's perspective, this is beyond the dreams of man! We must never
take friendship with God for granted, as though it could
have been expected!

Let us turn to St. Thomas Aquinas's understanding of
the greatest of all virtues, charity. He asserts that charity
itself is a friendship between human persons and God. He
explains himself by reminding us of what we have learned
from Aristotle: Every friendship is based upon a shared life.
Now God has deigned to share His life (and here St. Thomas literally says "His happiness") with us. *Charity is nothing
more than the mutual love between a human person and God that
is based upon this shared life.* (*S.t.* II-II 23.1) Recall the lines
from the Gospel of St. John quoted above: "These things
have I spoken to you, that my joy may be in you, and that
your joy may be full." Again, He shares Himself, by sharing
with us everything He has heard from the Father, so that

His joy, His happiness might be ours. Now we can love Him in a new kind of way. This is not simply the love of a lowly creature for an all-powerful creator, or of a servant for his master. This is the love of a friend for a friend. *This* love is called supernatural charity. *This* is only possible because God has shared His supernatural life with the soul. *This* is the highest of virtues. *This* is what endures, when all else has passed away.

From this vantage point, insights into our calling as Christians multiply. Let us consider a few of them. The Church has always taught that *mortal sin* deprives the soul of supernatural grace, which means among other things that the soul loses the supernatural virtue of charity. The *Catechism of the Catholic Church* states: "Mortal sin destroys charity in the heart of man by a grave violation of God's law; it turns man away from God, who is his ultimate end and his beatitude, by preferring an inferior good to him." (*CCC* 1855) We are now in a position to understand better *why* this love, the love of charity, is absolutely incompatible with mortal sin. We can put it this way: To commit a mortal sin is to act directly against the shared life of friendship.

We can see this point by looking to human friendship. We all know that there are certain ways of acting that would destroy any human friendship, such as stealing a friend's possessions. Similarly, mortal sins are actions that destroy friendship with God. The question might arise: Is this really the case in every kind of action that is considered seriously sinful? A look at Catholic moral theology from the outside might seem to reveal simply a long list of do's and

don'ts. Is it really the case that there are so many ways in which a person can ruin his friendship with God? Let us look into this.

If friends have a common goal, and strive together toward it, then it is clear that they have fundamentally similar desires. In other words, as regards the most important things in life (and usually much more than just the most important things), they have the same likes and dislikes. This point affords a critical insight into one of the central features of salvation history—*law*. Law is perhaps one of the most misunderstood of God's gifts to man. When St. Thomas begins his famous treatise on law (in his *Summa theologica*), he says that at its root law is a way that God *instructs* man. Law instructs in the form of a command or precept. But what does it instruct about? Law provides instruction regarding human goodness, or virtue, and how to achieve it.

Given this understanding of law, it should come as no surprise that the Old Testament Jews looked upon the Law of God as a gift of incomparable worth. The great Psalm 119 (176 verses long) is a song of praise and thanksgiving to God for His law. It begins: "Blessed are those whose way is blameless, who walk in the law of the Lord!" The psalmist continues:

> *Thou has commanded thy precepts to be kept diligently. O that my ways may be steadfast in keeping thy statutes! Then I shall not be put to shame, having my eyes fixed on all thy commandments. I will praise thee with*

an upright heart, when I learn thy righteous ordinanc-
es. I will observe thy statutes; O forsake me not utterly!
... With my whole heart I seek thee; let me not wander
from thy commandments! I have laid up thy word in
my heart, that I might not sin against thee. Blessed be
thou, O Lord; teach me thy statutes! With my lips I
declare all the ordinances of thy mouth. In the way of
thy testimonies I delight as much as in all riches. I will
meditate on thy precepts, and fix my eyes on thy ways.
I will delight in thy statutes; I will not forget thy word.
(Ps. 119: 4–16)

The Law was seen as guiding the people to what was at one and the same time a truly good life and a life most pleasing to God himself.

Now we must remember that in the New Testament God calls human persons to friendship with Himself. This sheds new light on the importance of God's law. Now we can see God's law as directing toward, and preparing for friendship with Himself. We can say that His law provides the necessary guidelines for friendship; it points to how we can "share our lives" with Him. This is how we should look upon His law—whether it be the precepts given in the New Testament, the natural law written in our hearts, or the laws of the Church. (St. Thomas explains that the Law of the Old Testament was a preparation for the Law of the New Testament. See *S.t.* I-II 107.1 and 2.)

The importance of this point should not be underestimated. Is this not a most beautiful and consoling insight?

God asks so much of me, as regards how I act, because He wants me to live as His friend! St. Thomas insists on this point. He says that "the chief intention of the divine law is to establish man in friendship with God." (*S.t.* I-II 99.2) He explains that "there cannot be any friendship of man to God, who is supremely good, unless man become good.... But the goodness of man is virtue...." (*Ibid.*) In other words, friendship with God, like any friendship, always demands certain things. And the role of law is to instruct us in what those things are. He ties this in with what we have seen above, when he argues that supernatural charity cannot exist without obedience to the law of God. Here is his striking argument:

> *For it is written (1 John ii. 4,5): "He who saith that he knoweth God, and keepeth not His commandments, is a liar . . . but he that keepeth His word, in him in very deed the charity of God is perfected:" and this because friends have the same likes and dislikes. (S.t. II-II 104.3)*

Friends have the same likes and dislikes. This is the final word on why God has given us a law, and on why charity is incompatible with mortal sin.

This is also the final word on why Aristotle was fundamentally correct in asserting that to be virtuous is to be happy. Recall that to have a virtue is not only to act in certain ways. It is also to *want* to act in these ways, and to *enjoy* it. God calls us to virtue, to the transformation of our desires and actions, *so*

that we might be completely united with Him in our desires and actions. And thus (and here again is something Aristotle could never have foreseen), God calls us *to make the supernatural virtue of charity the root of all virtues.* Charity, supernatural love for Him, should be *the inspiration, and the end or goal, of everything we desire and do.* Charity is the perfection of the Christian life, for the Christian life is about friendship with God.

Our consideration of friendship with God also gives us insight into our *prayer life,* or more broadly our *interior life.* Just as conversation is at the heart of human friendship, so it is at the heart of a person's friendship with God. We spoke earlier of the unique beauty of the conversation of friends; there is no conversation like the conversation of persons united by their love for each other, and their love for virtue. Friends' speech with one another is marked by an ease, a comfort, and a joy, and also an attentiveness and a seriousness not found in other speech. This conversation of human friends provides a model, though not a perfect one, for the conversation that we can and should have with God himself. St. Thomas speaks of the interior life of the person in the state of grace as a conversation with God and the angels. He says that this conversation, while imperfect in this life, will be brought to complete fullness in the life of heaven. (*S.t.* II-II 23.1)

As we look at our own prayer life, we might ask ourselves a few questions. First and most importantly, do I look upon conversation with God as essential to my relationship with Him, and thus as something that I should work on unceas-

ingly? Good habits are formed only through the repeated exercise of good actions. Second, do I participate in liturgical prayer (the Mass and the Sacraments, also the Liturgy of the Hours) with a spirit of entering into a unique mode of conversation with my divine friend? The *Catechism of the Catholic Church* states:

> *The liturgy is also the participation in Christ's own prayer addressed to the Father in the Holy Spirit. In the liturgy, all Christian prayer finds its source and goal. Through the liturgy the inner man is rooted and grounded in "the great love with which (the Father) loved us" in his beloved Son. It is the same "marvelous work of God" that is lived and internalized by all prayer, "at all times in the Spirit."* (CCC 1073)

Third, do I seek throughout my day to turn my heart and mind to my divine friend, for the kind of personal contact to which He has invited us?

It should be noted that those with an authentic friendship with God always retain a proper respect for His divine majesty. We do not give a "slap on the back" to our divine friend. He calls us to the most intimate of relationships, but it remains a relationship between the All Holy and a sinner, between Creator and creature, between Father and son. A son always retains a reverence for his father. Our reflections here should not be construed as suggesting that we treat God as "one of the boys." Friendship with God is literally an awe-some reality. It is an unmerited gift. It should be

approached with the appropriate sentiments of reverence, thanksgiving, and wondrous joy.

Charity as Friendship with God, Extended to Other Persons
Where does our neighbor fit into the Christian understanding of charity, especially since charity is a friendship with God? Christians have always held that there are two objects of charity: God and neighbor. The key to understanding charity towards neighbor is to understand how these two objects of charity are related to one another. This is a somewhat subtle yet extremely important point. God and neighbor are both objects of charity, but in such a way that there is really only *one* love here. How is this possible? God is the primary object of charity, and human persons are the secondary objects. When we say primary here we mean two things. First, God is loved more than neighbor, and second, God is *the very reason for the love of neighbor.*

Charity is first of all a love of God, above all things and for His own sake. God is seen as most worthy and lovable, as the source of goodness, and as goodness itself. As noted above, charity is a love for God that is possible only in the context of God's sharing His life, His happiness with us. Now when one loves God, with this love of charity, one will also want *other persons to share in the life of God.* Since God has called all persons to share in His life, a person with charity loves all persons, wanting them to "live with God." The heart of charity for neighbor is the desire for the neighbor to share in God's life, to live with Him in friendship.

We receive further insight into this point when we con-

sider that charity extends even to our enemies. St. Thomas turns again to his understanding of friendship in order to explain.

> *When a man has friendship for a certain person, for his sake he loves all belonging to him, be they children, servants, or connected with him in any way. Indeed, so much do we love our friends, that for their sake we love all who belong to them, even if they hurt or hate us; so that, in this way the friendship of charity extends even to our enemies, whom we love out of charity in relation to God, to whom (God) the friendship of charity is chiefly directed. (S.t. II-II 23.1reply2)*

What a beautiful insight into true friendship! Love for a friend extends even beyond that friend; it extends to friends, family, etc. of the friend. Of course, this does not mean that the friends of the friend are immediately loved because of who they are in themselves. The friends of the friend are loved *as being* the friends of the friend. (Though that relationship might then also become something more.) In the case of charity, a person loves his enemies as persons called to friendship with God. As one grows in charity, one grows in the ability to look upon other persons precisely as the beloved children of God.

Consider the example of a person who was filled with charity: Mother Teresa of Calcutta. What did she see when she looked upon a fellow human? She saw Christ. And further, she saw a beloved of Christ, one called to live His

life, with Him. This is supernatural charity in action, the love of God, extended to our neighbor. The Catechism states: "Charity is the theological virtue by which we love God above all things for his own sake, and our neighbor as ourselves for the love of God." (*CCC* 1822)

Some Final Thoughts on Human Friendships and Friendship with God

Aristotle was convinced that human perfection, or human happiness, happens most truly only in the context of human friendships. We must remember that friendship *with God* is something that Aristotle could not have imagined. The supernatural gift of friendship with God infinitely surpasses the greatest perfection that unaided human nature can achieve. We have noted how human friendships can prepare for supernatural friendship by helping us understand what friendship is, and by helping us develop habits of friendship, of "living together" with friends. But a question arises. Is charity, friendship with God and neighbor, something that is simply added "on top of" human friendships? Is human friendship then replaced by supernatural charity, now that there is something much higher and more important? The answer is No.

Charity transforms and raises up natural human friendship. In other words, *the human friendship that has been the main topic of this book is given deeper roots, and greater fruits.* A Christian seeks to grow in human friendship in the context of charity. The supernatural life of Christians gives them that much more as a common basis for friendship, as well as

that much more to look forward to, and to enjoy together as friends.

Let us consider this special situation of Christians as regards human friendship. Christianity provides a deeper understanding of such crucial realities as virtue and law. It also provides a much greater incentive to be virtuous— the personal invitation of the Creator, accompanied by the promise of His assistance through the Church and its sacraments. These things make a significant difference in the journey toward virtue, or what we can call holiness, which is the very journey that friends seek to make together.

Friends always want to be together, and they naturally dread separation. Christianity provides supernatural hope, and the promise that the ultimate life that they share transcends the mortal life of this world. Indeed, this ultimate life is not a mortal life at all; it is the life of the Blessed Trinity itself. What greater joy is there for those with a human friendship, than to know that as united in charity they *share together* in the Life of God Himself.

Practicing Friendship

Questions for discussion:

1. What is charity?

2. How is it possible that a human person be a friend of God?

3. Why does God give laws to us?

4. How does the importance of conversation in friendship apply to friendship with God?

5. Does charity necessarily extend to my neighbor? Why?

6. How does supernatural charity transform human friendships?

Questions for personal reflection:

1. Do I live as though friendship with God is the goal of my life... *in this life*?

2. Is my prayer life recognizable as a conversation between friends? How might I work on this?

3. Does my love for God truly extend to my neighbors? To the extent that it does not, why does it not?

Excercise:

Read the following Scripture passages and meditate upon the friendship that Our Lord had with human persons as He walked among us as a man. Mk. 6:30-32; Jn. chapter 6 (bread of life), especially vs. 66-71, chapter 11 (raising of Lazarus), especially vs. 28-44, chapters 13-17 (Last Supper and last discourse), especially 13:1, 13:23-25, 14:27-28, 15:11-15, 16:22, 17:6-19; Mt. 26:36-46 (Gethsemane).

~

Epilogue: Friendship in This Life and the Next

In the section of the *Summa theologica* called by many the "treatise on happiness" (the first five questions of the First Part of the Second Part), St. Thomas asks a question pertinent to our study: Is the fellowship of friends necessary for happiness? (*S.t.* I–II 4.8) As is often the case when St. Thomas answers such questions, he responds that we must a make a distinction. We distinguish between the happiness of this life and the happiness of the next life. As regards to the happiness that can be achieved in this life he says, along with Aristotle, that a happy human person *must have* true human friends. He explains that happy persons need friends so that they will be able to "act well." In other words, if one is really to act or live as a good and happy person does, one needs the fellowship of friends.

St. Thomas lists three reasons why a person needs friends: 1) so that the person can "do good" to them, 2) so that the person may delight in seeing them do good, and 3)

so that the person may be helped by them in living well. He explains the third point with this sweeping assertion: "For in order that man may do well, whether in the works of the active life, or in those of the contemplative life, he needs the fellowship of friends."

Let us think about this. To *do well*, whether in the works of the "active life," which is fundamentally the realm of the moral virtues, or the "contemplative life," which is fundamentally the realm of the intellectual virtues, a person *must have* friends. Thus, in this life, we can only be virtuous, and therefore, happy, if we have developed virtuous friendships with others.

But what about the next life, the life of the beatific vision in heaven? St. Thomas makes clear that even if there were only one soul in heaven, that soul would be in a perfectly happy union with God. Thus, *human* friendship is not absolutely essential to the ultimate happiness of heaven. However, this is not the complete picture. There *will be* other souls there, and one will have friendships with them. St. Thomas almost seems torn in expressing just how wonderful this will be, because he does not want to imply that there could be anything lacking in the central relationship with God Himself. In other words, if St. Thomas makes friendship with other humans in heaven sound too important, it might make it seem that friendship with God himself does not completely satisfy our desires. Yet he indicates that friendship with other humans will be a part of that inexpressible fullness of happiness. He quotes St. Augustine of Hippo, who says that those in heaven will "see one another

and rejoice in God, at their fellowship."

For help in savoring this point, let us turn to the great St. Aelred of Rievaulx, a twelfth-century Cistercian monk. His book *Spiritual Friendship* is one of the great masterpieces on friendship. He concludes with a sort of litany of the blessings of friendship. This litany culminates (and how fitting this is) in a consideration of the *prayer of friends* for one another, and how prayer lifts them toward their ultimate union in Christ.

> *Added to this there is prayer for one another, which, coming from a friend, is the more efficacious in proportion as it is more lovingly sent to God, with tears, which either fear excites or affection awakens or sorrow evokes. And thus a friend praying to Christ on behalf of his friend, and for his friend's sake desiring to be heard by Christ, directs his attention with love and longing to Christ; then it sometimes happens that quickly and imperceptibly the one love passes over into the other, and coming, as it were, into close contact with the sweetness of Christ himself, the friend begins to taste his sweetness and to experience his charm. Thus ascending from that holy love with which he embraces a friend to that with which he embraces Christ, he will joyfully partake in abundance of the spiritual fruit of friendship, awaiting the fullness of all things in the life to come. Then, with the dispelling of all anxiety by reason of which we now fear and are solicitous for one another, with the removal of all adversity which*

it now behooves us to bear for one another, and, above all, with the destruction of the sting of death together with death itself, whose pangs now often trouble us and force us to grieve for one another, with salvation secured, we shall rejoice in the eternal possession of Supreme Goodness; and this friendship, to which here we admit but few, will be outpoured upon all and by all outpoured upon God, and God shall be all in all. (Spiritual Friendship 3:133-134, pp. 131-32)

A Gospel Meditation

"The next day again John was standing with two of his disciples; and he looked at Jesus as He walked, and said, 'Behold, the Lamb of God!' The two disciples heard Him say this, and they followed Jesus. Jesus turned, and saw them following, and said to them, 'What do you seek?' And they said to Him, 'Rabbi' (which means Teacher), 'where are you staying?' He said to them, 'Come and see.' They came and saw where He was staying; and they stayed with Him that day, for it was about the tenth hour." John 1:35-42

The story is a familiar one. Jesus had walked by on the prior day, and John the Baptist had pointed Him out as the Lamb of God. That day, none of John's disciples followed Jesus. This day, Jesus once again walked by, and John once again bears witness to the Lamb of God. It is clear enough what Jesus is hoping for. How many times will He have to walk by before someone actually follows Him? This day John and Andrew arise and follow the Lord. Jesus has not as yet had any personal contact, or opened His mouth in

discourse with any of the men who will be His disciples. Feel the excitement of the fisher of men: His first two fish are on the line. Hardly able to contain Himself, He soon turns and asks *the question*; it is always the first question for those who would follow Him: What do you seek? He must have an answer; all depends on it.

The answer given is all that He had hoped for, that He had dreamed of. Given in a startled moment, it says it all. "Rabbi, Master"—they recognize Him as a teacher, one to learn from, one to follow—"Where do you live?" What they want is Him. They want to be with Him, they want to share their lives with Him. Nothing more, nothing less.

Oh, how this fits with His own desires! He solemnly extends an invitation. The Eternal Word of God, Yahweh Himself, has become Man that He might deliver *this* invitation: "Come and see." What more can He say? What more can God Himself offer to the human person? Come, and see, *where I live....* For where I am, there would I have you be. Be not surprised when you first see My dwelling. It does not look like the dwelling of your kings. Indeed at times it will be a little uncomfortable for you. But place your trust in Me. And I, the Lord of Hosts, swear by My very Self that you will find it to be a home, your home....

Our Lord has extended a call to friendship. What do friends do? They *share their lives.* But how can a human person live as God lives? There is only one answer, the one that the Lord Jesus gives: He must come, and see. And how few there are who do it, for the road is narrow, and not easy. During this life there are many hindrances to living out this

friendship, the friendship of supernatural charity. Indeed
the Lord warned that unless a person is willing to take up
the cross … he or she is not worthy of Him. That is, they
cannot *live together*, as friends do.

But to the one who comes and sees, lives and perseveres,
to this one the Lord will give all. And one great day, having run the race, this person will stand before the judgment
seat of the Almighty, having during this life strived to live
a friendship with One he or she has only seen through a
glass, and darkly. Then the mighty Judge will ask, "What
is it you seek?" "Master, where do you live?" "My friend,
come, and *see.…*"

~

Sources Cited

The Basic Works of Aristotle. Ed. Richard McKeon (New York: Random House, 1941).

Catechism of the Catholic Church. United States Catholic Conference, Libreria Editrice Vaticana, 1994, as revised in the 1997 Latin typical edition. Abbreviated *CCC*.

Commentary on Aristotle's Nicomachean Ethics. St. Thomas Aquinas, trans. C.I. Litzinger (Notre Dame: Dumb Ox Books, 1993).

Confessions. St. Augustine of Hippo, trans. T.J. Sheed (Indianapolis: Hackett, 1993).

Gaudium et Spes in *Vatican Council II, The Conciliar Documents.* Ed. Austin Flannery, O.P. (Northport, New York: Costello Publishing Company, Inc., 1998).

Holy Bible. All quotations are from the Revised Standard Version, Catholic Edition.

Plato: Five Dialogues. Trans. G.M.A. Grube (Indianapolis: Hackett, 1981).

Spiritual Friendship. St. Aelred of Rievaulx. Trans. Mary Eugenia Laker (Kalamazoo, Michigan: Cistercian Publications, 1977).

Summa Theologica of St. Thomas Aquinas. Trans. Fathers of the English Dominican Province (Westminster, Md.: Christian Classics, 1981). Abbreviated *S.t.*, followed by Roman numerals indicating the part, Arabic numerals indicating the question, then a period followed by the article number.

Resources

About Friendship

Aquinas, St. Thomas, *Commentary on Aristotle's Nicomachean Ethics*, trans. C.I. Litzinger (Notre Dame: Dumb Ox Books, 1993). See the commentary on Books VIII and IX.

Aquinas, St. Thomas, *Summa Theologica of St. Thomas Aquinas*, trans. Fathers of the English Dominican Province (Westminster, Md.: Christian Classics, 1981), Second Part of the Second Part (Vol. III) Questions 23-33 on supernatural charity.

Lewis, C. S., *The Four Loves* (New York: Harcourt Brace Jovanovich, 1960).

Rievaulx, St. Aelred of, *Spiritual Friendship*, trans. Mary Eugenia Laker (Kalamazoo, Michigan: Cistercian Publications, 1977).

About Virtue

Aquinas, St. Thomas, *Summa Theologica of St. Thomas Aquinas*, trans. Fathers of the English Dominican Province (Westminster, Md.: Christian Classics, 1981), First Part of the Second Part (Vol. II) Questions 49-67.

Cessario, Romanus, O.P. *The Moral Virtues and Theological Ethics* (Notre Dame, IN: University of Notre Dame Press, 1991).

Gray, Tim and Curtis Martin, *Boys to Men: The Transforming Power of Virtue* (Steubenville, OH: Emmaus Road Publishing, 2001).

Kreeft, Peter, *Back to Virtue* (San Francisco: Ignatius Press, 1992).

McInerny, Ralph, *Ethica Thomistica* (Washington, D.C.: The Catholic University of America Press, 1997).

Pieper, Josef, *The Four Cardinal Virtues* (Notre Dame, IN: University of Notre Dame Press, 1966).

Pieper, Josef, *Faith, Hope, Love* (San Francisco: Ignatius Press, 1997).

About St. Thomas Aquinas

Chesterton, G. K., *Saint Thomas Aquinas: The Dumb Ox* (Image Books, 2001).

Pieper, Josef, *Guide to Thomas Aquinas* (San Francisco: Ignatius Press, 1991).

~

What Is the
Measure of a Human Person?

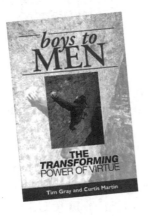

In a culture experiencing a crisis of human dignity, Tim Gray and Curtis Martin's "Boys to Men" is an invitation to delve into the heart of true humanity: growth in virtue, the pursuit of wisdom and the meaning of sacrifice.

In this 8-part Bible study, you'll discover an introduction to the virtuous life and the tools to pursue Christ's radical call to true humanity.

Ideal for use in groups or personal study, "Boys to Men" provides rock-solid advice on living a Christ-centered life, and leading others to do the same:
* Live a life of Christian virtue
* Experience the power of authenticity
* Discover God's plan for your life

To order, visit www.focusonline.org or call (303) 962-5750

FOCUS

Vision for Life

11 years. 236 vocations. 400 missionaries.

FOCUS, the Fellowship of Catholic University Students, is a national outreach that sends teams of missionaries to college campuses to introduce students to the love of Jesus Christ and the Catholic Church.

FOCUS missionaries meet college students where they are and invite them to examine the meaning and purpose of their lives. Compelled by the love of Christ, FOCUS missionaries bring a message of hope and truth to a world searching for something more.

How to Get Involved:
- Join a Bible Study
- Help with service projects and social outreaches
- Learn to share the Catholic faith and Jesus Christ with others

To join FOCUS or to bring FOCUS to your campus, visit us online at www.focusonline.org.

FOL

APR 2 1 2023

FOCUS • PO Box 33656 • Denver, CO 80233 • www.focusonline.org • (303) 962-5750

Liv Jan/14 ᴿ BARNY

OCT - - 2018 BW